Other *Leisure* books by Claudia Dain:

CLAUDIA DAIN

The Temptation

LEISURE BOOKS NEW YORK CITY

A LEISURE BOOK®

December 2003

Published by

Dorchester Publishing Co., Inc.
200 Madison Avenue
New York, NY 10016

ISBN 0-8439-5220-2

Visit us on the web at www.dorchesterpub.com.

CRITICAL PRAISE
FOR AWARD-WINNING AUTHOR
CLAUDIA DAIN!

MORE RAVES FOR CLAUDIA DAIN!

THE MARRIAGE BED

"For an unusual, sensual story set in a very believable medieval world, I strongly recommend *The Marriage Bed*. This is an author to watch."

—*All About Romance*

"Complex, challenging and one of the most romantic books I've read in a long time, this is definitely a trip worth taking."

—The Romance Reader

THE HOLDING

"A marvelous and fascinating read . . . this book hits the home run."

—Mrs. Giggles from Everything Romantic

"*The Holding* is a romance that brings historical detail and passion together. The strong characters hold appeal as does the backdrop."

—*Romantic Times*

TELL ME LIES
<u>RT</u> Award Finalist (Best First Novel)

"Ms. Dain has created memorable characters and a lusty tale. . . . This is an author with an erotic touch and a bright future."

—*Romantic Times*

"Claudia Dain has penned a sizzling tale that will warm your heart and sate your romantic soul."
—Connie Mason, bestselling author of *The Laird of Stonehaven*

"Claudia Dain heats things up from page one and keeps the reader at a slow burn throughout this appealing debut novel."

—Thea Devine, bestselling author

To Jennifer and Doug,
for lunch and drinks and message boards
and the best conversation I've had in years;
to Tina, who made the match;
and to Tom, for always and ever.

The Temptation

Prologue

England, 1156

The room was shrouded in the heavy dark of a cold and relentless night. Only a single candle burned, a single weak light against the pain and dark cold of the chamber. By that candle, hot and golden against the pressing dark, Elsbeth performed her duty.

"It is not proceeding well, Elsbeth. Something is amiss."

Elsbeth looked down at the woman she was to help, at the face swollen with strain and effort and pain. Ardeth, the whites of her eyes red with broken blood vessels, struggled for each shallow breath.

"You are only tired," Elsbeth said. "Hold fast. Your time is near. The babe is upon you."

Ardeth only shook her head and turned her gaze to the midwife, Jean. Jean pressed her lips together and said nothing.

"You know something is amiss," Ardeth said.

1

Ardeth said no more. Her pain was upon her again and she breathed into the face of it, straining for purchase and finding none. Her cry was ripped from her lips to end in a grunting sigh.

Elsbeth laid a hand upon Ardeth's mounded belly and felt the babe. He was moving downward, his hips easily discernible. He was coming strong and coming right. There was nothing amiss in this birthing. Nay, it was all as it should be. God had spoken true when He had declared that He would increase a woman's pain upon the child bed. She had not doubted it. Yet she did not relish the watching of it.

"He comes," she said, laying a cool, wet cloth on Ardeth's brow.

"That I knew, Elsbeth," Ardeth said with a half smile. "He will not come unheralded, it seems, though I would have preferred it. His herald is pain, and I must attend. A most unthoughtful child, though I love him even now."

The pain pressed at her again and she went silent in the face of it. Elsbeth clasped her hand and buried her wince at the pain of Ardeth's grip. Ardeth's belly roiled in movement as the babe was pressed downward again. He pushed against her bowels with his progress, and the smell of human excrement filled the air. Jean cleared it away with a swipe of a linen cloth, laying a clean cloth in its place to catch whatever else would be purged from Ardeth's body.

" 'Twill not be much longer," Ardeth said. "There are things I want to say to you, Elsbeth. So many things to say."

"The worst is past," Elsbeth answered. "Rest in that."

"Rest," Ardeth said. "I would rest."

Elsbeth could only agree, though she did not say the words aloud. God had ordained that, as a result of their fall from grace, a man must work the land and a woman must work to bring forth a child. She did not know a man who did not find joy in his work, be he knight, baron, or serf. Yet she did not see the joy in this birthing. This was pain. There could be no joy in it.

"It is harder now," Ardeth said on a grunt. "The pain sharper and heavier."

Elsbeth looked between Ardeth's legs as a gush of water soaked the bedding.

"Soon now, lady," said Jean. "Soon. Push when the pain comes again."

"I will push, but I know this has gone wrong somehow. I feel it in my heart," Ardeth said.

Her next pain took her hard and Ardeth cried out against it. Her scream bounced against the stone walls of the chamber until the echo of it flew out the single wind hole.

A cap of hair, dark as night, showed itself against the wet curls of Ardeth's womanhood. In the next instant, Elsbeth watched the skin beneath Ardeth's womb tear in a jagged line, a thin trail of blood seeping forth. Born in blood—that was the way into this world. There was no other path.

With the next pain, his head broke free and Elsbeth could see the line of his closed eyes. This was the hardest part, the passage of the head. Hard and large, larger than any woman should have to bear, it came forth push by push, pain by pain.

"He comes," Jean said. "Two pushes, mayhap three, and he is free."

Ardeth's pain suffused her and she cried, a screaming cry, her head thrown back and her mouth opened wide. A cry to mock the wolves and the beasts of the dark. An animal cry to mark the passage of her babe into the world of men.

His head was free, and Jean clasped him by the neck. Another push and his body came free into Jean's waiting hands. He looked small in her hands, but Elsbeth knew that was a lie. He was too big to have come from the body of a woman.

Face down, he was, but she could mark his sex. He was a manchild.

And he was dead. The cord was wrapped around his throat; with every push the noose had tightened, and with his exit from the warm dark of his mother, the cord had pulled tight, killing him. He lay in Jean's hands, a lifeless form of bone and skin and glistening hair.

"Push again—push out the afterbirth," Elsbeth commanded, turning her eyes from the child and onto the mother.

"I hear no cry," Ardeth said in a breathy whisper.

"Push!" Elsbeth said again.

The afterbirth slid out, and with it, a trail of blood. A trail that widened and would not stop. A running stream of blood that grew brighter and more lively as they watched.

"He is dead," Ardeth said. "As soon I will be."

She lay back on the single pillow that supported her head, her eyes closed, her breathing light.

"Nay! You must not and will not die!" Elsbeth said, pressing a wad of linen against the flow of relentless blood. "This bleeding will stop."

"There is so much left to say," Ardeth said, looking up into Elsbeth's face. "I love you," she said, a single tear winding down her tired face to mesh with her light brown hair.

"I love you, *Maman*," Elsbeth answered, her own eyes blurred with unshed tears. "You must not die."

"I am dying. I cannot stay God's hand and, of a truth, I do not care to try. Life is long and hard. I am glad to be going out of it, Elsbeth. Be glad for me, if you can," Ardeth said.

"I will be anything you want me to be," Elsbeth said,

blinking back her tears. She bent down to her mother and buried her face in her hair, finding pain-filled joy in the beating of her mother's heart and the rise and fall of her chest.

"Take my son," Ardeth told Jean. "Take him and clean him and prepare him for burial. I want him named Harald, after my father. Go now."

Jean left, the child a small, still bundle in her arms.

The blood between Ardeth's legs grew and grew, warm and wet, leaving her cold and empty.

Mother and daughter held each other, Ardeth stroking Elsbeth's hair, Elsbeth losing herself in Ardeth's vanishing warmth.

"I loved my husband very much," Ardeth said softly. "He was so very beautiful. He made me laugh. Did I tell you that? I could not see beyond his smile. I was lost in him and looked no further." Ardeth closed her eyes and sighed. "I am glad he is not here for this."

Elsbeth's father. Aye, she knew he had been well loved by his wife, had been beautiful, could be charming. And he was not here in his manor of Herulfmeade while his wife delivered up his eleventh child. Nay, her father was off in London, seeing to his pleasures while his wife saw to the ending of her life. Better there than here, that was surely true.

"I am glad as well," Elsbeth said. "Let us not think of him now."

"You must remember what I taught you, Elsbeth," Ardeth said. "You must not forget the lessons of my life. They will save you, if you heed them. You will not live out your life as I have done."

"Be still, *Maman*. I have listened. I have believed. Give no thought to that."

Elsbeth gently pulled away the sodden linen from between her mother's legs, hoping to find the bleeding had stopped. Blood burst forth steadily, defiantly. It

5

would not be stopped. Ardeth bled from high up in her womb, and there was no way to stop it.

"They cannot help it," Ardeth said, her voice high and meandering. "I do not think they can help it. God created them so, to be lusty and proud. The only thing to do is to be careful of them. A convent must be such a lovely place, so quiet and safe."

"Aye," Elsbeth said. "It must be so. Do not fear for me, *Maman*."

"I cannot seem to help it," Ardeth said with a weak smile. "I want so much for you. A different life than I have known. A safer life. Sunnandune is safe. Go to Sunnandune, Elsbeth, and if that gate is closed against you, then find your way into the abbey. Away from men and from all harm."

"I will. I have promised it. I will be safe," Elsbeth said. They had spoken of this before, for as long as she could remember. Throughout all her memories words of safety and of cloister echoed.

"I regret the choice I made for you so long ago. I would that you could have lived in Sunnandune all your life. Yet you will soon be of age, and then Sunnandune will be yours."

"Fear not for me, *Maman*. I am well and will stay so."

Ardeth clutched Elsbeth to her with arms made strong by desperation. "You must not give in to the temptation of men. They are masters of temptation. It is a long fall into desire and passion. Do not fall, Elsbeth. Be wiser than your mother. Be safe."

"I will be safe," Elsbeth said, making her voice strong, though her heart trembled in anguish. "I will not fall."

"I have not kept you very safe, have I?" Ardeth said.

"I am well, *Maman*. Rest in that. I am safe. You are a good mother. You have taught me well."

"You will beware the snare of men?" Ardeth said again,

her deep blue eyes clouding over as the blood poured free of her. "You will not forget?"

"I will not forget," Elsbeth said. She would not fail. She would fulfill all her mother's dreams for her. She would not tumble into the same traps, the traps of men.

"I wonder . . ." Ardeth said, her breath fading away before her thought was finished. Her soul was flown, high and bright and free, leaving the gray, cold world behind like a troubled dream.

Leaving Elsbeth to finish out the dream alone.

Chapter One

England, 1158

Elsbeth faced her father as she had practiced—composed, resolved, serene. She was not the girl he had sent from him those many years ago. Surely he would see that. All could see it. He could not be so different from all others, though he was her father and he had always seemed most different to her.

She did not think that he much valued her. Still, he was her father, and God did not make mistakes about such things. Perhaps he, too, had changed with the passage of years. With God, all things, even the nature of her father, were possible.

They were in the hall, he upon his chair, she standing. Just as it had been the day she left Warkham for Dornei. But not the same, for she was not the same. She would show him she was not the same.

All rested upon that.

The clerk continued reading aloud the letter from

Richard intended for her father; the letter which would declare just how much she had changed.

" 'And so, it is my prayerful belief that Elsbeth, her mind ever turned to heavenly things, is well suited to the convent life. Many upon many are the women God has created to be wives and mothers, but only once in a great while does God fashion a woman whose sole desire is for prayer and divine communion.

" 'The decision, as is right, is yours, Lord Gautier. I am confident that, with God to guide you, you will choose the life most precisely fitted for your daughter, Elsbeth.

" 'In God,

" 'Richard of Warefeld' "

Her father, Lord Gautier, only looked upon her and smiled. She did not return his smile; she was striving for serenity.

"So," he said when the clerk had rolled up the missive, "Lord Richard thinks you well suited to nun's garb. You have no liking for damask, Daughter?"

"I have no disliking for it," she said. "It is only that I would give my life to God, for His purposes and His will."

"So Richard says," he said. "Did you ask him to write on your behalf?"

"Nay, I did not."

All who knew her knew the direction of her thoughts and her desires. They were not of this world, but of the next. Richard was only stating the obvious, if her father would allow himself to see it.

"It was his own idea, then, to instruct me on how to run my house and my affairs? A most direct man, he must be," Gautier said, hiding his smile behind his hand.

"It is only that he cares for me," she said, defending Richard from her father's censure.

"Ah, and I do not?"

"I did not say that, nor did Lord Richard," she said.

9

"Yet, he has known me for three years now. He understands my hunger for the cloister. He supports it."

Aye, she hungered for the cloister, for prayer and for solitude, showing all the world that she did not hunger for a husband. She was not fit to be a wife. She had no desire for it and no inclination. Let her father only see that and the vow to her mother would be met.

"And why should he not? He is not going to lose an alliance because his child turns from the marriage contract."

"There is a contract?"

"Aye, written and approved," he said, smiling down at her.

So, the contract was set, the man chosen. That answered all. He was not going to turn. He was resolute, even in the face of her perfected serenity. He was as stubborn as she remembered him.

"Nay, Elsbeth," he said, smiling gently. "I can see, if you cannot, that God has called you to walk a different path. Has he not given you a healthy body and an equally healthy dowry? Such signs cannot be overlooked. When you have given your husband a few heirs to secure his place in the world, you can seek the life of the cloister, if your husband will allow. That will be between the two of you. But I do hope you will remember to pray for my soul when all your hours are devoted to prayer and matters eternal."

"I could pray all the sooner if I went now," she said. There was a desperate sound to her offer and in the timber of her voice; she could hear it yet not stop it. He was casting away all her hopes with a few smiling words.

Gautier laughed and slapped the carved arm of his chair in delight. "I had forgotten how amusing you can be, Elsbeth," he said and then all his smiles were done. "I have life in me yet. Your prayers on my behalf can wait."

"Yet can any know the hour of our death? The Lord calls us home when He wishes, His purposes His own. No prayer can wait with such urgency riding upon our hearts."

"His purposes *are* His own, Daughter, and they may stay His own. My purpose for you is clear, and as I am your earthly lord, you will do well to remember where your loyalty and your obedience lie."

"I know my duty," she said, meeting his eyes. He was still a handsome man, strong and dark. How that he had not aged or changed when she was so transformed?

"I know you do," he said. "You were ever and always obedient, though you struggled with it, did you not? If you are bound for the cloister at your life's twilight, obedience will be called for in good measure. Now is a good time to begin your life of quiet obedience. You will obey me in this, Elsbeth."

He had won. She could find no way out if he would not allow her to enter the cloister. She must marry. She was of an age. She had a sizable dowry. She was ready for the man who had been chosen for her.

Or at least, her father thought her ready. That was all that mattered in any regard. What she thought, what she wanted, was not part of any agreement she would be called upon to make. Her vow to her mother to remain unmarried and celibate was shattered in that moment at her father's word and whim. What chance had she to make good on that vow with her father standing between her and any decision she might make?

The Lord God had not made woman's load a light one. If only Eve had not taken the forbidden fruit. All would have been well if not for her.

But now the door was opened upon Sunnandune, and she could not find the heart to regret it. Sunnandune was hers upon the moment of her marriage or upon Epiphany of her sixteenth year. That momentous Epiphany, the one which she had waited for all her life, was nigh. Yet marriage and the freedom to fly to Sunnandune were closer yet.

Her mother had arranged it so, upon the counsel of her father in their early, joyous days together. Her mother had come to regret her choice, for it had been Elsbeth who had been made to live with it, yet all that was past now. Now, she was on the cusp of marriage, and with marriage came freedom of a sort. Now, she could have Sunnandune, taking it and herself away from her father's control. There was a sweet victory in that, and she savored it as fully as she could before her father's very eyes.

If only she did not have to manage a husband she did not want as part of the bargain. That was a puzzle she had to find a way to manage. She would not be married. Be it better said, she would marry if the convent was closed to her, but she would not stay married. And she would remain celibate, untouched and unviolated.

'Twas a maze and yet she knew she would find a way out, finding freedom from all men in her victory. Was God not her champion? How, then, could she fail?

Lifting her chin and concentrating on maintaining her serenity, she asked, "When is he come?"

"He is come now, Daughter, and is here. You might put on a pleasing face for him, now that he has heard you plead for release from this match. He should have a cheerful bride facing him, for he is come far to find you. Turn and behold the man I have found for you."

He was here? He had stood in the hall and heard her beg her father to allow her to enter the cloister rather than be married to him? This was not a pleasing start to any marriage. And it was just like her father to have him in the room when she first came before him after years of separation. He had likely hoped for just such a display from her. Such small acts of struggling rebellion amused him well.

She turned and looked about her. The hall was not empty. Many of the faces she knew from her childhood, yet some of the knights were new to her. Death and disease had taken some off in the ten years she had been away from Warkham, and new blood, new faces had risen to take their place. Yet who would her father have chosen?

Not the short, dark one with hair growing out of his ears. Her father would not have done that to her, no matter his humor. Though Gautier did enjoy his jests. He would be capable of it, just to charm a laugh every time he thought of them together. She must have been half the man's age, yet there was nothing unusual in that.

She looked at her father, a sidelong glance that had more open fear in it than was wise. He laughed loudly when he saw where her gaze had landed. He shook his head and gestured outward, encouraging her to look again.

There were too many men in the hall. She felt like a wife looking over the latest catch of fish, sniffing and pinching to find the freshest for her family. 'Twas shameful. 'Twas just like her father to force her to such an act.

One man stepped forward out of the shadows that hung like curtains over the corners of the hall. He was tall, golden like sea sand, and young. He stepped forward and kept coming, his eyes light in the dim shadows of the hall, his skin glowing with health and sunlight, his stride long and full of quiet purpose.

He was beautiful, in the way of a man. Strong, hard with purpose, sure of his place in the world. Certain of his worth. Safe in his beauty.

Her father did not have such grace in him as to give her a man of such beauty.

"You have spoiled my play, Hugh," her father said. "I rarely have such amusements, but if you will claim your betrothed, then I will not gainsay you."

His betrothed? Elsbeth turned to her father in amazement, her eyes unblinking. This was the man she was to be given to? This man with the face of a saint?

"Meet your betrothed, Elsbeth," Gautier said into the silence that had laid hold of her heart. "Meet Hugh of Jerusalem."

Hugh of Jerusalem. Who had not heard the tales of him? This man before her eyes was squire Ulrich's most favored topic, if William le Brouillard and Rowland the Dark were discounted. He was ever close to the side of the very King of Jerusalem, Baldwin III. A man, a Christian knight, born in the city of God. Could a man be any but holy with such a birthplace and such a calling? It was a match to make a maid's heart sing for joy, if the maid knew the tune to call a husband to her side.

She did not. She had no voice to sing for any husband; there was no such melody in her, and she had no will to learn. She knew only how to pray and in her praying, to plead for release from the married state and from the grip of her father.

And Hugh, not God, had heard her. He had heard her plead for an escape from this very marriage.

Nay, not plead, only tender a reason most reasonable as to why she should be free of betrothal. And that spoken before she knew the name of her betrothed. Or his look.

She faced him, this man who would be hers, and met his gaze. He studied her as she studied him, and she saw no condemnation in his eyes. She was no beauty, that was certain. She could not hope to match him in that. His look was solemn, not amused and yet not angry. She thanked him for that in her heart, that he should not take offense or unkind pleasure in the role her father had thrust her into. She was no prophet who could look about a hall and discern her husband at a glance. Nay, not even by the tumbled beating of her heart.

Her heart tumbled now. He was so very beautiful.

His hair was blond, golden from the sun for the roots were darker, almost brown. His eyes were the green of pine boughs in the sunlight, glistening and bright. He was tall, as she had known he must be from the tales of him; his tunic was the white linen of the Levant, with the emblem of the holy cross sewn near the region of his heart.

He was beauty and righteous holiness—twin temptations to which she must not submit, the very temptations to call most loudly to her heart. Her father had known it would be so. He knew her. He knew what would appeal to her, his daughter of no beauty and striving holiness. This man was all she could ever want. Her father must have known that well. This husband, this betrothed, would require a new kind of strength, a new type of serenity to keep him in his place. To keep herself intact.

For a moment, looking at him as the torchlight picked out the shining strands of his golden hair and the clean lines of his features, she wondered if she could do it. And then the moment passed and she knew she could. He was but a man, after all. Ardeth had taught her all there was to know of men and their ways.

She could not fail and would not. She faced Hugh of Jerusalem with her resolve in firm possession of her heart. She would not fall to a lovely face and form. She would not. She had more strength in her than that, and more faith.

"My daughter Elsbeth," Gautier said, introducing them finally. "She will not disappoint you, I think," he said to Hugh.

15

"Nay, I cannot think that she would," Hugh said. His voice was low and soft, like the wind in the trees after a rain. "Greetings, lady," he said.

"My lord," she said, lowering her eyes to the floor in a calculated display of feminine modesty. Even his boots were beautiful.

"Your daughter does not need time to adjust herself to this newfound marriage you have contracted for her?" Hugh asked her father.

"Nay, my daughter is adept at obedience, as all daughters should be," Gautier said.

Elsbeth raised her eyes and looked at her father. Yea, she heard his warning. She must be obedient if she was ever to find her way to the cloister. And Hugh of Jerusalem was now the door through which she must pass to reach it; he, as her husband, would either allow or disallow it. Her task was before her.

Hugh must allow her to find her way to sanctuary, the sanctuary of a world of women, their hearts and minds, their very bodies, given to God. If he found her unfit to be a wife, her hours devoted to prayer, her every thought and word given to God, he would release her. His repudiation of her was her dearest prayer. She would rather be free to live in peace at Sunnandune than in the cloister, but either would serve. She only wanted to be free of him.

What man wanted a nun for a wife? What man wanted a wife he could not possess? How she would escape his possession, his invasion into her body, she did not yet know. Yet she did know God, and He was able to keep her safe. Somehow, she would be safe.

"Then I follow your word, my lord," Hugh said, turning away from her completely to face Gautier, "for you know the heart of my betrothed better than I. I would cause her no dismay."

"You will not, but ask her yourself, if it please you," Gautier said.

Hugh took her hand in his and she let him. She was obedient to his will, showing them all the perfection of her submission, trying even now to find her way to the place where no man could find her.

"Show me your eyes, Elsbeth, for I would read your heart in them," Hugh said.

Her first act of obedience, and she felt the struggle within herself to perform it. He was too beautiful and the temptation to fall into him would be too great. Yet God was greater still.

She obeyed.

"Our path is marked for us, lady," he said, "but I would not have you stumble upon it, not being ready for the journey every marriage surely is. Would you wait, Lady Elsbeth, or will you trust that my arm is strong enough to sustain you, even as my heart yearns to fulfill our pledge? I stand upon your will, knowing that the God we both serve will guide you."

Perfect. Had any knight ever shown such well-balanced blending of courtesy, chivalry, and holy ardor? Nay, not even Ulrich in all his impassioned wooing had spoken so skillfully.

Yet she would not let a perfect speech from a flawless face move her, at least not overmuch. She must persuade him to relinquish her; she would be no man's wife. But he could not relinquish what he did not hold, and so her answer was clear. As clear as it was that her father would never let her remain unwed. If she could manage for Hugh to repudiate her, then Sunnandune would still be hers. If she could manage to convince Hugh that she was better suited to the cloister, then he would release her into it. Either way, she was free of the control of men. Either path led to freedom. Either path led away from her father.

"You are kind, my lord, to stand upon the will of a woman. Thank you for that courtesy." If her father heard a rebuke in that for him, let him. "I hear no call to wait, my father's will and God's being plainly heard. We marry at your will, the day and hour in your hands, as surely as my life resides in God's."

"Did I not tell you that you would suit each other well?" Gautier said.

"Aye, and you spoke true," Hugh answered. "Elsbeth is a comely damsel, her heart and mind set upon God's holy will. No man could ask for more of any wife."

"Aye, he can," Gautier said, grinning. "That her womb bear him many sons to carry his name and his blood forward. That is the best reward for a man in this life."

"In this life, perhaps," Elsbeth said with the smallest whisper of rebellion.

"My reward rests in God's hands," Hugh said, looking down at her, his expression solemn. "Let Him give me what He will. Or will not. I am content within His grasp."

It was a perfect answer. She could not have dared even to dream for more. She had no words to speak against the match or the man.

A most troublesome beginning to a marriage she did not want.

It was a marriage he wanted with all his heart, though he doubted Gautier knew it. Which was all to the good. No man would be invited into the dark and shadowed corners of his heart, nor any woman, even if she be a wife.

Hugh sat next to his future father-in-law in the vast, dark, drafty hall Gautier seemed so proud of. What was more, he was drinking bad wine, though Gautier did not seem to mark it. A most strange place, this England. He had heard the stories of it all his life, but he had not quite been prepared for the reality of the place.

It was damp. All over, it was damp. Within and without. A cold damp that settled in the very pit of his stomach and that no fire could burn away. And the sun was a weak thing here, shrouded in cloud and fog and mist and defeated by them all. He longed for the strong white light of Jerusalem and found it only in his dreams.

Ah, well, he had his duty to perform in England and then he was off, home again, to the land of God Himself. He would find solace in his dreams until then.

Elsbeth had gone to pray before the marriage ceremony and to bathe, rather like a man performing the vigil that marked the beginning of his knighthood. Well, and he could see the reason in it. Her life was about to change, and there would be no going back. Aye, let her pray through her fears; he would not condemn her.

According to her father, and even Lord Richard, she was a woman much given to prayer. He could see no fault in it. A woman's life was a secluded one. If she marked the hours by attending the Mass, sending her Latin heavenward, he would only praise her.

Aye, 'twould be a fair marriage, each of them content in getting what they wanted. And was that not the root of contentment? That she was comely was a boon unasked for; perhaps all the sweeter for that. She had the dark look of a woman of the Levant, dark of hair and eye, though her skin was the color of rich cream. Her features were bold and full and her gaze direct, which was not a feature of a woman reared in the land of Christ. He did not fault her for it. These Northern women did not have the same ways as the women of his own life.

He was very far from home, but it did not serve to dwell upon it. He was halfway to winning his goal; he dare not falter now by falling into dreaming of home.

Turning to his host, he said, "How did your daughter

come by her name? It is new to me," he asked Gautier, pulling himself out of his longings.

"She comes from a royal Saxon house," Gautier answered. "Her mother, Ardeth, was descended from a Saxon king. I married her to firm my bond to this isle and to gain good land. A wise marriage. Too bad she did not live to see Elsbeth wed."

"When did she die?"

"Two years past. She died in childbed, with Elsbeth at her side," Gautier said, licking chicken fat from his fingertips. "I married again and she is plumped, so all is well. Five sons I have, a rich legacy for any man."

"Aye, that is true. You are rich in sons. And in daughters. Elsbeth is lovely."

"It is good you think so," Gautier said. "A man finds pleasure in a pleasing face . . . and between soft thighs."

Hugh smiled and drank again of his wine, holding his tongue, keeping the peace.

"You do not wish to break free of the match, even knowing that she would prefer the convent?" Gautier asked.

Hugh smiled and set down his wine. The tablecloth was frayed and thin, much like the wine. "I do not fault her for having dreams as to how she would spend her life, especially a life devoted to prayer. She will make me a fine wife. I will not break free."

"Nor will she," Gautier said.

Hugh only nodded.

"You can have her today. I give her to you. The contract is written, the priest waits only upon my word," Gautier said.

He was a most anxious father, most anxious and eager to give his daughter into marriage. Still, Elsbeth was of an age to marry and Hugh eager to take her to wife. There was no cause to delay.

"I am ready. When she comes, I will take her. Let me

only say my own prayers to my divine creator before I join myself to your daughter. I would come to her clean of all sin," Hugh said.

"As you say," Gautier said. "Go to your prayers. I will not hinder you nor any man in his converse with God. Would that more men were of your temper, Hugh. The world we live in would have a different shading than it does now."

"Aye, it may be so," Hugh said, rising from his seat. There was a smudge of dirt on his white tunic from the dusty underside of the table. He turned his eyes from it and smiled his departure at Gautier.

Gautier smiled to watch him go and stroked the dog pressed against his side with negligent affection.

The chapel of Gautier's holding was against the east wall, a squat and dark building of stone and mortar scoured by wind and mossy with time. It looked like a stable. Hugh sighed and let his eyes find instead the beauty of the place. There was some small patch of brilliance, if one looked long and hard. He had. He had been in Warkham for a sennight, awaiting the arrival of his betrothed. The chapel did boast a splendid floor of cut stone and shimmering quartz laid in a design that awkwardly mimicked the brightly colored mosaics of the Levant. Still, it had a certain severe beauty, and he let the sight wash through him.

The chamber was quiet and still, the birds of winter cooing softly in the rafters, the air pleasantly scented by beeswax candles. It was a place to find God, to hear His voice amid the clamor of living. It was where he found Elsbeth.

She knelt in the nave, her dark hair a shining wave that flowed over her back. Her spine was straight and her head bent to her prayers. The sound of her voice was a soft murmur in the air, as pleasant and soothing as birdsong. He approached her softly, his boots silently marking his passage over the stone floor.

She did not look up. She did not stop her prayers. He had not expected such from her. A woman given to prayer would not mark the approach of a man, even though that man be her betrothed.

He watched her as he knelt at her side. There was a strength to her, a clarity of purpose that radiated from her eyes, a resolve that was unusual in a woman. She was small. And she was young. Yet those traits did not diminish her. A woman, this woman, would need her strength for what he planned to do in her life. Nay, he found no fault with Elsbeth. God and Baldwin had chosen well for him.

He bent his head to his own prayers, his words blending with hers to form a strange sort of spiritual song. If she heard it, she gave no sign. He did not think Elsbeth was given to showing signs.

In time, when the candles had burned down, their wax leaving smooth puddles on the floor, their prayers were silenced. Even Elsbeth, it seemed, could not pray all day. At least not while her betrothed waited at her side in her father's chapel.

"I have not yet bathed," she said, staring up at the rood. Christ upon His cross did not look down at them but cast His eyes upward, toward the Father and His reward. A fine lesson for them all in the way a man's eyes should be fixed upon the prize.

"I will wait," Hugh said, studying her profile. Her lips were full and her brow strong, yet her eyes were soft and deep.

The silence stretched out between them, a silence marked by nothing more significant than the sound of the wind in the rafters and the motion of the birds. Still, it was peaceful. Had he been born a woman, he might have found much solace in prayer and continual contemplation. But he was not a woman.

"I was not . . ." she began and then faltered.

He waited and did not press for more. Let her speak when she had found her words. Such gentle chivalry would go far with her, according to all Gautier had said.

"I did not pray to delay our marriage," she said, her eyes on the floor under her knees.

"I did not think you had. I would never think so ill of you, Elsbeth. I believe you to be a woman who does not give her words to the air, to be snatched off when the wind blows a different course," he said.

She looked up at him then, a fleeting look that showed first her surprise and then her pleasure at his words. Had she heard so few pleasing words in her life that these few would turn her head?

"Do you?" she asked and then turned away from him again, her eyes once more on the rood. "Do you know me so well and so quickly, then? Or do you only hope?"

"Perhaps it is only hope," he said, standing, giving her his arm to assist her.

She laid her hand upon his arm slowly, cautiously. It was their first touch, and well they knew it. Yet it was only a hand upon an arm. Only a hand, yet she hesitated. He could not fathom it. She had seemed more bold than to hesitate at this.

"And perhaps," he continued, taking her hand in his and laying it upon his arm, "perhaps it is that I trust. I trust in God, Elsbeth, as must you. I trust that He has gifted me with a bride who will suit. I trust that our lives will mesh, becoming one, as the Lord God intended. As Adam was given Eve, so I am given you."

Her eyes widened and she snatched back her hand. "Eve sinned grievously. Do not compare me to her, I beseech you. She did not do her husband any good turn that I can see. I would be better."

"It may be so," he said, taking back her hand and holding it in his, "and yet, she was fashioned for him and from him. And she peopled the earth, as God commanded. I find no fault with that."

"You are a strange sort of knight," she said, her dark eyes smoky with wonder.

"I am a knight of the Levant, Elsbeth. That is all I am," he said, meaning every word.

Chapter Two

She had listened to him, this man who would claim her, and tried not to drown in him. He was beautiful. His words were perfect in chivalry and in Christian courtesy. He was everything a maid prayed for, and he was to be hers.

She did not want him.

She tried to remember why.

By thinking of what was, of the hard terms and facts of her life and the counsel of her mother, Ardeth. That was the cure for muddy memory.

Her mother had instructed her for just such times as these. Hugh was a handsome man, and he called forth longings and desires in her that would not serve. Ardeth had taught her well what men did best in a woman's life; she had learned those lessons fully and so had no longing for the role of wife. The abbey was a kinder, safer life. 'Twas the abbey she desired, not a comely man from Jerusalem. So she must make him believe.

Yet why had he agreed to this betrothal? Why take Elsbeth to wife? There was an answer. There was always an answer, and it had nothing to do with Elsbeth and all to do with Elsbeth's worth.

Her father had taught her that.

Warkham was not the largest of her father's holdings, but it was still impressive. He was the holder of four great towers and two manors. A rich and mighty man who yearned to be richer and mightier still. His marriages had brought him more wealth, wealth in land and wealth in children. He had five sons and three daughters. He had known two wives.

It was her mother's dower land that made Elsbeth such an attractive mate. It was not her looks. It was not her deportment. No matter how Hugh looked at her. No matter what he tried to make her feel.

Elsbeth let the water of her bath slide over her skin, warming her. It was a chill day, dark and damp, the wind coming from the sea to the east and heavy with the smell of saltwater. She had missed the smell of the sea during her time at Dornei with Isabel. She would never see Isabel again. Her life as a bride would not require it, and her life as a nun would prohibit it. Nay, Dornei and all her people were past and could not be resurrected. Her future was in a different direction and bore a different name.

Hugh of Jerusalem.

He was a man who knew too well the words to woo a woman. How else to explain the way his words had touched her heart as surely as his hand had touched her own? His touch along with the words of warmth and welcome, had sparked a response in her that was only and always to be avoided. They were temptation and Hugh their wielder, though she would grant that he had not planned what he had aroused in her.

Aye, aroused.

For at that touch, that simple touch of hand to hand, her vision had clouded and her step faltered. 'Twas too simple a thing to cause a fall, the touch of a man's hand upon her own, though his hands be as callused and hard with fighting as her own were soft with prayer. She could not fall from a touch. Not even if the man be Hugh of Jerusalem. Not even for her betrothed.

Most especially not for her betrothed.

Elsbeth rose up out of the water, cold now, and reached for a length of linen to dry herself. She was clean and fortified with prayer, ready to say her vows and bind herself to the man chosen for her. Chosen by God, according to Hugh, and therefore accepted with peace and humility.

Could any man be so humble as all that? Even a man from Jerusalem?

He was a knight, first and last, a fighting man, a man of blood, as the church named all who fought their way through life. He was a man of blood, not heart, not soul . . . nay, she sinned by even thinking the thought. All men had souls, the most permanent part of their composition, enduring after all else wasted away in death. Yea, he was a man of soul, but so was she. And she did not yearn to be bound to a man of blood, no matter the gentleness of his words or the compassion in his eyes. Or his beauty.

It would have been a blessing if they had lied about his beauty.

He was so golden, so resolutely and perfectly golden. Even his eyes, as green as boughs in winter, held tiny flecks of gold in their deepest depths. A golden man with a golden name.

Hugh of Jerusalem. He dwelt in the land of the Savior, had walked in the very streets where Christ Himself had trod a thousand years ago. Surely, to even touch the stones where Christ had walked was to be transformed into holiness. And so it seemed, for Hugh was bathed in holy righteousness that shone out from his vibrant eyes.

Yet, he was still and always only a man.

But such a man.

He was close as a brother to Baldwin himself, the King of Jerusalem. He had been at the siege of Ascalon, or so the troubadours sang. Side by side with Baldwin, they had won the city after a siege of six months. Stalwart and patient, quietly relentless, they called him, and so he seemed to be.

He was to be her husband upon the hour. Did she want a stalwart husband? Would even a patient man give her what she wanted?

She did not know, and no amount of praying would divine the answer.

How did he find her?

He seemed well content with what he had seen of her thus far. Aye, and she was well-propertied, that was the extent of her attraction. The world was most predictable, once it was reasoned out. She would give him what he wanted: property. And she would then get what she wanted: a way out. He could give her that. He would have no need to withhold it from her. His place was in Jerusalem, his name made in this life, his course set. He had no need of an English wife.

She could be patient as well as any man.

If only. If only she did not have to be a wife. Yet, to be the wife of Hugh might be an easier task than to be the daughter of Gautier. Hugh had to be easier to manage; none could be more difficult than her father. How best to manage a man? She had never learned the answer to that, though Isabel had tried to show her. Her mother's counsel had been easier: Learn to manage yourself. That she could do.

With that thought in mind, she considered what gown to wear. Shivering in the linen wrapped around her torso, she dug through her trunk. The undergarment she had been searching for seemed to fly into her hand with a will; she chose to see it as a sign of benediction. Her choice was a wise one, God be praised.

Over her white linen chemise, she wore a pelisse of rich and vibrant red, the wool supple, the neckline and the narrow wrists decorated with a pattern of flowing leaves in creamy yellow. Her bliaut followed, a simple garment of flawless white, much like the surcoat Hugh wore. She arranged about her hips a girdle of golden rings; she would not wear a jeweled girdle. She would not come to him glittering and eager, her hips, the mark of her ability to breed, outlined, a sparkling temptation. She was just as holy as he, her garments and her soul just as pure as his, though she had lived her life in England.

He would not best her in holiness.

Her hair she brushed until it shone in waves to the middle of her back. About her head she fastened a headband set with small and modest garnets. It was her only adornment, worn in honor of their vows. Or so she hoped he would see it.

She was no beauty, but she was arrayed as one. A holy and untouchable wife. A woman with the scent of holy incense in her hair instead of perfume. Let him find a way to deal with that.

She would get what she wanted from him. She would, though he be her husband, though he be Hugh of Jerusalem.

Her father's wife awaited her in the hall. Emma was not much older than Elsbeth, with dark hair and blue eyes and a quick smile. She was also many months with child. Emma was happy about the imminent birth of what she was certain was a son. Gautier was not certain and, until he was, he was not overmuch interested. Emma still smiled.

"Are you frightened?" Emma asked.

"Nay, I am not," Elsbeth answered. She was not frightened. She was determined. Stalwart. Serene. She had hoped that it showed.

"That is good," Emma said. "I was frightened, and I was foolish to be so. You will be most content with such a husband, Elsbeth. Your father has done well by you."

He had also done well by himself, but Emma was not the sort of person to understand that. Pointing it out would not fit with Elsbeth's determination to appear serene and otherworldly.

"I am content," she said. It was what was expected of her and would serve her well if Emma repeated this conversation to Gautier. Which she likely would.

"You will be more than content with such a man in your bed," Emma said. "He looks able to get you with child by a look, and I can promise you, more than looks will be shared by you this night."

"Do you seek to counsel me, Emma? I can promise you, Lady Isabel and my mother were quite thorough in their education of me. I know what the marriage bed entails. It *will* require more than a look."

"Oh, nay," she said, laughing, holding on to the great bulk of her belly, "I do not seek to counsel you, only to encourage you. He is a worthy man, Elsbeth. He will bring you joy."

"I do not seek marital joy when I can have sanctity. The world has little to offer me that God, and God alone, cannot supply."

"Oh, Elsbeth, you are too serious," Emma said, grinning and running a fond hand down Elsbeth's hair, which tilted her headband. "Did not God supply the world with men and women and command them to multiply? There are some things that God cannot supply."

"You blaspheme. God is god of all," Elsbeth said, straightening her hair adornment.

"Aye, and yet He has made it so that a woman needs a man to bring forth a child, which is in the center of

His will, is it not? You cannot throw men away, Elsbeth. They must have a place in God's will as surely as you. And they are here to stay," Emma said, laughing lightly.

"Yea, I will agree to that," Elsbeth said, curbing her tongue. With Emma's runaway tongue, this was all sure to find its way into Gautier's ear. "As I said, I am content. Hugh of Jerusalem is a worthy man. I am most honored."

It was perhaps to be hoped that Emma would remember only what she had most recently heard and forget all the rest in her recitation to her husband and lord. It was not beyond hope. Gautier might never hear of her momentary rebellion. Even if he did, she would be gone, well in her husband's keeping, no longer the possession of her father. Aye, there were, after all, some good things to be said for marriage.

Mayhap one. Or two. She could be generous.

They had left the hall, which was oddly still and empty, and walked down the wooden stairs that led to the bailey. The wind was cold and wet, though it was not yet All Saints. A hard winter it looked to be. How her own holding fared, her dower lands of Sunnandune, she did not know. Her father had taken the keeping of it during the years of her fostering, though it was far from Warkham. It would be fine to see Sunnandune again, though a husband would share the moment with her now. It was his right, however, and she would not begrudge him that. Nay, not that.

Emma was still talking gaily, as if there were reason to be gay. Elsbeth was not gay. She was serene, composed, stalwart—all that a wife should be. Or at least the sort of wife she meant to be.

They entered the chapel and were confronted by a throng of bodies. She had not expected this, and it must have showed upon her face.

"Come, Daughter," Gautier said, "you did not expect anything less of me than the most public, the most celebratory of marriages? It is not often that a man of Hugh's merit comes into a damsel's life, taking it for his own. All want to see this joining."

So many witnesses, so many faces she almost remembered from her youth. When had she left Warkham for her fostering? Ten years and more ago, yet some faces rose in her mind and memory, a cotter, a blacksmith, a reeve, until she pushed all memory from her and remembered only her father at her side. So many witnesses. Aye, she understood him. None would say that the marriage between Hugh of Jerusalem and Elsbeth of Sunnandune had not been lawful.

"I would deny no man celebration when the cause has such merit," she said. "Have you taken names, Father, so that the clerk can record the number and weight of the witnesses?"

"Come, Elsbeth," he said, grinning and taking her by the arm. Perhaps so she would not run for the door. "You are too severe. This is your wedding day, long anticipated. We only want to rejoice with you."

She had nothing to say to that, nothing that would serve her present course, and so she kept silent. And she was not severe. She was serene.

Hugh stood at the front of the nave, his height and coloring like a beacon on a hilltop in that smoky, murky light. He watched her come to him, his eyes never leaving hers, his smile soft and warm, so unlike the cold amusement of her father. It was a welcome change, and she allowed herself to appreciate it.

Hugh was dressed as he had been, and she was glad to see it. They made a well-matched pair in their white and crimson, looking something like pilgrims about to set off for far-off lands. And so they were, in their fashion. Marriage was their destination, as he had said. If neither one knew quite what that meant or how to reach those shores safely, they kept their ignorance to themselves. As to that, none in the chapel, and it seemed to be the whole of Warkham, seemed to doubt that all would be well. On the contrary, they all appeared to find the whole notion quite exhilarating.

Of course, she was the one getting married, not they.

With her father on her arm, she was led to Hugh. If she had passing thoughts of a lamb being led to the slaughter, she suppressed them and kept her silence. As the lambs did. It would do her no good to fight now. Her course was set, and she would find her way through it. God was faithful. She had no doubts as to that.

"You are lovely, Elsbeth. A rare sight in this place," Hugh said.

It was kind of him to say so when he had no reason to be kind. Or pretend to be.

"Thank you," she said and then retreated again to the silence of composure.

Her father stood at her back, which was unnecessary. She was not going to run, even if she could find the door through all the people blocking her path. Could he not see her serenity?

"The contracts have been signed, Elsbeth," Hugh said. "Your portion declared, and mine. Will you hear the reading of them, or shall we proceed with the ceremony?"

She knew her father. All had been set down most thoroughly and most legally. He would have made certain that nothing would hinder this marriage and that there would be no cause for repudiation. A most thorough man, her father.

"Nay, I trust that all has been done according to the law. I have no complaint . . . or hesitation. I am yours, my lord; let the priest perform his function. I await your pleasure," she said, sounding exquisitely serene to her own ears. Let her father chew on that.

Her father chuckled.

The priest did not.

She remembered this priest from other days. He had been here when she was a girl. He had been young then and fair to look upon, his features finely molded and his smile quick and white. He was older now, as was she. She could not remember his name. It did not matter.

The ceremony proceeded, and she listened when she could; her attention was concentrated on appearing serene and composed. She had not much left in her for anything else.

She did hear the priest ask if they both consented to the marriage. She waited for Hugh to answer, wondering if he hesitated or if it was the pounding of her own heart which slowed time for that moment. Nay, he did not hesitate and so then, neither must she. She would match him, even in this. No one would be able to accuse her of anything less than cheerful obedience, a most necessary trait in any nunnery. It was all to her favor that there were so many witnesses in Warkham to testify to her willing obedience to her father and her husband.

Her husband. He was her husband now. The ceremony was complete. The kiss of peace was given to Hugh, and Hugh was turning to her, stooping from his great height to kiss her. It would be her first kiss from a man. A kiss she had hoped never to take. A kiss that sealed her place in life, shutting out all other possibilities.

But there were no other possibilities, only wishes. There never had been. She was a woman with a healthy dowry and a healthy body; she was bound for marriage.

And now marriage had her in its grasp.

Hugh's lips brushed against her own.

A shiver passed through her, from his lips to her heart; a shiver of foreboding, surely. A shiver to mark the end of hope. A shiver to mark the beginning of . . . what? A man, a husband, now had possession of her.

And she knew him not at all. She only knew the name of him.

And the beauty. Aye, she knew the beauty of him.

Which was nothing. The eyes deceived. God had declared it to be so, and so she believed, even as she watched him raise himself from her, his eyes soft and gentle, his expression calming and encouraging.

But she did not want calming. She was as beautifully serene as the altar of Christ, as undefiled as Christ's tomb, as untouchable as—

Elsbeth's knees collapsed beneath her; she would have tumbled into a womanish faint if not for her husband's arms about her.

Her last thought before all went gray was that her father would find it all very, very amusing.

"You are well, Elsbeth?"

It was Hugh, her husband.

Her husband.

Elsbeth kept her eyes closed and drew a heavy breath in through her nose. She did not know where she was. She did not want to open her eyes and find all of Warkham watching her. She did not want to open her eyes and see her father. She did not want to open her eyes. Still, it was very quiet. She did not think it in her father's nature to be so very quiet.

"Where am I?"

"In the chapel," he said.

His arms were about her. She could feel them. Her next breath was shaky. It was difficult to be serene lying on the chapel floor.

"Alone?" she whispered, pressing her eyes closed.

"Alone," he said, lifting her into a sitting position.

Slowly she opened her eyes. He was staring down at her, and the full impact of his green eyes and golden beauty assaulted her senses. She felt disoriented and closed her eyes again. Better. Except that she could feel his arms on her back and his chest pressed against her breasts. She took another breath, shallow, but sufficient.

"I have not often had a woman faint at my kiss upon her lips," he said.

Her eyes snapped open.

"I did not faint because you kissed me," she said, pushing his chest away from her, opening the distance between them. "And what do you mean, 'not often'?"

" 'Tis just a manner of speaking," he said, shrugging. "Then you fainted because you were overcome with joy at our union?"

He was teasing her. She hated to be teased. Her father was a master of it, and it had stopped being amusing years ago.

"As you say," she said. "I was overcome."

"I believe you," he said, helping her to stand. It was a blessing to be away from his overbearing heat. "I believe that too much has happened this day and that a maid, even if she be a wife, needs time to . . ."

"Needs time to what?"

He shrugged. "She just needs time," he said, holding on to her hand and staring down into her eyes.

What did he see? Did he think he saw some weakness in her? He did not. She was as ready for this marriage as he, as devoted to God's law and God's will as he. She did not need anything he did not need.

"I do not need anything," she said.

He smiled and turned with her, turning from the argument she longed to begin. "Then take what I offer, even if you do not need. Take time, Elsbeth."

"Time for what?"

"Time for . . . prayer?" he said, cocking a brow at her.

There was only one answer she could give, and she gave it gladly. This was the way out of a marriage that had barely begun. Let him see who she was and where

35

her devotion lay. "I will always and gladly take time for prayer, my lord. Would you join me?"

"Aye," he said, "I will join you. After the meal. Can we pray after the meal or must we bend our knees immediately?"

He was teasing her again. She could feel it. She was very attuned to this sort of thing, being her father's daughter.

"We shall do what pleases you, my lord, in this and in all things. I am, you will find, a most dutiful wife."

"Aye, and most . . . obedient?"

"Aye."

She had only to prove to him that she was better suited to the abbey, and then she could be free of him. Or too nunnish to bed, and then he would repudiate her, and she would fly on wings to Sunnandune. He was a righteous man from the holy land; surely he could see that she did not belong in the married state. He would lose nothing, nothing but a wife, and he would soon be awash in women. He was Hugh of Jerusalem—any woman would be glad of him. Except for her. She had mapped her life, and he could be no part of it. Even if he be Hugh of Jerusalem.

"Come, Elsbeth, I do not mock you," he said. "I only look to find your smile."

They were crossing the bailey, the afternoon wind blowing hard from the sea. The very air looked gray with water. Hugh shivered and pulled his cloak about him.

"Is it never warm here?" he muttered.

"It is warm now, my lord," she said. And smiled at his whining complaint.

"Ah, your smile comes out when you see your husband tremble in harsh weather. I think you will find much to smile upon, Elsbeth. I have been cold since I arrived here."

"This weather is not harsh," she said, trying not to laugh. He was a strange sort of knight.

"Not harsh? The sun has hidden its face for an age. The earth is ever wet and sloggy. I cannot keep my boots clean and I set great store in my boots. Fine red leather, they are, and well tooled. They have come as far as I and, I can tell you, they have no liking for this harsh clime any more than I."

"My lord, the earth is wet because it has rained," she said, biting her lip to keep her smile in bounds; men snared women by luring them to smile. Did he not try to snare her into warm camaraderie now? "There is no more to it than that. The weather does not conspire against you. Or your boots."

"Aye, you can laugh, lady, but I come from a land that sees little rain. And I like it so. The sands are warm, Elsbeth, and the trees silvered in the light of a pearl-white moon. A beautiful place is the Levant, and you would be a beauty there, as you are here."

She completely lost all urge to laugh that he could mock her so.

"I am no beauty, my lord. And I like the rain."

He stopped her as she climbed the stair to the tower and held her back. "You are a beauty, Elsbeth. I have no cause to lie. If the rain-drenched eyes of those who inhabit this distant isle, eyes ruined by lack of sun, cannot see the dark power of your beauty, it is their loss. You are all a man dreams of when he dreams of beauty in Jerusalem."

Nay, he did lie. He flattered, the same as lying. She was no beauty. Her looks were too bold and too small and too dark all at once. Beauty was blond and ruddy and tall. As he was.

No man dreamed of her, not even in far-off Jerusalem.

"My lord, I ask for no flattery. I do not need it. I do not want it. I know who I am," she said.

"I wonder," he said and quickly kissed her fingertips.

It was not flattery, not with words, but it caused her heart to skip and her breath to stop. She did not like it.

He said nothing more, for which she said a prayer of thanks, and they climbed the stairs to the hall. Supper had begun. Her father had not waited for her. She was not surprised.

"It was thought that you might have wanted to seal your marriage vows, Lord Hugh; hence, we did not wait," Gautier said loudly.

"Nay, I can and will wait, no matter my appetites or the appetites of my host," Hugh said, his green eyes cool. But only for the moment. In the next instant, he was smiling and guiding her to a place at the high table near her father.

She had little appetite. Hugh, at her side, ate lightly as well.

"You do not care for pork, my lord?" she asked.

"On occasion. Perhaps not this occasion," he said softly.

The meat was tough and the skin unevenly braised. Elsbeth passed Hugh a small tray of cheese.

"My father's wife cares more for the state of her womb than the state of the kitchens," Elsbeth said. "And my father has a hearty appetite; there is little that can dissuade him."

"And you, lady? What of your appetites?" Hugh asked, chewing a wedge of sharp white cheese.

"I fostered in Dornei, where the table is of supreme importance to Dornei's lady. I have eaten well in the past years and have learned the difference," she said, smiling in spite of herself. He was too quick to make her smile. It did not mesh well with her serenity.

"I, too, have learned to eat well. The tables in the Levant, especially in noble Jerusalem, are set with delicacies in bounteous quantity. I am spoiled, my palate ruined for other climes and other tastes."

"All things learned can be unlearned," she said, taking a sip of her wine. It was thin and had a sour aftertaste. Still, 'twas better than water. She was certain that Christ Himself had not been so particular about his food.

"As you say," he said, nodding agreeably.

She had rebuked him, even if softly. Should he not be angry, even to the lowering of his brow? But, nay, he turned the other cheek, as Christ had instructed. Elsbeth felt her serenity slipping away and blamed Hugh.

"Are you as others, other knights of Jerusalem?" she asked awkwardly.

He turned to look at her, his golden beauty making mock of her question. Was he like any other on the face of God's creation? Nay, there were not many like Hugh of Jerusalem. His beauty was a brand.

"I am Poulain, Elsbeth," he said. "The son and grandson of knights who took up the cross and followed in its way. There are many upon many like me in the Levant. We are Poulains. Children of the Holy Land."

"Men of blood," she said, her scant meal forgotten.

Aye, he was a knight in the most holy of places, fighting a foe only dreamed of in the North, surrounded by the Saracen and holding to the sepulcher of Christ.

"Men of blood," he echoed. "So the holy fathers name us and so we are."

"Men of blood," Gautier said. "I see more of bathwater in you than blood, Hugh. Though your blood may show itself in time."

It was an insult that none could mistake. No jest was this, but a sword smack to a man's honor and pride. None could doubt that.

None at that table did.

Hugh turned to face Gautier, his expression at peace though his eyes were once again cool.

"I could see little need to show you blood, my lord, when I was come to collect your daughter. A betrothal is surely the time for bathwater and not for blood, though if you would see me fight, name the time. Your daughter will be safe in my keeping. I can hold what I grasp. You need not fear for her," Hugh said, his voice low and soft.

"I do not doubt you," Gautier said. "You are the man for my daughter. There is no need to fight, not for me. You are called upon to prove nothing. Your very name proclaims your worth." Gautier smiled, breaking the tense moment. "I misspoke. You will forgive?"

"If you seek forgiveness, you shall have it, though you have done nothing to earn my wrath, Lord Gautier," Hugh said. "Yet forgiveness and blessing shall pour forth from me this day to any and all who have need of it. I have taken a bride today, and I tremble at the bounty of the gift."

All eyes then turned to Elsbeth, startling her. She knew not where to land her gaze; there was no soft and quiet spot on which to turn her eyes when all looked so resolutely and avidly toward her.

"Look upon me, Elsbeth," Hugh said softly. "I will be your haven when all others have flown."

"I need no haven," she said, looking down at her lap. "It is only that I am not at ease with such speech. I have said it; I have no need for flattery."

"Perhaps, then, it is your father who needed to hear from me that I would cherish his daughter. Sometimes, the need goes beyond ourselves."

She looked sharply at him, forgetting all thoughts of serenity at his prick. "I am not thinking of myself! Not in the way that you mean. It is no sin to run from empty flattery, my lord. I should think you would know that. And I can promise you that my father did not have need of any reassurance. He is well pleased with this union, if you had eyes to see."

"Oh, I have eyes to see," he said, his voice lowered to an angry pitch, "and ears to hear."

"My lord?" she asked, startled again by his intensity.

He had seemed to her all of courtesy and mildness, perhaps somewhat like the bathwater warrior her father had named him, though he came from Jerusalem. Perhaps *because* he came from Jerusalem. There were stories of their Levantine ways, an overfondness for bathing and good food, and the softness that was the inevitable result of such living. Yet no tales abounded of Hugh of Jerusalem's softness; nay, it was all his battle prowess and his golden beauty that were touted.

Yet what troubadour would sing of bathwater?

"I now must echo your father," he said, smiling. "I misspoke. Will you forgive me my harsh words and hasty anger? It is not the way of Christ—this we both well know."

"Yet it is of Christ to forgive, even to seventy times seven," she said. "I forgive and gladly. It is forgotten."

Except that she could not forget.

Who was this man she had married?

Chapter Three

He had married into a vipers' nest. The trouble was, he needed the viper's venom and so he must persevere. To have come so far and not to achieve his purpose would be a loss he could not bear, and one he could not bear to report to Baldwin.

All he did was for Baldwin and Jerusalem, and because it was for them, he would abide no regret and no defeat.

Hugh looked at the startled face of his bride and smiled to soothe her. He understood much of what she was and what she attempted. Even knowing, he found no fault with her. She was a woman caught in a net fashioned by ambitious men, and she only thrashed to be free of it. But she was caught fast, and he would not let her go. Not now. Not when he had come to the far northern reaches of the world to this damp and dreary isle on the edge of nothing.

He had need of her. He would deal gently, or as gently as he could, and then, perhaps, if all went well, he would release her to the cloister she hungered for. But that was far off. Now, there were other things to be done, words to be spoken and a part played out.

Whatever else happened, he knew he would manage Elsbeth well.

She was a woman who needed careful and soft management. That such a woman of striking beauty and abundant wealth could not see her own value, that she had not found the measure of her worth in the eyes of a distant admirer or the words of a protective father, were her bane. She had been much ignored, much discarded, but no longer. He was her husband now, and he would see all repaired. He would leave her better than he had found her.

Aye, he smiled to soothe her; it was a gentle and simple thing to give a woman the soft security of a smile. He gave her his smiles with an open and liberal hand. She was his wife. He would take care of her.

"You are generous, Elsbeth," he said. "I am a skittish groom. Perhaps all men are so upon their first marriage. I will, it is hoped, get better at this with time."

"You expect to say the vows and sign the contracts again, with another bride?" she asked, lifting her goblet for a small sip of wine.

"I do not know what to expect. The Lord of Hosts will

direct my steps along my lifepath. But I do know that it is rare beyond pearls for a man, or a woman, to live long with one spouse. The world is too hard a place and buffets human souls too often for long life, even when that life is shared as ours now are."

"What you say is true," Elsbeth said, setting down her cup. "We cannot know what tomorrow brings. You may well find yourself with another bride."

Did he hear hope in her voice? Aye, she could well hope for it. She had no great eagerness for this marriage, yet she had come into it well enough.

Her hands were as small as a child's, white and slender. The ring he had given her to mark her as his wife stood out upon her hand, a heavy weight of gold and sapphire that shone like darkest night and brightest day—the colors of Jerusalem. The colors of his pledge.

"But is it not odd to speak of next wives when your newest and first sits at your side? And at her bridal feast?" she asked. "Perhaps it is only that you speak your wish."

There was a light in her black eyes, a hidden and smallish light of devilment. He grinned to see it. Elsbeth was too much solemn and too seldom smiling. He wanted an unblemished and holy wife, as did any man, but he wanted her joyous. Flashes of unexpected joy were all that made life bearable until the gleaming glory of eternal reward.

"Again you see how little experience I have at marriage and bridal feasts," he said, taking her hand in his. "You must be gentle with me, Elsbeth. I have no hunger for another wife. You meet all my desires and every hunger well enough."

She gasped at the contact, and he lowered his head to hide his smile. She amused him. She was so innocent and so wary, so unaccustomed to the ways of a man, even the gentle ways of chivalry. Her education had been somewhat lacking in those matters, though her religious instruction was above the mark. Well, and he was more adept at chivalry than religion; he would instruct her.

"It must be odd for a husband to ask for gentleness in a wife. I cannot hurt you, my lord. I have neither the skill nor the means for it," she said, resting her hand in his.

"You are wrong in that, little wife," he said, lifting her hand to his mouth. "A beautiful woman has many weapons with which to wound a man."

He kissed the inside of her wrist, a light meeting of lips and blue-veined skin. Her skin was as soft as silken velvet, and his hunger for her leapt up like pulsing flame, scorching them both in its sudden heat.

Her eyes, black as a moonless night over the darkest sea, stared at his mouth upon her wrist. Her sigh was soft. Her pulse raced.

"I am not . . . I will not wound you," she said, slipping her wrist away from him.

"Nay? You wound me even now," he said, looking deep into her eyes. "Can you not see the blood you spill, Elsbeth?"

"Nay, I have not."

"Then give me your hand again and let me feast upon the silk of your skin. I ask no more of you."

"It is too much," she whispered, her gaze sliding to where Emma sat giggling beside Gautier.

"Then I will not ask it of you," he said. "Give me only what you will, and I will learn to live with wounding."

"Stop," she said, lowering her eyes. "I am not able to jest in this fashion."

" 'Tis no jest," he said. " 'Tis only a husband speaking to his wife. A first husband to a first wife."

She looked up at him then, and he could see the smile that hovered near her expressive eyes.

"Only smile at me, little wife, and all bleeding will be stanched, all wounds forgiven."

"You put much power into a smile."

"Nay, only your smile."

She smiled then and shook her head at his extravagance and his arrogance. Her mother had warned her of this, of this deception, this lure. These words were empty, yet they glittered, and she was mesmerized by the glimmer of them and of him.

He was a strange man, unlike any other she had known; even wild Ulrich could not match the smooth beauty of his words. He spoke of wounding, but it was she who was in danger of being wounded. With all others, she had the possibility of retreat, but where and how could a wife retreat from a husband? She knew of no such place. He was the master of her body and her life, both church and king declared it.

"When we are far from this hall, I will breathe in rhythm with your smiles, Elsbeth," Hugh said, leaning toward her.

"I have not so many smiles in me to keep you breathing," she said, edging away from him.

"Ah! A parry and a thrust from my little wife. You are learning, little one," he said, grinning. "Soon you will be calling troubadours to your side to hear their golden praise of you. And none shall hinder them. You deserve songs, line upon line, describing your beauty and your purity. But perhaps a troubadour from the Levant would better serve you. I do not trust what cold words might spew from a man living in these northern climes."

"I cannot keep pace with you, my lord. Your words are too quick. I am a mudfrog to your eel."

"Rather say you are a pheasant to my hawk, Elsbeth. I would not be an eel, even for you."

"There is the proof. I cannot even keep pace when striving for a metaphor. You have won the field. I stand silenced."

"Nay, not silenced, only stand," he said, helping her

to her feet with his hand on her arm. His hand was large and warm, even through her sleeve. "Stand and let all those in this hall feast their eyes upon you. We have tarried long here. Let us do what we are called by God to do. Have you the heart for it?"

She did not. Her inward parts were cold and watery, like the eel she had just named.

"Speak, Elsbeth," he urged, his head lowered to hers. "I would not drag you from the feast if you would stay."

She could not speak. She knew her duty was to obey, yet she could not. Had God led her here without a tower to hide her in? She knew it could not be so. God was not so unmerciful or unloving. With all her heart, she cast upward a prayer to heaven, praying as she sent it that God would listen.

God was silent.

"I have no wish to stay," she said.

"Then let us depart. We have an appointment, do we not?" he said.

"Do we?" she said, waiting for her miracle, certain it would come, that God had not deserted her to face what every bride must face upon the completion of her vows.

"Yea," he said. "Did we not agree to pray together after the meal?"

If he grinned at her in jest, enjoying her discomfort, she remembered again the pleasure men took in having women in their power. Still, God had answered. It was no miracle, but it was an answer. Yea, to pray. 'Twas what they had agreed upon. Hugh was not insisting upon his marital rights.

What she would do when he did insist, she was not certain. Nay, that was untrue. She was most certain. She would pray for a miracle.

The chapel was still when they entered it. They were alone and the light was dim. She was grateful for all. She needed time and privacy to cool the hot flush in her cheeks.

Her father had not let them leave the hall without comment. That his comments had been loud was to be expected. That his comments had been irreverent was also to be expected. That he had roused the hall to laugh and whistle upon learning that Hugh was taking her off to pray had been more than she expected and more than she was prepared to endure.

Hugh had not seemed to take offense, however, and for that she was grateful. Her father seemed to her to be a most offensive man. That her husband seemed somewhat fond of Gautier was a blessing. Familial discord was nothing to be wished for, though their home would be far from Gautier's. Another blessing.

"I do not know if it is the hour for Nocturn or Prime, the light is so uncertain. Does the sun never shine?" Hugh said as they walked toward the nave.

"The sun is shining now," she said.

"How can you tell?" he said, clasping her hand.

He had been holding on to her hand since they walked across the hall together; he had even squeezed her fingers as the whistles and catcalls of her father's men had risen to a din. She supposed he meant to comfort her. It was disturbing in the extreme that she was, indeed, comforted.

She looked up at him, at his smile, and saw his constant humor, his relentless efforts to make her smile. A most unusual man, to be so occupied and for so little cause. She did not need constant cheering. There was nothing amiss with her temper. Still, he did make her smile and feel light of heart. The look of him alone was enough to make a maid feel dreamy; he did not need to work so diligently. Yet when did temptation ever rest?

"The sun shines, even behind the clouds. You will

soon learn to discern darkness from daylight," she said, trying to pull her hand free.

He lifted her hand to his mouth and lightly kissed her fingertips. "Until I do, you must help me lest I stumble into Compline when all else are at their rest."

"I do not think it in you to stumble," she said, ignoring the feel of his mouth on her. Or trying to.

"You flatter me. I am glad to see that, though we are married and settled, you still think to stroke my vanity. It shows a wifely devotion and concern which are touching."

"I . . ." she began. "I do not mean to flatter you, nor stroke any man's vanity into greater size. God forbid I fall into such a practice."

They were at the nave, and he pulled her down onto her knees at his side. "I do not think you encourage me to sin. I never would. Be at rest, Elsbeth. Rest in me as you rest in Christ. Now, shall we pray?"

Rest in him? She could not rest in him. There was no resting with temptation, and he was pure temptation. He had to know it. No man could look as he did or speak as he did and not know the temptation he was to every woman in his sphere. As his wife, her temptation was multiplied a hundredfold. She was his, and yet she could not be his. How God was going to save her from this was a puzzle, yet if God could manage for Joseph to rise from slavery to become ruler of all Egypt, He could surely manage Hugh of Jerusalem.

She could rest in that.

With that thought triumphant over all her fears, she set herself to her prayers.

Why she held herself aloof from him he could not fathom. He was her husband. He had taken on the part willingly and with good cheer. He was a well-favored man in appearance and connection. He was cordial and brimming with courtesy. That he would take her from her father's house was surely a blessing she should thank God in all His mercy for. Did not every maid yearn for her own domain?

Perhaps it was the intimacy of the marriage bed which held her still and solemn away from him. Aye, that was logical and fit what he knew of women. Well, he had time and patience; he would win her trust and her smiles. He was confident of that.

She was a timid little thing, unused to raucous humor and the ways of men. He could not and would not fault her for that. Nay, not when the women of the Levant were tutored and protected to display just such traits. He had not thought to find such in his travels north. The women of Henry's kingdom were given more freedom than the women of his home, and he could not see that there had been any benefit to the practice. Women were unlike men in all their ways; they wanted protection, and a man shouldered that task gladly.

That Elsbeth was modest and quiet was right and well within the order of the world.

That she needed him was a gift he accepted gladly.

The matter of Gautier he would handle gently. That Hugh was adept at handling difficult men and uncertain times was the gift he brought with him from a lifetime living in the Levant, where men strove constantly against both ally and adversary. Baldwin had set much to rights when he took the throne, wresting it from the clenching grasp of his mother, Queen Melisende. She was a woman who understood nothing and learned nothing. Baldwin was as unlike his mother as a man could be, and Hugh his closest friend. There was much to understand of the world, and Hugh had been a willing pupil. The stakes were high: the very sanctity of Jerusalem.

But that was distant thinking, and his battle was here, with this wife, in this moment.

It would be a gentle battle. He would not harm her nor leave her scarred. Never would he hurt a woman, least of all his little wife who knelt so prettily at his side, her mouth moving in prayer.

Nay, he would not harm her, nor cause her the least distress. In that knowledge, he rested, his mind at ease, his purpose clear. He would leave England with no regrets.

There were only so many prayers she could say before praying was done. Nay, that was untrue. Did not the scriptures declare that all would praise God for the length of eternity and not run out of words proclaiming His greatness and His love? Aye, but there were no cold stone floors in heaven. She was becoming stiff. She was wanting to be done with praying, but the husband at her side prayed on. Could she let him outpray her, she who had a name for prayer and holiness that was finding its way into song?

Was it wise to make praying a competition?

She knew the answer, acknowledged it in her heart. And stayed kneeling on the floor. It was Hugh who complained of the cold, not she. He would rise first. She had only to wait.

The wait seemed overlong to her knees.

She shifted her weight and breathed a sigh she hoped he would not note. Let him think her unaware of earthly discomforts while her mind and soul dwelt on God. Let him know the nature of her devotion and her steelish bent toward all things heavenly. She would not make a good wife to any man. Her life must and would be found only within the cloister. Let him think on that and release her to it.

And soon, for her joints were like to crack.

"You tire, Elsbeth?" he asked, looking down at her. "Then let us depart. God knows the condition of our hearts, whether we be kneeling or walking."

"I do not tire," she said, ignoring the pain in her throbbing knees. "I could and will pray away the days and the nights. It is my calling."

"Ah," he said, smiling and lifting her to her feet despite her words, "but first you have been called to marriage, is that not so? And is not God's timing ever and always perfect? There are many hidden behind abbey walls who first have tasted of the world and then sought refuge. You may find yourself of that number. Perhaps."

Perhaps. He threw her a sop and she was supposed to cling to it. Well, she did not want to be a wife and then a nun. She would be all of nun and none of wife, no matter his charm or his look. It was most important that he believe that. He had to repudiate her. She was unfit to be a wife. She knew that well; it only remained to convince him of it before she was utterly lost in the temptation of him.

"It is also true that only God knows the future. Perhaps I will find my way into the nunnery sooner rather than later," she said, refusing his hand with as much dignity as she could manage.

"I think, Elsbeth," he said, taking her face in his hands, "that you will find your way into my bed before any nunnery has the gift of you."

Now was the time for God to deliver His miracle to her. Now, when Hugh's green eyes were looking down into hers, his smile soft and encouraging, his manner coaxing and light. Now, when the temptation of him rose up in her heart to wipe all wisdom and piety from her very soul.

To be in his bed. Aye, the vision of it was before her eyes, calling to her heart. She could feel her heart, traitor that it was, running hard to catch the vision of them twined together, his hands upon her, his mouth upon her, his heat filling her. She was pure, aye, but she was not made of stone.

She was adept at turning from many sins, many temptations, but not this one. Not the call of a man to the heart of a woman. Not the call of a husband to his wife. Not the call of Hugh of Jerusalem.

How well Ardeth had understood her. How well and ardently she had counseled her. How little it all seemed to matter now. Had her mother known this was how it would fall out?

Aye, she had.

His mouth lowered to hers, and she could not even think to turn her head. He smelled like wine and bread, like holy sacrament and sacred wine; the blood and body of Christ in His very sanctuary. All the things a man could not be, he was, this man from shining Jerusalem.

His mouth touched hers, his hands on her cheeks, holding her fast to accept his kiss. She would not have turned. Her will was gone, stolen by the scent of him.

A kiss it was, a kiss like none she had ever had. A kiss of longing and of tenderness and of passion breathed to life. A kiss to mark her as his own. A kiss to tangle with her soul until all was shadow and flicker of dwindling light. The light of her reason gone, doused in a single kiss upon the very altar of God.

A temptation that ensnared her with a single, warm whisper.

He lifted his mouth from hers; it had not been so very long, and yet she gasped a breath.

"You will not faint?" he said, laying his hand under her chin, studying her face.

"I will not," she said, but she did not speak of fainting; she spoke of all he held out to her, tempting her. She would not succumb to this. She would not run from all her plans. She would not gamble with her life, not even for Hugh of Jerusalem.

It was time for her miracle, and the prayer she sent shooting to heaven was blinding in its fervor. With such a need behind the prayer, did she wonder if God would answer?

She did not.

In the next instant, all was answered, and as surely as Daniel had been delivered from ravenous lions, so was she delivered from the hot temptation of desire.

Her courses had begun; she felt the hot trail of blood winding its way down her leg.

Chapter Four

"What say you?"

"I said, my courses have begun. We cannot consummate the marriage," she said, enjoying the look of shock on his face. He did not look so composed now.

"Now? Just now? You are certain?"

"Yea, just now." Thanks be to God and the perfection of His time. "And I am certain. This is not the first time for me, my lord. I know what I am about," she said. If her grin was somewhat superior, she did not suppose she could be faulted for it.

"But . . . we are wed today," Hugh said.

He seemed to be having some difficulty grasping the fact that she would not share his bed. Perfect. His taunt about her fainting at his kiss was almost forgiven. Almost.

"Aye, we are; yet, if I had been consulted I could have told the priest, my father, and you that now was not the best time for it. Yet I was not consulted. I know my body's rhythms; my father does not."

"Aye," he said, running a hand through his golden

hair, twisting the strands until all was a shimmering jumble of brown and gold and flaxen white.

He could do what he wished with his hair; he was not going to touch her. Not for a week at the very least. A week. A long week. Had God not created the world in a week? Surely it was well within His grasp to wrench her from this marriage in the same number of days.

It was the first time Hugh had not had to coax a smile from her. Nay, she smiled most freely. He did not seem to appreciate her good humor.

"You do not seem dismayed," he said, frowning slightly.

"Do I not?" she said, all sprightly cheer. "Well, I suppose I can wait a week for our bond to be set before God and church. Can you?"

He straightened at that and left off the ruffling of his hair. "I have been challenged," he said, looking down at her. She straightened and met his look; her own hair was perfectly ordered, as was her composure. "Aye, I can wait a week for you, little wife, but now I think that you will not be so content to wait a week for me."

"I do not know—"

"Ah, yea, you know," he said, cutting her off while he ran a fingertip over the waves of her hair. "I accept your challenge, wife. I will not be the one to pant after you; at least I will promise you not to be alone in my panting. Nay, for I shall wring a cry from you, and only when I have your cry upon my lips will I take possession of you."

The images were too strong, of taking and of crying out in passion and of his coming for her, pursuing her with all the relentless heat of dogs after a boar. She would be the boar for no man. He would not make her pant, and her only cries would be the soulful cries of devoted prayer. She would prove that to him, taking up the challenge he had set before her. He would not make her into something she was not. She would never be a woman who panted for a man.

"You will wait long, my lord. If that is your plan, then this marriage will never be consummated." Another oft-spoken prayer.

"You do not understand men, Elsbeth, if you say that. A man challenged is a man who must then win. What is more certain is that you do not understand me."

She did not want to understand him. She only wanted him out of her life so that she could escape the burden of men. Did he understand nothing of her wants and wishes? Nay, he did not. His thoughts were all of himself, which was very like a man.

"I cannot stand here," she said, wanting to be away from him and his vows and challenges. He was just like men as she knew them to be: self-serving, arrogant, and proud. She understood men well enough and had no wish to understand them better. "I bleed, I tell you. I must away."

"Then away, Elsbeth, and I with you. I am your husband, ever at your side, in need or without," he said, placing his arm about her and hurrying her from the chapel.

"I cannot walk so fast," she said, tripping over her skirts. "I do not need your assistance in this."

"Aye, but I am a husband of an hour. I need to be needed. I need to be with you, even if I cannot take you, planting my scent upon you and within you, feeling you shift beneath me, holding me within your heat."

"Stop! This is not speech a maid should hear," she said, putting her hands over her ears.

"Ah, maiden wife, you are right in that, but you shall hear it and feel the need for me grow in your belly and in your blood, until you beg to be freed of your maid-enhead. Until you pant my name and cannot think be-

55

yond having my hands upon you. That is what this week will bring you. That is my task."

"This is no worthy task," she said, pulling away from him, wanting her own space to breathe and think and move. She did not want his hands upon her. She never would. If only he would believe that of her, then this marriage could end today. God above, let this marriage end today.

"I have a maiden wife who will be a maiden still. It is the task I find before me. What can I do but meet it?" he said, grinning.

He caught her up against him and held her like a babe to his chest. The ground seemed leagues beneath her, and she held onto his neck without thinking. The smell of him was like goldenrod and honey, golden and sweet and wild.

It was certainly not how a knight should smell.

"My garments will be stained if you hold me like this. Let me down. Let me find my own way. I say again, I know what I am about."

"I am not afeared of blood, Elsbeth. I know the scent and look of it too well. If your garment is stained, I will buy you ten more to replace it, but I will not relinquish you. That price is too high. The feel of you in my arms is worth ten gowns and a cloak of ermine beside."

"You talk of cloaks of ermine when all this is about is a woman and her courses. Or a man who has found his will thwarted by the flow of blood." Aye, he had bumped against God's provision for her and was bruised. A lovely thought. Now, if only he would break and set her free.

He looked hard at her and then smiled, pressing her to him even more. He was a hard man and hot. For all he complained of the cold, he was so very hot.

"Aye, you speak true. My will is thwarted." He looked at her and pressed a kiss to her brow and then he whispered, "I want you. I want you, Elsbeth. I want the dark and solemn beauty of you to break over me like the rising dawn after a night of storms and wild winds. I want the softness of your skin to be my only contact with the earth. I want your breath to feed me. I want—"

"Stop!" she said, burying her face against his neck, shutting out the sight of him, but not the scent and not the feel. He surrounded her.

She could easily learn to hate him.

"Aye, I will, but only because we are at the hall. Let us put a happier face on this for your father."

"Nay! Say naught to him."

He looked into her eyes and smiled slowly. "I will say nothing. Let him think what he will think. Our time and our tidings are our own. I will not betray."

He took the steps in stride, the weight of her seeming no more than a cloak he carried. The lights and noise of her father's holding came to her first and then the smells. The way to the upper chambers lay across the hall. They would need to cross all of it to reach the room that was hers. She did not know how she would manage a passage of such distance with her dignity intact. Perhaps there was no way.

The sounds of the hall quieted as they entered. And then there came the laughter.

"Did she faint again?" her father called out. "She is too much at her prayers, that one."

"Nay, she did not faint," Hugh said, and she could hear the smile in his voice, the good humor he projected to the very rafters. "I am a husband newly made; am I to be faulted if I want the feel of my wife in my arms? Is Elsbeth not to be praised for giving in to my whims so readily?"

And so it ended before it had even begun. Her father was silenced, her dignity no more than bruised, and they were across the hall and climbing the stairs to her chamber.

"Take note, Elsbeth," Hugh said as he climbed the dark and twining passage. "If you would still a tongue, speak long and speak well, stilling all opposition by your very breath."

"It takes a mighty breath to still my father," she said, looking over his shoulder and back down the stair as the noise of the hall resumed its normal sound.

"As you say," he said, laughing. "But I have breath enough, have no fear."

"Of that, I do have no fear," she said, looking at his profile.

How that he could keep such good cheer about him? She never knew a man to be so winsome for so little cause. She had no cause to complain, except that it did make him more difficult to resist. Temptation's package was ever sweet.

He elbowed past the heavy door and then set her down in her chamber. All was dark within; the fire had not been lit, nor the tapers. The wind was rising without, dark clouds of purple and ash gray rolling across a darkening sky. The westering sun was hidden behind heavy clouds and thrashing treetops, moving relentlessly away, leaving them all in growing darkness.

The blood ran in ever growing force down her leg.

"Go now," she said.

"Go? Now?" he said, looking at her like a newborn calf.

"Aye," she said, pushing him from the chamber with her hands on his massive chest. Did women not bleed in Jerusalem when their courses ran? "Now!"

He backed up at her words, letting her force him from the chamber. "I will go, but I will remain without. I will not leave."

"Aye, I am much comforted," she said, shaking her head at his declaration. He could go back to far Jerusalem for all she cared at that moment. In fact, she would prefer it.

When the door was secured against him, she knelt by her trunk and pulled out her binding cloth and pad of lamb's wool. Lifting her skirts, she secured all somewhat clumsily.

Could she not hear him breathing at the door? And then she wiped the smear of blood from her legs with a dampened cloth. Thank God above she had chosen to wear a crimson garment. Her chemise had taken the worst of it; she needed to don a new one, which would require that she remove all and begin from the skin out.

Did she not hear her husband moving impatiently at the door? She drew the curtain that covered the door against drafts, shutting him out still further. With that last barrier in place, she removed her garments.

It was when she was completely naked that he knocked again, softly yet insistently.

She jumped and whirled, her chemise wadded to her chest.

"What is it?" she hissed.

"Someone comes."

"I can do nothing as to that," she said, pulling the chemise over her head. It was slow work; she was unaccountably clumsy.

He banged upon the door with his fist. "Let me in. I will not be found upon the doorstep."

"Aye, it is better to be found banging at my door. That will cause no comment in the hall," she said to the door, fumbling with her clothing.

He was not helping her, though she could not think that he would care as to that. He only wanted to get in. The state of her dress was not his concern. Nay, but it was hers.

"Better to find me breaking down the door of an unwilling and chill wife than to find me sitting in the doorway like an errant dog," he said, his mouth obviously pressed to the door.

"I am not unwilling, merely unable," she said. "I have done nothing. This is not my fault."

Her chemise was on, as was her pelisse. She could have let him in, but she was reluctant to receive him without shoes and stockings. And she needed to remove the pile of bloody garments on the floor.

"You have surely done nothing. That will be proved on the morrow," he said. "Or in the next instant. I think it is your father who comes."

She opened the door at that and pulled him inside. He closed the door behind them and bolted it. She tried to hide the bloody evidence of her flux with a kick of her foot, but he looked exactly where she did not want.

"It is true, then," he said, "though it is difficult to see in this dim light. Can we not light a taper?"

"I can see very well," she said. "And I do not lie. And some things, such as this, are private."

"So, is that your way of saying we cannot light a taper?" he said, smiling softly.

Why did he turn everything to jest and mirth and laughter? Could he not see that life was a solemn affair of duty and service? Could he not see that she did not want him in her life?

"Light it if you will," she said, turning from him to pick up her soiled clothes, "but I am not staying."

"Oh, yea, you will stay," he said, leaning against the door with his arms crossed over his chest. He had mighty arms and shoulders like an ox. He was more formidable than any iron bolt. "We cannot leave, not till morn when the whole world of Warkham will know and record that we have performed our marital duty."

"As I said, I do not lie," she said. "And I will not, especially not about this."

She was untouched and would remain so. Would that

the world would know she was a maiden still. The whole world, yet not her father. He would be most displeased that his plans had skipped and tilted against a will and power mightier than his own.

"Then do not lie, but lie with me this night. Our night will be chaste, yet I will have your company, Elsbeth. None other shall claim you."

"None other seeks me," she said. "I do not understand why you would want to . . . want to spend the night closeted with me when there can be . . . there will be no . . ."

"Consummation?"

"Copulation," she said.

"At least you did not say fornication. That would have wounded me greatly," he said, his smile as firmly in place as ever.

He did love to jest at her expense. She had no liking for it. Yet when did that ever stop a man?

"I have no desire to wound you," she said, still holding her bloody garments. She really had to get them in water. "Now I must away."

"Nay, you must not."

"You really have no idea what a woman's needs are at such a time, do you?" she said, pushed to the edge of her patience, of which she had a bounteous supply, easily a match to her famous serenity. A bottomless supply, until he had stumbled into her life.

"As much as any unmarried man," he said. "But I know what my needs are very well. I need only to have you with me this night. It is not so great a need to meet, is it, Elsbeth? It is a nigh great need in my heart. To have you lie with me, to touch your face, to watch you while you sleep and hold you in my arms, to talk with you as the owls scour the air on silent wings . . . all this is my need, and all you must do to satisfy it is to lie with me on this bed. Now."

He was too swift in words. He scoured her heart with

his words of longing and tenderness, leaving her blood-raw and aching for what would never be. For what she could not allow.

"Let me tell you what I need, my lord. You are now a married man and you should know these things. I will not lie abed all night, with you or without you. I will be up again and yet again to change the padded sling I wear that catches my blood-fall."

She hoped to shock him, or at least repulse him. He looked neither shocked nor repulsed.

"Then I will stay and talk with you the night through. I will wipe the blood from you, cleansing you. I will hold back the dark fall of your hair so that it will not hinder you in your self-ministrations. I will not leave you, Elsbeth. Let us share this bloody night together. A man expects no less than blood on his wedding night."

He was impossible. Worse, he had managed to embarrass her. He was beginning to remind her of her father.

"The church has rules about such things," she said. "I am not clean at such a time."

"Blood is blood, Elsbeth," he said. "No man wants to wash in it, though sometimes he must. I will not be defiled by sharing a bed with you," he said, stepping away from the door. "I will not touch you, if that is what you wish. I only will not leave you. That is my vow and my desire. What fault in that, little wife?"

God had given her this miracle of blood, and Hugh soiled its beauty by his presence. Had not God intended for him to leave her to herself? It was her desire, and her desires were ever in line with God's own divine will. She truly would make a most perfect nun, if only her husband would open his eyes and see that truth for himself. They could have the marriage annulled in time for Prime. It was a prayer worth praying. Let him stay, then, and see what manner of holy woman he had bound himself to. This night of blood and prayer might serve her cause well.

"Stay, then," she said, throwing her soiled garments in the corner.

He smiled his pleasure and his victory; yea, she saw it for what it was, and then he said, "Now may we light the taper?"

Oh, aye, he was the victor. None but the victorious would laugh so.

"Aye, and the fire as well," she said. "I would not leave you in the dark, since you seem to fear it so."

"Oh, wife," he said, laughing as he bent to the fire, fanning the chill embers. "You are a warrior at heart to strike so at a man you little know. I had not thought it of you—you who are given to much prayer and little speech. Or so it is said."

"I had not thought you a man to listen to gossip. It is not the way of the righteous."

"Say, then, that I have listened to the tales of you, Elsbeth, Prayer Warrior."

"You have said it. Prayer Warrior. I seek no other life. I do no other battle."

"Except with husbands," he said, straightening. He had kindled the fire, casting red and gold light throughout the small chamber.

"I know nothing of husbands," she said, her back to the wall, her bloody garments at her feet.

"Yet," he said, grinning. "But that will come, in time. You do know something, if the tales be true, of men and what they must risk in their quest for holiness."

"You speak of Richard of Warefeld," she said.

"Aye, I do," he said, crossing his arms over his chest, studying her in the flickering light.

"That is not my tale to tell."

"You are wise to say so, Elsbeth. Never would I urge it from you. Yet many in Christendom know what he did and marvel at his courage and his purity of heart. I wish I had been there."

"Nay, you do not," she said. "It broke the heart to see it, yet lifted the spirit to heaven itself."

"So it is said of all journeys to sanctity. The Lord of Hosts calls us to a narrow way, rocky and treacherous, yet there is no other path."

"Nay, there is not," she said. "It is the path I long with all my soul to tread. That path and no other."

She did not want to be a wife. She did not want a husband. She did not want anything he could give her.

He was a golden force in that darkened chamber, glowing with health and strength and holy purpose. It was this vision of him she feared the most, even more than his beauty. Her mother had not prepared her for this, and she felt ill-equipped to fight against holy ardor. It seemed immoral even to try.

Yet he was not pure. He was mortal, and mortal man could claim much, but never purity. Never perfection. No matter what the eyes declared or the ears heard, he was a man, and she would have naught to do with men.

"You would have it no other way, I think," he said, coming toward her, the size of him great with the fire at his back and the darkness all around him. She held her ground. She would not give way.

"There is no other way," she said, feeling the blood welling between her legs. It was near time to change her padding. This month she flowed hard and fast, praise God. "I do not wish for what is not. I only pray for what can and should be."

"You are wise to spend your time so," he said, closing the distance between them. "God has instructed us to pray without ceasing; there can be no better way to spend a life."

Yet how could she be a goodly wife if she spent her time so? Did he not see that? She could not pray without

ceasing and be a wife. Unless matters were different in
Jerusalem. She had not considered that.

He knelt at her feet and picked up the bloody garments, and she gasped in shock. This she did not want
of him. It was too foul and too . . . intimate. He was not
her servant. He was a stranger, though a husband. No
man should tend to such. What manner of men did Jerusalem birth?

"It is how I would spend my life," she said, "if I were
freed from the bonds of marriage."

"This I understand, Elsbeth," he said, looking down at
her. He held the soiled garments in one hand. "But I
can do nothing as to that. We are bound, the contracts
signed, our oaths given. Let be, little wife. Let God direct
you. Only trust, and all will be well."

"I do trust," she said. And she did. But not him, not
a husband, not a man. Her trust was all for God.

"Then rest in that trust, and tell me where to put
these," he said, lifting the bloody garments. "I would
help you, if and when I can."

In all he said, he seemed to say more, as if there were
a deeper meaning just below the golden light of his
beauty. But she never looked for hidden meanings unless they were in holy writ; she did not want anything
approaching meanings from the man before her eyes.
Only fools looked for the meaning behind raw temptation.

"If you would help me, then bring me a pail of water,
not too full. I must set the fabric in it and let it soak.
Also, I need more cloth for binding. Is this the work of
a knight of Outremer, my lord, to fetch and tend the
needs of a woman?"

She was angry, vulnerable because he made her so and
would not let her tend to herself. In all things, she was
a woman who did not need a man.

He only smiled, as was his way. Was there aught that

could topple him from his calm complacency?

"To tend to your needs is all I need know of duty, Elsbeth," he said. "Now I will leave and see to your requests, but you must vow that you will stay behind this door. I will not share you with any tonight. You are mine, wholly. It is our night, no matter what blood comes between us. Only blood shall separate us, and only for a time."

"I will stay," she said, but only because she could feel the pad filling. She did not dare to leave. "Only hurry."

He grinned and bowed to her, surely a mockery of all chivalry. "I will away and return as the hawk, so glad am I that you hunger for my return. Your desire for me grows upon the hour."

" 'Tis the padding I desire," she mumbled as he closed the door behind him. "Not you!"

He stuck his golden head back in, grinning as was his way. "If you will allow me to instruct? 'Twill only serve you well to flatter me."

"I have said I do not lie," she bit out.

He laughed as he closed the door. "I know you do not lie, little wife, yet I am not blind. I see what you feel for me. Your eyes reveal what your lips will not."

The door closed with a soft thud. If she were the type of maid to throw things, she might have thrown the stool against the hard surface of the door. It would have made a mighty sound. But she was not that sort of woman, though it appeared that he could drive her to it.

Her eyes revealed what her lips did not?

She should never have allowed him to light the fire; darkness served her better.

Chapter Five

Gautier was waiting for him in the long dark of the stair. He looked hard at the bloody garments in Hugh's hands.

"What are you about?" Gautier said.

"I am about the winning of a woman's heart," Hugh said. "She is in flux. There will be no bedding this night, nor for many nights."

"You have a task before you, then, to keep the marriage from being annulled."

"Aye, I do," Hugh said, passing him on the stair and going through the hall, heading for the kitchens outside the tower. He could only wish that Gautier would remain behind in the dark gloom of the smoky hall. Gautier chose to follow as far as the outer stair.

"She will fight you, but softly. It is her way," Gautier said.

"Aye, I know it," Hugh said to the night air. "She is a soft warrior, but still she fights."

It was no condemnation, though he wondered if Gautier understood that as the older man returned inside without a word.

"My lord?" Raymond, Hugh's squire, asked, coming to him from the stables. "May I attend you?"

"Nay, I need no aid, not in this," Hugh said.

"There is something amiss?" Raymond said.

Hugh smiled. "Nay. Aye. All is amiss, and yet 'tis nothing calamitous. Elsbeth has her courses upon her. I can do naught tonight, nor for many nights. The timing is most ill, yet God will test a man. So I am tested most hard."

Raymond chuckled and then swallowed the laughter building in his throat. He choked and then coughed, covering all. Covering nothing.

"You laugh?" Hugh said. "You can find mirth in it? 'Tis not your wedding night."

"Oh, my lord, it is hard duty to which you are called," Raymond said, laughing in spite of all his efforts.

"Speak not to me of hard. I am hard enough, and there is no escape from it."

"Yet how does Elsbeth fare in such a pass? Is she not as dismayed by this turning as you?"

"Dismayed? She is giddy with triumph," Hugh said.

"My lord?" Raymond said in sudden seriousness. "She will not seek an annulment. Not from you."

Hugh ran a hand through his hair and looked up at the sky, swaddled in clouds. "I think it may be in her to do such a thing," he said slowly. "She is a maid unlike any other I have known."

"My lord, 'tis not possible," Raymond said in suppressed outrage.

Hugh grinned and punched Raymond softly on the arm. "All things are possible, Raymond. Especially with this woman, I think. She has a core of steel to her that is uncommon, and her outward manner is cold and hard as well. In between, she is soft and womanish, yet how much of her is so? How much of her is able to be turned by a pleasing phrase or a timely kiss? That is what I do not know." Hugh smiled suddenly and said, "Yet the battle of Elsbeth will be a rare thing. I find myself looking forward to the challenge of her."

" 'Twill not be much of a challenge, not for you, my lord," Raymond said.

"Your confidence inspires me, boy. Now I had best be about the business of Elsbeth."

"How can I aid you, my lord?"

"By keeping your distance, and by ensuring the dis-

tance of all others who would stand between me and
mine. I will keep her to myself. There shall be no escape
for her from Hugh, no chance to rebuild her tattered
defenses. I will encompass her complete. She will fall
into my hand, but it will be a soft falling."

"Aye, my lord. I comprehend you."

"I go now to serve her needs. Do what you can, as far
from me as you can. My time is hers. If I have need of
you, I will call."

"As you say, my lord Hugh," Raymond said, disappearing into the murky edges of Warkham.

Hugh found what he needed in the laundry—bucket
and linen binding, water and soap. In the kitchens he
found things to win her—apples and honey and bread,
mead and wine, nuts and cheese. All for a wife who
would not leave her chamber; they would have a banquet in their bed.

Their bed, for he would make it so. He could not
claim her body, that way was lost to him, but he could
claim her heart. That way, though she fought his every
word, was open and open wide. He would win her and
win all in the winning of her. Her trust and her love he
had to have. All depended upon it.

He knew well his part. He would not fail. He had
never yet failed, especially in such matters as this.

She would fight him; she fought him even now, but
she would not win. She was half lost now, lost in his smile
and his beauty and his name. Aye, he knew what he
brought to the battle plain, and he knew his opponent.
Gautier had told him much of Elsbeth, one man to another, one man passing a woman of his house to another
man of another house, giving her freely. A gift given,
one man to another. Such was Elsbeth. A gift of bone
and sinew and dark, liquid eyes. A woman given against
her will, against every prayer that issued from her full,
solemn lips.

His wife. His wife now and for as long as she lived.

She did not want to be a wife. He knew that, and he found he could even understand it. But he needed her to be a wife, and so she was a wife.

A maiden wife.

But only for now.

Hugh left the soiled garments in the laundry and strode back across the dark bailey, the wind blowing hard against him, lifting his cloak into the night air. He had his weapons about him—food and wine and clean linen. Aye, he would win her, though she stayed a maiden for a while. There were many ways to claim a woman. To take her body was just one of many, and even that would come in time.

He trusted in God and in the perfection of God's will and time. He would take this other path. In fact, he could even find it in his heart to thank God for her blood on this of all days. Elsbeth was no common woman; this way was better, surer, truer. He would win her heart, and then her body would fall into his hands.

He had only to wait. And in the waiting, woo.

Hugh climbed the outer stair and crossed the noise and light of the hall, keeping to the shadows that bordered the room. Gautier watched him from his place at the high table, and Emma smiled to see him so burdened with homely gifts for his newly made bride. He ignored them both and climbed the twisting stair that would take him to Elsbeth.

With a knock, he entered.

"I am come," he said, pushing open the door.

She took the cloths from his hands and made to push him out again.

"Nay, I can assist," he said, setting the basket of food on the floor near the bed.

"Nay, you cannot," she said, pushing against his chest. She was a little thing, and yet she sought to push him out of his own chamber. It was amusing, though he knew she would not see it so.

"How do you know?" he asked, placing his hands over hers. "Perhaps I can assist you very well."

"Do you hear yourself?" she said, looking up at him, her black eyes wide in disbelief. "I have done this for many a year, month upon month, as do all women. Not a one of us requires, needs, or wants assistance. Just the opposite. Leave."

"Leave?"

"Leaving would be a great gift, if you would give something of yourself for me to treasure. Leave. Now."

"Your manners are most strange," he said.

"You can instruct me later," she said, crossing her legs. "For now, just leave."

"Your will is my guide, Elsbeth. I will leave. I will return."

"Aye, you have mapped it most nicely. Please, now begin it," she said, pointing to the door.

With a grin and a bow, he left her. She was a most strange, most amusing woman. It was well that he had married her. She was the perfect wife for him in all her ways.

It was only left to convince her of it.

He stood still in the black weight of the stone that surrounded him. England was a cold place, cold to the eye and to the bone. Jerusalem was also made of stone, yet the stone was warm as honey to behold and hot to the hand. A warm, sunny place, the center of all Christendom. England was no Jerusalem. Yet was there not only one Jerusalem?

He knew no other home, had no other memories to cloud his thoughts or dim his purpose. A blessing, most assuredly. He could see all clearly in the white light of Jerusalem. In England, all was dark with rain and cloud and mist, verdant green reaching to topple the sky. He felt smothered. He was half-blind with wood and sedge, his eyes reaching for a horizon he could never find. He had not seen the sunset for an age; he had not seen the sun in its shining glory for a month or more. The whole earth seemed gray and wet, or would if he lost the memory of Jerusalem. Jerusalem still blazed bright, if only in his thoughts.

Jerusalem and the dark lights in Elsbeth's eyes.

How that none here could see her beauty? She was not acclaimed as any great face. Gautier did not speak of her that way, mentioning no claim to beauty in the marriage bargaining. No troubadours sang of her dark power. No squires hung at her heels, groaning for the sight and scent of her.

A most strange place, England. All were surely blinded by the mist and clouds that hung so low, for Elsbeth was beauty as Jerusalem sang of it: dark, small, her bosom full, her black eyes intense with holy power and smothered passion. Her nose was strong and straight, her lips full, her brow noble, her skin without mark or blemish. In the Levant she would have been kept behind her father's walls; no man would have been gifted with the sight of her, for he would have surely fallen into temptation.

Yet he could not fall into such temptation. There was no temptation so great or beautiful as to make him forget holy Jerusalem and his vow to Baldwin, closer than a brother, honored as a king.

Little Elsbeth, caught in the plans of men. Well, whatever came, he would deal gently with her. She deserved no less, though he could give her little more.

"Elsbeth, I await," he said, his hand pressed against the rough wood of the door.

She was as small as a cat and moved like one, seeking no man's notice, quiet in all her ways. Yet could he not feel her presence beyond the door? Aye, he could. She had a soft glow about her that shone even through an oaken door. Or so he would believe. His task was to woo her; he must not let himself believe in the wooing, no matter her solemn beauty or her shy and reluctant charm.

"Elsbeth," he repeated, running his hand over the door.

He would win her with gentle caresses of voice and hand. He would pray at her side without complaint or frown. He would smile on all her dark humors. He would wring a smile from her before he was done. He would make her pant with longing for his touch, his kiss, his body pressing into her own. Aye, he would. He would do all. He would win all.

"Elsbeth, let me come into you. This hall is cold and dark; there is no taper. You taunt me, little wife, for all the light is there with you. Come, share your warmth and light with me. I ask naught else—only let me come into you."

She opened the door and stood there, framed by firelight, her dark eyes shadowed as she faced him. She wore naught but her chemise, white as starlight, and he could see faintly the binding about her hips. Her black hair was lightly waved, even from the crown, and whispered around her face like the wings of a falcon, strong and sure.

Aye, she was temptation. Thank God above that he was beyond temptation though he stood before its opened door.

"You are afraid of the dark," she said.

"I fear not the dark. I only seek the light, as should all God's creation," he said, looking down at her.

It was an answer chosen to please her, and he watched her as she fought the surprised pleasure elicited by his words. Words of heaven, words of the divine and the eternal—they were the path into her heart. He had guessed this from his hearing of her; having met her, he knew this path was true. He could run this path in the dark, and even the cold, wet dark of England would not make him stumble. He was from Jerusalem; he had drunk such words as a babe from his mother. He had breathed these words of salvation and redemption in the very air of Outremer. This was a battle he could not lose.

"Then come, my lord. I would not have you lose yourself in the dark," she said, holding wide the door.

He came in, smiling. It was going well. There was no fear in her. Such was the way to start with a woman.

"All is well with you?" he asked. Her soiled garments were soaking in the bucket he had brought her.

"All is well," she said. "I do not need a helper in these things. I am a woman. This is my path to walk."

He picked up the basket from the floor and set it on the bed. The bed was high and the mattress deep, the coverings of linen and wool and wolf pelt. A fine, warm bed with a curtain of red embroidered wool at the head to keep away the cold damp of English stone.

"That is well," he said. "All is well with you, little wife, and all will be better yet, for I have brought us a repast to share in the quiet of our chamber. Food and drink for a pair newly made in God's sight."

"I am not hungry."

"I think you will be, and as your husband, I take my charge to provide for your needs most seriously. When you hunger, I will feed you."

"I will not hunger," she said.

There was a stubborn core of steel to her that only made him smile. He had not yet met steel that he could not best, and so it was with the steely heart of his wife. Or would be.

"If I say that you need food, then of course you shall take it. I only seek what is best for you. I only serve where I see need."

"Look again, my lord. I have no need which you must meet. All is truly well with me."

"Aye, I will not argue it," he said, opening up a hunk of bread and releasing the warm wheat smell into the close air of the chamber. "It is only that I am prepared for what might come and would do you only good service."

"Eat what pleases you, my lord. Serve yourself good and well. I will abide on my stool. Give no thought to me."

"Abide on your stool? Give no thought to you?" he asked, his dismay and horror greatly exaggerated. "Is this the husband I am to be, named so by my wife? I will not abide your sitting on a stool when a good, warm bed is well within your grasp. Come, Elsbeth, share this bed with me, for I can promise you, I have given much thought to you and will always do so."

He picked her up and set her on the bed as easily as he spoke of it. Her blood did not put him off; nay, he had seen enough blood to wipe away any thoughts of defilement at her touch upon his arm. There could be nothing of defilement in Elsbeth, no matter what the priests might say.

She looked as if she would speak and then thought again, closing her mouth and breathing deeply, a sigh to set all to rights and to keep herself still. She sat upon the bed, her legs tucked beneath her, resting on her heels. She looked a child, a dark and pretty child, yet her eyes were all woman. Dark, deep, and wary, they were. There was little fault to find in that, and he did not look hard for fault in her.

He broke the bread again and held out a piece to her. She did not lift her hand to take it, though her eyes never left his.

"It is fresh," he said. "I will confess to finding that I have a weakness for the bread of Britain. Levantine bread seems a pale, thin shadow compared to it."

"It is the ale," she said, taking a piece, a very small piece, while he spoke. "Ale is added into the dough."

"Ah, well, that explains all," he said, grinning. "I have ever and always liked the taste of ale."

"And who does not?" she said, her eyes smiling if her mouth did not.

They ate in silence for a while, the flickering of the fire the greatest warmth they shared. And yet the warmth between them grew with each passing moment. Intimacy was built on such moments of nothingness, a shared meal, a shared and easy silence. There were many paths into the heart of a woman, and he knew them, every one.

When the bread was gone, a memory marked in crumbs, they sat upon the bed, looking at the fire together. It was a small chamber by the standards of Jerusalem, and the fire's light all but filled it. He did not look at her, but could feel her eyes on him, skittering glances that touched him like a lance-point. He let her find her way, her eyes mapping him, and did not think to press her hard. Such glances were a maid's first exploration, and it went best if gently done. He left her to it, holding still while she studied him.

He knew what she saw: a man come into her bed, her chamber, and her life. But not into her body. Not yet. That should give her ease.

"Will you leave?" she asked, looking at the fire.

"What? Again?" he said, looking at her with a smile.

She smiled and ducked her head. "I only mean to say . . . there is naught for you here. Tonight. You know that. My courses run hard. This is a night of blood for me, and not my maiden's blood, which a man does prize to see."

"I would never prize to see any blood from you, Elsbeth," he said softly. "The ripping of your maidenhead

76

will burn. It must be done, as God decreed, but I will take no joy in it." She looked into his eyes in more amazement than wariness; that was good, yet still she was wary. Well, she had been a wife for mere hours. Time would tear all wariness from her as her maidenhead would soon be torn. "Still," he said, "I do not count tonight a loss. There is much for me here, in this bed. There is you, Elsbeth. I would stay with you. You are the only gift I want tonight. Will you deny me?"

She looked down at her lap; her hands were folded there, and she studied them as if to see their inner workings.

"Do not deny me, little wife. I want to stay with you," he said, reaching out a hand to touch the wings of hair that framed her face.

"I will not deny you that which I can freely give," she said, still staring down into her lap. "Stay, if it please you."

"It will please me," he said. "It does please me."

She looked up at him, her eyes black holes of want in the shadowy light of the chamber.

"Because you please me," he said.

With just such drops, word by word, the hole in her heart would be filled.

She did not trust him. He worked a plan of his own devising, and where she fit, she did not know. But she trusted not.

Men used words as weapons, a careless entertainment upon which they sought to build a life. Well, if God could use men's steely weapons to win holy wars, that was His will and she would not fight it. But soft and silken words she would not allow to be cast about her; she would fight that. She was of stouter stuff than that and not a maid to swoon ... well, mayhap there was some small bit of swooning in her weaker parts, but she would master that.

"Thank you, my lord. You are generous of spirit," she said. "If your generosity will continue, I must again ask for privacy to tend my female needs."

He did not fight her this time. She managed all quickly, her blood flow slowing slightly; she might make it through the night without waking. If he let her sleep.

She bound herself well, using many layers to stanch the flow, and to keep her private parts well covered and still private to herself. How they would sleep, she did not know. Would he strip bare and require her to do the same? She would look a babe in swaddling, not a maiden's dream of her bridal night and surely no man's. She should have a thought as to what she wanted, so that when he pressed for his way in this, she would have weapon-words of her own, sharp and ready for his attack.

The night lay before them, long and dark and cold with only a small fire and a stranger to keep the dark at bay. So it was for each of them, but she thought that he would find the night longer than she did. For her this night was a victory and a blessing; she did not doubt that a husband newly made would not see it so. Ah, well. It was in God's hands. Let Hugh of Jerusalem wrestle with God if he disliked her miracle.

She watched him as he bent to stoke the fire to greater heat and height, the colors swirling from gold to blue to white. He was a man upon whom the weight of legend rested lightly. A man of Jerusalem, a man of blood, a man of golden beauty with eyes the soft green of fir and hemlock, and he knelt within her chamber with no other thought than to spend time with her in gentle discourse.

Or so he said. Could any man of blood be so mild as that? So easy in his praise and so soft in his expectations?

Nay, it was not the way of men to be so. Yet he was so. Or seemed so, be it better said.

Well, she was ready for him, no matter what attack he chose. Her weapons were few: blood, prayer, and caution. Yet they would serve.

He turned upon his heels and looked up at her, his hair outlined in fire so that he seemed to glow from within, like sunlight through church glass, holy and bright and pure.

"This fire should last us," he said, "if we are well abed."

Well abed. That meant naked and huddling, or cuddling, as he would likely name it.

"You are to bed, then?" she asked, ignoring the cold floorboards against her feet; she was of sterner, stouter stuff than to be chilled by an October night.

"Aye, I am," he said, rising to his feet. He all but dwarfed her. Did the sun of Jerusalem grow all creatures to such heights? "And so are you, little wife. The day is done. It is time for—"

"Sleep."

"Rest," he said instead.

"The prayers of Compline await us both," she said.

"I think the prayers of None and Vespers have served us very well," he said. "God will surely forgive our lack on such a day as this."

Another hour of prayer lost. Another hour of showing him that she was not the stuff of which wives were made. Yet to argue it would give the lie to her perfect submission, and that she could not do. Submissive, prayerful, mild, otherworldly: those were the traits in her arsenal. He must see that she was not fit for the life her father had chosen for her. She would not be a wife. Hugh must release her from it.

"Will you assist, or must I call my squire?" he asked.

Call his squire and let another man see the signs of her flux? Nay, she was not eager for that. Then, perforce, she must assist him in his disrobing. She did not want to get that close, yet, if she was in assistance, could she not then determine how much of his clothing was stripped from him? Aye, that would help her. He could sleep in his tunic, far to his side of her bed; that would well suit her.

"I will assist, my lord, if you can but help me with your mail," she said.

"I will assist you in whatever manner I may, Elsbeth, but you will find my mail light—lighter than the rings they fashion here in the North."

"It is most fine," she said sincerely. It was. His mail was silvery and shining, the circles of steel small and thin, and so tightly woven together that from a distance of but feet the whole of it looked solid. Few men could afford mail so delicately and finely wrought; few armorers had the skill to fashion it. "I have never seen the like."

"It was a gift from Baldwin, given after the taking of Ascalon," he said, his voice heavy for once. She had never heard such tones of sadness and longing in a man, and never in this man of many smiles and bright looks.

"He must hold you in high value, my lord. That in itself is a gift of rare price."

He looked up at her from his seat on the low stool, his eyes suddenly the bright green of spring grass. "Aye, he does, and so I do him. He is a rare man. There a few like him in this world."

"So it is often said of great men. You are blessed by God that you have known him and been loved by him," she said.

He looked at her, and she saw something in his face, something of melancholy tinged with regret and even joy. She had never seen such a look. She did not know how to name it. She did not know how to respond to it.

"Thank you, Elsbeth," he said, taking her hand and raising it to his lips.

His kiss was light and warm, and then was done. Yet the tingle on her skin lingered like a recent burn. She shook off the feeling and turned away from him to open his trunk on the far side of the bed.

"Your trunk is also fine, fit to house the garments you wear," she said. It was red leather, to match his beloved boots, and tooled with scrolls and diamond shapes.

"All things are fine in holy Jerusalem," he said, pulling off one boot. "Possibly because there is little mud."

She turned to look and saw that his boot was wet and misshapen and brown to the ankle. She smiled and swallowed a laugh to see the look on his face.

"Aye, I hear you laughing, little wife," he said, setting the boot by the fire and bending to examine its mate before he slid it off his foot. "You will not laugh so loud when the bride gift I have brought for you is riven and shriveled by English rain and English mud."

A bride gift? She turned to look at him, the memory of his kiss upon her hand still burning.

"I see I have your full attention now," he said, grinning. "In that, I deem that maids from Jerusalem to England are the same."

"Do you insult me?"

"Nay," he said, his smile fading. " 'Twas a compliment, Elsbeth. To be compared to a maid of Jerusalem is the best I can say of any woman. And in Jerusalem you would outshine them all. But enough of compliments. I forget, you care little for them. Care you to see the gift that has traveled continents and seas to find you?"

"I appreciate the effort," she said.

"That is fine, but I would rather have you appreciate the gift."

Appreciate the gift? Aye, how could she not? Never in her life had she been given a gift of any sort. If he pulled out a rusty and broken dagger, she would be delighted.

Hugh rose up and came toward his trunk. His boots

were resting by the fire, steaming and smelling of mud. She backed up at his approach, boxing herself into the corner made by bed, trunk, and wall. He seemed very large of a sudden, very broad and tall and male. Her pulse trembled within her skin, and her breath came into her lungs hardly at all.

He bent down and lifted and poked and pulled forth something wrapped in blue damask. All of itself, the damask would have been a gift most fine. It was rare cloth, catching the light and shining.

Hugh handed it to her and said, "May it please you, my wife."

She nodded her thanks and took the parcel from his hands. Her own were shaking. She coughed to hide her discomposure and opened the damask.

Inside was a cross. Small and golden and on a chain of finely worked links of hammered silver. The cross was inscribed with a strange and foreign script that held no meaning for her beyond its flowing beauty.

"It is lovely," she said, holding it in her hands, fingering the cross reverently.

"I thought so as well," he said. "Put it on."

She slipped the necklace over her head, and the cross lay against the rise of her breasts, warming instantly. She looked at it, her fingers touching it, memorizing the feel of it, the look of it, the beauty of it.

"Do you know what it says?" he asked.

"Nay."

"It says, 'It is finished.' "

"Ah, Christ's last words. I will treasure it all the days of my life. Thank you, my lord. It is a great gift. A great gift," she repeated, her eyes full of tears that did not fall. "I will never remove it."

But she would not be allowed to keep it when she went into the cloister; all of her past life must be cast away from her so that she might live her new life in poverty of all but spirit. Yet she would not think of that now. It was a gift unlike any other, and she cherished it. Besides, if she managed all well, she could finger her cross in her solitary life in Sunnandune, forgetting the giver while she cherished the gift.

"I rejoice that it finds such favor with you," he said.

"It does. It ever will. I will not forget this gift, my lord."

"Nor the giver?" he said, smiling, going back to his stool.

"How could I forget my first husband?" she said lightly.

"Ah, she wounds," he said, laughing. "Now I am to be the first of many? Yea, you would prick me with my own words, clumsily spoken, haltingly defended."

"You defended yourself very well," she said, coming out of her corner and into the light. Her hand still stroked the cross.

"I am pleased to hear you say so. Am I not a valiant warrior? I have learned to defend and to attack, but never against so soft an adversary and never with only words."

"Say not 'only words,' for words can be a mighty weapon, their meaning sharp and their weight heavy."

"Aye, 'tis so, yet never would I have my words wound you, Elsbeth," he said, lifting his hauberk from him, leaving his torso bare. "Say I have not."

"You have not."

He had not. He was a man, a mere man; he could not touch her with words. Yet her thoughts trailed away to nothing as he stripped off his clothing.

She could only stare, his words and hers a dim buzzing in the corners of her thoughts. He was a mighty man, wide and well muscled and as golden as her cross. Here the depth of difference between a woman and a man was revealed. Two, separate, as God had created them in His garden, yet made to come together. Out of man a woman had been formed. How they were to come together again she could not see, though Isabel had explained all very well and very enthusiastically. Yet he was too large, too strange. There was no place in her for him.

Yet was it not in every man to find his place in a woman?

But he would find no place in her. She bled, blocking him, shutting him out. She bled, and, as Christ had bled upon His cross, it was her salvation.

Her mother would have been most pleased.

Chapter Six

He had wooed her with soft words and gentleness and gifts. She knew him now as she had not known him at their joining. Her fears were lessened, her tongue loosened, her humor on the rise.

It was time they were to bed.

"Come, Elsbeth," he said. "Let us lie together."

"I have explained—"

"Keep your chemise and your virginity," he said, reaching out to take her hand. "I give them to you for this night and the next, for as long as your courses shall continue. Look well now, wife, for you shall see the man who claims you for his own."

He slid his braes off, baring himself to her. He was on the rise as well, his manhood high and hard with no release to be had in this chamber.

It would be a long, cold night.

Her eyes were on him and he rose higher. Let her look her fill. She needed to learn him; 'twould ease whatever maiden fears had settled in her heart.

"Come, be not afraid. I will not harm you, nor hurt you."

He stood before the fire, the warmth a welcome friend, and drew her to him. She was small; he could have lifted her with one hand or hidden her complete behind his back, which he would not do. He was saving the fire for himself. Elsbeth seemed to feel none of the chill of the room. Northern blood ran hot, mayhap. He was eager to find the truth of that.

"You are very hot," she said, echoing his thoughts. "Why do you say you are so cold?"

She stood before him, a hand's breadth away, her breasts a dark weight he could see and almost feel through her thin chemise.

"I am hot only when you are near," he said. "You are the fire that warms me."

"I am not," she said, looking down at the floor. "I am no man's fire."

"You are mine," he said, lifting her face with his hands. Her eyes were dark pools of confusion and caution—a maiden's look, to be sure. "My fire. My wife."

"Aye, mayhap, for now," she said, her breath warm on his hands, her eyes sliding into chilly repose.

"Now is all we have, Elsbeth. The Lord does not promise more. Our future is in His keeping. What can we do but obey in each moment of life He grants us? What more than that?"

"Nothing more," she said. "You speak the truth. There is only now."

He could read her well. Only now when she was in flux and he could not touch her. Or so she thought. There was much a man could do to a woman that would leave her maidenhead intact yet pierce and claim her heart. And he was just such a man to perform just such a claiming.

"Come then, little wife, and let us claim our now together. The bed awaits. The fire is high, the blankets deep. Let us avail ourselves of all."

She said no more, but meekly followed where he led. He led her to the bed and lifted her into it. She pulled the blankets up to her chin and watched him with wide and careful eyes. She was wise to be careful, for her life was on the brink of change.

She had to be careful, for some change was upon him. Gone was the gentle man of easy smiles and in his place a warrior with his battle before him. She knew well that she was to be his battle plain. A man could be counted on for certain things, and claiming a woman by laying his mark upon her was the surest yet.

He would not breach her maidenhead, but he would lay hands upon her, that she knew. His eyes betrayed all. And his manhood, high and hard and pulsing with intent. Aye, she knew what he would do if God had not taken the chance away from him. But what he would do while he waited for the days to pass she did not know. She only knew she was embattled and that her foe used his beauty as a weapon.

His beauty was formidable, and she knew enough of men to understand that he realized it. All men knew their weapons and kept them well honed. Even men from Jerusalem were only men, after all. Yet had her mother not warned her of this? Had she not said that sin entered through the eyes, consuming the soul? Elsbeth kept her eyes lowered in defense.

If the fire would die or the taper flicker out, her cause would be helped, but with his aversion to cold and dark, she did not see much hope. She closed her eyes, creating her own dark world.

It did not help much. She could feel his nearness and his heat as he slid into the bed. And then she felt his hands—nay, his fingertips—trailing down the center of her chest, between her breasts.

She drew a shaky breath and kept to her private darkness, ignoring the tremors he unleashed.

"The cross looks well on you," he said, touching it with his fingertips. "You have warmed it. It carries your heat, Elsbeth, and glows in the firelight."

She said nothing. All her effort was on breathing and keeping her eyes shut against him. The firelight would show the golden glow of his skin and hair. She did not seek out such an assault on her senses. Her battle plan was prudent and one of defense, her only recourse. Still, it would serve. It must.

"You hide from me, Elsbeth," he said, his tone amused.

"I am here. I do not hide," she said, pressing her lips together in irritation.

Ever and always the laughter was at her expense. Would that, just once, a man could feel the bite of her humor when it was aimed at him. It would be a gift indeed if she were able to attack. But she was a woman; that way was not open to her, not if she wanted to win her freedom from him. He held the key to all, and so she must fight softly, inching her way free. A bold attack would serve her ill.

"Nay, you do not hide. Only your sight is hidden. Or is it the sight of me you wish to hide from?" he said, releasing the cross and touching a finger to the hollow of her throat.

"I do not hide, my lord," she said. "I am but weary. The day has been long."

"Aye, a full day we have had between us. But the night will be longer still," he murmured.

His touch was light, a whisper against her skin, yet she felt it as a weight that threatened to crush her. She could not draw a breath that she did not will into her lungs.

Her very heart was pressed and flattened by the weight of his presence in their shared bed. Why could he not find accommodations elsewhere? Why share a bed with her when there was naught he could do to fulfill their marriage contract?

Why? He was a man and he wanted to stay, tormenting her.

"Breathe, Elsbeth," he said, his mouth hovering over her ear. "Breathe. I will not hurt you. Nor will I leave you, no matter how still and quiet you keep yourself."

"Stay, then. I have said naught to encourage you to go."

"Nay, you have done all that a wife should do. None could fault you. But if you would only open your eyes?"

She would not. "Did you not say that it was the hour for sleep?" she said.

"I believe the word I used was rest," he said, trailing his hand over her breasts. Her nipples rose up in alarm, throbbing their outrage. "Let us each find our rest in our own ways, little wife. I have found mine." He leaned toward her again and said against her brow, "I could fondle you for an age and not weary of the task. Lie quiet and still for me, if it is your pleasure; I will not complain, not when I am so happily entertained."

She could not help it: One eye opened a slit, just enough to admit light and the vague outline of him in the shadowy chamber.

"Am I your entertainment, my lord? Is that my function in your life?"

"Let us say instead that you are to be my pleasure," he said.

Aye, she could believe it. What man did not want a woman to share his bed and his body? What man would not want a woman to appease his lusts, satisfying his every base desire?

What woman would not welcome Hugh of Jerusalem

into her bed, welcoming his lusts, base or lofty?

Here, in this bed, she was the woman. She did not want him, nor did she want him to want her.

"Will you not say it?" he said, cupping her breast with a single hand. His other hand supported his head, the muscle of his arm bulging in the dim light.

She really ought to close her eyes again, but she could not seem to turn from him. Both eyes were opened now, mere slits, but open. It was most difficult to tumble into darkness when such a golden presence was so near.

"Say what?"

"Say that you are my pleasure, fashioned by God's own hand for me. For by my troth, Elsbeth, you are every-man's dream of a woman."

"I am not."

"I will not argue it, but I will defend. You are *my* dream of woman. The Lord must have read every dream of my boyish heart to have fashioned you so perfectly."

"I am not perfect."

"You are for me," he said, rubbing his hand over her nipple.

The sensation was intense, painfully erotic, an induce-ment to continue, to seek more at his hands, to hear more sweet words from his lips. Yet she could do none of those. Her path was set, and it was only folly to con-tinue on this course. How to stop him? He was her hus-band. He had the right to lay his hands on her. And what he would speak was his own affair. She could not stop him. She had not the right even to try. All that was left to her was to quietly resist. To let his words and his touch wash over her, a light wash of rain against her skin. She could not let him linger long enough to pen-etrate her heart. And she must never, ever respond.

"You are kind to say so. We both know I am far from perfect," she said, closing her eyes with difficulty.

He laughed and pulled her into an embrace. The

scent of him was of woodsmoke and wine, his skin as hot as embers. She could feel his manhood pressing against the soft mound of her belly, and her joints softened in response.

Response? She must not respond.

"I am not kind," he said. "A night in this bed will prove it, little wife. I mean to torment, you see. A night of perfect torment we will share."

She pulled back and looked up at his face. His jaw and throat rose above her, large and covered in a light brown stubble that caught the light of the fire and was lit to shimmering gold. He spoke of torment, he who had promised not to hurt her?

"Do not fear," he said, looking down at her from beneath his lashes. "It is the way of a man to say such. It is nothing to fear. I only have made myself a promise, little wife, to make you scream and moan for release."

She could well believe that. She was not far from screaming now. Her skin was hot and prickly, her breasts heavy and tender, his hands the cause of all discomfort within her. She had always found her skin most comfortable, before Hugh and his soft caresses and his careless laughter. If he would only release her and go to another bed, all would be well.

"The release of desire, the need for satisfaction," he said. "That is the torment of which I speak. You drive me to torment even now. Should not the wife of Hugh of Jerusalem share his fate?"

Nay, she should not. She would not. Her vow had been made before God, and He would not want her released from it. Some things were bigger than a man's desire; indeed, all things should be.

"I do not wish you in torment," she said, crossing her arms over her aching breasts.

"Of course you do not. You are not a cruel woman,"

he said, uncrossing her arms and holding them over her head.

Her chemise was stretched tight against her breasts, her nipples dark and erect beneath the fine linen. It would have been a fine night to wear wool—nice, thick, scratchy wool.

"What are you about?" she said. Her voice came out a squeak that would have rivaled a mouse caught in the talons of a hawk. An apt comparison.

"Only the torment of my wife. Fear not, little one, I will not harm you," he said. His eyes said otherwise. They were hooded and sleepy, green and sharp. "Close your eyes, if you wish. It will not help," he whispered.

He spoke true. It did not help.

She felt his breath on her skin first and then the soft weight of his lips. He kissed her cheek and then the corner of her mouth and then the underside of her jaw and then, and then her mouth. It was a gentle kiss, gentle and warm, and yet her arms were over her head, her wrists trapped in his hand, and the feeling of powerlessness she felt made the kiss not gentle at all. Nay, it was a kiss of power, and all the power was his.

She shifted against him, trying to politely pull her hands free.

"Nay, wife, you are just where I want you," he said, his mouth trailing down her throat. "Keep still and let me torment you at my whim. I vow that you will not be harmed, at least not permanently."

"What say you?"

"Oh, a bruise here, perhaps," and he bit her softly on the side of the neck, sucking gently. She tried to jerk away from his mouth, freeing her hands, but he only gripped her tighter, throwing his leg over hers for good measure. "Or mayhap here," he said, taking his mouth from her neck and lifting her breast to lay his mouth over her nipple through the linen.

"Nay! Do not!"

"Nay? Do not?" he said, lifting his head and looking into her eyes. His eyes were the green of spring, sharp and bright. "These words from a submissive wife to the husband who only seeks to worship her with his body? Nay, my little wife would not deny her husband what is rightfully his. Is your body not mine now, as mine is yours? Take of me, Elsbeth, I will not say nay to you. Or let me lead by example, if I must."

"If you must," she repeated on a snort of irritation. Aye, in that he would most willingly lead by example. What man would not?

"Would you torment me, little Elsbeth? Would you lie beneath my hand and lift your body to my kiss and open for me? Would you have eyes like a moonless night and skin like alabaster and breasts like fruit, ripe and swollen and heavy? Ah, but you already torment me. Do no more, else I shall never rise from this bed nor from your arms, all thoughts of knightly valor flown to the distant moon. Fight me, Elsbeth, else I shall tumble into you with no thought of escape."

Fight him? She could not fight him. He could not want her to. In one breath he wanted her to submit, and in the next he demanded that she fight. In truth, she could do neither. By all the laws of matrimony, her body was in his keeping; she could not deny him the joys of the flesh without being damned by God and priest. But she could not submit, not to this . . . invasion.

Still, her blood protected her from his ultimate siege into her. She was safe from that. Let him kiss her, touch her, fondle her; she would have to endure it, knowing she was saved from penetration. It was the mercy God had granted, and she was going to rest in that, submissive to her husband yet proving that she was not the stuff of which wives were made. He would let her go. He had to.

Besides, how much would Hugh want to toy with her without the release of consummation?

She did not know Hugh of Jerusalem.

He lay atop her, fitting himself between her legs. She thanked God again for her padding, for it blunted the feel of him. It was a blessing most generous. To feel the weight and height of Hugh on her was battle enough.

"You taste like bread and wine," he said. "Like the sacraments."

"Do not blaspheme!"

"I do not. You are the food on which I will dine every day of my life. Is that not a sacrament? Your body will sustain me, Elsbeth. There will be no one else, first wife. Only wife."

He kissed her then while the words rang in her heart. Only wife. Nay, he could not make such a vow. She wanted no such vow.

His kiss filled her. Almost she forgot that she could not move. Almost she forgot that she was to lie quiet and loose-limbed under his assault. Almost she forgot that this wanting was her enemy, and because he brought the wanting with his hands and his mouth, he was the enemy, too.

She could not forget that. He was the enemy. This was battle.

She sank beneath his kiss, his tongue finding hers, his breath invading her, his scent filling her.

He untied her chemise, lace by lace, and uncovered her breasts. His hands were gentle, as gentle as a warrior's battle-roughened hands could be against a part of her that no man had ever before touched. She sucked in a hard breath when his palm skimmed over the peak of her breasts, teasing her by touch. Tormenting her.

A man of his word, was Hugh of Jerusalem.

"I will be your first," he said, his mouth on the skin of her breast. "I will be the man you remember, even in the cold cloister, where even memory is banished. I will live on. You shall not forget me, Elsbeth. You shall never forget this."

He pressed against her, his hips to hers, and she lifted to him in spite of all vows made to God and to Ardeth and to herself. She lifted to his weight, feeling the man weight of him and wanting more. His mouth suckled her breasts, tugging a nipple past his teeth, and she cried out at the surge of sensation that thrust down into her womb, sharp and sweet, a pulse that was ignited and burned in the glow of him. Because of him.

"Do you say then," she gasped, turning her head upon the mattress, snarling her hair, gasping for reason and remembered vows. "Do you say that you will release me?"

He looked up from her breast, her nipple between his teeth, his eyes hooded and sharp as the falcon's. She met his look and felt her inward parts convulse. Had ever a man looked so? Nay, never upon her.

He bit her nipple softly and she jerked in response, her eyes trapped in his gaze.

"Release you? Nay, do not think of release, little wife. Think only of now, this bed, this oneness we are commanded to achieve. That is your duty now. That is your divine calling. Be one with me," he whispered. "Be one with me and you will make God smile."

"I am in flux," she said, pulling against his hands. Her breasts heaved toward him, and he smiled as he licked her. "I cannot."

"Nay, you cannot," he said, moving his mouth up to her throat, kissing her, a trail of kisses that would leave marks any hunter could follow. "There is only torment here tonight between us. We will be one in our torment. That is the oneness we will share. I share even that with you gladly, Elsbeth. You are a maid to make a man lose his reason. Am I not wary, I will lose myself in you."

Nay, it was not so. He was not wary. He was wild, and

he was calling to some secret wild desire in her that had no place in her life. She was calm and reasonable. She was composed and holy in her aspect. She was not in torment, no matter what he tried. Only God could torment a soul.

Yet Hugh could torment her body. And so he did.

The pain of frustrated longing built in her. It was a fire that, once ignited, burned hot and bright. She had no way to dampen it. He held her arms above her head, kept her hips imprisoned by his leg. With his mouth and a single hand upon her body, she writhed in an agony she did not know the earth possessed.

Her breasts were heavy, throbbing, her nipples swollen and aching, tender to his touch yet craving it. 'Twas madness. Her eyes she kept closed and she turned her head from him, trying to deny what he unleashed with every lick and bite and nibble. This could not be. It must not be. She thanked God that He had given her the gift of her blood, for now she understood that it had been a gift to save her from herself and not from Hugh. She could not have turned from this branding, this call of heat and fire and smoke. She was turning toward him even now, craving him; only her blood protected her in this darkness of desire.

It was as Ardeth had said. It was all as she had said.

"Are you praying, little wife?" Hugh said, taking her earlobe into her mouth. "Are you praying for release from me, or from the torment you suffer at my hands?"

He kissed her then, his tongue a living flame that consumed her. Her breath was his. Her will was his. Her very heart beat at the sound of his voice. She was lost. Only her blood kept her safe.

"Or are you praying," he said, his mouth hovering above her, his lips brushing against her lips, "simply for release?"

"Release me," she said, pulling again against his re-straining hand.

"Nay, that is not the release I was speaking of. This fire in you has but one release. When your blood stops, you shall find it. I will give it unto you."

"Give it to me now," she said. "Let me go. In all ways, let me go. Please." She had to escape him; before her blood passed, he must be gone from her life. Her vow to Ardeth could not be sold for a kiss from a golden man of a golden city.

"Open your eyes, Elsbeth. See me," he said softly, his hand against her cheek.

She did. The room was dark and yet too bright, the fire too hot, the air too still. Her skin was tender, and she shivered at the look in her husband's eyes.

"You are in torment," he said. "Say it."

"Release me," she whispered. Her throat was parched as if she had not drunk in a week.

"Say it," he said, "or you will find no rest this night, as I will not, to have such a woman at my side and be un-able to have her. I want you, Elsbeth. This wanting is a fire, bright and hot, and I am burned. I only wish to share this torment. Do not let me burn alone."

He looked embattled by desire, his pulse jumping in his throat, his forehead damp with sweat, his eyes fever-bright. He looked a man tormented. Something surged in her, like a wave upon rocks, something violent and elemental. In a single instant God and her vow were cast aside, for just an instant. For just a moment in time, she gave him what he asked for. She could not deny him in that moment, and that was a torment of a different sort, a torment of the soul.

"You torment me," she said, her voice throaty with suppressed desire. "I am tormented. My skin burns. I ache. I want."

He looked deep into her eyes and then he released

her slowly, his hand trailing down her arms, soothing them, igniting her.

"I also want," he said, kissing her brow. "I want you. I will find no rest until I have you."

She crossed her arms over her breasts, closing him out. He smiled and pulled her arms from her self-embrace and laid his head upon her breast, wrapping his arms around her, holding her to him. His breath was on her breasts, and she stirred in carnal discomfort. She could feel him smile against her skin.

"Find what rest you can, little wife, as I find mine. We have found our oneness for tonight. Sweet torment, Elsbeth."

Sweet torment. He said it well.

The night would be long indeed.

Chapter Seven

"Away! I must . . . Away with you!" she said, pushing him from her.

Hugh leapt from the bed, his hands fisted and ready to attack, his eyes blinking. He looked at her. He looked behind him. He looked at her again.

"What is it? Where is the danger?"

"Can you not get you gone? The danger is here," she said, pointing to the juncture of her legs.

"Ah," he said, nodding, brushing the hair out of his eyes. "Can I help?"

"Yea, by leaving you help much," she said, sliding out of bed with her hands pressed between her legs.

After he had backed out of the room, she approached the bucket. It was almost full. She was almost out of wadding. She was thirsty. She was cold. All to the blame of

Hugh. Had she slept alone, all would have been well. He had made it so that she could not well attend to her own needs. He had done it apurpose. He had nearly said so. All because he had wanted to torment her. Well, he had succeeded and succeeded well. Perhaps she should have encouraged him to stay and watch while she dealt with her blood flow; that would have been fair recompense. A torment of her own devising.

"A rare sort of torment, to have a man like him in your bed and yet not have him at all," Jovetta said in the quiet of the kitchen.

"I do not think Elsbeth thinks herself in torment," Marie said. "I have heard it said that she has no liking for men."

"What sort of woman has no liking for men?"

"A woman with the lord of Warkham for a father?" Marie countered.

They stood in a bolt of light cast upon the worn wooden floor. Dust and flour and stems and cores and bones were littered about them. The kitchens of Warkham were not well run. The cook of Warkham, John, had a particular loathing for the lord of Warkham and used his ladle as a weapon of resentment. It was his misfortune that the lord of Warkham had an inferior and unrefined palate; he noticed nothing beyond whether his food was hot or cold.

"Do you think she will decry?" Jovetta asked, wiping a rag over the worktable.

Marie shrugged and went to fetch a broom. John might have little care for his kitchen, but she disliked endless hours of idleness.

"It would be a rebellion of sorts. I do not think it in Elsbeth to rebel," Jovetta said.

"I think anyone may be pushed to anything," Marie said.

"You do not know her," Jovetta said. "We are of an age, and she was ever well set in her tasks—Ardeth and Gautier both made certain of that. A most dutiful daughter they managed between them. I do not think it in Elsbeth to defy her father."

"Ever since Eve it has been in every woman to defy any lord. Given the right cause," Marie said.

"Hugh of Jerusalem is hardly the right cause," Jovetta said with an audible sigh.

Marie laughed and kept sweeping. "Throw yourself in his way and see if he will not catch you," she offered. "He certainly must be hungry for a woman, since his own is forbidden to him."

"You think I have not?" Jovetta said with a grin. She had a lovely figure, and knew it well. There were few men in Warkham who had the means to marry, and the one who did was paying court to Marie. Jovetta found her amusements where she could, with whom she could. "He pays more attention to his horse and squire."

"In that order?" Marie asked, laughing.

"Aye, in that order," Jovetta said. "But his squire is a man to make a maid look again and yet again. I wonder if the men of Outremer are all so fair as these two. Mayhap it is the holiness of the very air that makes them so beautiful."

"He is a comely man," Marie agreed.

"Comely? If you did not have Walter of the mill at your heels, ready to offer marriage at the crook of your finger, you would not say merely comely."

" 'Tis better for me to remember Walter, a man I might attain, than to think of men so far above our sphere and reach."

"Above our sphere, aye, but above our reach?" Jovetta laughed lightly. "I think I can reach Raymond. I do not want to hold him long, only hold him hard between my legs. I think I can reach for that and find success."

"And the babe that might come from such reaching?"

"I will take care. I know a thing about stopping the making of a babe."

"Really?" Marie asked, laying her broom aside. "And who taught you that?"

"Oswina, the midwife's apprentice."

"She was a scold! Besides, she has run off. I would not lay my life on any words of counsel from her lips."

"Scold or not, she was an apt apprentice. She had practice enough in serving Warkham."

The dust was disturbed by the entry of a man into their midst. The very man of their speculation.

"May I beg a drink?" Raymond asked.

Jovetta turned and smiled with all the abandon of a woman on the hunt. Marie blushed and averted her eyes.

"Surely, Raymond," Jovetta answered.

"You know my name?" he asked as she went to fill a mug of ale for him.

"Aye, and the name of your lord and the name of his horse," Jovetta said.

Raymond smiled. "Then you know more names than I. What is yours, wench?"

"Jovetta."

"A lovely name."

"I thank you, though I had no hand in the choosing of it," she said with a grin.

Raymond smiled in response, taking the ale from her, their fingers brushing, and then turned to Marie. "And your name?"

"Marie."

"The name of our Savior's mother. What name could be more beautiful?" he said.

"The name of our Savior?" Marie answered tartly, resuming her sweeping.

Raymond grinned and said, "Ah, a warrior maid and her weapon, a broom."

"Nay, my weapon is my tongue."

"Then wield it against me again, Marie. I know well how to defeat a woman's tongue."

"And what weapon do you use in this battle, Raymond?" Jovetta asked.

"My own tongue, of course," he said.

"What talk is this?" Father Godfrey demanded, coming into the kitchen as the rain began to beat down in the bailey. "This is not proper and does not lead the heart and soul down the path of righteousness. I had thought better of the men of the holy city," he said, looking hard at Raymond.

"Your pardon, Father," Raymond said, bowing.

The women bent their heads in contrition, whether because they were truly contrite or only shamed at being caught, only they knew.

"Well you should ask my pardon. Will you lead these weaker vessels astray?" he asked, sweeping his arm toward the servant girls. "Is this how you serve Hugh and the needs of Jerusalem?"

"Nay, Father," Raymond said. " 'Twas only idle talk."

"And does the Lord smile on idleness in any form? He does not. I am about the business of the Lord. I would strongly urge you to be about the business of your lord. I am most certain Hugh does not encourage this in you."

"Nay, Father, he does not," Raymond said in perfect solemnity. "I stand in submission to your will and his."

"Good," Father Godfrey said, leaving the kitchen with a warning glance for the women.

"Did you speak true?" Jovetta asked when she was sure the priest had left them. "Is your knight so hard of purpose?"

"Hard?" Raymond asked with a smile. "I would not

give any answer that would shame him or me. Let me say only that I have yet to earn his displeasure for speaking to a woman."

"And so we are back to the topic of your tongue and what you may or may not do with it," Jovetta said.

"Jovetta!" Marie said.

"What did Jovetta say?" said a voice from beyond the kitchen wall. In the next instant, a small, dirty, fair-haired girl ran into the kitchen from the rain. She was also very wet.

"Denise, you should not be here," Marie said. "Lady Emma will not be pleased that you are not where she has left you."

"I am not pleased that she keeps leaving me," Denise said. "I do not see why she cannot have a turn at being displeased. I have had turns enough."

"Who is this chit?" Raymond asked, throwing back the end of his cloak.

"Chit?" Denise said, eyeing him. "Who is this gangling lad of wrist bones and knuckles?"

"Lad? I am no lad. I am squire to Lord Hugh of Jerusalem."

"Lord Hugh must have been very easy in his choosing," Denise countered.

"Denise!" Jovetta hissed. "Back to the solar with you."

"She is fostered here?" Raymond asked. She looked a villein by her dirt, yet her clothes were of fine weave and color, and none but the lady of the holding and her women entered the solar.

"Aye, I am," Denise answered. "What are you doing here?"

"I do not answer to a child!"

"Do not or cannot?" Denise said with a smirk.

"Denise," Marie said, taking her by the hand. "You must be where you belong."

"He does not belong in Warkham's kitchen. Why does he not leave?"

"I am leaving," Raymond said.

"Good," Denise answered, grinning.

"Must you leave?" Jovetta asked.

"Aye, he must," Denise answered, crossing her arms over her flat chest.

"Aye, he must," John the cook said, coming into the kitchen from the rain. He was a huge man of dark complexion and much hair. He did not look at all like a cook. "I must begin the day's meal, and all who do not belong in Warkham's kitchens must depart." He looked at Raymond and Denise. Marie and Jovetta became very busy with cleaning, heads down and mouths closed.

"You must leave," Denise said to Raymond.

"As must you," Raymond countered.

"I live here."

"I am a guest."

"Guests do not belong in the kitchen."

"Neither do children."

"Out!" John thundered.

Denise and Raymond bolted out of the kitchen door, arguing as they disappeared into the rain, which was lightening to mist.

Out of the mist came Hugh.

"Master Cook," he said upon entering the warm glow of the fire, "I would beg sustenance for my lady."

"For Lady Elsbeth, the larder is ever full and ever open," John replied. "Take what you wish, my lord."

Hugh nodded his thanks and took a loaf of bread from a lively looking wench.

"The laundry will have what else she needs, my lord," a more subdued wench supplied.

"I thank you and my lady thanks you," Hugh said. So, all within Warkham knew of Elsbeth's condition. Well, there were few secrets in any holding, and this secret was one that all women shared in their monthly time. "If I could send my squire in for ale? My wife and I have simple needs, and we will break our fast in the quiet of our chamber."

The comely lass giggled. Hugh grinned in response and winked at her. She dropped a tray of crockery.

"Would there be any water for a bath for my bride? I think it would soothe her," Hugh said.

"Aye, 'twill be ready in but a few moments," John said. "Though 'twas your needs we had heard were best met by hot water, my lord."

Hugh shrugged and grinned. "I confess it freely. I have the Levantine fondness for water and soap and freshly scented cloth against my skin. Think you I can tempt Elsbeth into sharing my weakness?"

"My lord, I think it in you to tempt a maid to anything," Jovetta said.

Hugh only laughed in answer and they all laughed with him, with the exception of John, who kept his countenance a careful blank.

The cook handed Hugh a basket of apples, declaring that Elsbeth had a fondness for them. The quiet lass came with a handful of wadding and clean linen. The lively lass bent to pick up shards of crockery, the cook giving her a fearsome frown. All were bent on helping Hugh, a situation to which he was well accustomed.

He left the kitchens to find Raymond loitering about with a scowl to match the heavy clouds above them on another gray English dawning.

"Fetch ale from the kitchens for my lady, Raymond," he said. "I have no more hands to do her service."

"You look well laden," Raymond said, banishing his scowl.

"Aye, and well purposed. I will take another step, mayhap a leap, upon the path to winning her this day."

"And can a damsel be won with apples and bread?"

Raymond asked with a grin. "Nay, do not answer it. I know. If the man be Hugh, then the maid be won."

"My wife would call that flattery," Hugh said, grinning. "I call it stating the truth."

"Go to, my lord, and win her love. Then we can be gone from here. The maids are mostly sour in this soggy land. I would to the south, where smiles are sweeter and flesh plumper."

"You are too young to be so jaded," Hugh said. "And too much the man to give in so quickly. If you must fight for her, then fight." Hugh shrugged. " 'Tis what a man must do, and ofttimes the winning is the sweeter for the fight. I have a fight of my own with Elsbeth. Do I tremble? Do I scowl? Nay, I smile and whet my blade."

"This one is no Elsbeth. Your lady is sweet-tempered and mild."

"Mild?" Hugh said, laughing. "You know not your women if you call my lady mild. She is all blade and mail; I have never known the like. Nay, she is a worthy battle for me. In fact, I find I am most engaged by her."

"My lord, you are engaged by every woman," Raymond said.

"Quiet, boy, I am a married man," Hugh said with a smile. "Those days are past."

"Aye, my lord," Raymond said with an answering smile.

He reentered the chamber without even a knock. They had come that far in intimacy in a single night. What would prevail after a sennight, she did not want to think.

However, he had a fresh bucket of water, more wadding, more linen, and a loaf of fresh bread.

"No ale?" she said and cursed her contrary tongue even as the words slipped out.

He grinned at her churlishness and cocked his head in entreaty. Two mugs of ale appeared from the hall suspended on longish arms and grasped by bony hands.

"Who?" she said, darting behind the bed.

"My squire, Raymond," Hugh said. "Would you meet him?"

"Nay! Just give me—" she said, reaching for the linen from behind the bed, ducking, grasping, not reaching, and snapping her fingers in her dire need.

"Oh? My wife thinks to snap her fingers at me? This shall not be borne. Would I be any knight at all if I allowed my little wife to snap me about like a child of two? Nay, I would not."

Meanwhile, he had closed the door upon his squire. She was thankful for that, though it was small enough service considering the circumstances.

"The linen!" she hissed. "Have your fun later, my lord. My need is great."

"So it is, and I will meet it," he said, handing her the linen and setting down the new bucket. The bucket of sodden cloth he set outside the door. "See to yourself, Elsbeth. I will have a bath sent for us. You have need of it today."

"You will leave, then? To see to the bath?" she asked. She could wait no longer.

"I will," he said. "I will return anon. Be quick, if you can."

She would be quick because she must, which showed how little he knew of things. The matter was well in hand when she heard the knock upon the door long moments later. She bid whomever was without to enter, expecting Hugh. What she got was a lad she did not know carrying a large washtub most awkwardly.

"My lady," he said, tipping his head.

She nodded in return, glad that she had dressed in a clean chemise, pelisse, and bliaut from her trunk. She had chosen her deepest green pelisse with red cording at the wrist and throat and a rose-hued bliaut. Her girdle was of small golden links set with unglittering and serene onyx. She felt well protected from any further torment at her husband's hands. The sun was up. It was past time for prayer. Yet this lad had a tub which he was setting in front of her fire.

Hugh came behind him carrying a smallish basket of apples.

"Set it there, Raymond," he said. "See to the water and bring more wood for the fire. I would not have my lady feel the chill of an autumn morning."

"I am not chilled," she said to Hugh, crossing her arms over her breasts.

"You will be," he said, offering her an apple, grinning.

"My lord? You are ill-attired," she said. "Shall I leave the chamber to you? I have seen to all my needs."

He stood in his bare feet and his tunic, naught else. Of braes he had none. He was more bare than clothed.

"I can well understand why you complain of the cold if this is your common attire," she added.

"Elsbeth! You rebuke me? I was but seeing to your needs," he said, pointing Raymond out of the room. Raymond went without looking back. "And I see to them now, again. You are soiled, my little one. The water is coming which will cleanse you. I think you should disrobe, though that is a very fetching pelisse. Did you choose it for me to admire?"

"I did not. It was the closest to the top," she said.

"Hmmm. Take it off," he said, taking a bite of his apple.

Elsbeth drew herself up. "I have prepared to face the day. My prayers are tardy. I will away. Avail yourself of the water, if it suits you so well."

"Ah, it suits me very well, and so it will suit you. Take off your clothes," he said again, taking another bite. His jaw worked hard on the apple, the muscles of his cheeks contracting in rhythm with the movement of his throat. Never had the eating of an apple been so sensuous.

"I do not rebuke you, my lord," she said, reaching for calm composure and finding a blond giant in its stead. "I only seek your pleasure. Take the water—it is yours."

"I will take the wife instead; she also is mine. Shall I assist—?"

It was at that moment that Raymond returned with the bathwater, halting their joust of wills. He was followed in by two men of Warkham carrying more water. They quickly filled the tub and left.

"I will take your silence for assent," Hugh said. "I think it wondrous fair that you want me to disrobe you, Elsbeth. It speaks of seduction and intimacy; 'tis rare for a wife of mere hours to lure her husband so."

"I will do it!" she said, backing from him with an outstretched arm.

"You will?" he said, stopping, his expression comically confused. "You are ever changeable, little Elsbeth. A man must keep his wits sharp when in parley with you. You will befuddle me in a sennight, am I not wary."

"Will you leave me to my ablutions?" she asked, ignoring his attempts at jesting.

"Nay," he said, shaking his head in false regret. He ate his apple, core and all. The stem he threw into the fire. "I am not afeared of a woman's body, in flux or out. Do not fear for me, Elsbeth. I do not need protection from you."

She supposed the women of Jerusalem found him wondrous, handsome, and of jovial temperament. She was not of Jerusalem. In England, his humor wore very thin.

Or perhaps it was she who was wearing thin. This constant proximity was more than she had expected upon getting a husband. He could not share her bed as a husband would wish. Did he have to share her company? She had never heard the like. Their union was for begetting; so said church and king and Gautier. Never had she heard it said that a husband would insist upon watching his wife bathe.

'Twas most strange.

'Twas equally unwelcome.

"I cannot bathe without turning all the water to blood, my lord. Take the water for yourself; I give it unto you with a glad heart," she said.

He stopped and appeared to consider her words.

"I had not thought of that," he said, running a hand through his hair. "Let us then do this: I shall bathe first, and then you may have what you wish of the water."

"I wish nothing of the water, my lord. I have no need of it."

"Ah, but you do, Elsbeth. Are you not blooded? I would have you clean of it, even for an hour."

"You understand little of these things, my lord. My blood will not withdraw for an hour."

"Yet water will not harm you, and it will give me great pleasure to cleanse you myself, even if the cleansing last for only a moment. It was on your lips that your desire was to give me pleasure."

"Did I say that?"

"Aye, I remember something of the like," he said, smiling pleasantly. All his smiles were pleasant, yet none of the pleasure was passed to her. Nay, why should he not be pleasant when he expected to have his way in all things? "Do you not remember the same?"

She was not going to answer that.

"I will leave you, then, my lord. You have an appointment with your bathwater, and it cools even now."

"Nay, do not leave, for my pleasure only grows to have you near me. Can you not see how pleased I am?"

Aye, she could see. His manhood stood out from his body, stiff and long, lifting the tunic away from him.

"Is that because of me or the water?" she said and again regretted instantly the tartness of her tongue. This was not the way to open abbey doors to her.

Hugh laughed and lifted the tunic over his head, throwing it on the bed. "Why, for you, Elsbeth. Have no doubt as to that. You shall know what causes me to rise soon enough, once you have left behind the name Maiden Wife."

He stepped into the water. "Wash me, Elsbeth, as I will soon wash you. Touch me. Know me."

"I know you very well," she said. As well as she needed to.

"But not as the Bible says a man shall know his wife. That knowing is still to come," he said. "Learn at least a part of me, before that final knowing is upon you. 'Twill make it easier, I think."

Easier for him, she had no doubt. She had no desire to touch him and she did not want to know him.

"You think of me, my lord, or is it of yourself? I think that a man will always find a way to get a woman's hands upon him."

"You think wrongly then, little wife, for a man will always find a way to lay his hands upon a woman. What she does with *her* hands hardly matters."

"You hardly think well or much of women, my lord, to say so," she said, keeping her distance and her arms crossed over her breasts. They were strangely sensitive, no doubt a result of his fondling last night. It was going to be very difficult to concentrate on her prayers with aching breasts. Another reason, if one was needed, to drive this man off.

"Nay, I think very well of women. It is only that I understand men most clearly. But come, Elsbeth, I will not hound you to this. Come of your own will. I only ask for what you can easily give. Come, bathe your husband. 'Tis lawful and right, and you will do a goodly service to a knight of the Levant."

Put thus, how could she say nay? She could not and

still be the wife of docile submission she must be, and so, with a bent head and a heavy sigh, she knelt by the tub and rubbed his shoulders with some soap wrapped in a piece of linen.

Shoulders, aye, he had them and to spare. No man could have need for such an expanse of bone and muscle and tendon. He was wide and hard, yet without great bulk, more a buck than an ox, if she had to make comparison. Which she did not. She did not need to think at all; she only had to wash.

But as her hands slid over his skin, her eyes soaked up the sight of him. Eyes were cursed things, leading thoughts where they did not need to go. No wonder the Scriptures warned that if thine eye offended, pluck it out. Would that she had the strength of heart for that. Her eyes were all of offense because they would not turn from Hugh. It would have been like turning from the sun when all was shrouded in mist. He was a radiance that lit the stone chamber like a fire, pulsing with laughter and warmth and beckoning beauty. In the darkness of the world, in the dim shadows of stone and dirt and wood, he was light. She could not turn away. She had not the will to dwell in shadows when sunlight and firelight called to her.

If not for her courses, she would have been lost.

'Twas most humbling. She had thought herself more resolute, more stalwart, less of feminine weakness and more of prayerful might. She did not like what having Hugh in her life showed her of herself; he was a most unyielding mirror. Still, she would not lie to herself, no matter how unflattering the mirror's reflection. She found him compelling, beautiful, mayhap even irresistible. All the more reason to escape this marriage quickly. This temptation was too great; she would surely stumble. She must fly out of this marriage with all speed, before her courses ended and left her vulnerable.

"You are quiet, little one," he said. "Have I frightened you?"

He said it well. He did frighten her, though not in the way he supposed.

"Nay," she said, hiding behind him, trying not to see the tangled golden strands of his hair. "You are a most gentle husband, my lord."

He grabbed her hand and pulled it to his mouth, kissing her wrist softly. "For that I am glad. I would not frighten you for all the world, Elsbeth. Let us find our footing gently on this marriage path. There is no harm to be found in slow startings. Step by step, we shall find our way."

"Aye, that we shall," she said, pulling her hand free with care.

Step by step, she had to find her way out of this. If he had his way, he would devour her.

She seemed frightened unto death. He could feel the fear in her; it was like a mist that shrouded her, closing her in and shutting her off behind gray walls. He wanted to reach in behind the mist, pulling her into the sunlight, but ever she eluded him. No matter how he reached out his hand or gave her his smile, still Elsbeth stood a pace off. Wary. Shuttered. Untouchable.

That was the fault of her courses. When her flow ceased, all would change between them. He would take her as a man took a woman, marking her and making her his, and then she would have no cause to be wary.

It was all he wanted.

It was better said that it was the first of what he wanted. From their bonding all would proceed, all that he desired, all that he had come to England to find. All began with her. He had understood that from the start, and he had accepted it. The terms were well understood, and he was well set to meet them. All that hindered him

112

was this untimely flux. Yet it was what marked her as a woman, and it was a woman he had come to England to claim.

He could not begrudge her the mark of her fecundity and the stain of her femininity. Nay, he would not. He wanted her and he needed her; 'twas much to be said of a woman. Elsbeth was a woman who would hold that crown of value well. She deserved the value set on her. He could see that now, knowing her.

Perhaps it was best that she had never seen Jerusalem and Jerusalem never seen her. If she were a woman of the Levant, all men would have flocked to her dark beauty, and the engaging humility which shrouded her would never have taken root in her heart. He was much engaged by that humility coming from a woman of such rare beauty, piety, and riches. 'Twas a rare thing.

And she was his. At least for now.

For now. A man could find delight living in an eternal present, his past forgotten and his future locked in God's hands. Some man could, perhaps. He was not such a man, though this present with Elsbeth as his wife pleased him very well.

He only wished that she could be as pleased by him. Oh, she liked his look well enough, but she was still wary of the man. He could not fathom it, but perhaps he did not need to try. He had only to win her, not understand her. He knew how to win a woman. He would win Elsbeth of Sunnandune. It was only a question of when.

Now would suit him very well.

"Will you kiss me, Elsbeth?" he asked, running his hand up her arm to lay a wet hand on her breast. "Will you bend down to me and give me a willing kiss? I will not hold you as I did last night."

"My lord, you hold me now," she said, staring into his eyes, her bliaut stained wet with the mark of his hand upon her.

"Against your will? Do I hold you against your will, Elsbeth?" he asked, pressing his hand against the soft weight of her bosom. He felt her nipple rise up against his palm, answering his question.

"What will I have is in submission to your own," she said softly, not moving. Her eyes were dark and deep, the eyes of a woman falling into temptation. Aye, he knew how to win a woman.

"Well said, Elsbeth. Words to please any husband, even one from far Jerusalem," he said, squeezing her nipple gently. She surged toward his hand and pressed her lips together, swallowing a moan. "Kiss me, Elsbeth," he commanded softly.

She leaned down to him, her hair falling forward into the water, curling as it lay in black swirls, twisting, moving like lazy snakes in the sun. Her eyes were heavy-lidded, somnolent, exotic. He was for an instant caught, trapped by the look of her before he shook free. It was *her* will which was to be subjected, not his own. No woman was worth that price.

He felt her breath, soft and light, on his mouth and then her lips. Her kiss was tentative, shy, yet she touched something within him; some chord was struck, some note ringing clearly in his heart, before he escaped. Many traps had Elsbeth to catch a man unwary. He was wary. He would not be caught.

With a sigh, she escaped him, lifting her mouth from his.

"You are kissed, my lord," she said, backing away from him and his touch upon her breast.

"Aye, I am kissed," he said. "Will I need to ask for every kiss I want from you? Will you never come to me and kiss me of your own will and wish?" he asked, searching her face.

"Is not my answer to be 'your will is mine'? What else is left for a wife to say?" She took another step away from him and then turned to face the fire, avoiding his eyes. He took it to be a good sign, a sign of her weakness and the strength of a desire she did not wish to feel. Aye, he understood her very well.

"It is the answer I would hear, but only if it be from your heart. Do not deceive me, Elsbeth. Your submission does not please me if it is deception."

She turned at that, her wet hair flying heavily against her breasts. "I do as you ask and I am called a deceiver? That charge is unjust. I have never deceived you; you know what I want very well, my lord, is that not so?"

"My pardon, little wife. I meant no insult," he said and then he smiled. "Do you then mean to say that you wanted to kiss me, to feel my hand upon your breast?"

She crossed her arms over her breasts again and turned back to the fire. "I have said what I meant to say. There was no mystery in it," she said.

"Well said," he replied, chuckling, then ducking to rinse himself. "And well washed. Thank you, wife, I feel as clean as fresh linen. Now, may I attend you?"

She turned again to face him at his words, shock upon her strong-boned features. "Did I not say that it was not my time for bathing? It cannot be done, my lord."

"It can always be done," he said. "And should be. Have you not noted the strange, sour, odorous fog that hovers over England? You may think it is only fog, but it is not. It is the smell of the unwashed. The skies of Jerusalem are clear and clean, I can assure you. It is not coincidence, I think."

He rose from the water and stood, his hand out for the length of linen which would dry him. She reached blindly for the cloth, her eyes on him. Let her look on; the sight of him pleased her, he knew, though she would choke before she would admit as much. He was steady and hard, and had been since awaking in the night with her head nestled against his shoulder, her body warm and soft against his side.

How long did a woman's courses run? How long was he to wait?

Elsbeth was a temptress in her own right, giving a man a glimpse of what he could not possess.

She handed him the cloth, her arm fully extended, her eyes lowered and her breathing quick. She would not avoid him that easily.

"Will you assist? Wrap the cloth about me, if you would. I welcome any reason to feel your arms about me," he said, lifting her chin with his hand and looking into her bottomless eyes.

"You say it most plain," she said, looking at his mouth and not his eyes. "Why do you taunt me? I would be no man's amusement."

"Nay, you are not my amusement, Elsbeth," he said, touching her lip with his fingertip. Her lips were the pale coral pink of shell, as smooth and as flawless. "You are my torment," he breathed. "Come, torment me again."

He heard the catch in her breathing and watched her eyes close against the sight of him. But he was still before her and they both knew it; she could not push him from her by the simple closing of her eyes. She dropped her head and wrapped the cloth about his shoulders like a cloak and stepped away from him.

"Nay, nay," he said. "Come, do it well if you will do it. Wrap it about my hips, low and tight so that it will not fall."

"I cannot," she said.

"Why can you not?"

"I . . . cannot."

"Then do not," he said, wrapping the cloth about his hips himself and stepping from the tub. "I will never ask of you what you cannot do nor demand what you cannot give. Rest in that, little one. Find your rest where you may," he said almost to himself.

She looked up at him, her face as solemn as ever, yet also curious. She did not know what to think of him; he did not meet her expectations of husbands or of men. Having spent even a short time in England, he could understand it. The men of the north were closer to barbarians than they would ever admit. The best of them had gone south to the holy land two generations ago; the worst of them had stayed behind, hiding behind wooden palisades and smelly moats, unwilling to risk their blood to save the land of their very Savior. They were hardly knights as he knew knights to be. Yet they were the only knights Elsbeth had ever known.

"You are gentle," she said, giving proof to his observations. "I did not think it in a man to be gentle."

"Do not tell your father he has given you to a gentle knight. He may regret our bargaining and take you back unto himself," he said lightly. "Now lift your skirts and I will wash you."

She backed up, catching her foot on loose kindling laid near the fire, her hands pressed to her skirts, holding them down. As if that would stop him.

"Nay!"

"Aye," he said, grinning. "Come closer, Elsbeth. 'Tis time for you to be bathed, as well you may while your courses run. Or must I come and catch you? That would be fine play. I am willing, if you are."

"My lord, this is wrong. You must keep away. You will defile yourself."

"My lady, there is nothing wrong about it. I will not keep away. You have not the power to defile me. I am not to be put off by a trace of blood."

" 'Tis more than a trace!"

"Then change your dressing yet again. I will wait. Yet

I will wash you. My lord Christ did so to his followers; can I do less for you, my wife?"

"His disciples did not bleed."

"Well, perhaps they should have for deserting Him as they did. They were vassals to His holy will and they abandoned Him. A little bloodletting would not have been amiss."

"Do we now talk of Christ and His twelve or of me? I am lost."

"Then be found, Elsbeth. All words lead to Christ, Lord of all under heaven. Can He be far from any discourse man can speak? I think not."

"I never did hear verse where Christ spoke of a woman's flux," she said, her anger and confusion barely hidden.

Hugh smiled and shrugged. "Did not the apostle John say that all the books of all the world could not hold the words and deeds of Christ? I must then believe that He did speak of it, yet it was not recorded into Holy Writ."

"This is blasphemy, my lord. The Word of God is complete."

"Aye, it is. I do not argue it. Now lift your skirts, Elsbeth, so that I may do what I *will* do."

"Do not ask this of me, my lord," she said, her eyes panicked. "You said you would not ask of me what I cannot give. I cannot give this."

He smiled at her and dipped the cloth into the water, now holding the chill of autumn and stone. "You can. I will show you that you can." When she only looked at him with eyes gone wide in shocked embarrassment, he said, "I want to touch you. I want you to lift your skirts for me. I want to see what no man has seen. I want the most intimate part of you, Elsbeth. Give yourself to me. I will not abuse. I will not harm. I will deal gently, always and only. Trust me. Please."

She could not. She could not lift her skirts for any

man. 'Twas too much. Too much of sensual bonding. Too much of intimacy. Too much of desire. Only women who took men into their bodies lifted their skirts. She would not be such a woman. She would not even act the part.

And yet, she felt the thrill even now of what it would be like to lift her skirts and watch his face as her legs were revealed to him, inch by inch. She would tempt him with the act. Aye, he would be tempted, and she would revel in holding him in thrall for that little while.

She could not. Not because she feared him. In that moment, she only feared herself and what he roused in her. Had not Ardeth and even Isabel spoken of this? This desire to tempt a man, this was to be avoided as it was the first step on the path to destruction. She had known that truth all her life.

"I cannot," she said. "Do not ask it of me, I pray you."

"You fear," he said, his green eyes soft and smiling. "Let me tell you then what will be, so that you will not fear."

He stood in his linen, his hair dark with water and brushing the tops of his shoulders. He stood, his masculinity an assault she could feel in her very bones, turning her heart to water, melting her joints to wax. The sight of him was a battering ram to her defenses; his words were arrows that pierced her heart and her resolve. Yet she stood and prayed for deliverance. God would answer. God was true.

"I will kneel at your feet. I will lift the hems of your very pretty green pelisse and your fine rose bliaut, tangling them in my grasp. I will grasp the hem in my hands, lifting it softly. You will feel the slightest brush of air, first on your ankles and then on your calves as I raise it, raise it, raise it to your knees. When I see your knees, I will be overcome and I will lean forward to kiss one perfect knee. You will tremble and you will shift your weight from foot to foot. You will duck your head and sigh, yet I will hear you and I will smile. You make me smile, did you know that, Elsbeth? You have the rare ability to make me smile."

"You laugh at me," she said, her voice a croak. The images he painted were too strong. He was too adept with words; it was his gravest fault.

He took a step toward her, the linen moving about his feet. "I do not," he said. "Believe that. If you believe nothing else, believe that. I would not wound you even with a misplaced laugh. You simply ease my heart, that is all. And yet it is so much."

"Your words . . . you have too many words," she said.

"You are right. I use words because you have stopped my deeds. I would show you what I want for both of us, yet my hands are stopped against your iron will. Only my words are left. Will you take those from me, too, and leave me stripped of all the ways a man may win a woman's heart?"

"You have my body, my lands, my riches. What need have you for my heart?"

"I want all of you, Elsbeth," he said, his face suddenly intent. "Without your heart, all else is dross."

She saw another side of him then, another besides the grinning, pleasant face he wore for all the world and his wife to see. He was capable of much more than smiles, this man from Jerusalem, but what that meant for her, she did not know. His smiles had all but undone her.

"Let me touch you," he said, dropping to his knees at her feet. The fire was behind her, yet it was cold and dark compared to the heat and light of Hugh.

"You ask my leave?"

"Nay, I beg it," he said, his voice a throaty murmur.

Too many words, and all of them perfectly designed to cast her into a fall from which there was no rescue. She had no weapons against such temptation. When her courses stopped, she would fall. She was walking to her very death and could not seem to turn aside.

"Touch me, then," she said and did not recognize the voice as hers.

He lifted her skirts as he had predicted. The air touched her ankles, her calves, her knees, yet she felt no cool draft; all was heat and fire and longing. Her very blood pulsed out of her, pushed by her desire. She was defiled, disgraced, and still he lifted her skirts and still she let him, gasping her longing. Lost in smothered desire.

Lost.

"Is it not as I said?" he asked her, his breath on her legs, his head near her thighs.

It was all as he said. Every word beat against her mind as his eyes devoured her, his hands caressed her. Where was her sanctuary from such an assault?

"No higher," she said, trying to back away from his hands. The fire was behind her; she had nowhere to go.

"Nay?" he said, looking up at her as he held her skirts bunched in his hands. His eyes were shaded by the spikes of his lashes. He looked as wild as any cat. "Then I will wash what I have revealed."

Hugh took the cloth she had used on him and rubbed her legs with it, from ankle to knee, in soft, slow strokes. The water was only a little warm and the room was cool, even with the fire at her back; her legs shivered as he wet them, and she trembled, as he had said she would.

He rinsed the cloth in the tub and then touched her again, more slowly, caressing rather than washing. And higher. Higher, though she had said nay to that. She did not say nay now. His hand stroked upward, past knee to thigh, to the very joining of her thighs. To the very padding that shielded and protected her.

"You are so hot, Elsbeth. I had not thought the fire was so high and hot as that, but you prove me wrong.

Your skin burns under my hand. Without this cloth to shield me, I would be scorched and blistered."

Nay, she was not hot. She shivered and trembled. Her heart shook within her ribs. She could not draw a breath without a gasp to mark it.

"Open for me," he said, the cloth high up on her thigh. Her legs were pressed together, closed against him, closed against the blood that flowed out of her. Which did she want more, her blood or his touch? She did not know. She had fallen that far.

She did not know which was blessing and which was curse.

"Open," he repeated, his breath soft against her thigh. His hair was drying, golden and shining against her skin.

She opened for him, just a bit. Just a slight shifting of her feet. She could not see anything but the golden halo of his hair. She could not think beyond his next touch, his next stroke against her thigh. She could not even think to pray.

His hand stroked up the inside of her thigh, his fingertips just brushing the wadding of her protection. His hand came away, sheathed in white linen touched by a tint of red.

"You bleed," he said.

"Aye," she said, swaying on her feet, the fire at her back and the fire between her legs consuming her. She laid a hand upon his shoulder, steadying herself. "I told you."

"Aye, and I believed. Still, I would cleanse you as best I may."

He stroked again, the cloth dipped clean in the water of the tub, wiping bloodstains from her thighs, igniting desires she had not known dwelt within her. He turned her. He turned her so that her back was to him, her skirts left to fall in front so that her posterior was exposed to his sight and to his touch.

"Nay. Enough," she said.

Now she was begging and she had no will to stand on pride. He was destroying her. Gently, softly destroying her. She would have no will left to fight if he did not stop now.

"Not enough," he said, and she could feel his breath on her derriere. She clenched against the sensation and felt the pulsebeat of desire pound within her core. "Never enough," he said. "You are mine. I want all of you. Even the blood. Even your shame. Give me all and I will be content."

"You said no harm."

"I will not harm. I have not harmed. I have barely touched," he said, stroking her derriere with the cloth, edging his hand between her cheeks, running his damp hand down the inside of her thigh.

"You have touched all," she said, gasping, trying to drop her skirts. He held them fast and laughed.

"Spoken like a maiden. When this time of constraint has passed, you shall learn the difference, little one. I will have all of you. You will give me all of you."

"Nay," she said, turning within his arms, facing him, the enemy to her vow.

"And you will want all of me," he said, pulling her down to kneel in front of him. " 'Tis the way of marriage, Elsbeth. One body, one flesh, as the Lord commands. Will you disobey?"

"I will follow God's path for me," she said, knowing her meaning was different from his.

"As will I," he said. "We can do no more. We must do no less," he said, throwing the blood-tinged cloth into the tub, where it floated softly before sinking to disappear in the dark shadows of the water. "I torment myself. To touch you, lay my hands upon you, dwell upon your beauty, is torment when I cannot have you. When I know that you do not want me . . . yet."

He was wrong. She wanted him. It was her torment. She did want him yet she would never choose to have him.

Even kneeling as they were, he was taller by a head. His heart beat in his breast, and she could count the beats beneath his golden skin. He had very little body hair, just a thin line that hovered low on his torso, trailing down to his manhood, darkening as it went. His cloth held about his hips, for which she thanked God most profoundly. A thin barrier, yet welcome.

"Do not ask for what I cannot give," she said, closing her eyes against the vision of him.

He pressed her head to his chest, comforting her, running his hand down the long fall of her hair.

"I will not," he said, and she was comforted. Until he added, "You will want to give me all. I will see to that."

Chapter Eight

"The timing was most unfortunate."

"God is the master of time and His will made perfect by it. I am not constrained nor concerned. All will be well."

Gautier looked at his daughter's husband. All would be well? Only a Levantine would find a bleeding and unclean wife to be a matter of no concern. Perhaps he did not have it in him to take a woman. The Poulains were soft, as were all who were born within the shadow of the holy sepulcher and lived out their days on the rim of the Great Sea. They smelled too sweet to be men of blood. They loved the bath, not battle. They lived in cities behind thick walls of stone; when did they battle but over the choice of damask for their bedhangings?

Hugh of Jerusalem was all too fit a match for his prayerful daughter. They could well pray each other into heaven before this marriage was consummated, which would not serve. He needed this marriage. He had arranged it most carefully. If not for Elsbeth's flux and Hugh's fear of blood, all would have been settled by now. If Hugh would only lift his fleshy sword and poke it into his daughter, the matter could be set to rest.

Gautier looked askance at his newfound son. He looked a pretty man, mayhap too pretty to do his service to a maid. There were many tales told of the men of the Levant, tales that would not serve his goals. It was certain that Elsbeth would not encourage him, not with Ardeth's counsel shaping her as it did. This marriage must be consummated, sealed and set. 'Twas up to Hugh to do his part. It was up to him to point the Poulain in the right direction.

If Hugh could not manage to find his way into Elsbeth, securing her as his, then Gautier must consider other means for gaining what he sought from this union. He was not a man to shrink from any course. Nay, he was a man made for anything.

"You are confident," Gautier said. "I must take comfort in that, drinking of your confidence."

"Your confidence is not misplaced," Hugh said. "All *will* be well."

Gautier shrugged. "She is most devout. She will not welcome you, I fear," Gautier said.

"To be devout is no sin," Hugh said, looking over the curtain wall to the fields below. They walked the battlements, seeking fresher air than that to be found in the still confines of the bailey. "I am most pleased by Elsbeth. You did not speak false concerning her."

"I did not speak false on anything," Gautier said, ignoring the fields below, studying Hugh instead.

"That pleases me as well," Hugh said lightly, "and I

did not doubt but that you spoke true. Your good name has traveled far, even to Outremer."

"That is well. I have done good service in my life, and while my reward will surely find me in heaven, to be praised on earth is equally satisfying."

To be praised on earth was all the praise a man would get, his eternal praise robbed to feed it, according to the Gospels. But if Gautier did not know his Scriptures, Hugh would not be the light to blind him with the truth.

They had an agreement, the two of them. An agreement which hinged on Elsbeth. Knowing her better, knowing her father better, made the agreement more unpleasant to him, yet he would not disappoint Baldwin. Baldwin and Jerusalem needed him to succeed in this distant and cold land, and so he would succeed.

He would not disappoint. He would not fail. It was well within his power to achieve all ends, though his heart did not yearn for the battle ahead. Nay, his heart had been touched by Elsbeth and, once touched, was changed.

He had not expected that. He had come to take a wife, but he had not come to find his life changed. It was unwelcome, what she aroused in him: an urge to protect and defend which had nothing of Baldwin in it. The soft warmth he felt when he made her smile was surprising. She did not smile often, that he knew. He felt like the victor of a great battle with every smile won from her shuttered heart.

Still, a man did his duty and asked his heart to bear the burden of it. He was Poulain. He knew where his loyalty lay. God would see to Elsbeth if men failed her, as they surely would.

"Does she know yet that you stay at Warkham?" Gautier asked, pulling his cloak tighter against a sudden sodden gust.

"Nay, she does not know she will not see Sunnandune.

Yet, until her flux is past we must stay where we are. Travel would be difficult as it stands now with her. She will not wonder at it."

Gautier laughed and looked up at the sky. "All the world must seem wet and unwelcoming to you now, Hugh. Take another woman of my holding to ease your wait. I will not look amiss on such an act. A man's needs must be met elsewhere when his wife rains blood upon the sheets."

"Do not men welcome rain?" Hugh said, pulling his own cloak about him, cloaking his tongue in courtesy. "Elsbeth is not unwelcoming, she is simply unable. I can wait for Elsbeth and will wait for her. I need no other woman. Patience, Lord Gautier."

"You counsel yourself. I am not the man who must wait for a woman to become ready to receive my seed. My seed is set."

"Your lady wife looks well. She will deliver you a fine child," Hugh said, turning the talk away from Elsbeth.

"She may," Gautier said casually. "There is no way to tell until the child is loosed from her. I have seen this many times."

"How many times a father are you?" Hugh asked out of courtesy if not curiosity.

"This will make eleven, I think. What matter the number unless they come loose living, kicking free of the womb, grabbing hold of life with both hands? Of living children, I have eight. Of living wives, I have one," Gautier said, laughing.

Hugh smiled along with Gautier, but the urge to laugh was far from him.

"Your flow is still strong, Elsbeth," Emma said in sympathy.

"It is but the second day," Elsbeth said. "I know how my courses run. I am not dismayed."

127

Nay, hardly dismayed. Overjoyed. She needed this blood, this time, to gather her resources and her strength, for Hugh awaited on the other side of her flux and she was much afraid that she would not withstand his assault. In truth, she was near certain that she would be near helpless against it.

Never had she imagined the power of desire, the pulse of need and wanting that crowded out all thoughts but one. Possession. Surrender. This was what her mother had tried to explain to her. This was the danger of men. This need was what drove women to lay their bodies down, their very wills subject to the throbbing want that pounded in their hearts and bodies. This need, this damning need, was what destroyed them. She understood better now. And from understanding would come strength.

"You are not dismayed," Emma said with a small laugh, "but is the question not whether Hugh is dismayed? A man does not think to have to wait on his wedding night, nor on any other night, as to that. What did you do all the long night? I know he stayed with you, which is more than Gautier would have done, but how did you pass the long hours of the dark?"

Elsbeth looked at her father's wife from across the chess board. She did not want to talk of what men and women did in the dark. She did not want to remember the sweet torment of last night. She did not want to stir those memories, those feelings, to remembered life.

"If you do not tell me, I will imagine all sorts of delicious things," Emma said, moving a pawn.

Her imaginings could not be more delicious, or dangerous, than the reality of that night, yet Elsbeth could not admit that either.

"We talked," she said.

"All night?"

"We also slept."

"Together?"

"Of course, together. There is but one bed," Elsbeth said a trifle sharply.

"And the bed is not overlarge," Emma said, grinning. "He must have . . . touched you, then. Did you like it?"

"Have we not already agreed that my flux is still rampant? There was little of touching."

"Little, but some?" Emma said cheerfully. She was the most irrepressibly cheerful woman, but then, that would serve her well in her marriage to Gautier.

"Some," Elsbeth said, moving her queen to a position of more ready aggression.

"Really," said Emma with overt and obvious interest. "Tell me. Tell me everything. He really is a man of courage not to be put off by a woman's blood."

"He did not touch me *there*." But he almost had, this morning. Was it courage or foolishness that prompted him?

"Then where? Tell me," Emma said, her eyes avid and alight. Her life really must be deadly dull to want such information. "Your breasts, I would guess," she said sagely. "You have fine, shapely breasts."

"Emma!" she said, horrified. "I will not discuss this. We should be at our prayers."

"Sext is not for hours," Emma said. "So, did he fondle you?"

"Your king is in peril," Elsbeth said, looking down at the board.

"My king is yours if you tell me what happened." Elsbeth looked up at her, surprised beyond words. "My life is empty now, waiting for this child to come forth. Your father keeps his distance. Denise, Warkham's fosterling, is still at her playthings; she is no companion and too young to train to anything more than needlework. Talk to me, Elsbeth. I need a woman in my life."

Elsbeth could understand that. A woman's life was better and more happily spent with other women. Which described the abbey life very well.

"Could we not talk of other things?" Elsbeth said.

"What else is of more import than your wedding night? This night will live in your memory for all your days. Do you not wish to speak of it?"

That was her fear, that it would live in her memory for all her days. She did not want to think of his eyes on her, his hands on her, his mouth tasting her, because if she did, then she remembered all he made her feel. Her body had been traitor to her will. 'Twas not a pleasant memory. Yet it was a memory that burned slowly in her thoughts, smoldering like embers, too ready to flash to brilliant life.

She could not take such memories into the nunnery with her, and she would not foul Sunnandune with them.

"It was not a wedding night, not the way the church defines," she said. "I have naught to say. We talked, he was kind and patient, we slept when the night was old. There is nothing more to say."

Emma sighed and shook her head. "That is too bad. A wedding night should be more. But never despair, your flux will pass and then you will have a night to remember."

Elsbeth sighed and nodded, glad for the passing of this questioning.

"So," Emma said, considering her next move, "did he kiss you?"

"What did she tell you?"

"Very little, my lord," Emma said.

"Did he touch her?" Gautier asked.

"Aye, but her blood still flows strong. There is naught he can do till it passes."

They stood at the hearth in their hall, the tables

stacked along the wall. It was hours yet till the meal, and the hall was near empty. Still, they kept their voices low. This was not a conversation for other ears.

"Yet he did touch her," Gautier said softly, stroking his chin. "She is very like her mother; touching may well have broken passion loose in her. Did she seem distraught?"

"Elsbeth? I do not think it in Elsbeth to be distraught. She did not like my questions, that is all I am sure of," Emma answered.

"So, he waits until her blood stops," Gautier said, looking off into the shadows of his hall. "Well, there is nothing for it but to wait. Hugh thinks he knows what he is about, how to win her. Whether he speaks true or nay, Elsbeth will show us. I do not like this waiting."

"Nor does Hugh, I would say," Emma said.

Gautier smiled down at his wife. "You say that aright. This is a wait no man likes, yet we must each face it, month upon month."

"We women face it, too. I do not like the time spent without you," Emma said, leaning into him.

Gautier only smiled and rubbed a hand down her back.

"This waiting is most hard, my lord."

"Speak not to me of hard, Raymond. I ache even now," Hugh said, throwing his squire a casual grin.

"Yet the marriage is legal, is it not, my lord? None can be blamed for non-consummation."

"None can be blamed, and yet the marriage is not consummated. I cannot think that the church would honor any claim to dissolve this union, her flux being an act of God and nature. Yet, without penetration, my claim is tenuous."

"She would not deny you," Raymond said, his eyes alight with fervor at the implied insult.

"I do not think it is in her to rebel against both her father and her husband, yet she does not want to be a bride. Her maiden state suits her temper very well," Hugh said.

He and Raymond walked the land just outside the gates of Warkham. It was a damp day, as all English days seemed to be. The town of Warkham was a single street, muddy and rutted, not worth the title "town" at all, a blemish upon the earth when held in comparison to the towns of Outremer. There, a town had a thousand years to sink down roots and grow into a flourishing settlement that welcomed all. Here, a piss pot had more permanence.

Raymond had come with him the long distance from Jerusalem and was of that land, as Hugh himself was. They shared the same mind on many things, and Raymond knew why Hugh had come north and approved the deed. All who knew Baldwin must approve his purpose here, and Raymond loved Baldwin as well as any man.

"You can change that with a smile and a sigh, my lord. All the maidens of Jerusalem attest to that," Raymond said.

"But we are not in Jerusalem, Raymond," Hugh said, "and this English bride does not fall to a smile. Her heart is of firmer fiber, though she be a woman still."

"If she be a woman, then she is won if you seek to win her."

"Your confidence cheers me; still, she is not yet won."

"You have only to wait, my lord. When her flux is past, then the way will be clear."

But he did not dare wait. Elsbeth was too strong against the match, her very soul striving against the married state. If he waited to win her by the claiming of her body, she might yet escape him. He could not wait, nor count on the stirrings of her loins to tie her to him. Nay, he needed to hold her heart; if he could do that, then her body would perforce follow.

He understood a woman's heart, and this woman, with her father's careful counsel echoing in his ears, he understood better than most. The way to win her was through the chapel and the nave, keeping the office of a monk with the caress of a lover. Well, and he could do that. Was he not from holy Jerusalem? A little girl from England could not beat him at a game of holy ardor.

The nave was cool, and it suited well her mood. The memories of last night had risen new and hungry with the questioning by Emma, as she had feared. The cold dim of God's own house would press the images from her. Her prayers were soft in the gloom, yet her heart was firm.

She felt him enter long before she heard his step upon the stone.

"I thought I would find you here," Gautier said, his voice just behind her. She did not turn; she was at her prayers, or was supposed to be.

"Here I will ever be," she said, struggling to be free of him in even this small way.

"If your husband so decides," Gautier said at her back. He did not kneel. She felt very small and vulnerable with him rising up behind her, but that was foolish. She was in God's own house. She was perfectly safe.

"I will abide by his decision for me," she said, her head bent more to avoid the sight of him than out of holiness. "I am content."

"I would only that you be content, Elsbeth," Gautier said. "As any father would for any child, so I am for you. I chose well for you, did I not? He is a man to make a maid swoon."

"I did not swoon because of him," she said, lifting her

head. "I had not supped. 'Twas hunger that made me light of head, nothing more."

"Hunger?" Gautier asked, and she could hear his silent laughter. "I will not argue it. He is a man to make a maid hungry, and there are many kinds of hunger. Has he taught you that?"

He excelled at this form of verbal sparring; she had learned long years past that she could never win such a game with him. All was turned to his purpose, and his purpose ever seemed to be to find amusement in her embarrassment.

"If I could return to my prayers?" she said, lowering her head again, shutting him out. She could hear him chuckling and stiffened her spine against the assault of his humor.

"Aye, I would keep no woman from her divine duty. But remember also your duty to your husband. He has a hunger of his own that must be met, Elsbeth. Do not forget it. He most certainly shall not."

"I need no reminder, Father. I know my duty."

"Then may you find the joy of it. I wish you that. I wish for little else."

"And if I wish for more?" she said against all wisdom and experience.

"Then do what you must to achieve all your desires, Elsbeth," he said. "Give Hugh what he wants from you. God willing, he will then answer your every desire, even your desire for the abbey. But deny him and he will give you nothing. Remember that. Be only wise and submissive and you will win what you desire most."

"I know what I must do," she said, keeping her head bent against him.

"I know you do, and I know that you will do it very well," he said, laying a hand on her head in benign approval.

She did not move, she scarcely breathed, and then he

moved off. She heard his footsteps fading, and then he was gone and she was again alone in the chapel. Alone with her thoughts and what should have been her prayers. Yet she could not pray. All her thoughts were of Hugh and the battle that was even now being set before her.

She did not know how she would succeed, but she must. Hugh was the temptation of a lifetime. If she could stand against him, her body and her heart intact, she could stand against Lucifer himself.

She heard him come and breathed deeply in resolve.

"I knew I would find you here," he said.

"Here I will ever be," she said in rote repetition.

"Then here I will be, at your side," he said, kneeling next to her. "I will pray the day away with you, a warrior of blood and prayer at your side."

She did not need a warrior at her side. She needed only God. She would tell Hugh so, when she could find her breath. Her heart raced and pressed against her ribs. It was most difficult to remember the words of her prayer when all she could remember was the feel of his hand running up her thigh.

"There are other things which must call you," she said, her voice a whisper.

Let him think that she was devout, not consumed by flaring desire to have him so near. She did not even dare to turn her head. The sight of him would be more temptation than she could bear right now.

"You call to me," he whispered. "You, Elsbeth. I want to hold you. I want to talk with you, learning your mind and thoughts and heart. Let us look on this week of waiting as a blessing most divine. I will know you before I possess you, and I will not fault the time. I see God's hand in this delay of our physical union. Do not you?"

Yea, but not the way he meant. God's plan was for deliverance. She was certain of it.

"Yea, I know this is of God," she said, her head bowed in prayer, her hands trembling.

"All is of God. A man is a fool who fights against His will and His ways. I will not fight," he said, his voice a thread of feeling in the middle of her prayer. "I would not fight. He has given me you. God's ways have never before seemed so perfect in my eyes and in my heart."

She would crumble into dust if he did not stop. No man wanted a woman he did not know with such ardent longing and such willing devotion. She did not slight herself, but she knew enough of men to know that what he said could not be.

But it was so tempting to believe.

"It is good that God's ways are now seen perfected in your sight. That, surely, is His will for all of us, that we see and acknowledge His perfection and His power," she said.

"Yea, Elsbeth, and you are the vessel He has used in my life," Hugh said, running a hand over the length of her hair. "I am blessed."

"We are all blessed," she said, leaning into the touch of his hand without volition. Where was she in her prayers? She had forgotten. All was lost in the heat and light of Hugh.

"Keep to your prayers, my little wife," he said. "I will stay at your side, my voice in harmony with yours. Did Jesus not say that where two or more are gathered together, He hears our prayers most well? I will make the pairing. Our prayers will find God's ear. Pray on, little warrior—I stand guard at your back."

Pray? She could not pray with him so near. God Himself seemed to be receding like mist in the sun.

"You must have tasks of your own," she said.

"None so dear to me as this," he said.

"But . . . should you not practice arms? Your skills will

grow dim if you linger in the shadows of God's sanctuary."

"I lose them willingly. To be at your side and in God's presence more than makes up the lack. Besides, will God not give me strength and skill when I need them? I trust in Him to keep me strong. I will abide here, with you."

Nay, he could not. She did not want him so near. She did not trust his intent. His words were all of worship and prayer, yet she did not believe a man could be so devout, even if he be from holy Jerusalem.

"Then I will leave, my prayers done," she said.

She did not want to share this place with him. Her time with God was sacred and private. She would not let Hugh turn God's house into a place to tempt a woman into sin.

He rose as she did, his arm on hers, leading her from the nave without hesitation, his purpose revealed. He had not wanted peace. He had only wanted to destroy her prayer. That was so like a man.

"Then I will follow you, our paths one," he said. "What now, Elsbeth? The day is young. I think," he said, poking his head out of the portal, looking up skeptically at the leaden sky. "I cannot tell. Is the sun up? Can you tell the hour?"

She did not find his complaints about the weather charming; had not God created England as well as Jerusalem? The air was soft with rain. She found it most pleasing.

"It is not yet Sext. The meal will be upon us after that."

She did not look forward to eating. Hugh would be at one side, her father hemming her in place on the other. Nay, she did not yearn for the meal.

"What shall we do until the hour for prayer at Sext?" he asked, still holding her arm.

"You might enjoy warming yourself by the fire," she

said. "I know how the chill of autumn has buried itself into your very bones."

"You are cross that I have shortened your hour of prayer," he said, smiling ruefully. "Be not cross with me. I only want your company."

"I fear I am not available, nor am I pleasing company today. I must away."

"Away to where?"

She tried to walk away from him, but he would not obey her will. He stayed at her side, all concern and care. She believed none of it. Rather, he was all temptation and deceit.

"I think you must know," she said.

"Ah, is the bucket full again? Need I fetch you another?"

"You need do nothing. I can take care of myself and my needs very well, my lord. Occupy yourself as you will."

It was the wrong thing to say. She knew it as the words left her tongue.

"My will is to stay at your side. There is no other occupation I seek, Elsbeth. Let me help you."

"For someone who seeks to stick to my side like a burr, you have remarkable trouble remembering my words. I do not need help. Seek your amusements elsewhere."

"Your flux has soured your temper," he said soothingly.

"It has not!" she snapped, pulling her arm out of his grasp. "My temper is constant. I am calm," she said. "I only remark that you do not seem to be listening to the words you beg from me."

"I listen. I have heard you," he said, his eyes going a bit cold. "You do not seek the married state. You seek a life behind abbey walls."

"I have not deceived you," she said, slightly alarmed that he sounded offended. Would he repudiate her if he were insulted? That might serve her purpose, though it did not seem a man's response. It was more likely he would want to keep her close and punish her for giving him offense. That was like a man—all pride and little tolerance. "I wanted the cloister long before I even knew your name."

"Ah, so now that you have come to know me, you are content in your marriage to me," he said.

If she were of a more suspicious nature, she might believe he was goading her. "My heart does not turn so quickly, my lord. Nor my vows. And never my will." Let him chew on that. She was determined and devout; there was no more to her than that.

"Yet you have taken a vow before God to me, Elsbeth. I will not let you forget that. And wills can be turned, even at the eleventh hour. Do you not remember the thief upon his cross? Did he not turn and was he not welcomed into Paradise that very day?"

He looked very severe, in a seductive sort of way. How was that possible?

"I have not forgotten," she said, staring up at him.

How that he could talk of Christ's crucifixion, her binding vow of marriage, and death . . . and still manage to seduce a ragged breath from her?

Where had she been going? It was difficult to remember. He seemed to drive out every thought which did not center on him. She had never felt so confused in all her life.

"That is good," he said, taking her chin in his hand, holding her gaze up to meet his. "Though it would not be amiss to remind you of the bond we share, the caresses we have exchanged—"

"I have not caressed you!" she interrupted.

Hugh paused and seemed to consider it. "Do you know, you are correct in that. That is something we must change. We will go now to our chamber, and after you have seen to your needs, you will see to mine. I will be caressed by my wife. I must insist, Elsbeth. You will touch me." He smiled. "You will enjoy it."

"Because you say it, does not make it so!" she said. She was a fool even to talk to him; he twisted everything to his own design.

"Oh, yea, it does," he said, grinning. And then he kissed her lightly on the lips. He took her hand in his and crossed the bailey with her in tow like an errant child.

The only reason she went with him, she told herself, was that she did need to change her padding, after all. She only hoped he remembered that.

"Hurrying back to your chamber?" Emma said from the top of the stair.

Elsbeth held her tongue. Emma would only think one thing, no matter what was said. Unfortunately, she would be right in this instance.

"My wife has need of privacy. I go to assure her of it," Hugh said, gifting Emma with a warm and winsome smile.

Emma looked starry-eyed. Emma had no call to look starry-eyed; she was a fortnight away from delivering herself of a babe.

Emma was left behind as they crossed the hall, empty but for the servants setting up the board in the misty light. The torches burned softly, steady and quiet in the rain-soaked air. She was only glad her father was not about to note her progress and her company as she was hurried up to her chamber.

"Should I carry you again?" Hugh said. "We could make a tradition of it."

"Nay, I need no such traditions in my life."

"You have little romance in you," he said, looking back at her as they came to the stone stair that led to the upper floors.

"I have little need for it," she said, meeting his gaze.

"Then perhaps you should have it all the more," he said, his eyes suddenly very solemn.

He turned from her then and did almost carry her up the stair, so rapid was his ascent. Her progress would have been easier if he had let go of her hand. But he did not let go. She should have been more annoyed than she was. Yet she was not.

Such was the depth of her danger.

They came to her chamber, coming out of the dark of the stair to find Raymond within. He was lighting the fire. A pile of cord wood was next to the hearth, fragrant and fresh, smelling of pine and oak.

Elsbeth turned to Hugh in the doorway and said, "You have prepared for this. You knew. You planned to bring me here. Now. At just this hour."

Hugh did not even have the grace to look repentant. He waved Raymond out of the room and when the door had closed behind him, said, "Of course I did."

At those words, he threw the bolt, locking them inside.

Chapter Nine

"You are not even contrite!"

"Contrite? Because I want to be with my wife? Because I want to have her hands on me, her mouth, her hair trailing over my skin—"

"Stop!" she said, putting her hands over her ears and turning from the sight of him. "There is more to me than hands and hair, my lord. If you cannot see that—"

He turned her to face him, his hands on her shoulders, and wrapped his arms about her. She was pressed to his body, her face buried in his chest. She should have pushed him away, but suddenly she was drowning in weariness.

He never could let her rest; always he came at her, with his hands and his flattery and the weapon of his beauty. She was so very weary of fighting the battle of Hugh. It felt so good to rest against his strength, just for the moment, finding a temporary succor with her foe. Naught would come of it; they were fully clothed.

"Of course I see that there is more to Elsbeth than hair and hands and even mouth," he said, his chin resting on the top of her head. "You are soul and mind and heart. And I would know all of you, little wife. I want to know you. I want to find all there is to love about you. Your beauty I already know," he said, smiling. She could hear the smile in his voice.

"Do not mock," she said, fighting the urge to wrap her arms around him and just rest, buried in his warmth.

"I do not," he said, his voice the gentle hum of distant waters, soothing and calm. "I never would. You are beautiful. And . . . I am commanded to love my wife by God Himself. How can I disobey? I do love you, as commanded, but I also look to find a way to love the Elsbeth in my arms, to make obedience easier. I am human. I do not look for the stony path climbing to the mountaintop when the sandy path leading to the meadow is within my reach. I want to know you, wife, so that I may love you better."

Words of deceit, surely. No man wanted to love his wife; there was no chivalry, no honor, in that. And she did not want his love. She only wanted release. Why did he speak of love?

Because he understood women. What woman did not yearn for words of love?

She was that woman.

Ardeth had made sure of that.

"Better? You mean to say easier."

He pulled back and lifted her face with his hands. "Better and easier. Now it is you who mock me."

"Nay," she said, aware she was losing herself in his eyes and unable to find the will to stop. "I do not mock. Or I will not."

"A truce, then?"

"Were we embattled?"

He smiled and kissed her brow. "You know we were."

"I do not want to battle you," she said, and it was the truth. But what other way was left her?

"That is a fine beginning to any marriage. Firm footing," he said, kissing her again just at the crest of her cheek.

Firm footing, he said, when all was crumbling beneath her feet. Worse, she did not even fear the fall this rest in his arms would cause. He was so strong, so sure, so smiling-bright. It was easier to resist temptation when temptation was dark and cold.

So said all who had fallen.

He kissed her face, gentle kisses on brow and cheek and chin. Her mouth tingled for a taste of him, a sign of the crumbling path she walked. He was temptation, and she yearned to fall into him. Was it only yesterday that she had stood so firm against him?

There was little of the warrior left in her; she had not been very mighty, after all.

Hugh kissed her softly on the mouth, and his hands rose up to caress her breasts. They tingled and grew heavy, aching, swelling at his touch. A sudden response that seemed ages old. She leaned into his kiss, sighing her submission to his touch, watching her resolve fade into the mist.

She would not die of this. She was still safe, her blood her surest shield. She would allow herself to fall this far. This far and no farther.

"I like our truces better than our battles," he said, lifting her hair from her nape with both his hands. "Your hair is your glory, as Scripture declares. I could drown in your hair and die with a smile."

He had exposed her nape and whispered kisses there. She closed her eyes, lost in the fog of passion he had thrown over her like a cloak. Lost in kisses and whispers. Nay, not a warrior. Only a maiden cast under the hands of a man who understood maidens too well.

"There is more to me than hair," she repeated, reminding them both.

"Aye, and more than skin as soft and sweet as a wild Damascus rose. More than eyes as dark and deep as night. More than lips that call forth my manhood even as they murmur holy prayer. More than breasts as lush and ripe as pomegranates."

"Enough," she said, pushing against his chest, wanting this assault to stop, yet wanting his hands on her as much as she wanted her next breath. "I do not know what pomegranates are," she said with a nervous laugh.

Hugh leaned back from her and smiled, untying her laces, layer upon layer, baring her shoulders.

"Pomegranate is the lushest, sweetest fruit in God's creation. Red and round, hard on the outside, full of seeds sweet and tart within. I could live on pomegranates, and tried to, as a boy."

"Tell me of your life in Jerusalem," she said, watching through a haze of desire as he inched her bliaut from her, baring her body to his eyes. And his hands. "Let me know you."

"I want you to know me. To know all of me. To want all of me," he said, smiling softly down at her.

The fire was at her back, yet all the burning was in front. He burned her with a look, his hands and mouth the salve that saved and destroyed at once. He was her torment, as he had promised.

So quickly she had fallen. Where was her resolve? It

had disappeared under the power of his hands. She was ill-equipped for such a battle as this.

How was it that Hugh was not?

"Jerusalem," she said as his hands cupped her breasts, her nipples rising hard and fast in welcome. "Tell me of Jerusalem."

His hands stilled and he looked past her into the fire, his expression distant and full of dreams. "Jerusalem shines white in the westering sun, her pinnacles spires of holiness and history. The sun is ever bright and the sunsets—ah, Elsbeth, the sunsets last an eternity. Red and cerise and gold and violet bands across the heavens, a gift from God for every night. A miracle of color that ever changes yet is ever the same."

"The sun sets in England, too," she said, defending her home.

He had let her go, his hands resting still and quiet upon her shoulders, his mind in other, far-off places, his eyes on the hot glow of the fire. She had stumbled upon a weapon in this truce; Jerusalem was his weakness, his distraction from her seduction. Jerusalem, holy city, would serve her well, if she had the will to use it.

"You do not know sunsets," he said, grinning and hugging her to him, his eyes still on the fire. "Here, the sun simply disappears, lost in mist and cloud and gray blankets of rain or else swallowed by trees, hidden and cold. Nay, in the Levant, the sun casts its glory to the sky and earth, and all men stop and admire the handiwork of God. There is little power to the sun in England."

She held her tongue. She knew no other than England, that was true, but she loved it no less, though she had no comparisons to make. England was soft air and green hills and seas crashing against stone. England was as old as the Levant, for, though Christ had not walked here, had not God created all the earth on the same day? There was nothing in Holy Writ to point to England

and these northern lands as being an afterthought. Christ was Savior in England, too.

"You long for Jerusalem," she said instead. It was clearly true and would not insult. And his hands were still as his thoughts dwelt upon Jerusalem.

"I long for her as any man longs for home," he said. "Her streets are crooked and many, white and gold and tawny in the light, her banners many and many-colored. Her people rich in many tongues and diverse ways. As old as time is Jerusalem, sacred, holy, the city of Christ and of David and of Solomon, his son. The world began in Jerusalem. The world will end there in Armageddon. Jerusalem must not fail or fall."

"Why would Jerusalem fall?" she said.

He started and then smiled, running his hands over her again, teasing her breasts for a response. She had misspoken somehow. He had remembered her. His hands roamed.

"Jerusalem will not fall," he said. "Am I not a knight of the Levant? I will protect her to my death and die laughing, knowing my life to have been well spent. Nay, there is naught to speak of that. Let us speak of you, my wife. Tell me, in this moment of confessions, tell me of your life here, in this place."

"You must already know all. You were here to meet me. You must have spoken with my father ere I came," she said.

He slipped the bliaut from her, letting it fall to her waist, where it was held by her jeweled girdle, her arms trapped within the sleeves of her undergarment. She was bared to the waist, her breasts high and eager for his touch. She shamed herself by such a response. It was within her to resist. Or it should have been.

"Tell me of your life," he said, thumbing her nipples. She swayed into his arms with a moan. It was a cry for mercy, surely. It could not have been the sound of swelling desire. "You are not going to faint again?" he asked, wrapping his arms about her.

She might. It was a good excuse to keep his hands from her breasts, and she took it up readily.

"Aye, I feel most strange," she said. It was unfortunately true. "Talk to me awhile; your voice soothes, my lord. Tell me of the land of my Savior. Tell me of the paths where Jesus trod."

He tugged and pulled her free of her clothes, unfastening her girdle, letting all fall to the floor. Only the linen wrapping her hips and the padding to catch her flow were left in place. A girdle most strong to keep a man at bay—how she thanked God for it in this hour when Hugh stripped her bare and laid his hands upon her at his will. As was a husband's right. If only she could quell her body's response to him, to his touch and look, but she seemed doomed to fail in that arena. He called forth from her some passion that she had not seen in herself.

He tempted her most perfectly. Could such a thing as temptation be perfect? If it bore the name of Hugh of Jerusalem, then, aye, it could.

"Please," she said. "Please talk to me."

She stood before him, her body bared to him, his touch, his gaze, and he looked his fill. She should have sheltered herself from his eyes, but she did not. Nay, she found herself standing straight and tall, her breasts high and proud, her eyes meeting his. She wanted this, this look, this appraisal, and she wanted to be found desirable. It was the truth. She did not want it to be so, and yet it was.

What had he done to her in a scant day? Had all changed because she now belonged to him? Had it been so quickly done? Would God close all doors to escape?

Nay, for what of her vow to Ardeth? God would not

let her fail in that. That vow was sacred. Yet where was God in this smoke of desire?

"Aye, I will tell you of Jerusalem, but you must make a promise to me that I will hear in equal measure of your life in England. My grandsire came from here more than fifty years past, yet all I have are tales of the place. I would have you give flesh and bone to what has been spirit and mist till now."

Hugh ran his hands over her skin, over bosom and belly and hip, and then lifted her and laid her on the bed. The blanket was rough against her skin, and she writhed against the feel of it, finding an odd pleasure in the soft pain.

"Say yea to me, Elsbeth, or else you shall find no rest upon this bed," he said, lying down at her side, supporting his head with his hand.

"Yea," she said, looking up at him, his clothing still perfectly ordered, his hair falling in a golden tumble around his neck and arm. "Yea, I will tell you all you wish to know."

He grinned and ran a fingertip over her breast, across her nipple, and down to her linen wrapping. She gasped and closed her eyes.

"That is good, Elsbeth. I cannot wait."

Could she? She needed to pray for more strength, more forbearance, more resistance. Could she remember how to pray?

"Is it beautiful?" she asked. "Jerusalem?"

He smiled and kissed her on the mouth. "It and you are both beautiful," he said. "Jerusalem is wondrous fair—a citadel of white stone upon a hill, and the Temple with its golden crown, apart and separate from the throng of city life." He lay upon his back, Elsbeth forgotten for the moment. "Whate'er you wish to buy, it can be found in Jerusalem. Spices? There are three hundred if there are three. Silks of vibrant azure, brocades with silver thread, baldachino from Baghdad, damask from Damascus, samite from Byzantium, taffeta from Persia, satin from Zayton—all soft and supple and rich with color, reds, purples, greens and glowing white. Jewels and jade, coral and pearls for sale in any quarter." He lifted himself up to a sitting position and looked down at her, his emerald eyes alight. "And the people . . . from Zipangu, Java, Cathay, Tartary, Ceylon and Malabar. You have not seen the like in this distant place, this England, Elsbeth. The Levant is the crossroads of the world!"

"You love it very much, do you not?" she asked, looking up at him, seeing something she needed very much to see, though she could not put form to it.

He grinned and lay back down upon the bed, his hands behind his head. "All men of Christendom love Jerusalem. We fought to reclaim her. We will die to hold her. She is our city, our holy city. Would any man say otherwise?"

"Nay, I do believe none would," she said, studying his profile. "And what of Baldwin?"

He blinked and paused and then turned his head to look at her, the holy light in his eyes dimmed and dulled. Only passion dwelt within him now. Only passion. And Baldwin's name hovered in the air between them.

"Baldwin is my king, my liege lord, and my friend."

"You have known him long, long before he took his kingship," she said, holding very still, reading all there was to see in her husband's face, though studying him was like trying to search the face of the blinding sun.

"Aye, I have known him long," he said, turning again to face her, his hand reaching for her. "I mourned with him when we lost Edessa to the Saracen. I was with him when we attacked Bosra. I rode side by side with him at

149

the siege of Ascalon. He is my king. My place is at his side."

"And yet you are in England," she said.

"And yet I am with you, my wife," he said, his smile as brilliant and as hot as a thousand fires. "My first wife," he said, grinning and pulling her to him for a kiss that should have melted all thought and all fear in her.

Yet it did not.

The name of Baldwin hovered in the air like a chill fog, cooling her, calming the bright light of Hugh so that she could see. See the face of the sun. See the center of her husband's passion.

Hugh was interrupted in his seduction by more than her sudden and profound chill. It was the hour of Sext and time for prayer. The priest rang his bell within the chapel, calling all to his presence and the presence of the Lord.

Hugh grumbled with a smile and kissed her mouth again, his hand trailing down the outline of her shoulder, breast, and ribs. Her nipple rose at his touch, but halfheartedly. He did not seem to note it.

"Sext and then dinner," he said. "All designed, I am suddenly certain, to keep me from you. Well, I will go to all with cheer for it cannot be helped, but I would rather stay sequestered with you, little wife. Even more than food, I would have you. Only prayer takes precedence, as is proper, but even that I would rush through, to have you again in my arms."

She watched him, her eyes solemn and studious. He spoke very prettily. Why and for what cause? What need had any knight to speak so prettily and so well?

He sat and pulled her up with him, running his hand lightly over her hair, brushing it back from her face.

"Up. We must away and you must dress. I fear you cannot attend Sext as you are. 'Tis my fault, yet I cannot repent. I drink the draught of you with every meeting

150

and yet I am not satisfied. You are heady brew, Elsbeth. Better than the finest wine. I fear I am drunk on you."

"You speak clearly enough for a drunken man," she said, pulling up her chemise and straightening her bliaut. "I must ask for privacy again, my lord, before I go down to the chapel. You need not wait."

"You speak wrongly." He smiled, helping her arrange her clothing, fussing with her golden girdle. "I do need to wait. I need to walk at your side. I will not go without you."

"Wait, if that is your will," she said, brushing his hands aside carelessly. "If your wait could begin now?"

Hugh laughed and bowed to her, a gesture somewhat overwrought, it seemed to her, and left the chamber to her. She stared at the swinging curtain that hung before the door, pondering her husband, his ways and his words. Well, she could not make sense of it all in a moment. She would think on it and pray most heartily for wisdom; then she would act, finding her way out of this marriage. Perhaps now she had the means to find her own release from the vow that bound them. Perhaps. It was worth contemplating.

With that thought uppermost, Elsbeth lifted her skirts and saw to her needs. Her blood still flowed strong and bright. God was most merciful, indeed.

Something had changed in her; he knew not what. He had stripped her quickly of her clothes and she had not hampered him. Nay, she had all but melted in his arms, her black eyes smoky with passion, her limbs soft and unresisting.

Hugh paced the upper hall, waiting beyond the oaken door for his wife, turning it all over in his mind. She had asked about Jerusalem and he had told her of it. Nay, more than that, he had sung a song of praise and devotion. That had not been wise. She might have felt her England slighted by the comparison, and had she not said some words in its defense? Aye, she had.

It was no way to win a woman by slighting her homeland. He knew that well enough, well enough not to stumble in that way. Better to ask her of England and Sunnandune; that path into her heart was surely wider than the road to Jerusalem.

Hugh lifted his head and ran a hand through his hair. Well, that problem was solved. He had sought and discovered his misstep with Elsbeth, and he would now put all to rights. He could do little more to secure her body and her longings; it was time to ease his way into her thoughts by spending hours in converse with her. Women liked that sort of thing, having their thoughts and dreams treasured by a man. He had some experience with such things; he would not misstep. Let her talk. He would listen.

She came out of the door then, and he greeted her with a smile of welcome. She did not smile in return. He was not dismayed; Elsbeth was not the sort of woman to smile often, yet when she did, the very sky seemed to lighten as by the rising of the sun. She made him want to work to win a smile from her, he who had been smiled upon by women since he first came of age. Yet it was different with Elsbeth. Her smiles meant something, as if a victory had been won and her smile the prize.

"You look lovely," he said, taking her arm.

"I look as I did moments ago. Nothing has changed," she said, letting her hand rest on his arm.

"Did I say anything had changed? Nay, you looked as lovely in our chamber, covered only by the dark fall of your hair. It is your fate, I do perceive, to be complimented upon the hour," he teased.

"Or even upon the half hour," she said and then ducked her head to hide her smile.

"Oh, do not hide your smiles from me. I work too

hard for them," he said in mock seriousness.

"Is it work you do with me, my lord?"

"Call it rather a labor done in love," he said as they reached the bottom of the stair. All was quiet in the hall; the torchlight flickered on emptiness.

"I use your word for it," she said as they crossed the hall. "You do not find the companionship of your wife either soothing or restful?"

"You are right," he said, releasing her arm, running his hand down her back and over the mound of her derriere. "I have no rest in your company until I have the rest of possession. You are mine, yet not mine. I want you. I will not rest until I have you."

She stumbled and caught herself, and he could not stop the smile that crossed his lips at her discomfiture. He had the power to move her and he enjoyed it greatly. Given what her father had said of her, he had been in doubt. Now all doubt was gone. Elsbeth was a woman of strong passion, both spiritual and physical. Both were well approved by him.

And he spoke true. He did want her. He wanted her more with every hour he knew her. She was a mystery, a puzzle in a way that no woman had been before. A life of prayer was what she sought, yet with a touch, a look, a kiss, she tumbled into passion that burned them both. Such a woman should not bury herself in the cloister. How that she could not see that?

After her courses passed, he would prove it to her. Most happily, he would prove it to her.

These thoughts were not helping. Hugh adjusted his braes with a nudge of his hand and a shifting of his weight. His plan was to talk to her, get her to speak and share the longings of her heart; that was the path open to him. That was the path he would take.

Until her flux passed.

How many days did a woman's flow occupy? It seemed

a week had passed and yet it had been just a day.

He looked askance at her as they left the hall and walked down the stair to the bailey. Would she tell him when her blood left her?

Nay, she most like would not.

She did not yearn for consummation, though her body softened at his touch. Nay, all she yearned for was the abbey. He would do well to watch her closely, his eye ever on the bucket in their chamber. When the blood ran thin, he would mark the day and take her the next.

But how long was he to wait?

She could hardly wait. As soon as the office was sung, she would talk to the priest. He would advise her; it was his duty and his calling, after all. If only she could remember . . . what was his name? She had not been to Warkham for ten years, and his name was lost to her.

He was older now and had the neglected look of a recluse; it was not how she remembered him. She only hoped he knew what he was about. She had need for good counsel, and there was no one in Warkham whom she trusted with the suspicions that had arisen within her when she had heard Hugh speak of Jerusalem and King Baldwin.

The hour of Sext ended, the incense rising to the vaulted beams above them, disappearing, merging with the mists of autumn. All rose and moved, eager to be back within the lofty hall, where the meal awaited them. All except Elsbeth.

Hugh remained kneeling at her side and whispered, "Will you pray on, Elsbeth? I will stay at your side, our prayers rising in one voice, if that is your will. But perhaps we could fill our stomachs and then return to pray?"

"You need not wait for me if your appetites call you

elsewhere," she said, keeping her head bowed reverently.

"What? And have it said that my wife outprayed me? Nay, if you stay on your knees, your heart bound toward God, then I am at your side. I will not be outdone in so solemn a thing as prayer."

He was jesting. She could hear the laughter in his voice. His leaving would be nothing but pure blessing.

"I do not compete with you," she said, lifting her head just a bit, looking at him from downcast eyes.

"Nay, 'tis I who compete with you, little wife. I will not be found less holy than a maid from England; I, who walked in the path of Christ from the moment I could walk."

"I am sure there are many in my father's hall who would dearly cherish hearing of your holy walks in shining Jerusalem," she said, looking at him directly.

That had been a mistake. He looked distinctly challenged. Elsbeth sighed. Now he would never leave. No man left a challenge unanswered; it was the mark of their sex.

"I have wounded you," he said, taking her prayerful hands in his, turning what had been a holy exercise into an embrace most profane. "It is true, I love the land of my birth, but I have a great heart; I will love England with as fierce a love. If Elsbeth will instruct me in her finer points."

"If you will only go in to dinner, I will tell you all you wish to know of England. Later."

"Then you stay now to pray? I will stay with you."

He really was a most obstinate man. He was quite the match of her father.

"I do not stay to pray," she said, rising to her feet. He helped her up. She did not need his help. "I would speak with the good father on a matter—a private matter."

Hugh looked down at her and raised his eyebrows. "Oh?"

" 'Tis not unusual," she said defensively.

"Nay? For a bride who has not been breached, it might be found unpleasantly predictable," Hugh said.

He looked stern. It was a new look upon his face that she had yet to learn. Still, there was no mistaking it; he was not pleased.

"There is no cause for you to be concerned," she said, lifting her arm from his hand.

He let her go, but he took a step nearer. She swallowed hard and looked up at the great mass of him. He was a goodly sized man, almost a giant by some measures.

"Ah, my little wife proclaims that I need not be concerned. Her blood flows, she is not breached, her heart is not in this marriage but in the convent, where she longs to fly," he said softly. It was the soft touch of whispered menace. "Nay, Elsbeth. I think you have it wrong. There is much to concern me."

The vault above them was dark with age and shadowy with smoke and mist. The softness of his voice echoed within the stone chamber, rising up to the dark to fall back down on her, a wave of sound that crashed against her with muted intent. Yet there was no mistaking his meaning. He thought she meant to have the marriage annulled, or feared she would. If he would only repudiate her, then she could let her suspicions sink back into shadow, leaving him as she had found him. Why would he not release her? Did he not always find her at her prayers? Aye, when she was not stripped and leaning into his hands and mouth, curse her weakness.

It was no easy thing to slip out of a marriage. Unfortunately.

But now did not seem the time to discuss any of that. They were alone, the priest long fled, and Hugh was looking most unhappily determined to keep her.

"I think you have misread my intent, my lord," she said. "Besides, the priest is at his meal by now, as is all of Warkham. Shall we not join them? I have missed my time."

"I hope I have misread you, Elsbeth," he said, his look still stern, his hands at his sides. "And it is I who have missed my time. I wed a woman, intent on making her a wife; time was against me. Yet I am a patient man and determined. I will have you, Elsbeth. Let there be no doubt in your mind as to that. I will have you."

Yet she had many upon many doubts as to the nature of her husband. She only needed the priest to make things clear. But she held her tongue and said nothing to Hugh.

She was learning quite well the manner of a wife.

Chapter Ten

After the meal, when she would have made straight for the priest of Warkham, an event of profound importance happened. At least, Hugh thought it so.

"Look, Elsbeth, the sun shines!"

Multiple shafts of warm yellow light spread through the air and onto the wooden floor of the hall, lighting the dark interior to a cheerful glow.

"Aye, my lord, as it does every day," she said.

"Every day you say?" he said, grinning and grabbing hold of her hand. "Nay, the sun may rise but it does not shine, not in this land of mist and cloud. Come, we must away and enjoy the white shine of it while it lasts."

So saying, he clutched her hand and all but dragged her from the hall. She could feel her father's sardonic amusement pressing against her back. That was enough to propel her out, no matter the pull of the sun.

Yet when she was out and down the stair that led from hall to bailey, she could not fault her husband for his joy. It was a glorious day. The air was clean and sharp, the sky a bowl of lapis adorned by the golden specter of the sun. Clouds floated high and far above, white lambs in a scattered flock that raced happily across the sky. Aye, it was a day for gamboling and grinning, a day for walking out and skirting mud puddles, a day for—

Hugh pulled her straight into a wide puddle, sending mud up in all directions. Her bliaut was instantly sodden and stained. She jerked her hand from his and lifted her skirts away from her legs.

"My lord, have a care," she said tightly.

"My lady," he said, grinning like a boy, "I care only for the sun this day, and to take you out in it, sharing my joy with you."

" 'Tis no joy for me to be soaked and sodden."

" 'Tis naught that water and soap cannot cure," he said, reaching out for her again, taking her hand. "Come, Elsbeth, let your smile shine as free as the friendly sun. This is a day for play. Come play with me."

Of course, he would make her feel churlish for not wanting to cavort in the mud. Of course, he would speak softly in entreaty when other men would harangue a shrewish and ill-tempered wife. Of course, she would bow to his wish, because he was Hugh and because he smiled with all the shining splendor of the sun.

"As you wish, my lord," she said reluctantly. "I will cavort with you, but may I point out that my shoes will not withstand another puddle?"

"Yea, you may point that out to me, little wife. I will take care to keep you from puddles. I am a knight of some renown; I will destroy the next hostile puddle I see."

"Very well, my lord," she said, fighting a traitorous grin. "I now feel safe with you for, you see, I did not know that you were at your best when fighting puddles. What is your name, then? Lord Hugh of the Muddy Water?"

"You can mock me now, wife, but when the next mud flies, we shall see who you turn to in your distress," he said, laughing back at her.

They were through the bailey and into the outer ward. A nod to the porter and they were out of Warkham and making their way across a well-trod path that led to the not-so-distant sea. The air smelled of salt, and gulls, white as cloud, flew above them, crying into the sky their own peculiar joy at so fine a day.

They walked together, her hand in his, and said nothing for a time. A peaceful time it was, his stride shortened to hers, though she could feel the urge in him to run for the pure pleasure of it. The wind blew stronger as they neared the sea, and with it came the smell of fish.

"It reminds me of Jerusalem, though the air here is brisk and the sun a weaker shadow of itself," he said, his face to the sky. "I could live all my life within the sound of the sea and count myself blessed."

"Is Jerusalem near the sea?"

"Nay, not so near as this. It cannot be walked, but the bounty of the sea comes to us yet, from the Sea of Galilee most near."

She watched him, watched the memories sliding over his face, moving behind his eyes.

"You miss it very much," she said.

"Jerusalem is home," he said, looking forward and then smiling down at her. "Yet with Elsbeth is where I want to be."

So he said upon the hour, yet . . . there was something in him when he spoke of Jerusalem and its king, Baldwin, something that no amount of talking of Elsbeth and England could mimic. He was a knight of the Levant, so he said with regularity, yet why was he in England? Sunnandune was in England, and Sunnandune was the only land they owned; he had come to her rich in money, but poor in land. Where would they live but in England? Would he spend his life loving Jerusalem from afar?

What did it matter where he spent his life as long as hers was left intact?

Yet it did bear thinking on. If he would not repudiate her, would he at least leave her safe in Sunnandune while he fought for Jerusalem's king? That would answer. He could live out his life in Outremer while she abided softly in Sunnandune, her husband only a name upon her lips, her body untouched. Her life untouched.

'Twas a possibility, if he would agree to it. Yet now was not the time to ask it. He was well set on having her, a man with his blood up and chasing after a maid. Time would cool that. Perhaps even before her flux was ended his blood would chill and he would look elsewhere, to other maids and other victories, leaving Elsbeth to herself.

Aye, it did bear thinking on.

"I think that where you want to be is running through the grass, the wind singing past your ears," she said instead, turning the conversation onto a smoother course. "Go your way, my lord. I will not hinder you."

He looked at her, a question in his brilliant eyes, half undecided and in doubt.

"Go, my lord. Away with you. I fear no puddle," she said on a rising laugh, anticipating his disappearance from her life.

"Well, if you think you can manage it . . ."

"Go!" she said, pushing him along.

With the word and a parting grin, he was away, running for the joy of it. His legs carried him far, for they were very long legs and his wind was good. He disappeared around a spur of wood, and then she was alone with the gulls and the wind. It was good.

When was the last time she had been alone, out from behind the curtain wall of hall and tower? When had she last breathed air that did not smell of woodsmoke or incense but only of the sea and sun? When last had her thoughts been free of all save the beauty of a perfect day?

So far back in time that she could not remember it. And suddenly, that seemed too long a time. Her mother had kept her close and then had kept her away at her fostering. Of freedoms, she had known few. Only the freedom and sanctuary of prayer had been her solace, with Ardeth's warm encouragement. A fitting occupation for a daughter. A better occupation for a nun.

At that thought, Hugh came running back from beyond the wood, his cheeks ruddy and his hair wild and tossed by the wind from the sea. And with the sight of him, all thoughts went flying to mingle with the gulls. He was a beautiful man. He was a plainly beautiful man, and he was hers. With a jolt of realization, she knew that she wanted him.

So temptation ran into her heart, straight and hard and with the smell of the sea to mark it.

It could not be so. She had sworn in her youth never to submit to a man's touch, no matter what desires enflamed her blood. She had promised her mother that she would not fall into temptation with any man. But she had not conceived of such a man as Hugh of Jerusalem.

It was more urgent than ever that he leave her.

"No puddle has attacked you, I see," he said, laughing lightly, his breath coming out in well-spaced gasps. "I came hurrying back, certain you were in peril most grave."

She shook her desire from her, breathing deeply the clean air of the sea, forcing out the shallow breath of passion. She would not fall to this. She would not give herself over to this.

"I think, my lord, that you came back because you had run the length of your course."

"You think me doddering, to tire from such a jaunt as that?" he asked, still laughing.

Why was he always laughing? She had never known such laughter in her life. It seemed almost unnatural.

"I did not say doddering, my lord. You inflict yourself with such a word."

"Oh, Elsbeth, you know your words are daggers, though the knifing is so sweetly done that I cannot say I am ever offended."

"Nor ever do you bleed," she said, completely against her will.

She baited him, teasing him with words that maids used to catch the attention of a comely knight or squire. She was no such maid, nor ever had been. What was it about this man that made her want to throw herself into the wind, trusting that she would not fall to the rocky shore below?

He grabbed her round the waist and twirled her in the air, her skirts flying free behind her. She buried her face in his neck and held on, laughing softly, surreptitiously, hiding her mirth mostly from herself.

"Have a care, Elsbeth, or else I shall throw you into yon puddle and watch the mud wick its way up your skirts. Then where will you be, maiden of mud, defeated by water and earth?"

"Where will my knight and husband be, he of Muddy Water renown? Will his name not fail if it be known that I was defiled by mud and he so near to save me?"

"It is not mud which will mark you, little wife," he said, slowing his twirling and letting her feet touch to ground.

He bent his back low to set her gently down.

"Water, then?" she asked, looking up at him. His eyes were the deep green of a shadowy wood.

"Nay, not water, though you live in a land where water is in the very air you breathe. Nay, it is blood which will mark you, Elsbeth, as you know it must be."

Her mood settled at that, as did his. 'Twas for the best. Such laughing gaiety was unnecessary and only put her in harm's way.

"My blood marks me now, my lord."

"Aye, it does. A fine wall it is between us. Yet it will not last, though I begin to think you pray that it would." She started slightly, he was so close upon the mark, but she held her tongue. He continued, "Yet it is not your woman's blood but your maiden's blood which I want and which I will have."

She lowered her gaze and turned from him. He held her by one arm and turned her around to face him.

"There is no running from that, Elsbeth, no matter what you pray or how ceaselessly you pray it. I must have you. I will have you. Find your peace with it, I beseech you. I would not hurt you for the world."

"Then do not hurt me," she said, looking at the grass and stones beneath her feet.

"I cannot promise what I cannot control," he said. "That is the first of many lessons for a knight, and I learned it well. I can only promise that I will deal gently and that, if I could, I would take all pain upon myself. I must do no less as your husband, and I would do all that and more. Only trust me, Elsbeth. Trust me."

She wanted to. The temptation was strong. She wanted to lay down the burden she carried, letting him carry all. Trusting him as every wife must needs trust her lord and husband. But she could not. No matter what he said or how sweetly he said it, in the end, he was only a man.

He was the man of her temptation and he must leave

her. He must return to Jerusalem. With a distance of a thousand miles between them, she would be safe. Only memory would haunt her, and she knew how to manage memory.

"Do not ask what I cannot give," she said. "Let that be the vow which marks our union. You would not hurt me. I believe you. I would give you all that is in my power to give. Believe me, my lord. I withhold nothing from you out of a spiteful heart," she said, looking up into his eyes, letting him imagine that he could see into her, into her very heart.

He smiled slowly and then bent to kiss her on the mouth. It was a soft kiss of reconciliation and peace and even of trust.

Raising his lips from hers, he said, "I do trust you, Elsbeth, and I will endeavor not to ask of you what it is not in you to give. Are you content?"

Smiling up at him, she said, "I am content."

From the woods bordering the track, a pair of eyes watched them, taking their measure. Hidden and watchful, the man followed them as they made their way back to Warkham.

Hugh would, of course, see to it that she would want to give him all he asked. That was the very nature of every discourse between a man and a woman, even if that woman be a wife. To tempt her into wanting, that was his task, for, however lovely she was, she held herself aloof and wanted it to remain so. It could not. God and all His saints knew it could not. Mayhap even Elsbeth knew it could not, yet still she struggled to keep all as it was, to keep herself apart from him, her body and her life her own.

How that she thought she could have a marriage unlike every marriage under heaven?

But she did not want a marriage, did she? She wanted

to be the bride of Christ. To be Hugh's bride held no appeal. Or so she wanted him to think.

What a rare battle this was; never had he thought that the wife he finally took unto himself would treat him with anything but love and gratitude. Elsbeth was not grateful; she was desperate, as her father had predicted. Gautier had been blunt in his appraisal of his daughter, and he had struck the mark soundly. Elsbeth yearned for the cloister, not the conjugal bed.

Well, he was the man to turn her toward her rightful place. She could pray away her years when her hair turned silver. Now, she was for bed. His bed.

He had no doubt that he could get her there, eager to give him all he asked of her. He looked down at her now, at her dark and petite beauty, at the uncertainty and fear that hovered like gray mist in the blackest night, shrouding her heart and all her thoughts. Why such fear? Why this yearning hunger for the cloister? She was devout, aye, but so was he, and he was content to live in the world of men. He had no yearning to hide.

Little Elsbeth, so serious and severe, so vulnerable and afraid. In all his words designed to win and woo, he had spoken true. He would take care of her, love her, for she was his wife and he saw the value of her. But they would consummate the marriage, despite her blood if he must. He would not relinquish her, no matter her fears. No matter what she said to the priest of Warkham.

Turning to her, wrapping an arm about her waist, he began walking back toward Warkham Tower.

"Do you still wish to see the priest?" he asked.

He felt more than heard the hesitation in her answer. "Aye, I do."

"What will you say to him, or is it a question you wish to ask? I may be able to answer you myself. Will you not trust me with your confidence?" he asked, smiling down at her.

She kept her eyes on the horizon, green and golden in the sunlight, the grass heavy with seed and swaying in the coastal breeze.

"Do not make this a matter of trust," she instructed, her spine rigid as she walked at his side. "There are certain things which must find the ears of a priest. This is one of them."

"Oh, so you have sinned since Sext?"

She stopped and glared up at him. "I have not. Not all matters having to do with priests are of sin."

"Praise be to God," he said in mock seriousness.

"Praise Him indeed," she said, nodding.

"So, it is a matter of repentance, then? You wish some penance to observe?"

"I have done nothing requiring penance, at least today," she said.

"Ah, I do not doubt it, little wife. You are most unrepentant today."

"I think you find yourself very amusing today, my lord, but I do not jest about matters divine. Repentance is no man's game. Not even if he be from Jerusalem itself."

"Elsbeth!" he said, clutching his heart and falling back a pace. "A strike! A strike upon my soul, my honor, and my very home, the home of our blessed Savior. You are a brave maid to strike so. And most in need of penance."

She pressed down a smile and tried to ignore him, her mud-stained skirts swinging heavily against her legs as she walked away from him. "I will leave that to the priest," she said. "It is his province."

"Aye, leave it to him; he will decide if repentance is called for this day."

"And by whom," she said.

"And still she bites," he said, patting her on the derriere. "When shall it be my turn to bite into glorious Elsbeth?"

She swung away from his touch to face him. "My lord! This is not seemly."

"Perhaps not," he said easily, "but I want my wife, now, under the sun, and later, under the stones of her father's tower. When shall my needs be fulfilled?"

She stood still, her breathing shallow and uneven. "I cannot answer as to that."

"Then what will you answer to, Elsbeth? Will you say you want me? Will you say that your body will lie unresisting beneath mine as I learn the depths of you? Will you give yourself to me?"

She stared up at him, her eyes wide and her lips parted. "Do not ask that of me."

"Why not?" he said softly, taking her hands in his.

"I do not know the answer," she whispered, looking past his shoulder to the sky above them. "I do not want to know."

She did not know the answer, but he did. She would in time. She would give herself to him, not because he demanded it, but because he would bring her to the place where she would want no other path before her. She would want him. She would want him as much as he wanted her.

She was halfway there now, and perhaps that was the root of all her fears. She did not want to be a wife, and he was making her a wife. All her dreams for herself were fading in the sun, and all she did to hold the shadows to her failed. She was a wife, his wife, and he would not relinquish her. If only she could accept that, all would be well.

"Be at rest, Elsbeth," he said, pressing his hand to her back. "Find your ease in me. I will not betray."

They walked along, the breeze freshening the air, blowing through the trees on their right hand. To the left lay the long slope of the sea, hidden now by earth and bush and clumping grass turning golden and heavy with seed in the autumn air. 'Twas the twilight of the harvest season and they were nigh onto November, the blood month when all the livestock that could not be overwintered would be killed and preserved through the lean months.

She hated November.

"What are winters like in Jerusalem?" she asked, ignoring the touch of his hand on the small of her back. Or pretending to.

Hugh smiled. "You ask much of Jerusalem," he said. "Are you truly so interested?"

"It is your home, is it not?" she answered. "It is the home of our Savior; for that reason alone I would ask."

"Hmm," he said. "A worthy answer. Tell me, Elsbeth, are you not attempting to flatter me?"

"Humph," she said, lifting her skirts and skirting a puddle. "I am not."

"You do not need to say it with such pride."

"Pride? First I flatter and now I am prideful? Nay, my lord, Jerusalem is the prize we fought for and won, to reclaim the land of Christ. I would hear of it from you, who have seen it from your first toddling steps. I do not flatter. You did not choose the place of your birth."

Hugh laughed and slapped her lightly on the derriere. She tried to ignore that, too. "Well said. Well met, Elsbeth. I stand abashed for so provoking you," he said. "I will not further insult you by remarking that your eyes glow like the eyes of a wolf when you are provoked. So," he said, "you would hear of Jerusalem. Well, I could speak of Jerusalem and her king all the hours of daylight."

"You are close to Baldwin?" she asked, keeping her eyes on the ground before her.

"Closer than a brother," he said softly.

"He is a handsome man, they say."

"Aye, he is that, but there is more to him than beauty.

168

He is a man of great heart. Let him meet you but once, and your name is not forgotten by him, even to the lowliest servant. He reads constantly, his head full of the knowledge of things past and present, and yet he is the finest horseman I have ever seen." Hugh paused and looked into the middle distance. Warkham was a gray shape on a hill, but he was not seeing Warkham. "He is the first king of Jerusalem to have been born there, and there is a rightness to that. He knows her and loves her, yet he is not blind to her faults."

"What faults can there be in the holy city?" she asked.

Hugh blinked, pulling himself back to England, and looked down at her. He smiled, but it was a sad smile. "Even if something be loved, it does not mean it is without flaw. Even the kingdom of Jerusalem has its flaws."

"And Baldwin? Does he too have flaws?"

Hugh smiled widely, all sadness gone from him. "If you can find any in him, you would be the first. He is loved by all. It is said of him that he came to the throne at exactly the right time and with exactly the right qualities. Do you know that when he took Val Moysis, built by his father and lost to the Turks, he won it back without the loss of a single man? Aye, he is well loved, and rightly so."

"You love him," she said, all her questions bound up in that statement, for it was no question. He had made it plain; still, she would be sure.

Hugh looked down at her, his green eyes mirroring the green all about him, his hair as golden as the waving grass, his form as mighty as the oak. She knew what he would say before he said it.

"Aye. I love him."

Chapter Eleven

They were just entering the gate of Warkham when a small girl ran out. She was dusty, her gown torn at the hem, and her light hair was a tangle. She was looking behind her as she ran and so hurtled straight into Hugh's legs. She would have fallen if his quick hands had not caught her.

"Hold, girl," he said as she fought his restraining hands. "I intend no harm."

Sniffing, she looked up at him, her head going back and back again to take in all of him. He was a tree of a man. Her small bliaut had the look of quality and the color, an intense blue, but she was shoeless and dirty. Elsbeth had never seen her before, yet she had an idea who she was.

"You are Denise?" she asked.

Denise hesitated and then nodded slowly.

"You are where you are supposed to be?" Elsbeth asked in a slightly reproving tone.

Denise suddenly looked like a bayed fox, all staring eyes.

"Come, which of us knows exactly where we are supposed to be, unless it be in the center of God's will," Hugh said, laying a large hand on the girl's slender shoulder. "Are you out of God's will, little one?"

Denise shook her head and then shrugged.

"Ah, a scholar," Hugh said seriously, his eyes alight. "Which of us can say the exact moment when we step out of the divine path? You are wise for one so small."

Denise giggled.

"You are also very quiet. A man likes that in a woman," he said, looking over her head at Elsbeth.

Elsbeth looked back, her brows raised.

"Come, Denise," Elsbeth said. "Where is it you should be?"

"In the solar," she said.

"Then you must return to the solar," Elsbeth said, taking her by the hand. "What occupies you there?"

"Nothing," Denise said.

"Come, that cannot be," Elsbeth said. "What is Emma teaching you? Embroidery? Weaving? Sewing?"

"Emma does not come often to the solar. I am supposed to sit there all day. She comes when she can," Denise said.

Elsbeth stopped walking and shared a look of concern with Hugh over the child's head. To be left so alone? It was not done. Denise had been committed to Emma and Warkham for her fostering, to be trained in all the duties of a lady. To be shunted off into the solar, solitary and silent, was not fostering done well.

"Well, she is grown great with her burden," Elsbeth said, continuing to walk into Warkham. "Now that I am here, I shall teach you."

"But . . . but you are not here for long, are you?" Denise said. "You are to Sunnandune?"

'Twas a worthy question. When would they go to Sunnandune? She longed to return, to be out from under her father's watchful eyes, to go to the only home she had on this earth. She could as well convince Hugh to release her from this marriage there as anywhere. Sunnandune. She had been Denise's age when last she saw it, a well-placed manor with a single knight and a steward to hold all secure for her while she completed her fostering and came of age to hold it. Isabel and Dornei were behind her now, her fostering complete, and she came of age the day she married Hugh; Sunnandune was her future and her legacy.

"Aye, when are we to Sunnandune?" Elsbeth asked, turning to face Hugh.

"We are to Sunnandune," Hugh said, "but not today. Do not trouble as to that, Denise," he said, refusing to meet Elsbeth's eyes. "Now you have the Lady Elsbeth to yourself. Enjoy her, learn from her as you may. Do not worry about your tomorrows."

"God is in my tomorrow as surely as He is in my today," Denise said.

"Why, that is most correct, Denise," Elsbeth said, bending down to her, leaving the matter of Sunnandune to another, private time. The girl's eyes were an unusual shade of blue, almost green, and as light as her hair. "You are well spoken in matters spiritual."

Denise returned her look and then gazed up at Hugh, taking his hand in hers so that they formed a loosely connected threesome as they made their way deeper into Warkham.

"Except that God is not very much in my today," Denise said lightly.

Hugh and Elsbeth shared another look over the top of her small head. God's mercy, the child had been totally neglected! If Lord Gautier were not careful, he might find himself in legal trouble over the mismanagement of this child's fostering. Not to mention the sad state of Denise's soul, to be so unaware and unconcerned about God, His place in the heavens, and her small place on His earth.

"God is in all of our todays," Hugh said. "There is much rest to be found in that truth. Surely you want that rest, Denise? To know that God will not abandon you? That He is ever at your side? That a single sparrow does not—"

"Fall to earth," Denise interrupted, continuing the

verse, "but that God does not note it." She stopped walking and looked up at them. "Yet still, the sparrow did fall. And I would rather have a piece of venison than rest. I rest all the time."

Emma appeared at that moment, her face flushed as she hurried down the outer stair from the hall to the bailey.

"Denise! You are not in your place!" Emma said, rubbing her belly with a soothing hand. "My lord Gautier expressly told you to remain in the solar, and Lord Hugh does not wish to be bothered by such a one as you."

"Bothered?" Hugh said, keeping Denise's hand in his. "This beautiful, engaging girl could bother no man. Nay, I thought that she could attend me at my bath and learn her scents and soaps by doing so. It is time she learned how to attend a guest in her home, is it not?"

"Most assuredly," said Elsbeth, understanding Hugh's intent upon his first word. Her father had decreed that Denise was to remain behind the solar wall? Let Denise then come out and defy her father; she would only endorse the effort. "Let her come with us, Emma. She will be well tutored. You need not worry."

"Nay? Then I thank you. She is very much for me to manage just now," Emma said. "I will arrange for water to be brought to you."

But they had already passed her by, climbing the wooden stairs to the tower with Denise clutched between them.

"Am I truly to give you a bath?" Denise asked Hugh.

"Do you not wish to?" Hugh asked.

"Nay, it is only . . . you are very big. It will take a long time."

Hugh laughed. "Then I will make an offer. Shall I not bathe you? You are very small. It will only take a moment."

"My lord, it is not necessary," Elsbeth said. A knight

to bathe a child? 'Twas not done, no man would stoop
to it.

"Mayhap it is not," he said as they crossed the wide
hall to the stair that wound its stony way up to the next
floor. "Yet if Christ could wash the dirty feet of His disciples, then surely I can wash this small and pretty child.
Why, she will hardly dirty the water, she is so small."

"I am not *that* small," Denise said as they entered the
chamber.

The afternoon sun was low, slanting golden light
across the stone, turning all to amber and topaz. Low-
lying clouds hung like slivers on the horizon, just above
the waving trees. The sun would vanish into cloud ere
long. Hugh would have lost his moment in the sunshine.
Yet now he made the golden chamber glow by his very
presence.

"Oh, nay," he answered, "not *that* small. Why, in Outremer, we have flies that are larger."

"You do not," she said as Elsbeth stripped off her
bliaut.

"Your speech is not respectful," Elsbeth said softly.
The child needed another bliaut; the one she wore must
be washed.

"You do not . . . my lord," Denise said.

"Most polite," Hugh said, grinning. "I think that was
much improved, do you not agree, wife?"

"Oh, aye, we have a long road here," Elsbeth said,
shaking her head, but smiling nonetheless.

"All roads are long," Hugh said. "The trick is to make
them smooth."

"Are you going to make me smooth?" Denise asked.

"I am going to make you exceedingly smooth," he
said, "and white. What color is her hair, do you think?"
he asked Elsbeth.

"My hair is flaxen," Denise said. "My mother told me."

"Then you must be flaxen-haired," Elsbeth said. "A mother, by God's design, is always right."

"Your mother must have loved you well for you to say such," Hugh said. "Or is it that you only speak your wish? You are close upon becoming a mother yourself, are you not?"

"Am I?" Elsbeth said, holding his gaze. "I would not have said so. And my mother was a noble lady who loved me well, her counsel to me most sound, most true."

"I but tease you, little wife; be at ease. I do not mock," he said, looking at her . . . tenderly. Aye, it was tenderness. She did not know what to do with tenderness. Her mother had told her many things, but had never spoken of tenderness.

"He thinks you are little, too?" Denise said, looking at Elsbeth.

The child was stripped of her clothes as the tub came in; it took only three men to fill it, but the buckets were unusually large. In moments, the bath was prepared.

"Aye, he does," Elsbeth said. "I believe," she pretended to whisper, "that it is because he is so large. Even a destrier seems small to him."

"Ladies, I am no giant," Hugh said, his hands on his hips.

"Have you ever seen a giant?" Elsbeth asked him, winking at Denise.

"Well . . . nay," he said.

"Then how do you know you are not one?" Elsbeth said.

"Aye, how do you know?" Denise said.

"Well," Hugh huffed. "Mayhap, then, I am a giant, but I will be a good giant, and no soldier of God will have need to kill me with a stone."

"You can kill a giant with a stone?" Denise said, sitting upright in the water, her hands clasped around her knees. "A big stone? From a trebuchet?"

175

"Nay, a very small stone," Hugh said, scrubbing her back with a soap that smelled like lavender. "But in the hands of a godly man, even a small stone can do much."

"Of course, David also used a sword. It was with his sword that the giant was killed," Elsbeth said.

"Oh," said Denise, "well, if he had a sword—"

"Nay, nay, you must not discount David so quick. He got the giant to the ground, his wits befuddled, with a mere stone. Such is the greatness of God in a holy fight. It was with the giant's own sword that David cut off the giant's head. And then all the Philistines ran," Hugh said. "Which is only right."

"I would not like for your head to be cut off," Denise said as he scrubbed her left arm with a strip of linen.

"Most courteous of you, my lady. I should be very lonesome without my head," Hugh said.

"I think my lord Hugh can defend his head right well," Elsbeth said, digging around in her trunk for a smallish shift that the girl could wear until a bliaut could be found. But in her heart, even as she said the words, she wondered. How much did a man fight in the Levant? They were known for their holiness, aye, but also for their love of luxury and for their softness. Did he not now even wash a child? What sort of knight did that?

A most strange one, certainly.

"Thank you, lady," he said, bowing his head in her direction as she came back with the shift. "I am a knight from a faraway land. My prowess here is not known, I think."

He said that true enough. She had heard of Hugh's friendship with Baldwin and his beauty. Of his warcraft, little was spoken beyond the siege of Ascalon. Perhaps he was not much of a warrior; he did not have the scars to mark his trade, that was certain.

"You must be a very good knight," Denise said. "You have not a mark upon you."

Elsbeth flushed to have her thoughts echoed by the girl, yet her own conclusion could not have been more different.

"Ah, all my wounds are upon my heart, and in this very room is the little warrior who slices me," Hugh said, pointing at Elsbeth.

"Elsbeth?" Denise said, her eyes round.

"Nay, not Elsbeth," Elsbeth answered, frowning at Hugh. "My lord enjoys a jest, Denise. There is no more to his words than that."

"And there you see, Denise, another wound inflicted. My wife does not believe I have a heart to bruise, nor does she believe a word I say in praise of her. It must be a trait of English women, for I have ne're had this trouble before."

"I would believe you if you praised me," Denise said.

Hugh laughed and motioned for her to stand in the tub and be dried. "Would you now? And you claim to be English? Hmmm, I shall have to make a test of it, I think," he said, rubbing his chin in thought while Elsbeth dried Denise with a length of clean linen.

"You truly do have flaxen hair, Denise, and eyes the color of a Southern bay. You will break many hearts with those eyes, my girl," he said.

Denise poked her head through the opening of the shift. "I will?"

"Aye, you will. Do not say you doubt my word and break my heart. I have had enough wounds to my heart since landing on these shores."

"I believe you!" Denise said. "Do you believe him, Elsbeth? Will I break many hearts?"

Elsbeth looked down at her; her hair lay in a wet trail which Elsbeth dried with the linen strip. She was a most comely child, bright of eye and white of skin. Her hair was the pale yellow of flax, as her mother had said. And she believed every word from Hugh's mouth, or wanted to. They were not so different, the two of them, for did Elsbeth not want to believe Hugh as well?

"I think," Elsbeth said, looking at Hugh, "that you may believe what my lord tells you."

"I do," Denise said, as if invoking a vow.

I do; Elsbeth felt an echo in her own heart. *I do. I want to believe you. I have fallen that far.*

"Then the testing is done?" Hugh said, looking at Elsbeth.

"Aye," she said, holding his gaze.

The testing was done. She would believe him when he praised her, though she would never understand his need to pour sweet words over her like costly perfume. Perhaps it was the fashion in Outremer to speak in honeyed words, to woo and win when all was won, to praise and pet a wife who needed no petting. She knew who she was, and she knew her value. And she did not need wooing.

"Did I pass?" Denise asked.

"Aye, you did pass," Elsbeth said, smiling down at the girl. "Yet there is more to be done. You must have shoes and a new bliaut, and you must learn at least some of your soaps, or else Emma will find my lord a liar."

"I would not be found a liar, even if I am a giant," Hugh said. "Come, Denise, what was the scent you were bathed in?"

"That is easy. Lavender."

"Exactly," said Hugh.

"And this?" He held a bag to her nose and let her sniff.

"Rose," she said.

"Ah, but not just any rose. This is Damascus Rose, and you will not quickly find its match in all of England."

"May I have a bath in Damascus Rose?" Denise asked.

"Nay, for I brought it as a gift for Elsbeth. It is for her, when she next bathes."

"Oh, I cannot wait to smell you after your bath in Damascus Rose, Elsbeth," Denise said.

"Nor can I, Denise," Hugh said, laughing. "Nor can I."

"Well, all must wait," Elsbeth said, looking uncomfortably at the floor. "But we cannot wait for your shoes and bliaut. Let us go and find something for you. Did your family send a trunk with you to your fostering?"

"Aye, but I know not where it is," Denise said.

"Well, we shall find it," Elsbeth said, leading her from the room. When Hugh made to follow them, she said, "My lord? If you would not be found a liar, you must bathe, for did you not tell Emma you required assistance at your bath?"

"Aye, and if you do not assist me, will you not be found a liar?" he said.

"But, my lord, I do not care if I am found a liar," she said, grinning as she walked out with Denise's hand in hers.

"Proof indeed, since that is surely a lie," Hugh said. Hugh's laughter followed them down the winding stair, lightening their steps and giving smiles to their faces.

Raymond awaited in the stair hall outside their chamber. He stood as silent as a torch, and they passed him by with a nod and a smile. He nodded in return, but did not return their smiles.

When the ladies were well gone, Raymond entered the chamber as Hugh was slipping off his tunic.

"My lord, Lord Gautier would speak with you."

"I am about my bath," Hugh said, tossing his tunic onto the bed.

"My lord," Raymond said.

Hugh looked at his squire, his expression curious.

"He is most insistent," Raymond said.

"Lord Gautier is consistently insistent, is he not, Raymond?" Hugh asked with a sigh. "It seems my bath must then wait. It would not do for Baron Gautier to find his insistence ignored."

"Nay, my lord, it would not," Raymond said, helping Hugh back on with his tunic.

"Tell me, Raymond, how do you find Lord Gautier?"

"My lord?" Raymond said.

Hugh walked behind him and closed the heavy door. "How do you find this man who holds our plans and our purpose in his hands?"

"He is . . ." Raymond said, his brow furrowed in thought at the seriousness of the question. "He is a powerful man. He can give us what we came to England to find."

"Aye, he is a powerful man," Hugh agreed, fastening his belt. "And powerful men are wont to accrue power, not give it away."

"My lord? You do not think he will renege?"

"Renege? Nay, perhaps not that. But I do not think he is eager to meet his end of our bargain. I cannot think what man would be, yet the deal is struck. We must make certain that he fulfills his vows. I would not return to Baldwin defeated, empty of all we came to find."

"Nay, my lord," Raymond said. "It will not come to pass. Baldwin put his trust well in you. You will succeed. Gautier will meet his bargain."

"Aye, he will, though I begin to wonder if he knows it," Hugh said as he ran a loose hand through his hair.

"You do not trust him."

"Nay," Hugh said, laying a hand on his arm. "I do not, yet we are here and will not leave until we have in our hands that which we sought," he said, smiling at Raymond. "I would that this were all past and we were on our way back home."

Away from Elsbeth who was growing in his thoughts like a weed in constant rain. He was beginning to think of her too much, to seek her smile, to find joy in her very nearness; she was a temptation, and he had no room for temptation now. For all he had come to England to find, he had not thought to find such a woman as Elsbeth. There was no place for her in his plans, and so there should be no place for her in his thoughts.

"Aye, and I as well. Before the winter sets down its cold hand on this isle."

"You do not find the damp pleasing?" Hugh said with a laugh, once again forcing his thoughts away from his wife.

"My lord, the walls sprout mushrooms!"

"Aye, that they do. Let us finish here. With God's aid, we will be home for Epiphany."

"With God's aid," Raymond echoed, sending that prayer to heaven.

They ran down the stairs and across the hall. Elsbeth was in the hall, Denise at her side; they faced Emma, who sat with her feet upon a stool before the hearth. Emma was in for a reckoning from Elsbeth. Hugh did not envy Gautier's wife.

Quiet Elsbeth was, but she was an unrelenting and unyielding warrior. With a wave to Denise, who watched him as he passed out of the hall, Hugh left the cold comfort of stone behind and ran down the outer stair to the bailey below. Raymond whispered and pointed, and Hugh turned toward the practice yard, finding his wife's father testing his blade against the air.

At his approach, Gautier looked up.

"Does she still bleed?"

Hugh stood his ground, literally, and smiled into the older man's curious face. "You know she does. It has been too soon for aught else."

Gautier shrugged and studied his blade. "Difficult for a man to win a woman when he can't get at her."

"For some men, perhaps."

"But not for you?"

"But not for me," Hugh said.

"I would not have given her to you if I thought that you could not find your way with her."

A lie. Gautier would have given Elsbeth to any man who would suit his purposes best. Hugh was that man—the right man for the right time. Elsbeth was his now. There was no other truth for any of them. It was past time for Gautier to understand that his daughter was not his concern any longer. She belonged to Hugh, and Hugh would see to her.

"I will find my way. I find it even now," Hugh said.

"Do you?" Gautier said, lifting his head. "A different sort of man, then, they breed in Outremer."

"Aye," Hugh agreed. He could not have agreed more or been more joyous at the differences. "There are many ways to possess a woman's heart. Elsbeth is nearly mine."

"Well, when she is all yours, then you will have something to tell me," Gautier said.

Hugh swallowed his retort. He needed this man too much to strike an offense when discretion better served his purpose.

"Yea, I will. I will come to you and tell you when this thing is done. The matter of your daughter's blood need not concern you," Hugh said stiffly, holding on to his anger.

"Need not?" Gautier asked, smiling. "Perhaps you are right, yet Elsbeth has always been the daughter of my heart. We were close once, before her fostering, before Ardeth stepped between us, souring the sweetness we shared."

"You have told me this. I sorrow for you that your wife's temper became uneven. Yet that is past now. Elsbeth is mine. I will see to her," Hugh said. He had heard all about Ardeth and the destruction she had wrought in Gautier's house, but Ardeth was dead. Those days were done.

"Elsbeth is yours?" Gautier asked sharply, his smile wiped away by his sudden anger. "She is not yours. That is the problem. Make her yours, and then I will be content."

"Let lie, Lord Gautier, I will manage all. For now, shall we battle?" Hugh asked, looking for another, safer outlet for his rising temper.

"*Do* you battle?" Gautier asked. "I have seen little sign of it."

Hugh could feel Raymond shift behind him, his breath expelled in outrage. Hugh only smiled. "Only when I must. Still, I would not like to have my calluses go soft; it takes so much blood and toil to rebuild them, does it not?"

Gautier grunted and lifted his sword in answer. Hugh lifted his sword free of its jeweled scabbard and advanced upon his bride's father. With his sword in hand, even foggy England began to feel like home.

With a cold grin, he advanced, eager to show Gautier the skill he had brought north from Outremer.

Elsbeth and Denise had found Emma sitting by the fire in the lord's chair with her feet up. Her ankles were swollen to the size of loaves, and she looked miserable.

"You have bathed her," Emma said, her hands rubbing lazy circles on her abdomen. "She is quite pretty, is she not? Lord Gautier remarked on it when she first did come to Warkham."

"Yea, she is pretty, though she needs a clean bliaut," Elsbeth said, holding Denise's hand. The girl's hand was chill and tinged with blue. It was no pleasure to walk without shoes in such damp cold. "If you will tell me where you have put her trunk, I will attend to her. I can see that you are much occupied."

"Aye, this babe takes all of me. I do not know where to find my next breath," Emma said.

She truly did look most uncomfortable and as big as a carthorse.

"When is the babe due?" she asked.

"At Martinmas, I think," Emma said. "Though it could be sooner. I would not complain of it."

"You do not fear the birthing?" Elsbeth asked.

"Nay, I want him out of me too much for fear," Emma said, "though I would not have said the same even a sennight ago."

"You are very big," Denise said.

"I am," Emma said on a breathy laugh. "I wish to be smaller and quickly."

"If you would tell me where you have put Denise's things, I will attend to her," Elsbeth repeated. "Perhaps you would be more comfortable in your bed? I will bring you whate'er you need."

"Thank you, Elsbeth," Emma said. "But I cannot lie abed. My legs tingle and my back aches. Nay, I have slept sitting up for the past month. Yet I would be most thankful if you would see to Denise and keep her close by you. She has not had the best of me of late. Her things are in my chamber."

"I will see to it," Elsbeth said. "And I will bring you a cup of wine when I have seen to Denise. Perhaps that will ease your breathing."

"I will never turn my face from a cup of wine, Elsbeth," Emma said. "Thank you."

Denise was shivering by the time they turned to the stairway.

"I did not think it would take so long. I should have left you in my lord's bed," Elsbeth said in apology to the girl.

"I would rather stay with you," Denise said. "Emma looks very bad, does she not?"

"Bad?" Elsbeth said, looking down at the child's bright head. "She looks uncomfortable."

"I think she looks bad. Her breath is loud and harsh. Her feet are swollen. Her face is red."

"It will pass when the child comes out of her," Elsbeth said as they entered the lord of Warkham's chamber. "Now, which is your trunk?"

"The red one," she said, pointing.

Elsbeth got down on her knees in front of the small red trunk and opened it. It was not locked. It should have been. Inside were two bliauts, two pelisses, three shifts, four pairs of stockings, and a pair of well-worked boots. Below all was a beautiful comb of carved rowan wood.

"My comb!" Denise said, reaching for it.

"It is lovely," Elsbeth said.

"A gift from my father," she said, running it through her damp hair.

"A most fine gift," Elsbeth said. "Now, on with your boots and stockings. Which bliaut would you prefer? The green or the amber?

"Which do you think suits me best?"

"Suits you best? I would say the warmest, to judge by the color of your lips. Here, wear the green bliaut with the blue pelisse. A striking combination. It suits you well."

"Do you think Lord Hugh will like the green?" Denise asked.

"Lord Hugh?" Elsbeth said, burying her smile. "I do not see why he should not. When you next see him, you can ask him how he likes the look of you in the green. I am certain you will like his answer."

"You do not mock me?" Denise said as she pulled the bliaut over her head.

"Nay, I do not mock you," Elsbeth said, arranging the girl's hair down her back.

"You are not . . . jealous of his attention?" Denise

185

asked, passing Elsbeth the comb when she reached out her hand for it.

"Jealous?" Elsbeth said. "Nay, I am not."

"Why not?"

"Because . . . because . . . he is mine," she said, shocked by her answer. Unhappy with the deep weight of contentment that settled on her with the words.

"I think that you are very kind."

Elsbeth stopped combing and put the comb back into Denise's small, white hands. "I am not kind. It is no great mark of kindness to see a child properly dressed. It is no great deed to bring a cup of wine."

"Yet you did not have to," Denise said, stroking her comb. "My mother says that if you do not have to do something for someone and yet you do, then that is kind and generous. You are generous, too."

"You put too much on me," Elsbeth said with a laugh. "The clothes are yours, Denise; the wine is Emma's."

"But you did not have to."

"It was easily done."

"You did not *have* to," Denise insisted.

"Nay, I did not have to," she said, giving up the battle.

"I like you," Denise said, looking up at her. "I like you almost as much as I like Hugh."

"High praise," Elsbeth said, "and most welcome. Now, put on your boots."

Denise did, with effort. They were a bit small.

"You could try them without the stockings—that would help," Elsbeth said.

"But my legs would be cold."

"Aye, it is a choice, and I leave you to make it. The toes are yours."

"I will wear the stockings. Mayhap the leather will stretch," Denise said.

"Very wise," Elsbeth said. "Now, will you assist me in

186

bringing wine and perhaps a small cheese for Emma, or will you hunt for Lord Hugh to show him your green bliaut?"

Denise chewed her lip in thought and then said, "I want to find Lord Hugh, but the kind thing would be to take care of Lady Emma first."

Elsbeth said nothing as Denise looked up at her.

"You will not press me to be kind?" Denise asked.

"If I have to press you to it, how much of kindness is there in such an act?" Elsbeth answered.

"Humph," Denise said. "I will assist you with the wine, but I wish now I had never spoken of kindness. I think my mother knew this would happen."

Elsbeth smiled and laid a hand on the girl's back as they left the chamber. "I think she probably did."

Chapter Twelve

Gautier was sweating heavily, his arm shaking with exhaustion by the time Hugh was finished with him. 'Twas a lesson he had longed to lay upon Gautier's head since first meeting with him, yet he even now wondered at the wisdom of his action. He had listened with a strangled tongue to Gautier's soft insults cast upon the sons of the Levant, to the rumors of their debauchery, their soft lives, their love of luxury. Their baths. These men who had held off the Saracen for fifty years, to be held in scorn by this lordling of a dreary isle? 'Twas intolerable. Yet he had tolerated it.

But now he had Elsbeth. And having her, he could let loose his anger a bit. He would not openly offend, but he would no longer hold his tongue and his sword arm against insult. Gautier now knew the truth of that.

"You are skilled," Gautier said.

"No more than any who dwell in Outremer," Hugh said, laying down the gauntlet for all his kinsmen.

Gautier grunted his answer and wiped his face with his arm.

"Where did you foster?" Gautier asked.

"In the household of my king," Hugh answered.

"Baldwin," Gautier huffed. "Tales are told of him."

"They are more than tales. They are the sterling truth. He is a king unlike any other."

"Henry is a king to be feared," Gautier said, glaring.

"Henry is a king, and if men fear him, then that is good. But Baldwin is loved."

"Is it better for a king to be loved? What strength lies in that?"

"It is because he is strong and wise and fierce that he is loved," Hugh said. "A man may turn from fear, having grown weary of it, yet no man turns from the thing he loves, for in loving, he is strengthened and fed. Such is the strength of Baldwin and of those who serve him."

Gautier looked at Hugh appraisingly, and Hugh returned the look.

"So, you were fostered at his court and you learned to love him."

"Aye," Hugh answered, his chin raised. "I learned many things at his court. Especially how to fight."

"Aye, you did learn that, I can attest," Gautier said. "Whether you learned how to inspire love, that is still to be seen."

"I have given my vow to it."

"Aye, but a vow without the force to see it done is an empty promise. You must win her love and her trust. Her will must bow to yours."

"And so it shall," Hugh said, his face solemn. "This is old ground. We have run this course when you tutored me in all the ways to win her. I am her husband now. I am close upon the mark."

"Yet not on it," Gautier said. "You must consummate. There can be no grounds for annulment or repudiation."

"I will not repudiate her."

Gautier laughed. "You do not know her. She could well bring a case against you in ecclesiastical court. Bed her. Close that gate and then talk to me of winning her. We cannot have what we each want until you have her in your grasp."

"I cannot take her whilst she is in flux."

"Then pray that she waits for you to penetrate her. For myself, I think she thanks God hourly for this reprieve. And plots a way out of an unwelcome and unsought marriage," Gautier said, sheathing his sword.

"I am bending her will to mine even now."

"So you say," parried Gautier, "and mayhap you even believe it. Yet I know Elsbeth. You are not on solid ground."

Hugh said nothing. There was nothing more to be said, and he was weary of arguing the same point again and again with a man who had no wish to be convinced.

"Find your wife," Gautier said. "Do what you must to fulfill our bargain. I stand ready to meet my obligation to you."

"I am pleased to hear it," Hugh said with a tight smile.

Hugh watched him walk off, his squire at his back. Gautier stood ready? Hugh had grave doubts as to that, but for now, there was nothing to be done. Nothing except win the heart and will of Elsbeth. From that, all would follow.

Hugh could fight. Gautier had not expected it of a man so soft and smiling. 'Twas a wrinkle in a plan that he had mapped well.

Gautier sighed and ran his hand over his hound's head, thinking hard.

They had a bargain, the two of them, and he would meet his end, if it came to that. But were there not ways to get what he wanted without losing a thing? There had to be. There always was.

Hugh might need to die and his squire with him.

Aye, that would clear many obstacles. Yet he could not see it done in one-to-one combat; that had just been proved. It must be done by stealth.

"We must go now and speak with the priest," Elsbeth said to Denise.

"With Father Godfrey?" Denise said. "Why?"

Father *Godfrey*. So that was his name. Thank the saints that she had not been driven to ask; she would have been shamed past bearing.

"Because he is our priest and we should talk to him."

"About what? It is but hours till Vespers. Can we not see him then?"

"Yea, we will see him then, but we must speak with him now."

"Why?"

Elsbeth suddenly understood why Emma looked so exhausted.

"Because I am concerned about your soul."

"My soul feels fine. I think," Denise said. "I am not troubled by it."

"Aye, and that is part of the problem," Elsbeth said.

"You want me to have trouble with my soul?"

"Nay, nay, but I want you to feel the weight of it, this eternal part of you. Your temporal parts will wither and age, dying as all things of this world do. It is your soul which lives on. We must see to its health."

"If my soul lives on, why must we see to its health? Will it not live on, no matter what?"

"Denise," Elsbeth said, taking firm hold of her hand and marching her across the bailey to the chapel, "we are to see Father Godfrey. Make up your mind to it."

"Oh, aye, I know we are, but I still do not understand why."

"I will leave that to the father to explain to you." She only prayed to God he could.

They entered the chapel, which was already dark in the failing light of an autumn afternoon. The clouds had built up again, thick against the floor of heaven, pressing against the treetops, turning all the world to pearl. Beautiful. Candlelight shone warm and golden against the stone walls, yellow orbs of heat and welcome in a gray world. The light of heaven itself, welcoming a soul within its bosom. Or so she hoped Denise would see it.

"It is very dark," Denise said. "And cold. I am glad of my boots. Do you think Lord Hugh will like my boots?"

"I am certain he will like your boots very much. He has boots of his own which he cherishes highly. Perhaps you can spend an hour by the hearth, comparing the workmanship of your boots."

"Elsbeth?" Denise said, looking up at her in puzzlement at her tone.

"Nay, I am not mocking you," Elsbeth said. "I am cross of a sudden. I do not know why."

"Mayhap you miss him? It has been *hours* since we were with him."

Aye, it had been hours, but what of that? She did not need him, or want him. When she disappeared into her own life, a life apart from his, she would be year upon year without the sight of him or the sound of his laughter. What mattered hours now?

He was hers, but only for now.

"It has also been hours since we last prayed. Think on that, Denise, and let us find Father Godfrey."

"He is easily found," Denise said. "He is always in his

toft, working the soil your father gave into his keeping."

"He works the soil?"

"Yea, when he is not at his prayers. What do you do when you are not at your prayers, Elsbeth?"

She was never not at her prayers. Her prayers sustained her, giving her life purpose and structure, imbuing her mind with peace and security.

"Are we not instructed to pray without ceasing? This I do."

"Even Father Godfrey does not do that," Denise mumbled.

"I am sure he prays mightily."

"But not all the time."

She was not going to get into another debate with a child of eight.

"Show me to his toft, Denise. I will speak to him today."

"It is through the side door," she said, pointing to a small arched door at the side of the nave.

They found him on his knees as the rain began to fall in large splattering plops. He stood at their approach and dusted his hands, ignoring the rain.

"You find me at my labors," he said. "Do not tell me it is the hour for Vespers. I cannot have been so remiss."

He was a kindly looking man, now that she looked again, her memories of him stirred to life. He had been a handsome man ten years past and had always had a smile for her. His hair of ginger hue splattered with silver, his cheeks ruddy with health, his eyes the blue of a soft sea—a most regular and comforting looking priest was Godfrey, just the sort of man to guide Denise.

"Nay, Father," Elsbeth said. "It is hours yet. We have come because . . . well, because . . ."

She did not quite know where to begin.

"Let us move into the chapel. It is ofttimes easier to

speak under the shadow of the rood," Father Godfrey said.

"Aye, that is so," she said with a relieved sigh.

When they were gathered beneath the comforting arms of Christ on His cross, Father Godfrey said, "Now, what need does a bride of a day have for a priest?"

"Oh, it is not I who has need," Elsbeth said.

"Oh?" He looked down at Denise.

"It is Denise," Elsbeth said. "Her spiritual education has been lacking."

"I see her at the Mass."

"Aye, but she does not seem to ... believe," Elsbeth said.

"Not to believe—that is a most serious charge," he said, looking down at Denise. She met his look for a time and then looked down at her feet. "Tell me what you believe, Denise."

"I believe in God, in the Holy Trinity, in heaven and in hell," Denise said.

"And?" he asked.

"And I believe in the miracles and in the saints and in the blessed Virgin."

Father Godfrey looked at Elsbeth. "Her belief seems most complete. From what springs your concern?"

"I do not think Denise believes that God cares for her, that He is her bulwark against trouble and her strong tower against enemies. There is no rest in her belief," Elsbeth said.

Father Godfrey looked carefully at Elsbeth and smiled. "It could be said that she is young yet for such precision. It could be said that Denise lives in a strong tower and so feels not the hunger for protection that David did when he wrote those inspired words. It could be said that all belief is perfected by God Himself in its proper time. And it could also be said that this child needs guidance in her beliefs," he said, looking again down at Denise.

"I would say that I live in a strong tower, but that I would like a pair of boots that fit properly," Denise said.

"Would you?" Father Godfrey said, scowling down at her softly. "And has anyone asked what you would say?"

"Nay, Father," she said, dropping her head.

"Have you thanked God for the boots you have and for the strong tower which shelters you?"

"Nay, Father," she said, slipping her hand into Elsbeth's.

"Well, kneel now and give your thanks to God for what you have. He will see to what you do not have. And when you are done with thanking God, you will come to me after Compline each day and we will search God's will for you, I your willing tutor in matters eternal. You will come, Denise?"

"Yea, Father," she said, kneeling in the nave, her blond hair picking up the golden light of the candles.

"Thank you, Father," Elsbeth said. "I was concerned, as was my lord Hugh."

"She is young," he said. "Such stumbling steps are common. I have known her longer than you, and Denise is a stout soul; she will find her way, with my guidance. But what of you, Elsbeth? Have you not a care of your own?"

"Father?" Were her suspicions so plain then?

He led her away from Denise, who was mumbling her prayers in hurried Latin. When they stood at the back of the church, the shadows enfolding them in chilly comfort, he said, "I remember you well, Elsbeth, and I know how to read a troubled heart. Tell me what concerns you." He laid his hand upon her arm in comfort; she shook off its weight before answering.

"Of concerns I have few. Perhaps I have a question or two which I had thought to put to you," she said. Now that the opportunity was upon her, she could not get the words past her constricted throat. He knew her well? She could hardly remember him at all; finding his name had been a task beyond her skill.

"Questions? I will answer what I may, yet is it not the fear of sin which clouds your eyes?"

"Should not the fear of sin cloud every eye?" she said, evading him.

"Aye, it could be argued," he said. "But what troubles you, Elsbeth? Speak plain. I am your priest and would only serve your soul."

Her priest, yet she did not know him. He was a stranger to her. How could she speak her fears to this man of God who lived out his life in Warkham under her father's very nose?

"I have not sinned, yet . . ." she said, halting. "Yet . . ."

She could not name the thing she feared. She could not lay Hugh out to public shame in Warkham's bailey. With any other priest, at any other holding, she would have spoken freely. But not here.

"All have sinned. It is only unconfessed and unrepentant sin which damns us."

"Aye, that is true," she said. "Do you then tell me I have no cause to fear?"

"I can tell you nothing, Elsbeth, beyond what I have said. In confession and in repentance we are set free. And instructed to go and sin no more," he added.

"A difficult task," she said. "Even for a knight from Outremer."

Surely the priest had heard Hugh's confession and knew whether he had unnatural desires. Let Godfrey only say that Hugh had turned from his sin. Yet why should she want that? If Hugh sinned and by his sin she was released from this marriage, would that not answer all? She should want to find the evidence of Hugh's continuing sin. Coupled with their lack of consummation, it was the key to set her free. Yet she did not want to believe what her heart whispered against him. 'Twas little wonder she could make no sense of what Father Godfrey was saying; she could make no sense of her own thoughts and wishes. She was the very woman her mother had warned her against becoming.

"Sin knows no boundaries, Elsbeth," Godfrey said softly. "Lucifer is no respecter of persons. Even a knight from Outremer may fall into his maw," he said solemnly.

"Father, I am not comforted."

Did he tell her that Hugh was guilty and that he had not repented of his sin, or did he blame her for the courses that barred the way of her husband into her? Or did he speak of theology with no thought to Hugh or Elsbeth or the working of things behind Warkham's walls? He was not a plain-speaking man, this priest.

"Elsbeth, comfort is only found within God's strong tower. Comfort and safety are His promises. 'He alone is my rock and my salvation; He is my fortress, I will never be shaken.' Heed the words of the psalm. Heed them and be at peace."

"Father, I am at peace," she said again, more firmly. "I know this verse very well."

"Aye, I taught it to you years past," he said. "I am pleased that you remembered it, though I was forgotten."

"I did not—"

"Nay, do not lay the sin of deceit upon your soul," he said, smiling softly. "I have changed. I know it. The years pass and the burdens of life grow heavy."

Elsbeth smiled. "Yea, Father, and thank you. You are most forgiving."

"Lay it not as praise upon me," he said. "Is the dispensing of forgiveness not my province? I but do as I am bid by my master. Elsbeth," he said, his smile fading, "forgiveness is what we are each called to. Mayhap the burden that you carry with you now could be lifted from you if you could find the grace to forgive."

He was guilty. Father Godfrey could not say it outright, but Hugh was guilty of sodomy. Perhaps even with Baldwin, the king he openly loved. Perhaps even with Raymond, his handsome squire. Father Godfrey wanted her to forgive him. Father Godfrey wanted her marriage to stand, and he wanted her to forgive the sin Hugh carried upon his soul.

Yet this was her way out. If Hugh had committed sodomy, would not the church release her from marriage to such a man? Especially as there was no consummation? What held them together? Not their bodies joined as one. This union could be broken at a word.

"And will God forgive a woman who repudiates her hus—"

"Ah, I have found you," Hugh said, shaking the water from his hair as he entered.

Elsbeth jumped as if struck and whirled to face him. "My lord," she said, dropping head in greeting.

"My lady," he said, bowing. "And my small lady Denise," he added as Denise came toward him. "How fetching you look, and how fine are your boots."

Denise grinned hugely and stole a quick look at Elsbeth, who smiled and shook her head in surrender.

"I have said my prayers, Father Godfrey," Denise said. "Do you like my bliaut, Lord Hugh? Do you think the color suits?"

"Father Godfrey," Hugh said, ignoring Denise for the moment, "I looked for you in your toft, even in this rain, for I know how you must work your soil every day. Only two such worthy ladies could pull you from your self-appointed tasks."

"All tasks are God-appointed, Lord Hugh," Father

Godfrey said with good humor. "Even the task of teaching small ladies how to pray."

"You speak not of my wife, certainly, for though she is small, she is a prayer warrior of great renown."

Father Godfrey only smiled.

"Do you not like green?" Denise said.

"Be still, Denise. You must keep still," Elsbeth said.

"I have an amber bliaut," Denise said softly to Hugh. "Do you like amber?"

"Denise," he said, his eyes mild and smiling, "you must listen to Lady Elsbeth. Let her show you what it is to be a woman. You could not see a finer example though you traveled the world."

"Well spoke, my lord," Father Godfrey said.

"It is only the truth," Hugh said, looking down at Elsbeth.

She suspected him of sodomy and still he could touch her heart with his smile. Ardeth had spoken true of the way of things between a woman and a man. She had vowed to walk a different course, and yet she was momentarily blinded by a smile from a beguiling man, her mother's lessons lost in mist.

She did not need his praise. She had never needed any man's praise. What, then, this stirring in her heart? Was she as weak as all that? It could not be so.

"I will suffer from the sin of pride if you keep on, my lord," she said.

"It is not pride to know your worth," Hugh said. "Nor is it folly for me to give praise where it is deserved. And so," he said, turning finally to Denise, "may I say how comely you look in your green bliaut with your shining hair, Denise? You are as bright and fresh as spring grass in a meadow. I like your green bliaut very well."

Denise glowed with pleasure and smiled up into Hugh's face with all the open adoration of a hound. Elsbeth was afraid her own look was not much different.

Had she learned nothing from Ardeth? Would she walk the same path to the same end? She had to do better, to be better. She had to run from this temptation.

She stayed where she was and tried to find the prayer that would lead her away from temptation.

Had she prayed yet today? Had she sought the comfort of the chapel? She had not. What had become of her plan to show her husband her eternal devotion to prayer and chastity? It had disappeared somewhere on the cliffs beyond Warkham tower.

"My lord!" Raymond said, hurrying into the chapel. "You are sought, or rather, your lady is. The lady Emma has begun her labor. You are required, my lady," he said.

She had begun her labor. Elsbeth closed her eyes against the words. Bloody work was what she must now face.

"Lady," Hugh said, "she will have need of you."

She opened her eyes and said, "I am come. Tell her I am come."

"He comes," Emma said from her chamber.

The lord of Warkham's bed was high and wide—too high for Emma, who had more comfort in sitting than in lying in any case. She sat upon a small stool, her knees spread wide, her breasts resting on the restless mound of her belly. She was naked, her skin flushed and her breathing shallow. The room was crowded with servants watching her, prepared to help yet not moving beyond the circle of their curious interest at the event of another soul coming into the world.

"I see," Elsbeth said. "It is your time." She turned to the other women and said, "Get you gone. Marie, bring me a cord from the kitchens and a knife. Clean linen also. All others, depart. I cannot do what needs must be done with so many eyes upon me."

They left, mumbling their discontent at having their

amusement curtailed by strange notions of privacy and concentration. Emma did not seem to note who or how many were in her chamber; her mind was all on her child.

"Have you sent for the midwife?" Elsbeth asked.

"She is dead," Emma said. "Died not a week ago. There is no one to take her place. Except you, Elsbeth. You have done this before, have you not?"

Aye, she had done it before, been trained in some small way in the matters of childbearing, as would befit the lady of a holding. But she was no midwife. She knew nothing beyond what all other women knew, and mayhap less. She had never borne a child and never would if her prayers were answered.

"I have," she said to Emma, hiding all her fears in soothing calmness. That was what Emma needed and that was what she would provide. "I know what to do. Take what ease you can in that."

"I am past ease," Emma said, huffing as Elsbeth watched the spasm work itself over her belly.

"How often comes the pain?"

"Often enough."

"Can you lie down?"

"I cannot breathe when I lie down. This babe presses against my wind, squeezing my heart."

Marie returned with the cord and the knife. "Where is the linen?" Elsbeth asked softly.

"The laundress has most of it, and it is still wet from washing. She is drying a length near the fire. It will come as soon as it may."

"Is there none more?" Elsbeth asked, knowing it was she herself who had used the linen as binding.

"Nothing clean," Marie said.

"And is there no one in the village who knows something of midwifery?" Elsbeth whispered as another pain ran its course over Emma's distended belly. "No apprentice?"

"Nay. She had an apprentice, but the girl ran off last spring. No one knows what became of her."

Elsbeth straightened her spine and tossed back a length of her hair. "Then bring me wormwood and lady's mantle and set yourself to pray."

"Aye, lady," Marie said, turning and leaving the room.

Elsbeth almost wondered if she would see Marie again. Certainly she herself would not return to this chamber unless compelled to do so, which she had been by Emma's dire need.

"Elsbeth?" Emma said.

"Aye, I am here," Elsbeth said, turning to face her father's wife.

"I am . . . I am afraid," Emma said, her eyes shining with terror.

"I know," Elsbeth said. "I know."

The hours of Emma's labor were long. The day slid into a gray, damp twilight. Night came softly, yet nothing in the lord of Warkham's chamber was soft. Marie sat quietly in a corner on the floor, praying softly, aiding Elsbeth when she could.

Emma squatted, trying to push the babe from her, her arms over her head to give her more breath. The babe was not dropping, not moving down; only Emma moved, her belly heaving and roiling as her body tried to expel a babe who clutched his mother's womb with both fists. Elsbeth had given Emma a draught of wormwood for the pain. Whether it had helped or no she could not tell.

"Give me something," Emma said softly, her face red with effort.

"I have given you all I can."

"Give me something . . . to stop this. I will die. Let me not die in pain."

Elsbeth laid a wet length of linen on the back of Emma's neck and rubbed her distended belly. "I cannot. There is naught amiss. It takes much labor to bring forth a child."

Emma laughed weakly and shook her head. "I know what is happening. I know."

"What do you know?"

"The child is dead."

"Nay. Only God can see into a woman's womb. This is only a difficult labor, as most first birthings are."

"Elsbeth," Emma said, looking into her eyes, "I watched my mother die in just such a way. Give me a way out of this pain."

And had Elsbeth not watched her own mother, Ardeth, die in just such a way? And with her husband far from her? Elsbeth had been called from Dornei to help her mother in her labor at far Herulfmeade and she had gone to her most willingly, though not Gautier. Her father had been in London when her mother had died giving him yet another child. A woman's course was short and hard.

"I will give you hops, it will calm you."

Emma strained against another birth pain, her hands clutching her belly.

"Do not leave me!" she said through the pain. "Do not leave me to die alone."

"You will not die," Elsbeth said, but she was not certain. It had been many hours and nothing had changed. The babe did not come, though the pain did not relent. Women died in childbed every day. Every day. Every hour. "And I will not leave you."

"My child is dead or dying and I will die," Emma said. "I know it."

"We all die, Emma," Elsbeth said, gripping her hand

and holding on to her, "but not today. You will not die today."

"You will help me?" Emma said weakly.

"I will help you, but not to die. I will only help you to live. You and the babe together."

"My lord will be pleased if he has a son of me," Emma said.

"Think of yourself now, not of him," she said. It was Gautier who had brought Emma to this pass; he did not bear thinking upon now or all thoughts would turn to curses. "Think of how strong you are."

"I am not strong," Emma said. Her lips were white and dry, her nose pinched, her brow prominent on a face gone suddenly sharp and old. "Yet you are strong, Elsbeth. Push this child from me. Pull him out. Get him free of me."

And so she did. She pressed and pushed against the mound of belly. She had Emma lie on her back by the fire and reached inside the wet dark of her to feel the babe and try to coax him out. She even held a lighted taper to the opening of her womb and called, "Come forth, child! Come into the light of Christ our Savior!" but the child did not come.

"He will not come," Emma said. She sounded resigned, or mayhap only tired, eternally tired from her bones to her skin, tired unto her very soul. "I will take him with me into heaven today. It is day?"

It was night, darkest, blackest night without a moon to light anyone's way to heaven or to hell. It was not a night to die, without even a friendly light in the sky to guide a soul to heaven and to God's eternal rest. Yet would not the angels guide the way for a woman whose life was lost in the making of a child?

"It is day," Elsbeth said, looking away from Emma to the high wind hole set into the stone. "It is a fine, bright day."

Emma nodded and stared into the smoking fire, her head braced upon a folded fox pelt. "Have you sent for Father Godfrey? Send for him now. Cover me with my cloak. I am chilled. Strange to be so chilled on such a fine day."

Elsbeth said nothing. She went to the door and opened it. In the narrow hall stood Hugh and Denise and Raymond, their faces solemn and gray in the flickering light of the torch.

"Bring Father Godfrey," she said.

Hugh nodded and took the first step away from her, Denise at his side. "Denise, go to your pallet," Elsbeth said. "This is no place for you."

"I only wanted—" the girl said.

"I do not care what you wanted!" Elsbeth said sharply. "Do what I say. Go."

"Come, Denise," Hugh said. "This is wise counsel. Go to your place, as Elsbeth goes to hers. Raymond, see to it while I fetch the priest."

He looked at her as he said it, his eyes dark and wide in the shadowy light. He understood. In that moment, she knew he understood all that she felt. Terror at her helplessness and rage that such a death was being played out before her weary eyes: That was what she felt. She should have been able to help Emma and the child. She should have been able to save them both. She should have . . . been in a convent where no woman was required to push a child from her, bloody and wet. And where no woman was required to watch.

It did not bear contemplation, not now. Not when she still had so much left to do.

She closed the door on them and turned back to her father's young wife. Her first marriage and her first child, both to end here, in this chamber, in this cold and dark chamber of stone. Emma deserved more. More than this short earthly life that ended in pain and terror.

Elsbeth poured more wine and wormwood into Emma's cup. "Drink deeply, Emma. This will soothe your pain."

"Thank you," she said, drinking lightly of the cup and setting it beside her on the floor. "I am very tired."

"I know you are."

Emma felt the cloak with her hands and pulled it higher. "He will marry again."

Elsbeth ignored the twisting in her heart and rubbed Emma's belly. The contractions had stopped. The babe was still and quiet. Even the hour was quiet. All the world was quiet in the hour of Emma's death. Even Gautier was quiet; asleep somewhere warm and dry, no doubt, while his wife labored on, naked and afraid.

"Rest," Elsbeth said. "Give no thought to anything but rest. You have labored hard, Emma."

"I have," she said. "I did not think it would be so hard, though God has promised us so, has He not?"

"He has also promised that a place has been prepared for you. His house has many chambers, and one has been made especially for you. He has promised you rest and peace, and He has said there are no tears in heaven."

Elsbeth ignored the tears sliding down her own cheeks.

"And streets like gold," Emma said. "What must that be like?"

"I do not know," Elsbeth said. But Emma would. Emma would know in moments. "It will be beautiful, that is sure. A place without hunger or cold or fear. No tears in heaven, Emma. Think on that. Trust in that," she said.

Father Godfrey entered then and knelt at Emma's side. He prayed, his head bent, the sacraments in his hand, his voice a lonely echo that followed Emma into paradise.

Chapter Thirteen

Gautier took the news of Emma's death with equanimity. He yawned when Hugh told him what had befallen his wife and child. He had been asleep, as Elsbeth had supposed, in the chamber given over to Hugh and Elsbeth's use. There was no good reason in his mind why a good warm bed should lie empty when Elsbeth was otherwise occupied with Emma in his own chamber.

Whether that was the reason Hugh had been waiting through the long night in the hallway outside Emma's chamber, she never knew. Nor had she the heart to ask. She wanted to believe that he had waited and prayed out of concern and compassion. She let herself take comfort in that belief. If it was untrue, it mattered little, but believing was so very comfortable.

'Twas because Hugh encouraged such belief to rise in her that he was so very dangerous.

Elsbeth shook off thoughts of Hugh and set her thoughts on the funeral Mass for Emma and her unborn child. The chapel was full; all the folk of the village and tower and field had come to mourn the death of Warkham's lady. Even Gautier looked somber and saddened. He had much experience at wearing such a look; had he not looked the same at Ardeth's death a mere two years past? His oldest child, a cherished son, had died five years past; a daughter born to him had died a year before that. He had learned to grieve very well and very efficiently.

How long before he took another wife and plumped her with his child? How many months before another young bride came to Warkham, certain of putting her mark upon it and leaving behind only a grave? It would not be long. Her father did not wait long. He was determined to leave his mark upon the earth, and that meant leaving sons behind. Her father had five sons, a worthy number for any man, yet not enough for Gautier. Anything could overtake a child. The world was full of ills and dangers. The world was full of death.

Her eyes had strayed to her father, her breath quickening in her anger. She forced her eyes downward and slowed her breathing. This was for Emma. Thoughts of her father had no place here.

Hugh stood at Elsbeth's side and could think only one thing: How would this death affect the consummation? He had blood and now death to surmount in sliding her beneath him and marking her as his; how much more tribulation could God send a man and the man still meet the task?

More upon more. He was a man who was accustomed to trials. He could bed a fair damsel and win her heart in the doing. He was the man for that. And so he had been sent, the likeliest of all in Baldwin's court to win praise from Northern barons and their fair daughters; and so he had come upon Gautier and his daughter, Elsbeth, finding a baron hungry for gain and a daughter hungry for prayer. Well, she could pray after he bedded her, or even during, if that gave her solace, but he would have her.

This waiting wore on him. He was eager to be home, back in the heat and sunshine of Jerusalem, back in a land where his name and his worth were as bright as the sun. Or would be, when he had accomplished his goals here.

Win Elsbeth, win her heart and her will, and all else would follow. Honor. Renown. Power. And Baldwin's highest regard. Above all, he wanted that. He had his love, aye, but he wanted his regard, his respect. He wanted to close the gap between them, loving as equals. He would succeed. All he had to do was win Elsbeth.

She was half won already.

He looked down at her, at her dark and flowing hair and her proud nose and beckoning lips—a rare beauty and a woman of uncommon dignity. What woman possessed dignity? None he had ever known. Certainly it was not a trait sought in the sheltered women of the Levant; beauty, aye, and modesty, and charm, but dignity—that was for warriors and kings and emperors. Yet Elsbeth had dignity. How that a woman in a misty land surrounded by earthen huts and crumbling mortar put on dignity as her mantle?

He liked her. 'Twas not required, but he liked her. 'Twould not matter, but it was a surprise. He had never thought to like the woman that he married.

It was a blessing from God that she wanted a life in the abbey, but did God not know all, making all paths straight to His ends? This, surely, was His end. Hugh only wanted what God Himself must want. Yet, for all to begin, Elsbeth's courses must stop.

When would Elsbeth's blood cease?

The Mass ended at its proper time, and Emma was cast before God, time having stopped for her. There was peace in such stillness. The chapel echoed the peace of God in some small measure; 'twas little wonder, Elsbeth thought, that she found such haven in prayer and with it, the joy of solitude.

Hugh leaned close to her as Father Godfrey gave them the blessing.

"Do you need to return to our chamber?"

She knew well where his thoughts led his tongue. Well, God's time was perfect and she still bled, though not as heavily as before. Still, her blood was a barrier, and she smiled, secure in her defense.

"Aye, I do," she said.

"Then I will come with you."

"We have trod this path before. I do not require a helper."

"Nay, but a companion?"

"You know better," she said.

They progressed down the aisle, their feet mixing among the others of Warkham to make a sound like the march of the saints to the very throne of God. Would that it were so. Yet they were only the feet of the people, dirty and rough-shod, and they made their dusty way out to the open air of another gray autumn day.

"Come, Elsbeth," he said, wrapping a long arm around her waist. "I would not leave you alone today. Much has befallen that I would carry for you, if I could."

"You cannot," she said, ignoring the feel of his hand on her waist. His hand just brushed the underside of her breast. 'Twas surely immoral to leave the church in such a manner.

"Yet I would try," he said softly. "She was mother to you, and you—"

"Emma was not my mother. She was scarce two years older than I."

"—and you were by her for the whole, long length of her labor."

"And accomplished nothing but to aid her to her death," Elsbeth said.

"And so you need me, Elsbeth. Your very words are proof, for you did not aid her to her death; but in her death, which God ordained, you were the voice and the hand which eased her. 'Twas mighty service and well done."

"Well done?" she said, stopping, looking at the mud beneath her feet. Hugh's boots were a wreck, looking hardly different from the lowest serf's. This English weather would be the ruin of him. Could he not see that in returning to Jerusalem all would be well? He might even save his boots. But he understood nothing. He was a man and he spoke often, his words impressive to himself, though they were empty of meaning. " 'Tis not well done to watch a woman die and her child with her. 'Tis not well done to have no more to say than 'Fare thee well' as the blood leaves her face and the stink of her bowels empties onto the floor. 'Tis not well done to—"

"Stop, little one," he said, wrapping her in his arms and burying her face in his chest. He smelled like lavender and leather. And man. He smelled like a man. "Stop."

"Stop? I cannot stop. I will not stop. Emma is dead. She is the one who is stopped."

"We all must die, and it is God who appoints our hour."

Elsbeth pulled slowly out of his arms and continued across the bailey.

"Elsbeth?" he said, walking just behind her like mud she could not shake off her skirts. "Elsbeth, you know that as well as I. This lies with God, not with you."

Aye, but it had not been God who had held Emma while she writhed in unrelieved pain. It had been Elsbeth.

He followed her up the stair and through the hall, quiet for the time, and up the inner stair to the chamber she was forced to share with him. Someone had left a pile of clean lamb's wool and linen for her. Someone had also emptied her bloody bucket of stained linen and water.

"I thought you would have need of more," he said when he saw her looking at the fabric.

"You did this?"

"Aye," he said.

"Why?"

He shrugged. "I thought you would have need. I am here to meet your needs, Elsbeth."

"I can see to my own needs," she said. "And I can see to them privately."

Hugh smiled and ran a hand over her head, smoothing her hair. "Did you know that your hair curls around your brow when it rains? I wonder if your hair would be as straight as a lance in Jerusalem."

"Will we ever know?"

Hugh started and then laughed softly at her. She did not laugh with him.

"Why should you not see Jerusalem? It is my home." He said it very nicely, very sweetly. But he would not look into her eyes, and her question was not answered.

"Aye, it is your home, yet England is mine. Tell me, my lord; we serve different kings in differing lands, how did you come to claim a wife in chilly England? How did you come to me?"

"I came to you on angel's wings, Elsbeth, guided by God Himself."

"A pretty answer," she said, reveling in the sensation of the blood softly making its gentle way down her leg. "Yet not an answer. Let me ask another question, my lord. Where will we live?"

"Where would you like to live?" he asked, facing her, yet looking at her hair, not into her eyes. Hiding.

"I would like to live in Sunnandune, my home. I have longed for it far longer than you have longed for distant Jerusalem."

"How long has it been since you slept within Sunnandune's embrace?" he asked gently, his face mirroring the compassion in his voice most perfectly.

"A decade, my lord. A long decade. I was just a small child, of fewer years than Denise is now, yet I long for my home as you long for yours. I ask you again, my lord,

211

where shall we abide? With your king or mine?"

Always he spoke as if this marriage were a thing to be grasped and cherished, yet never did he speak of where they would live. Would he leave Baldwin? Nay, she could not see it. And she would not leave Sunnandune. Never would she relinquish the only home she had ever dreamed of. So she would stay at Sunnandune and he would run off to Jerusalem. Not a bad bargain, if she could only get him to speak of these things. Let them speak of this and not of his coming to her on angel's wings. She was no child. She did not need the comforting lie of empty flattery.

He did not answer; nay, he was spared an answer by the running arrival of Denise, with Raymond hot behind her.

"My lord!" she cried, wrapping her arms about his legs. "My lord, I will not go!"

"Where will you not go?" he asked, unleashing her arms and taking her hands in his. He looked down at her with tenderness and good heart. Of course with good heart, Elsbeth thought; had he not Denise to thank for her distraction?

"She will not go to the solar," Raymond said. "I have told her that is where all ladies must abide."

"Aye, it is where ladies spend their days," Hugh agreed. "What is amiss in that, Denise?"

"I do not want to," she said.

"A life is not constructed of wants, Denise," Elsbeth said. "Best to learn that early." As she had.

Hugh looked up at Elsbeth, his eyes soft and warm. "Let her stay," he said, speaking to Raymond. "If that is your will?" he asked Elsbeth.

With Emma gone, the matter of Denise was in her hands now, the girl her charge until another fostering was arranged for her. Yet Elsbeth would leave Warkham in a matter of days, if she followed her will. What Hugh's will was she did not know, but this was a way to find out what he had planned for her.

"Denise will need a new fostering," she said. "I will take charge of her until she is away from Warkham, or until I am away from Warkham. How long will that be, my lord?"

"I know nothing of her fostering," he said. "That is for a future time. For now, can she not be released from her bondage to the solar? Is it in you to grant her that freedom?"

How carefully he phrased it. How well he strung his words. How impossible he made it for her to do any but his will. He even made it so that she wanted what he wanted. How that a man could so form her to his will, making her the vessel for his desires? Ardeth had been right about that. Ardeth had been right about all.

Yet one desire he would not slake on her. Her blood still flowed, and in that blood was her deliverance and her salvation. For a time. In the time given to her, she must accomplish much. There was no time for delay or hesitation.

"You are freed from the walls of the solar, Denise," she said, looking into Hugh's green eyes. Hugh smiled his approval; it was the smile of a victor, and she felt resistance harden into resentment. "You will stay at my side. I will be your companion, teaching you what I know until another house is arranged."

Hugh's smile dimmed, and she smiled. Denise would be her shadow. Hugh and his torments would fade into nothing with Denise ever at her side.

"Surely—" he began.

"Surely such a small child, who has so recently lost the mother of her fostering, needs another woman now? Just for now," she said, pressing the word back upon him like a weight of stone.

"Just for now," he said, smiling grimly and shaking his head at her.

"Now is all that concerns me," she said, smiling slightly.

"Aye, I understand that very well," he said. "Raymond! Take my lady's small companion to the hall and make certain she has some ale and cheese. Surely her need for sustenance is great."

"I am not hungry," Denise said. "I want to stay with you." She pressed her face into his legs, burying herself in the tall strength of him.

"But I would stay with my lady," Hugh said, looking a bit frantic.

"But her need is so great and mine is so small," Elsbeth said, grinning in pure victory. "Surely you must see to her. Just for now."

"You put much reliance on 'now,' my little wife. I think you will find it will not support you for long."

"Yet long enough," she said softly. "And for now, you have won at least one heart in England. Have a care with it. She adores you."

"All hearts that I win into my keeping I treat with care," Hugh said, looking deep into her eyes.

"I am sure Denise is relieved to hear it," she said. "And now, I must encourage you all to leave."

Hugh smiled slightly, a crooked smile that went all the way to his eyes. "Come, Denise, let us see if Raymond has my sword sharpened. I would test it on something, for I find my blood is up."

Aye, it would be. She had thwarted him for the moment, and he could fault her not. This battle between them had been too much of victory for him and too much of torment for her. Denise in her adoration would tilt the scales in her favor.

They went down the stairs, a noisy trio, Denise talking happily, her every wish made real. Elsbeth did not linger

NAME: _____

ADDRESS: _____

_____

_____

TELEPHONE: _____

E-MAIL: _____

_____ I want to pay by credit card.

__ Visa   __ MasterCard   __ Discover

Account Number: _____

Expiration date: _____

SIGNATURE: _____

*Send this form, along with $2.00 shipping
and handling for your FREE books, to:*

Historical Romance Book Club
20 Academy Street
Norwalk, CT 06850-4032

*Or fax (must include credit card
information!) to:* **610.995.9274.**
*You can also sign up on the Web
at* www.dorchesterpub.com.

Offer open to residents of the U.S. and
Canada only. Canadian residents, please
call 1.800.481.9191 for pricing information.

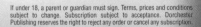

to listen at the door. Hugh's blood may have been up, his sword hard and in need, but hers was flowing down and splattering on the floor.

She could not have been happier.

"But you said you would fight," Denise said. "I want to see you fight."

They had left the tower and were in the bailey. The sky was the color of charcoal, the warm gold of autumn earth a blanket of color at their feet. The trees were tawny spires thrust against the heavy sky, and the stones of the curtain walls gleamed pale in the spotty light. It would rain. Again.

"Would you have me fight in the rain?" Hugh said.

"Do knights only fight when the weather is fair?" Denise asked, her hand in his.

If the truth be told, he feared he held her heart as well. Somehow, he had won himself a very small, very lonely damsel. The wrong damsel. Yet he could but smile at Elsbeth's maneuvering. She was an adversary most resourceful, most resilient. He had not thought it possible for a woman to resist for so long with such heated ardor beating against her resolve. England truly did birth steelish women. Though he had won Denise easily enough.

"In Jerusalem, the weather is always fair," Raymond said.

"Do you only fight in Jerusalem?" Denise asked, still looking up at Hugh.

"God willing," Hugh said on a chuckle. "The best fights are in the holy land, where the fighting is all of God and for God."

"Then God likes it when you fight," she said as they crossed the bailey to the armory.

"Yea, for I fight for His land, His home," Hugh said.

"I thought God lived in heaven," she said.

"Jerusalem is the home of God's son," Raymond said. "Do you know nothing of the Scriptures?"

"I know enough," she bit back. "Father Godfrey said so."

"An English priest," Raymond muttered.

"Are the priests of Outremer any better?" she said, her voice rising to match her anger.

"If Father Godfrey is content with your spiritual condition, then none shall gainsay him," Hugh said, giving Raymond a censorious look.

"Aye, listen to your priest," Raymond said, refusing to look at the girl.

"I shall," she said, ignoring him equally.

They entered the dark bastion of the armory, a chamber of stone and weapons, weapons that glinted with purpose and power even in the rapidly failing light.

"There are the swords," Denise said, pointing. "You had best be about your duty to your lord," Denise said to Raymond.

"I know my duty," Raymond snapped. "I need no child to—".

"I am no child!"

"Ha," he said, his shout of derision loud within the stone. "You are all child, all mouth, all trouble."

"I am not! Lord Hugh likes me!"

"Aye, I do," Hugh said, stepping between them, shoving Raymond toward the swords with a scowl. "I like you exceedingly well. As I also like Raymond. I value him. He is my squire. I cannot allow you to berate him."

"Then I will not," she said. "Because you ask it. But only because you ask it. *I* do not like him."

"And I do not like you!" Raymond said, spinning around. "We have much to do here, and we do not need a child of two toddling at our heels!"

"Raymond!" Hugh said, his voice thunderous. "Enough."

Denise stood her ground as she faced Raymond, but her eyes held the smallest and most proud of tears at their corners.

"Aye, enough," Raymond said, breathing hard. "I forget myself, my lord. Forgive me."

"Done," Hugh said. "But hold your tongue and your impatience. All will be well if you do this."

"Aye, my lord," Raymond said, lifting a sword to hand to Hugh.

Hugh took the sword and weighed the balance of it in his hand. Denise was all but ignored. In fact, she was completely ignored.

"I forgive you, too. But only because it is my Christian duty to forgive up to seventy times seven. But I am counting," she said ominously.

"Denise. . . ." Hugh warned, looking askance at her.

"Count as high as you can," Raymond said. "We will be gone before you can count to even ten."

"You will be gone?" she asked, looking hard at Hugh. "But where are you going?"

It was not a question Hugh was eager to answer. And Raymond knew it.

"Did you think Warkham was mine?" Hugh asked, evading her question with one of his own.

"Nay, but you are wed to Elsbeth," Denise said.

"And Sunnandune is Elsbeth's," Hugh said.

"Then you go to Sunnandune?" she asked.

Hugh held his tongue, throwing Raymond a look of deep irritation. Whate're was said to Denise would be repeated; she had neither the skill nor the desire to hold her tongue. He knew that well enough. A lie would be told as quickly as the truth, and he wanted neither to be bandied about Warkham's walls. This questioning was too close upon Elsbeth's own. What was it about women that made the place of their abiding of such devoted interest?

When his answer faltered, she asked, "But do you not have your own holding? Where is it? Will you go there soon? Will Elsbeth go with you?"

"Is Elsbeth not my wife?" he asked in answer.

"Yea," she said.

"Then that is your answer," he said. "Come, Raymond, give me a fight to test my skill and my nerve. I have much anger in me of a sudden."

"Aye, my lord," Raymond said, hanging his head in expectation of what was to come.

"I shall come with you," Denise said.

"Nay, you shall not," Hugh said, "and I will brook no argument on this. Go instead and find my lady. Give her aid, if you can. And if you cannot, give her comfort and cheer. Even if it be in the solar."

He was past indulgence with her and she read him well enough not to argue his edict. Denise turned, her shoulders slumped in resignation, and left the armory. She was a small weight of disappointment and depression, casting a heavy shadow upon the earth as she passed over it. Yet she did pass, leaving them alone. 'Twas all he wished for, at the moment.

"You spoke amiss and too clearly," Hugh said, the sword an easy weight in his hand. "There is no excuse for such laxity."

"Aye, my lord. I do know it. It is only that she pressed me—"

"She is a child! If you cannot control her and yourself with her, then you are not made of the stuff of knights and will remain a squire all your life. Is this your father's dream for you? Is this your dream for yourself?"

"Nay, my lord," Raymond said, his eyes earnest and shining. "I will control my tongue and my ways. Such will not happen again. I will not betray, even to the child Denise."

"Especially to the child Denise," Hugh said. "She will

be ever under Elsbeth's hand now, and Elsbeth must not think of where we will dwell or when we shall leave Warkham. That is not to my purpose, as you know better than any. None shall hinder me in my task here. Including you, Raymond," Hugh said, his fierceness showing through his amiable charm like a ray of shining light through dark cloud. "Consider that."

"My lord," Raymond said, kneeling, "I am your man as you are Baldwin's. I will not speak amiss. I will not betray. I will not hinder."

"Good," Hugh said, clasping his shoulder in forgiveness. "Now, give me the fight I yearn for. My blood is high and hot, and I may slake my needs on none here but you, Raymond. Only you have that high honor."

Raymond smiled and bowed to his lord, obedient to his every will.

He was waiting for her in her chamber. But then, were not all the chambers of Warkham his? He could go where he would; there was no lock against the lord of Warkham.

She stepped into the room cautiously. Her father's temper was uncertain, and she had learned to walk carefully when walking in his way.

"You have denied him," he said. He was leaning against the bed, his arms crossed and his legs out before him. A most casual pose, yet nothing her father did was casual.

"I have not," she said. "I am in flux. I am unfit and unable, nothing more."

"Unfit?" he said, smiling. "You never could be unfit, Daughter. You are all that a wife should be. I am most proud of the woman you have become."

"Thank you, Father," she said, letting his words wash over her like water, sliding, smooth, and then gone.

"He is a well-favored man," he said. "And a fighter of some skill, I can attest."

"You fought with him?"

"Yea, and took his measure. Or perhaps he was taking mine," he said easily. "But what was certain was that he was a man in need of a maid. He has needs, Daughter, and you must meet them."

"I will. When I can," she said, keeping the open door at her back.

"You can now. It can be done," he said. "If your mother were here, she could tell you."

"Yet my mother is not here," Elsbeth said abruptly. "And I will not go against church doctrine. Now is not my time."

"Yet what of his time? The time is hard and hot for him, Elsbeth," he said, grinning at her. "Does the church not say that a woman must give herself to the man who claims her? He has given you his name. It is your part to give him your body."

"I cannot."

"*Will* not says it plainer," he said, standing suddenly. He was a tall man, tall and dark and still in the prime days of his strength, or so it seemed to her. "Think, Elsbeth," he said. "Think what will serve you best."

"I know what will serve me best," she said grimly.

Gautier laughed softly and shook his head at her. "I know what you would say, Daughter, yet the contracts were signed before I knew of your passion for the cloister. What could I do? I would not make an enemy of Baldwin and his liege man over a simple betrothal. There is no wisdom in that course. Nay, I was trapped as surely as you. He stood in my very hall and heard you beg for release from the married state."

He would remind her of that.

"I did not know he was there. I did not know of the betrothal," she said.

"As I did not know how a betrothal to Hugh of Jerusalem would distress you," he said. "We were companions in our ignorance. Yet now you are his wife. And being his wife, you must perform your wifely function. If you would ever see the inside of an abbey, you must gain his goodwill."

Aye, she knew it. What did he tell her that she did not know?

"Give him what he wants," Gautier said. "Without childish delay, meet his needs."

Gautier came to her and took her chin in his hand. Smiling softly down at her, he said, "Do this, Elsbeth, and you are more likely to get from him what you want. An even exchange. A well-ordered bargain."

A bargain, aye, and with her body as the tool to achieve her ends. It did not sit well with her. Then again, nothing her father said was likely to sit well with her.

"Think on it," he said, dropping a kiss upon her brow before he left the chamber.

Think on it. Aye, she would.

What would Ardeth have to say about such bargaining?

Chapter Fourteen

"Denise, I do not need any aid," Elsbeth said as she gathered food from the kitchens.

"Lord Hugh told me that you did, or would, or might, and so I am here," Denise said. "I am to stay with you."

Elsbeth reached down a hand and brushed it over the girl's shining hair. Well, there were worse things than the company of a small and very earnest companion. Her own fostering had been slipshod. Isabel of Dornei had a kind heart, but a wayward will, and her instruction had been . . . inconsistent. She would not wish such on Denise; her success as a lady of a great holding would depend upon her skills. It did not matter so much for Elsbeth, as Ardeth had taught her early and taught her well all that a lady of this world must know to thrive. She had learned well, listened well.

She knew how to pray and how to sew, how to manage a house and how to discipline a servant, how to submit and how to survive. She was very adept at submission. All who knew her said as much and more. Even Hugh would come to say the same, and from there, it was a small step to gaining his permission to enter the convent. A small step, but so perilous. It looked less likely by the hour that he would disavow her, but would he let her run to Sunnandune without a husband at her side? He seemed to want her most desperately.

Nay, she was being foolish. Hugh was a charming, carefree man, given to smiles when other men were given to anger. He would release her. He needed only to understand that she would make an unfit wife. And he would see that. She would make him see that.

She would make him see that before her blood deserted her. That was very important. She must not and would not be breached, no matter what her father counseled. Or perhaps because he counseled it. To have him encourage her to open her legs to Hugh made her clench them together all the tighter. She did not want to give him what he wanted, though his arguments had been all of her and how she could best achieve her goals. No matter. There had to be a way of achieving her ends without the opening of her thighs and the breaching of her maidenhead. There had to be.

"Where are we going?" Denise asked, picking at a crumb on the table and popping it into her mouth.

Elsbeth corralled her thoughts and pinned them on

the duty at hand. "We are going to the village to see who might need an extra crust or a wedge of cheese. Perhaps there is a child who sits untended at the edge of a toft or by a cold hearth who would be thankful for a small bite."

"Shall I hold the basket with you?"

"Nay, you carry the sack of apples; I shall carry the basket."

"But the cook will not like that his apples are gone missing."

"You speak from experience, to judge by the whiteness of your cheek," Elsbeth said with a smile. "Fear not. These apples are very small. I am certain John will not miss them."

"Well, if you are sure," Denise said, looking around for the cook, who was not to be seen at the moment. "Perhaps we should hurry."

"Denise," Elsbeth said, lifting her chin with a hand. "I am the daughter of Warkham, the lady here until my father weds again. I can take what I will from all of Warkham's bounty. None shall gainsay me. This is a lesson to be learned."

"This is a good lesson," Denise said, her eyes glowing with possibilities. "I will remember this lesson."

Elsbeth laughed. "Just be sure you remember that your duty is to see to all of your holding, and not to see to yourself."

"Lady," John said, coming into his kitchens. "Can I serve you?"

"Nay, John, we have served ourselves, taking what can be spared for the villeins of Warkham," Elsbeth said.

"Take what you will and more, lady. 'Tis good service you do. And 'tis well to take the child with you. You make a likely pair, full of goodwill and good heart. Take this pie with you. The crust is scorched on the rim. I would not serve it at Warkham's table, but it may serve down below."

Denise's eyes were as big as cats' as she watched John hand over more provender from Warkham's stores. Elsbeth only smiled and took the pie. She had seen far worse arrive on Warkham's table, but she held her tongue as to that.

"Many thanks, John. This will be well received."

They left the heat and smoke of the kitchen and went into the breezy chill of the bailey. Hugh was not to be seen. She was relieved. And puzzled. Where was he?

"But," Denise asked, the apples bumping against her leg, "can I never see to myself?"

"Hmm?" Elsbeth said, her eyes scanning the curtain walk, looking for a blond head tousled by the autumn wind. She only wanted to find him so that she could avoid him, that was her reasoning. Her father's words she had banished from her memory. It was her mother's counsel on the affairs between women and men that she would heed, and using her body as a tool was no part of Ardeth's counsel to her daughter.

"Does a lady never get anything for herself?" Denise asked.

"A lady takes care of all around her—her husband and lord, her children, her land, her home, her people. It is then that God smiles upon her. And when God smiles, life is rich indeed."

"How can you tell when God is smiling?"

They passed the tower gate and walked down the hill to the single street that made up the village of Warkham. Pigs scattered at their coming, snuffling in the dirt of the street.

"How can you tell when *you* are smiling?" Elsbeth asked, looking down at Denise and pulling her close. A certain pig, one with a mottled snout, looked quite fierce, eyeing them boldly.

"How can I tell?" Denise said, looking up at her. "I can just . . . feel it."

"And how does it feel?"

"It feels good."

"And so it feels when God smiles upon you," Elsbeth said, smiling. "It feels good. You feel good."

"Hmm," Denise said, pondering.

"Hmm," Elsbeth echoed, grinning at the girl.

A boy of about Denise's size came running into the street with a long stick, herding the pigs down the road, away from them. The angry pig with the mottled snout resisted the boy. The boy ignored his resistance and thwacked the pig on the rump with the heavy end of his stick. The pig grunted and ran into the throng of his brethren, his resistance done.

"Sorry, my lady," he said. "You here special? Looking for someone?"

"Nay, only to give what aid I can with a few small apples and loaves."

"And cheese," Denise added, looking him over.

He was missing two front teeth—his milk teeth to judge by his age—and had rough-cut hair the color of wet slate. He was perhaps a year or two older than Denise.

"Are those your pigs?" Denise asked.

"Four of them," he said with some pride. It was not every family who could boast the ownership of fine, healthy pigs. "We'll be killing two of them soon, in the blood month."

The blood month. November. When fodder was scarce, animals were killed, feeding those who could not afford to feed them. It was the same everywhere, even in the halls of the richest barons. None could sustain themselves without the killing that defined the blood month.

It was the smell that Elsbeth disliked. It tainted the very air with the metallic stain of blood.

"Will you miss them?" Denise asked.

"Miss them? Pigs?" he said and laughed.

"They will likely not miss you, either!" Denise shouted at the boy's retreating back.

Elsbeth looked down at Denise. Denise looked down at the dirt.

"You have a quick tongue, and a quicker temper. It will do you none but ill in this life," Elsbeth said.

"He did not have to laugh at me. I was only trying to be kind," Denise said.

"And succeeded very well," Elsbeth said, turning Denise to face her. "It was kind of you to ask about his pigs."

"Then why did he laugh?"

"Think, Denise. The best of his family's riches are in those pigs, yet he would starve, as would the pig, if it were not killed in the blood month. Would you have him give his heart to something he cannot keep? Would you have him admit it if he struggles against ropes of tenderness for a mere pig? He had to laugh. You asked him a question he could not answer, not even in the quiet of his own mind."

"Oh."

"Come, let us find some soul who has need of what we bring. That will cheer you."

"Is that another lesson?" Denise asked, kicking a pebble.

Elsbeth laughed in spite of herself. "You are learning me too well. Yea, it is another lesson. Never forget that—"

"That helping others is the greatest reward and that God will bless us for the act."

"That is so. I see someone else has taught you this. Or tried to."

"I learned it," Denise said. "I do not yet know if I believe it."

"Then let your belief follow on the heels of the act. Faith is sometimes built upon just such a foundation."

Denise held her tongue and kept kicking the pebble. Elsbeth was content with the silence.

Where was Hugh?

Her eyes scanned the fields, hardly empty even though the harvest season was past. All who had legs to stand were in the fields, repairing fences, keeping watch on the oxen left to graze in the gleaned fields and meadows, the women about their laundry or their brewing, the smell of barley and hops strong in the wet, cold air. All required fruitful work upon the earth to feel merit; 'twas how God had designed a man.

Even men of age, bent and gaunt, still looked for work among their own, and found it more often than not. A village was a busy place, busy about the business of farming and grazing, growing and tending. How quiet and soft a village must be without the lord in attendance. Did they wait and wonder when the lord of Warkham would leave for other holdings?

She would have.

She and Denise waved to the villeins as they worked in their tofts and crofts, and handed small crusts and tiny wedges of cheese to the children who crawled in the dirt of their virgates.

" 'Tis a fair and generous act, lady," said a weatherbeaten man, the miller by his look.

" 'Tis very little I do," she said, sliding away from his praise. "It looks about to rain," she said, glancing up at the sky.

"There has been much rain and much sorrow this year, lady. My prayers are with you on the untimely death of Lady Emma and her child," he said.

"You are kind," Elsbeth said. "Yet is it not my father

who needs your prayers? He has lost much in a single hour." Mayhap with prayer, he would remember it. He seemed to go about his life with nary a scowl to mark his wife's absence.

"Aye," the man said. "I can say that all in Warkham pray for him with a will."

Something in the way he spoke, some gleam in his eye, prompted her to ask, "Have we met before? I seem to remember you. Or perhaps it is you who remembers me?"

"I know you, Lady Elsbeth," he said. "I remember you from when you were no bigger than this one," he said, gesturing toward Denise.

"And your name?" Elsbeth asked.

"Walter, my lady. Walter Miller. Do you truly not remember me?" he asked, looking hard at her.

"Nay, I do not think I do," Elsbeth said. "Yet have I not seen you recently?"

"I am courting Marie, who was with you when Lady Emma and her babe died."

"She did good service. How are you progressing in your suit?" Elsbeth asked with a smile.

Walter shrugged. "Marie could answer you better. She is a widow once already. I am a widower three times. 'Tis hard to lose the woman of your hearth again and again. Yet I like the married life. And I am prosperous. I have a good name built here."

"My father's name is Walter," Denise said.

"A fine name for any man," the miller replied easily. "And it does look to rain," he added, looking up at the treeline as he changed the subject. "A wet autumn it has been. The crops not what they should have been, much of the grain ruined before I could grind it. And still more rain."

"And Lord Hugh's boots will ruin," Denise said.

Elsbeth cast her a glance and then nodded her farewell to the villein, guiding Denise with a hand upon her shoulder. If Walter watched them walk away for longer than she liked, she ignored the tingle of warning that his gaze aroused in her. It could mean nothing, after all.

"That was ill-spoke," Elsbeth said, turning her thoughts again to Denise.

"Why? The rain *will* ruin his boots. Hugh cares very much for his boots."

"He will care even more when his stomach growls for food that cannot be found. The crops are worth more, to more people, than the shine of Lord Hugh's boots. To compare them to—"

"But Lord Hugh loves his boots!"

"Denise," she said, bending down to her and taking her by the hands, "there is more to the world than what makes Lord Hugh happy."

"But he is your husband."

"And still I say it."

"Should you not be making him happy? Is that not what the Holy Scriptures say is your divine duty?"

Elsbeth straightened and turned again to the hill of Warkham tower. "God says I am to submit to my husband. That I do. No mention is made of his happiness."

"Then God does not care if we are happy?"

Elsbeth sighed in frustration. "Of course He cares. It is only that . . . He is more concerned with our righteousness than our happiness."

"I would rather be happy."

"We are to want what God wants for us, either happiness or righteousness. He is Lord of all, even to the very desires of our hearts."

"It is the desire of my heart to be happy."

"And if He desires something different for you?"

"I still want to be happy."

"Against God's will? That is blasphemy, Denise. You surely see that. We cannot reach for what is outside of

God's will. His will is most perfect. No whim of man can hope to match His limitless sight and His everlasting love."

"If He loves me, He should want me to be happy. I do not see how that can be against God's will," Denise said.

"His ways are above your ways, His thoughts flying high above ours."

"Then it should be easy for Him to give me what makes me happy," Denise said.

Elsbeth had not known it was possible for a small child to be so obstinate; she herself certainly had never been so contrary.

"And what would make you happy?" Elsbeth said, hoping to shift the conversation.

Denise did not even have to pause. "I would like it to stay dry, so that Lord Hugh's boots are not ruined."

Elsbeth should not have been surprised; Denise's thoughts seemed to fly no higher than the height of Hugh's head.

"I think there is no sin in that prayer. Pray for dry weather," Elsbeth said. "It will help the villeins as well. That, surely, is a more selfless prayer and one for the greater good."

"I do not think it fair of God to value what a villein wants over what Lord Hugh wants," Denise said as they crossed beneath the tower gate. "I like Lord Hugh."

Elsbeth was suddenly exhausted. Emma's decision to sequester Denise in the solar became more understandable by the hour.

"He likes you," Elsbeth said, deciding to let Father Godfrey manage the bulk of Denise's spiritual instruction.

"Do you think so?" Denise asked, her blue eyes shining.

"Yea, I think so. I know so."

Denise grinned her victory and her joy. It was a warning to Elsbeth. She was in danger of just such a fall, just such a look. And it could not be. No man was worth it. Not even a man from Jerusalem.

"How are your lessons proceeding with Father Godfrey?" Elsbeth asked, pushing Hugh from her thoughts.

Denise shrugged and made a face.

"How?" Elsbeth asked again.

"I proceed," Denise said. "He talks. I listen. He talks again."

"A most thorough summation," Elsbeth said wryly.

"I do not like to be out in the dark," Denise said. "Must I go after Compline? There is no one about, and it is so cold . . . and dark."

Elsbeth looked down at her and wrapped a comforting arm about her shoulders. "I think after Compline is most convenient for Father Godfrey. Would you like an escort to your lessons?"

"Do you think Hugh would come with me?" Denise said, her face alight.

Elsbeth smiled reluctantly. "Would I not do?"

"Well, it is very dark. And you are not very big."

Elsbeth gave her a quick hug full of quiet laughter. "I am not very big, but I shall tell you a secret."

"Really?" Denise said avidly.

"Really," Elsbeth answered, bending down to whisper in the girl's ear. "Lord Hugh is afraid of the dark."

"He is not!"

"He is!" Elsbeth said in quick answer.

"But, he is so . . . big."

"Aye, I know it. Perhaps it is darker up where his head is. Did you think of that?"

"Nay, I did not," Denise said, wide-eyed. "Well, I would be glad of the company. Thank you, Elsbeth. You will not leave me alone with him, will you?"

"Alone with him? With Father Godfrey?"

"Aye. I would like it if you could stay," she said softly.

Elsbeth looked down at Denise's shining hair and delicate form and said the last thing she had expected to say. "Then I will stay."

"Thank you," Denise said quietly.

Elsbeth's eyes lifted from the girl at her side to scan the bailey, looking for her husband. She saw him leaving the dark archway of the armory, a sunbeam just lighting his hair to glimmering gold. Like a torch in the night he was—a glow of warmth and welcome in a cold, dark world. At his heels came Raymond, a smaller glow of light and beauty. They seemed so united, the two of them, these strangers from Outremer in the mists of the distant North. How alone they must feel in soggy England. How close they must be drawing to each other, the warmth of the familiar tightening the cord that bound them, one to another.

How very beautiful they both were.

"Lord Hugh!" Denise called, running across the bailey. "Lord Hugh! We fed the villein babies, and I will pray that it does not rain!"

Hugh smiled, watching her run to him. With a whispered word, Raymond drifted away along the curtain walk, his head down and his gait measured. Why did he go, Elsbeth wondered, when the sum of his duty was to attend his lord?

"The two are connected," Hugh said with a smile, "but I cannot make out how. Shall someone not enlighten me?"

"Have you been in the armory all this time?" Denise asked. "Did you not fight?"

"You are to pray for no rain?" Hugh asked at the same time. "I will join you in that prayer, but we must be quick, for it starts even now."

The sky had grown thick with cloud, black and loaded with water ready to burst forth. As he said, even now the first drops splattered heavily and singly to the ground. Elsbeth stood and watched him laughing with Denise, grabbing her round the waist and lifting her to his shoulders. A most congenial man.

Why had he not answered Denise's question?

"To the chapel, then," he said, bounding off, Denise squealing in horrified delight. "We must hurry to our prayers and stop this flood. You are coming, are you not, wife? We go to pray, and you are ever eager for that."

"I will always hurry to my prayers," she said to his retreating back, "as a true warrior of God hurries to his appointed battle. You *do* battle, do you not, my lord?"

Hugh stopped and turned, his smile fading like mist in a chill wind. "Am I not battling now, little wife?"

"I see no arms, no shield, no raiment of war," she said.

"Ah, but I battle for the heart of my wife."

Her heart tumbled out of his reach at the words. He did strive to win her—she could feel his effort. And his success.

"And prayer is the way to win her?" she asked, striking to find his intent and his method.

"Prayer is the way to win all, Elsbeth. Surely a prayer warrior of your renown knows that better than I, a mere knight of Jerusalem."

Their eyes held, a measuring that left them knowing little more than they had at the start. He wanted her for some cause. She rejected his possession for some reason. And in spite of all, there was respect. Perhaps even fascination.

"I am getting wet!" Denise said. "We must be at our task."

"Aye," Hugh said, looking softly at Elsbeth. "We must certainly keep to our task."

Elsbeth said nothing. Her throat had closed at the look in his soft green eyes. She was his task; the winning of her, his mission. Yet why this was so she could not fathom.

The weapons of his battle she was coming to understand. He wanted her body, soft and willing beneath his. He wanted her heart clasped firmly in his hand. He wanted her as wife; in all ways, as wife. He was wooing her to win her, to have her, a fit wife for any man. For him. For now.

It would not be so. He would fail. She was unfit to be any man's wife, even Hugh of Jerusalem's. Even for now. She would not lose herself to that temptation, not even for Hugh.

She would convince him she was unfit. She had the time to do so; God had given her the time.

Even as she thought the words, she could feel the seep of blood at the edges of her padding. Her blood called more urgently than prayer, called her away from Hugh and his smiles. God be praised for even this small mercy.

"I must away," she said. "I have an urgent task of my own."

"I will come—" he said.

"You must keep your divine appointment, my lord, and your promise to Denise. I have no need of you," Elsbeth said with a smile.

"Ah, Elsbeth, you have great need of me," he said. " 'Tis only that you do not yet know it."

"Come, come, I am as sodden as any cloak!" Denise squealed, her hands over her head as the rain began to pelt down in long strips of silver.

With a final grin, Hugh turned toward the chapel, away from Elsbeth, releasing her from the grip of his smile. Elsbeth turned and ran gently toward the tower stair, lifting her skirts in her hands. When she reached the stair, she turned back toward the chapel. Hugh was outlined there, Denise at his side. He grinned and raised a hand in farewell and then turned into the chapel.

It was with some dismay that she found herself standing in the rain until she could no longer see him.

"I did not think to see you today," she said.

"My time is not my own," he answered. "I come when I can. I look only for you."

"How can I know that?"

"You must take me at my word. My word is sound and true. You need only trust."

"Trust? A woman is a fool to trust a man."

"Where did you learn that doctrine?" he asked, smiling. "It is not sound."

"I learned it here, in Warkham. And I find it most sound doctrine."

Raymond walked to the well and helped Jovetta with the water. She smiled up at him and then tossed back a thick strand of her hair. It was brown, darkening to black in the rain. He had not remembered the color of her hair. He had only remembered her smile and the bright shine of her eyes.

"Our doctrine differs. In Jerusalem, a maid trusts a man, if he be honorable."

"If he be honorable," Jovetta said, carrying the water to the kitchen. "The same is true here. Are you honorable, Raymond?"

"If you have to ask, then my cause is lost with you before it is begun," Raymond answered. He was safe in his answer. Jovetta wanted too much to play at love. She would not abandon him so quick as that.

"Aye," she said, looking up at him, her gaze direct. A challenge. "It is."

And with a smile, she left him in the rain. Raymond stood in the mud looking after her. This was not how the game was played. This had most assuredly never happened to Lord Hugh.

"Wait," he said, running after her. Jovetta had reached

the kitchen door when he caught up to her. She stood on the threshold, out of the rain, forcing him to remain drenched by it. "How that you discard me with such an easy nonchalance, Jovetta? I had thought—"

"You had thought to play at love with me, Raymond. I am no girl," Jovetta said. "I do not play at love. None at Warkham play at love."

" 'Tis a fine art and a better entertainment," Raymond said. "There is much courtesy in such gaming. I could teach you—"

"I have been taught the games a man can play by other men, in other times," she said, her voice brittle and cold, as cold and sharp as pelting rain. "I play no more games. If you want me, say so."

"I want you," Raymond said, stunned by the look in her eyes. Her eyes, now that he looked, were blue. Blue like a stormy sea, dark and restless.

"I know," she said and turned, going into the kitchen, leaving him in the rain.

Chapter Fifteen

The meal was done, the prayers of Vespers said, Denise tucked away on a pallet in the solar, the candles flickering wildly in the gusts of wet wind that came through the wind holes when Hugh looked at Elsbeth across the chessboard.

"It is time to bed," he said.

His eyes glowed green, hotter and more intense than the hottest fire; his hair was a gleaming helmet of golden waves, like ripples in golden sand. She did not want to go to bed with him. Rather, she did want to go to bed with him, but she should not want to. Chess was a more palatable way to spend an evening with Hugh of Jerusalem, and she hated chess.

"Should you not pray? It still rains," she said, staring down at the board. She could not think whether she should move her queen or her pawn.

"I have prayed. If God decides in His wisdom to send rain, I will not oppose Him. My boots are ruined anyway."

"You are weary of praying. Let me take that mantle from you. I will pray away the night. If God wills it, you will rise to sunshine and white clouds." Let him think that it was all she wanted, prayer and more prayer. It was a better way to spend her life than trembling for a man.

Hugh laughed and lifted her chin with his hand. "You will not pray away the night, little wife. You will spend the night with me. I am more than certain God wills that."

"I know God's will for me better than you. What has He revealed to you that He has not revealed to me?"

"Only that a wife's place is within her husband's embrace," he said softly.

"I still bleed, my lord," she said, tossing back her hair, freeing herself from his touch.

"I am still a husband, my lady," he said. "I have needs."

"I am not fit to meet those needs." She never would be. He had to see the truth of that.

Hugh laughed. One of the dogs came over to sniff him in curiosity. Hugh petted the dog's head and then sent him off with a careless wave. He probably would do much the same with her. His curiosity was up; he would touch her, come to know her, and then wave her off when his interest had cooled. Even the dog looked morose at having been sent away from Hugh. Would she fare better?

"Oh, you are, little wife. I shall teach you all manner of ways to meet my needs."

One of the men-at-arms snorted into his ale. Was it not just like a man to embarrass her so?

Elsbeth lowered her head. "This conversation is not prudent."

"Nay, it is not," he agreed, standing. "What is prudent is for us to leave this company and make for our chamber."

She stood reluctantly, her gaze going again to the man who had snorted in laughter at her. Her father was at his place at the high table, holding his goblet in both hands, staring down at her and her husband. His gaze was intent. He had lost a wife in the first hours of the day, yet she did not think he looked sunken in grief. Nay, he looked to be plotting. She knew him well; he was most definitely plotting. She wanted to be very far from her father when he was in such a mind. She wanted to be equally far from Hugh when he was determined to act a husband.

"I am most tired. I was up with Emma last night, and this has been a day of grief," she said, reaching for an escape.

"I know you are tired, little one," he said, wrapping an arm about her waist. "I will not press you."

"That is well, my lord," she said in obvious relief.

"At least, not too hard and not too long," he finished.

Two men-at-arms laughed, one burying his face in his folded arms. Prayer in the quiet sanctity of the chapel was infinitely better than this public humiliation. Did he think to shame her into compliance?

"Hugh!" her father said. "A word?"

It was an escape of sorts, even if it did come from Gautier. She was too determined to fly to be choosy. God could use even Gautier, she supposed.

"I shall be about the hall," she said, slipping away as Hugh looked at Gautier.

"I shall find you," Hugh said.

Well, he would certainly try, of that she was certain.

Hugh walked up to Gautier as Elsbeth slipped out of the hall. Gautier looked terrible, tired and disheartened. He had lost a wife and child that day, and Hugh supposed he looked just the way a man should look in such a circumstance. Gautier offered him a cup and the wine, which Hugh accepted.

"You are still in pursuit of her," Gautier said.

"I am," Hugh said.

"How goes the chase?"

Hugh shrugged. "I have no complaints. Elsbeth is a beautiful woman. Any man would be glad of her."

"When you get a child of her, then you will have reason to be glad," Gautier said, taking a swallow of wine.

"This has been a black day for you. My grief does not match yours, but Emma was a fine woman. I grieve her death, and that of your babe."

"Emma was as all women, neither better nor worse," Gautier said.

"Then you have been blessed with fine wives in your life, Gautier," Hugh said, choosing the higher path in this conversation. "Tell me, what was Elsbeth's mother like?"

Gautier looked off into the middle distance at the smoke that hovered in the firelit hall.

"Ardeth. She was brown-haired and clear-skinned," he said, "and came with rich Sunnandune in her hands. A good match for me and a good mother, though she gave Elsbeth some odd notions. She birthed ten children, mayhap eleven, before she died. A woman of passion, once I had taught her to taste of it. That is what I remember of her."

A short list for the woman he had taken to his bed and into his lineage. Still, such was the list for many a woman. Daughter, dowry, wife, mother, death; what else was there for a woman?

He knew. There was one thing more. The bride of Christ. A woman could marry herself to God and never know the joy of motherhood. Or the pain. And death.

Of course. He understood why Elsbeth wanted him to find her unfit, why she wanted a life without the knowledge of a man's touch and a man's possession. She feared the pain and risk of childbirth. A worthy fear, if he could judge. Her mother had died but two years past in childbed and now Emma this very day, the same cold and bloody death. And Elsbeth there to witness both. The two women of her father's choosing had both died the same way. Would she not fear to come to the same end? Aye, Elsbeth would have cause to fear what came of the heat of the marriage bed.

"You have not taken her," Gautier said.

Hugh pulled himself away from his speculations. "Not until her blood stops."

"Take her now," Gautier whispered, his eyes glazed red with smoke and wine.

"In her blood? 'Tis not done."

"All things can be done," Gautier said, "if a man be a man. You know the battle you are in with her—I prepared you well for that—but I can see what you will not. You soften," he said on a sneer. "Your heart softens for her. You will not see it done. She will unman you if she has not already done so."

"I am not unmanned. I am a man, and the man for this," Hugh said. "In all ways and in all times."

"Are you?" Gautier asked, looking askance at Hugh. "Perhaps your squire would tell a different tale."

"I do not comprehend you," Hugh said. The man was drunk on wine or grief, he knew not which. He spoke in circles that no hawk could track.

"Do you not?" Gautier asked with a crooked grin. "Ask Elsbeth if she comprehends. I'll warrant she sees what I see and fears what I fear, knight of Jerusalem."

"What do you see?" Hugh asked, setting down his cup. "And what fear could Elsbeth have in regard to me? I have been patient. I have wooed her. I will have her, this she knows. All is as it should be."

"All is as it should be? You have not breached her. Perhaps it is not in you to do this thing. Perhaps I chose stupidly for my daughter when I chose a man from Outremer." Gautier took a sloppy drink, wine dripping down the sides of his mouth to his bearded chin.

"Our bargain was struck, and I will meet my part. I have more to lose than you, Lord Gautier, if this goes awry."

"More to lose?" Gautier said, his eyes glittering in the flickering light. "What do you lose, Lord Hugh? You have no land, no power other than what you won by my daughter's hand. You have naught to lose. You have gained all in gaining Elsbeth. No matter what befalls, Elsbeth will remain yours, and with Elsbeth, Sunnandune."

"Baldwin and Jerusalem encompass all I cherish and all I need, Lord Gautier. I lose Baldwin's trust if I fail here in my quest," Hugh said. "I would rather lose my life."

Gautier looked long at Hugh and then he laughed, a slow laugh that built to a roar of hard and bitter humor.

"You doubt me?" Hugh said, his hand on his dagger.

"Nay," Gautier said, laughing and wiping his mouth with the back of his hand. "I believe you well enough, and for that I pity my daughter. I am also sure your pretty squire believes you. I am even sure that my daughter, for all that her eyes are cast heavenward, is coming to understand where your . . . interests . . . lie."

In an instant, with Gautier's bleary eyes upon him, Hugh understood the depth and depravity of Gautier's charge.

"Of what do you accuse me?" he said. "Name it."

"Accuse you? I accuse no man. Nay, that is between you and God," Gautier said. "Have we not all sinned? Is one sin worse than another? Nay, I only wonder . . . can you meet our bargain? Will your cock rise for a woman when your pretty squire is so near? Can you breach my daughter? Can you make her yours?"

"I can. I will. And I am guilty of no—"

"Tell your confessor, not me," Gautier said, raising a hand to stop Hugh's words. "Where you find your amusements, in what dark hole, is a matter for priests. I am no priest. I am a father who has wed his daughter to a man who has yet to rip her maidenhead from her. This you must do. Unless you are afeared of the smear of a woman's blood."

"I fear nothing," Hugh said tersely. "Not even you, Lord Gautier."

"Fear me? Why should you fear me?" Gautier said, shrugging and drinking again of his wine. "Are we not allies in this campaign? Do we not all gain when Elsbeth is your wife in fact and her heart and will in your keeping? All win, even Elsbeth, if you stay true to your course. Falter and we all fall."

"I will take her. I will make her mine. I will mold her will to my own and get from her what we both want," Hugh said. It was a vow. He would not fail.

"Then find her and get it done," Gautier said and then buried his nose in his goblet.

When Hugh was gone, Edward, Gautier's chief man-at-arms, left his place by the fire and came to stand at his lord's side.

"You heard what they said to each other over the chessboard?" Gautier asked, setting down his cup.

"Aye," Edward answered.

"And?"

"And he still fights for her. She is not breached, she

is too skittish still for that, yet she is entangled in him, if I can judge," Edward said.

"Any man may judge that. 'Tis writ clear," Gautier said.

Edward said nothing. He waited, his eyes scanning the hall. Jovetta was in the corner, sweeping. He caught her eye and motioned with his head. She returned his look with one of her own and then nodded her agreement. All was set. When he had done his duty by his lord, he would do his duty as a man. Perhaps they would meet in the stables; the hay would be soft with rain, as sweet as any woolen blanket.

"Give him one day more," Gautier said, ending Edward's plans for the moment. "One day to do what he has sworn to do. If he fails, kill him."

"What of his squire?"

"Kill them both. There must be no tongues sending this tale out of Warkham."

"Yet, even when he is dead, you will not have what you seek," Edward said.

Gautier looked up at him, his black eyes murky as pitch. "I will get what I seek. No matter who must fall."

Edward said no more. He swallowed hard and did not let himself think beyond the pleasures to be found with Jovetta. Tomorrow would take care of tomorrow, as it always did.

He had only to wait where she must return, like a snare set for a rabbit at its hole. There was one place to which Elsbeth must come, one place she could not avoid. Hugh awaited her there, his foot upon her bucket of bloody linen floating in stained water, his mind leagues away with Baldwin in Jerusalem. Away from the foul stain of Gautier and his smirking accusations. Silent accusations that his daughter might share. Was this why Elsbeth ran from every beat of desire he roused in her? Did he disgust her for the sin she thought she saw in him, or was it only that she feared the trial of childbearing? Was ever any woman such a maze as Elsbeth of Sunnandune?

No matter. He had to take her, no matter her fears or her disgust. He would prove to them both that the tales they'd heard of the Poulains were false.

Raymond came to him quietly, ducking his fair head into the room, his glance expectant.

"What?" he asked in gruff preoccupation.

"My lord, there is something about Warkham, about the maids of this place," Raymond said.

"Do not talk to me of the maids of this place. I have a wife who is still a maid. I cannot think of aught else tonight. Leave me, Raymond, until the morrow. I am not fit to talk of anything now."

"Aye, my lord, it is only that—"

Hugh shook his head and waved him out.

They thought him guilty of sodomy.

Hugh grunted and ran a hand through his hair. Let Gautier think what he would, he would breach Elsbeth, finding his way inside her, turning her will to his, branding her with passion, ruling her heart. Let them think what they would; he knew what was said of the knights of the Levant. They were soft, unused to war, unused to women unless they be behind thick walls and many veils—such were the tales. No tale could have been more false.

No wars? The Holy Land of Christ was ripped by wars, ceaseless wars, with enemies on all sides, allies changing sides, men changing alliances. He had breathed war from his infancy; he was bred on war. He had no fear of war. These Northern lords in their squalid mounds of mossy rock knew only raids and threats; he knew war against the very army of the devil himself.

No women? Nay, he knew women. Women as soft as cashmere with voices like gently ringing bells had surrounded him all his life. Women who had the world and its treasures in the next street or on the next caravan. Women who understood that men ruled the world and that women were the feast upon which the conquerors feasted.

Elsbeth knew none of that. She had a will that did not bend to his and a heart set upon God when it should be set upon her husband. Elsbeth was not a woman as he knew women to be.

Yet he liked her. His task would have been easier if she had remained only a woman instead of a person who had managed to claim his regard and his respect. He had not expected that of her or of himself.

What was it about her that caught at his heart? It was more than her refusal to fall into the temptation he laid out before her. It was more than her beauty, more than her reluctant smiles, more than the sharp, sweet edge of her tongue. Nay, it was all of that and yet still more. She was like no woman he had ever known. She was a maze, and though he felt himself growing lost in her, still he could not turn from her. Such fascination was dangerous because it did not serve Baldwin. His very life was given over to serving Baldwin. Elsbeth must not stand in the way of that service. He could not and would not fall into that temptation.

Hugh shifted his weight and went to stand at the wind hole. The night was full upon the earth, stealing all color and form until only the black weight of darkness lived on. Elsbeth was like the night. She encompassed all, consumed all, her dark beauty a weight that pressed against his plan and his duty. But even the night must pass, giving way to the sun. Jerusalem was the sun, the light of the world, the home of God's Son; all must be sacrificed to the light. Even the soft beauty of the encompassing dark.

Even Elsbeth, who had a mind of her own and a heart and a will she guarded against all but God Himself. Els-

beth could not stand between his love for Baldwin and
his duty to Jerusalem. He would not hurt her, but he
could not spare her.

He heard her foot upon the stair, light and firm and
quick. She had need of her bucket and clean linen. She
had no need of him, or so it was now. He would teach
her to want him, to want his will, to give herself into his
desires and plans, her will submitted wholly to his. He
had begun it well, and tonight he would continue her
lessons in need, blood or no.

She opened the door and stopped when she saw him,
her dark eyes going wide and wary. And then she was
calm and composed, putting on the face she wore for
the world. But not for him. Not any longer.

"My lord," she said on a sigh of air. "I did not expect
you."

Hugh laughed softly. "I am certain you did not or you
would not have rushed so quickly here, would you, my
wife? 'Tis the bucket which calls to you, stronger than a
husband, more urgent than desire."

"I desire to use the bucket. I need to cleanse myself,"
she said, shutting the door behind her. It closed with a
thud that echoed softly around the stone walls of the
chamber. It was a sound of portent and of purpose; even
Elsbeth seemed to sense it.

"But you have no desire for me," he said lightly, leaning against the far wall, studying her.

What did she think? That he had practiced sodomy
and would have no inclination for her? What did she
think about anything? All he knew of her was that she
yearned for a life of prayer sequestered from the de-
mands of men, and that she had no great love for her
father. Perhaps the two were bound more fully than he
had yet considered.

Was it her father she longed to escape by hiding herself away in the convent? Gautier was a hard man, and

Elsbeth must have battered herself against the stone of him for year upon year. It was certain that her father knew her well, having given him the battle plan to win his way with her. Gautier had not guided him amiss; Elsbeth was all he had predicted and more. Very much more.

"I do not know what you mean," she said, stepping into the room, her hands inching toward the apex of her thighs, "and I do not have the leisure to ferret it out. I have need of the bucket and require privacy. Please, leave."

"Oh, but I will not leave, though I am more than eager to give you what you need. All that you need, my little wife," he said, straightening from his slouch and taking a step toward her. She watched him, unmoving, refusing retreat. She was a brave little thing, most valorous considering his present mood. "Use the bucket and the linen, I will only aid you. But privacy? That you shall not have. Not again. Not from me."

Her gaze was wary and shuttered as she said, "My lord, I do not comprehend you. This is no insult to you. I merely ask for what all women in their monthly time must ask. I cannot do otherwise."

"Can you not?" he said, smiling. "I think you can. I think you can lift your skirts and crouch down upon your heels and unwind your binding linen from your waist and from between your legs. I even think that I can help you, which is all I want, Elsbeth, to help you in all your tasks." Help her? He wanted to devour her.

"Not in this," she said, her eyes huge and dark.

"Aye, even in this," he said softly, reaching out to brush his fingertips over the smooth waves of her hair.

"My lord, nay, do not," she said, her voice a whisper of entreaty and longing tied in a knot of confused desires. He was lost in the depths of her, even now when he wanted to punish her for refusing him. Even now, when she suspected him of sodomy. Even now, when she stood so alone and so resolute in the face of odds she could not best.

What an odd, precious warrior she was. What a rare dignity she held about her soul. Even now, when she insulted him with every breath and every thought, he was drawn to her.

"Can you not say my name? Even now? Even as we are alone, the darkness pressing against our heat, our bodies pulsing with longing?"

"Nay, I do not pulse with anything beyond the measure of my womanhood. My lord, I must unwrap and cleanse myself."

"Nay, you must not," he said. "I must. I will. I will perform this act of devotion and intimacy, since you deny me all other ways into you. This one I shall take. This road is open to me."

"It is not," she said, pushing his hands away from her. "This way is not open. This is perverse, my lord. I will not partake of it."

Hugh smiled and shook his head as he knelt before her. "You English. So much of the world and its people are perverse to you. Did you never think that it is you who are perverse?"

"Nay, I never did," she said, batting away his hands while pressing her left hand hard against the soft mound of her womanhood.

"Then think again, little wife. Think of what I will do to you," he said, his breath brushing against her legs as he lifted her skirts with a single hand. "I am lifting your skirts, admiring your pretty legs, watching the blood flow in a thin and lively stream down your left leg. Your blood is very red, Elsbeth. Tell me—I have wondered—does it hurt a woman to bleed so much and so often?"

"It only hurts when I am made to talk of it," she said, turning her back on him, twisting her heavy skirts upon herself in a woolen trap, straining to reach the bucket and her clean linen.

Hugh laughed. "Then I will not hurt you. Keep your secrets, woman, and I will keep mine."

Aye, he had secrets, she thought, secrets that he shared with Baldwin and Raymond and even Gautier, but not with her. Surely that was perverse. Perhaps it was that his secrets were perverse. She could not but think it. He smiled and laughed and charmed, but told her nothing of himself. She knew as little of him as she had at the moment of their bonding. He played this game as all men played it, holding every weapon and asking a woman to trust in mercy. But she would not trust. She knew there was no mercy in a man, and she had taken up weapons of her own.

"Release me, my lord."

He sat on his heels, his hand clutched in her jumbled skirts, smiling up at her.

"Only if you say my name, Elsbeth. I have a name, you know. A good name from a good family."

She could feel her blood sliding into her shoe; it was the moment when her composure broke. Surely she was justified. Even as she felt the words tumbling into her mouth, her mind swirling in anger and frustration, she could only think that she was more than justified. He had pushed her hard and long and over nothing. She bled. She had needs. He mocked all.

"Tell me of your family and your life, my lord. I would know of this distant kin in fabled Outremer. When do you return to them? You long for Jerusalem with every breath. Tell me again of her winding streets and markets and ever shining sun. Tell me how your destiny is bound by Jerusalem's walls and Baldwin's will."

"Every man's destiny is bound by his liege lord, Elsbeth. There is little to tell beyond that," he said, dropping his hold on her skirts. They swung free and settled about her ankles. Her blood was hidden, but she could feel it still, cold and wet against her legs.

"Little to tell? I think there is much to tell," she said, her voice as cold as fractured ice.

"What of your blood?"

"My blood is mine. I will tend to it. Until I do, speak to me of your family, your holding, your life."

"You are fierce, Elsbeth," he said, standing and taking her in his arms. "What cause have I given you for fierceness? Am I not a man who has yet to find his way into his wife? Should I not be fierce?"

"Aye, you should, if you would act the man," she said stiffly, holding his gaze.

"If I would act the man?" he growled, releasing her. "I am a man and I have been none but gentle with you. Have I played false? Or have I shown you that men are other than what you have known in damp and dismal England?"

"It is not gentleness to hound me at every turn. I have needs which I must attend. How this is an insult to your manhood I cannot see."

"See to your needs or let me attend. I will tell you whate're you wish, another night. Another time. I would have us share everything."

"Except your life, or the knowledge of your life," she said.

"You make much of little," he said, handing her the clean linen and woolen padding. "There is time for talk. We have the night before us. Do what you must now."

"Will you leave me?"

"Nay, I will not, yet I will not provoke."

"A first," she said, turning from him, her back a shield as she lifted the front of her skirts.

And then she thought better of her modesty. Let him watch. He wanted this? Let him have it, then. And by watching him watch her, perhaps she could see if perversion truly dwelt in his eyes. It was a thing to know about a husband, if he carried the stain of sexual perversion on him. It was a thing to see, if one was not afraid of seeing.

She turned back to him, the fire between them a timid flicker of flame and smoke. Hugh raised his brows in surprise, but said nothing. It was wise he did not, but she had never thought him a fool.

Elsbeth lifted her skirts about her waist, clutching the heavy fabric in both hands. Her private parts were wrapped in linen stained bright red with her blood. A trail of blood ran down her legs to her feet, a thin trail but it marked her well. She bled still. Let him see it. There was no way into her, not now. Let him see and understand that truth.

He could not touch her.

Not with his hands. Only with his eyes. 'Twas more than she wanted, but she could endure it.

He did not know how much more he could endure with his smile still sitting easy on his face. In his heart, he did not smile. Nay, for she was not a woman to smile upon. Not Elsbeth. She was a woman to make a man pant with longing, to make his heart pound. She was a woman to take and hold, her very breath captive to his.

Her legs were slender and pale in the smoky light of a room lit only by fire. Her bandage hid her dark, wet curls, twisted with her blood. He wanted her blood, wanted to see the mark of her maidenhood on her thighs and on his. Wanted to rip past her composure and her pride and her questions, leaving all behind in the hot silence of passion spent and subdued.

He wanted her.

Her dark eyes met his, challenging him, mocking him. It was her blood which mocked him. That blood barrier

251

that stood between them, holding her away from his hand and his control.

He wanted to control her. He had never wanted that with a woman before. But then, she was unlike the women of his land. She was bolder and harder, her mettle fired by forces he could not see and little understood. Her life in this cold, damp land had been clutched from the mists of rain and snow, starvation and death.

It was tenacity, that was what he sensed in her, pure and undiluted tenacity. She clung to her dignity and her independence the way other women clung to husbands or fathers. She clung not to her father. She refused to cling to her husband.

That would change.

She stared into his eyes as she unwound the strip of white linen from her waist, holding her skirts high with her left hand. It was awkwardly done. He was acutely aroused by the sight.

Slowly she was revealed to him, her belly and her woman's hair, dark and wet as he had known it would be. She dropped the sodden fabric into the water-filled bucket, grabbing up the end of the soiled linen, damp now, to scrub her legs and private parts. She did not lower her eyes. She did not blush or smile or twitch. Nay, she watched him watch her, daring him to look away. Daring him to touch her with her blood still shining upon her skin.

It was a dare he would take.

He walked to where she stood by the bucket just as a cold wind sliced through the wind hole into their chamber. She refused even to shiver as that chill shaft of air lifted the ends of her hair.

She looked a wanton, a warrior maid with the blood of the kill fresh upon her.

She looked as if she could kill and find no need for repentance.

In that moment, she looked more perfectly like Elsbeth than he had ever seen her. This was the woman, the prayer warrior, the stalwart and stony heart he had heard tales of. This was a woman to achieve sainthood if ever any mortal soul could. This was the woman who held his future in her bloody hands.

Her hand still held her skirts, smeared with dots of blood. He looked down into her eyes. This time, he did not smile. This was no woman to wash with smiles. Nay, he would wash her with kisses and bites and caresses until she knew no name but his. Until she spoke no name but his.

If he could have wiped the name of God from her soul in that instant, he would have.

He grabbed up the clean linen and knelt before her. With his fingers, he touched her, touched that place of blood and heat, cool now and clean, but not for long. Yet there was time enough for him to touch the soft folds of her, cupping her, feeling her shape and warmth against his palm.

Soon. Soon her blood would stop and he would thrust his way into her, bleeding her again. He wanted that. He wanted her blood on him. Even this blood. Even though it was forbidden. He wanted her. Even now.

He heard her intake of breath, felt the stiffening of her body, and made himself release her. Made himself follow the commandments of God and church. Made himself deny his want and his need for her.

He began wrapping the cloth about her hips and between her legs. Her skin was smooth and cool beneath his fingertips, the smell of blood and water strong on her. It was as perfume to him, the smell of her.

Without a word between them, he wrapped her up against his touch, keeping her blood away from them both. When he was finished, she dropped her skirts, covering herself. A wasted effort. He would not forget the look and feel of her, nay, nor the smell. Even with her blood upon her, he could smell her female scent.

"Are you content?" she asked, staring down at him as he knelt at her feet.

He looked up at her. Her black eyes flashed with . . . what? Annoyance? Victory? She had won no victory, not over him. Not over herself. He would prove that to her before the night was done.

"Nay, I am far from content," he said, rising to tower over her. She was a small woman; only the strength of her will made her formidable. "Yet I will be."

She said nothing to encourage him. She did cross her arms over her breasts. Good. He made her wary. That was good. He was sick unto madness of making her easy in his company.

"How will you be content?" she asked. Very wary. Very good.

He closed the distance between them and stood over her so that her arms brushed his chest.

"Your blood is upon you, yet it is not upon me. There are no impediments for you."

"I do not comprehend you."

"Of course you do not," he said, lifting a twisted strand of her hair and running it across his cheek. "You are a maiden. I will tell you what you will do."

She jerked away from him, pulling her hair free of his hand. He let her. There was nowhere for her to run in their small, smoky chamber. She would not escape him. "I do not like to be told what to do," she said.

Hugh laughed in spite of his determination not to. "I know that very well, Elsbeth; there are few in this life who enjoy obedience. Yet it is required of us all."

"Whom do you obey, my lord?" she said.

"I obey God and I obey my lord Baldwin," he answered readily.

"And do you find your obedience burdensome?"

"Nay. Do you think to trap me into blasphemy? How shall I answer such a question? Or do you even want me to try?"

"I do want you to try," she said, her voice suddenly small and tight.

"It will not delay what is to come," he said, his voice soft with a compassion he had no wish to feel. Her father had warned him of this, of this softness, of his loss of purpose. He could not bend to her will now.

"Do not speak of what is to come," she said. "Speak instead of your bond with Baldwin."

Hugh stared down at her, his brow furrowed in suppressed anger. "Speak of Baldwin? There is no hesitation in me to speak of Baldwin; often have I done so with you. Why this weight upon your heart concerning Baldwin? And why now?"

She looked up at him, and he could see that she trembled. Her eyes were wide with unwelcome expectation.

"If you will speak of Baldwin, will you also speak of Raymond?" she asked.

"What is this you ask?" he said, grabbing her up against him. "What dark snakes writhe in your heart, Elsbeth? What sins whisper my name?"

She stood in the face of his anger, expecting the worst and ready to face it.

"Why will you not answer?" she whispered.

"Why will you not name my sins? Tell me, of what am I accused?"

"I do not accuse you," she said softly. "I will not judge."

"You judge me even now, lady wife," he ground out. "You want me to confess to . . . what? Can you name my sins, or would you have that of me, too?"

"We all have sinned," she said. "All have fallen far short of God's glory. I do not judge you," she said again.

"Then what would you have of me if not judgment and condemnation?"

"I only want the truth. Please, tell me the truth. For once, Hugh."

Hugh considered her. The width of the chamber separated them, yet, in some strange way, he knew they had never been so intimate or so close. She wanted the truth? Which truth?

"If my answer is what you fear, will you seek to annul the marriage? 'Tis what your father thinks you will do. He has warned me of it many times," he said, watching her carefully.

How deep did her plotting and her fears run? Did her father manage her as he tried to manage him? Did she seek a way into the convent that would not rely on his goodwill? Did she seek to leave him at any price?

Had he won her heart not at all?

"Did he?" she asked, her eyes hard as granite. "My father has warned you of me, has he? Well, he does not know me as well as he would like to think."

She paused, and he could feel the workings of her mind. She had not wanted a husband; she had plotted a different path for her life. Yet she did not want to bend to her father's will; that way of escape carried too high a price. Or so he gambled.

He had not yearned for a wife, at least not the sort of wife a man could find in the Levant. But Elsbeth? He could yearn for her. She was a woman unlike any other.

"Speak true, Elsbeth," he said. "Let us have this settled between us."

"Speak true? I ever speak true. I will not seek an annulment," she said.

"No matter what truths pass between us this night?"

She held his eye and shook her head, her hair shivering with the motion.

"No matter what truths, my lord."

Hugh straightened and lifted his chin. He was prepared to answer her charge. She would not like his answer at all.

Chapter Sixteen

"Baldwin is my friend and my king. I love him. My heart is bound to his will and his fortune, as his is bound to the future and sanctity of Jerusalem. Our goals are one."

It was as she had feared.

Hugh continued, "Raymond is my squire, the son of my uncle's wife. I have known him long and cherish him as family. He and I share a trust that goes deep, our minds and hearts focused on the same goal: the preservation of Jerusalem."

Yea, they were close, she could see that. All could see who had eyes for such a thing. Sin did not hide well from eyes seeking the truth.

"I have committed the sin of sodomy with neither Baldwin nor Raymond. I have never committed sodomy, Elsbeth," he said. "I am no soft man from Outremer, a Levantine who seeks soft pillows of silk and whose best sword hangs from the center of his hips. I have not sinned, not in this way of man to man. I am a knight for Christ, my thoughts and will and strength given to God and king. I am not the man you thought me. I am not the man your father thought me."

Elsbeth's head jerked up. "My father? Where does he fall in this?"

"I have answered your questions, Elsbeth. Is it not time you answered mine?"

"What part in this has my father played?" she said again, her efforts at composure falling away from her like leaves in an autumn gale.

"The same part any father plays in the betrothal and marriage of his daughter. He only seeks to protect you, as any father would," he said, his anger fading. "What fears haunt you, Elsbeth? What is the source of this suspicion?" he said, coming near to her, his hand out.

He touched her and she kept herself from flinching, holding very still, breathing very slowly. Had her father said anything to make her think so ill of Hugh? She could not remember. It would be like him if he had. He loved nothing better than stirring up discord.

"Did he accuse you of sodomy?" Elsbeth asked. "Did my father lay this charge upon you?"

"The only charge your father laid upon me was the proper husbanding of his daughter," Hugh answered, an answer which could be interpreted in many ways.

Her father. Would he care if she was properly husbanded? Nay, he cared only that she be a proper wife.

And if Hugh now lied to her and he was guilty of sodomy, there was nothing she could do. She had promised him that she would not seek an annulment, and she would abide by that vow. Her father had sparked this confrontation somehow; she could feel his hand in it, and she would not play in any game he started. It was her father who could not be trusted. It would have been just like him to whisper some remark that set her mind on sodomy. She wanted to find a way out of this marriage, but she would do it without acting as her father's pawn in a game against her husband.

"I ask you to forgive me, my lord, for my suspicions," she said. "I did not understand the depth of your devotion to your king. I understand now."

Hugh instantly frowned and studied her. She wondered what she had said wrong. Had she managed to misspeak her apology?

"What is it you understand?" he asked.

"I understand that you have a bond with your king that I do not have with mine," she said, striving for a lighter mood. If she could get him to speak of Baldwin and Jerusalem, he would forget her entirely and she would be safe from his attentions. For now. "I have never met Henry."

"I have," Hugh said, smiling with her. "A most able king, is he not?"

"He must be. Those who know him, speak well of him. More of Henry I cannot say," she said.

"You are prudent in your praise," Hugh said.

"Better if I were prudent in my condemnations," she said wryly. "Will you forgive me, my lord? I know little of the world."

"You know enough," Hugh said.

"I think not," she said, smiling.

"Enough for me," he answered, "yet not enough of me. I do not know why you would think such of me, Elsbeth. I have given you no cause. Yet mayhap I have. I am a husband who knows not his wife in the very way that God commands I should know you. And you do not know me. There is the sin I carry, Elsbeth. We must become one flesh, as God commands. We must not deny each other the fullness of desire and satisfaction. That is our sin. Come, Elsbeth, learn the man who has taken you for his own."

"What must I learn that I have not yet done?" she asked, pulling away from him, keeping just far enough off so that he could not touch her. He turned their physical union into a matter of obedience and divine directive; she had no ready answer, no counterassault which would aid her.

"Learn *me*," he whispered.

"My lord?"

"Learn my name, for a start," he said with a smile.

"I know your name."

"Then say it. Say it, Elsbeth. Touch me with even that intimacy and I will be charmed."

"I do not seek to charm you," she said.

"Say it," he said. "No more games between us, no more tests, or sparring, or distrust. Let us begin anew. Let us start with my name."

Yet was this not a new game? This smiling intimacy, this cordial conversation, this easy forgiveness; he wielded all in order to win her body and her will, that she knew. He labored on and on for the thing she would not give him—herself—and still he smiled and charmed and wooed.

A man would always want most what he could not reach.

She considered him. He stood before her, his strength and size an easy weapon, yet he stood weaponless. Or so he wanted her to believe. And so she could believe, for a man's strength was only a weapon against a woman if he chose it to be so. In other places, with other men, in other times, a man's strength was a woman's greatest protection. But not for her. Not in this time. Not in this place.

He asked for his name. She could give him that. She lost nothing in giving him that.

"Hugh," she said. It sounded like a sigh of longing on her lips when it was no such thing. She had had good cause not to call him by name when his name sounded so seductive on her lips.

"I thank you," he said softly.

She smiled and ducked her head against the look in his eyes. Such tenderness she seldom saw. It did not help her now to see it. She had no ready weapons to defeat tenderness.

"What else must I learn?" she asked.

"Are you eager, then, for lessons?" he said, grinning comically.

She knew he played with her, yet the game had snagged her and she could not turn from it or him. He was a rare man to so work a woman to his will.

"I was only curious."

"Then your curiosity shall be sated. As shall I. As shall you," he said, his smile fading like a dwindling fire extinguished by a cold wind.

"Sated?" she said, taking a step away from him. It was not a word she liked.

"Sated, yet do not fear," he said. " 'Tis only another lesson. There is nothing in this chamber to harm you."

He was wrong. He was in the chamber. He could harm her, hurt her, tear holes in her that God Himself could not unmake.

"What is the lesson?" she asked.

"Learn the color of my skin," he said.

"My lord?"

"My lady?" he mocked.

"Your skin is white. There. The lesson is learned."

"Is it? White, you say? White like milk? White like soft churned butter? White like bleached linen? White like—"

"White like the sand at low tide," she said almost against her will.

"Ah, and yours is the golden white of flour as it rises in the heat of the day. Hot white, that is what you are, and yet I know that your skin is not hot, but only warm and smooth like butter or cream or—"

"I understand you," she interrupted.

"Do you?" he said, and his voice was low and hoarse, his look intense.

"Aye, my lord. I put you in mind of food."

Hugh laughed, and she smiled with him. "You have said it better than you know. When I am with you, Elsbeth, I am ever hungry and you are the banquet on which I long to feed."

Nay, that was not good. Such words were all against her purpose. She would be no man's meal nor sate any man's appetites.

"Warkham's larder is full, my lord. Sate your appetites there."

Hugh took a step toward her, his humor flown, all playing behind them. "Do not even hope for such an escape, little wife. All my desires shall be met in you."

"That is not possible, my lord. My blood——"

"Your blood will not stop me, Elsbeth. It is time for us to fulfill the vows we took before God. I must make you mine. I must find a way into you."

"There is no way into me," she said coldly.

"Ah, you speak your wish, but you do not speak what is true. I can find my way into you. And I can even tell you how to satisfy me. Your blood is no barrier to that."

Images filled her head, shadowy and disjointed. Dreams of terror from the darkest of nights closed about her like an instrument of torment. Panic filled her throat like thick smoke, and her chest closed against the invasion of his words. She could not breathe and began to cough against the pressure on her throat. She could not seem to get any air into her otherwise.

"My lord, I am not well."

"You are well enough," he said.

"I cannot get my breath."

"Then take mine," he said as he took her in his arms and kissed her. She began to choke into his mouth, turning her head from him, frantic for air and space. He released her with a frown, studying her in the dim light.

"Your pardon. I cannot——" she said.

"You can," he said. "You are bound by fear. Needless fear. I will not harm you. I only want to——"

"To what? To take my body? To use me to meet your desires? To sate yourself on me?" she asked, her panic still fresh and new upon her.

She threw at him the most vile charges she could. The taste of the words was bitter on her tongue as she accused him of what she knew he was guilty of. This was wrong, all out of joint. She did not want him. He could not make her want him. He could not make her have him.

"Elsbeth, there is nothing amiss in those words. I am your husband. You are my wife. It is as God designed. We are to meet each other's needs, sate each other's desires. This was the vow we took before God, and, before God, we shall accomplish it."

"I cannot," she said. "It is not in me to do this thing. Can you not see that? I am not fit for this life. I cannot do this!"

"You can. I will see that all is done by God's holy will."

Her anger rose up at his arrogance. He would not use God against her. "He is my God as well as yours, and He has set before you a blood barrier that it is forbidden to cross. You must wait. You know this is so. To do otherwise is to sin. Would you force me to that? Would you?"

She could feel tears itching behind her eyes and had no thought as to why such an entreaty should make her cry. She spoke only the truth. There was no need for tears. Hugh was a godly knight; he would not plunge them into sin. She could trust God for that. Could she not?

The tears escaped from behind her eyes and slid down her face. She wiped them away, signs of her weakness, and faced the man who had taken her life into his keeping.

"I must have you, Elsbeth," he said.

"At any cost? For any price?" she said, swallowing hard against her tears.

She had heard the echo of those words before and she had cried then, too. Yet she could not remember more; all was lost in mist and shadow. Happily lost in the darkest corners of forgotten memory. She turned from those shadows.

He considered her, his eyes soft and shimmering

green in the shadowy darkness of the chamber. He was as bright as a beacon on a stormy night, shining gold and warm in a cold, dark world. Yet in darkness was safety; she did not need the light he cast upon her. She needed him not at all.

With a low voice, rough in its intensity, he answered her. "Aye. At any cost."

"Nay! You must not sin! You must not cast me into sin!"

Had she said those words before, in some long-ago time? She did not know, but they rang within her, stirring old fears and dark terrors.

"I must take you, Elsbeth. You must be mine in truth, your body pierced by mine; even if your blood covers me, I must have you. Let us do what penance we must for this tomorrow. For now, I must have you."

"For now, you must," she said, rubbing away her offending and demeaning tears. "Aye, for now. What a man wants, he must have, even if it be only for now. But what of tomorrow? What of me?"

"What of you?" he asked as he lifted off his tunic, revealing the width of his chest and the muscled length of his arms. "You are my wife."

"For now," she said sharply. "That can change if you only release me, Hugh. I do not want to be a wife."

"I will not release you," he said on a soft growl.

He stood before her in his braes, the firelight turning his skin and hair to molten gold. She did not care how he looked. She could not let him touch her. He must never do that. She had other plans for her life, a life untouched by any man, even a golden husband.

"You married me and gave me no thought; my plans for myself are nothing to you. Am I supposed to let you ride me hard, taking your pleasure at your will and whim? What of my needs? What of me?"

"You are my wife," he said, stripping off his braes in

one smooth motion. "That is who you are and who you will remain. All else is in God's hands. All else is for tomorrow. Now you are mine. I will not give you up, not even to your dreams."

"I am my own," she said, staring into his eyes, refusing to look at his nakedness and the power of his form. "For now and for always, I am my own," she said, her voice ending on a crack of humiliating emotion.

"God says you are not. Will you fight Him, Elsbeth? Will you question His will, for has He not brought us together in the divine perfection of His will? Is He not working out His plan for your life? Will you doubt the very omnipotence and omniscience of God?"

"You will not turn this carnality into theology," she shouted. "You will not turn the achieving of your will into divine obedience and the seeking of my will into abject sin. You will not rob me of my faith and my devotion by a twisting of words. Lucifer did the same in the Garden. I will not play Eve for you."

"How have I turned my words?" he said, his anger a pulse of raw flame. He came near her, laying his hands hard upon her arms, lifting her up on her toes to meet his eyes. "If God be God in truth, then He moves us where and when He wills. I am your man, my vow spoken before God. What trick is in that? You pledged your body and your life to me. Did you lie when you spoke that holy vow?"

"I did not lie, but you knew I did not want this. You heard me speak against it before I even knew of you."

"Yet you made your choice. I heard that as well. When did I become Lucifer in your eyes, Elsbeth? How have I deceived you?"

"You deceive me with every soft word. With every flirtation. With every look."

"How that you see my wooing as deceiving? How that you cannot see I want only to win you?"

"Win me? By your very words, I am already won. Am I not yours? Am I not bound to you until death? Will it take my death to free me?" she said, wrenching her arms free and dropping hard upon her heels.

He took a heavy breath and ran a hand through his hair. She did not look at his hair. She looked at his manhood, pulsing in her direction, seeming to seek her out. She backed up a step.

"Elsbeth," he said softly, letting his anger run out of him like wine from a pitcher. "Elsbeth, I understand your fears. I can do—"

"What do you think you know of me? I fear nothing, nothing you can name," she said harshly.

"Aye, wife, I know what you fear."

"You hardly know me," she said stiffly.

"Yet I do know you," he softly argued. "I cannot fight God for you. If He will have you, then you must go to Him. Yet is it not mercy to fly to the Father of us all? Eternity awaits. Paradise. 'Tis no thing to fear."

Elsbeth looked at him, her mouth agape, and then she began to laugh. A small and quiet laugh it was, barely heard, mostly a sharp exhalation of breath. He spoke the truth, in part, and it would serve her well. She did not want him in her and she had no yearning for motherhood; too often it was the path to death, and she had no wish to die. If he thought fear lay behind her determination not to be a wife, then it would serve. He might release her, if his heart could be softened to it.

He stared at her, his member shrinking at her laughter. She laughed the harder, watching him go soft and small. She could not remember such joy as watching the look of bewilderment grow on his face. 'Twas easily the sweetest moment of her marriage.

"You are full of wise counsel, are you not, my lord?" she said when she could speak again.

"Your laughter is unseemly. I only sought to comfort you," he said stiffly.

"My laughter is unseemly? Odd to hear you say that when you have been trying to win a smile from me since the moment of our meeting. I would think you would be much pleased that you have been the cause for such merriment in me."

"Elsbeth," he said with barely concealed anger.

"Oh, be not angry, my lord," she said. "I understand you well enough. You wanted me to laugh *with* you, not at you."

He pulled himself up to his full height, towering over the entire chamber. Even the fire seemed smaller and more subdued when faced with the specter of Hugh of Jerusalem in the full force of his anger.

"If you think that by pricking my anger, you will escape being pricked my me, you have no knowledge of me."

She laughed on a sharp note. "Oh, I know enough to know that when a man's prick rises, he can do naught else but follow."

Hugh raised his brows in surprise at her choice of words. She had some small measure of joy in shocking him.

"If you want our coupling to be tainted by anger and hard words, keep on, little wife. No matter what you say, I will pierce you, be it in smiles or frowns."

"Or beating fists?"

"I would not beat you."

"But I may beat you," she said. "Could you fault me? I am only trying to save my life, according to your wisdom."

Hugh took a calming breath and turned to walk back to the fire. He had a fine form even from the rear, his muscles marching in precision from his legs to his buttocks and up to his very shoulders. He had led a harder life in Outremer than she had supposed, to be so well hewn.

His face to the fire, he said, "I want only to help you, yet I find I cannot do what needs to be done to ease your fears. It is all in God's hands and none of mine." He turned to face her, his green eyes intense. "But, Elsbeth, if I had it in my power, I would take this fear from you onto myself."

"Would you?" she said, unwillingly moved by his obvious sincerity.

"Yea, little wife, I would," he said.

"Well, that is something," she said. "It is not enough, but it is something."

"Not enough?" he said, rubbed raw by her refusal to be comforted.

"Nay," she said, sitting on the stool near the fire and shaking her head softly, suddenly exhausted. "It is not enough. You have not the words to soothe me. I am beyond such comforting, my lord. It is no mark against you. I am simply beyond your reach."

"Elsbeth," he said, crouching down before her, taking her hands in his, "you must trust God with your life. What else can a man do?"

"What else can a man do?" she repeated softly. "A man can fight and die fighting. But what is left for a woman to do? A woman can die on her back and bleed out her life without a weapon to aid her, death coming for her by inches."

"To die is to die, little wife. What matters the weapon in your hand when death comes for you?"

"What matters? It matters much to me. Tell me, my lord, is your mother alive?"

"Nay," he said reluctantly.

"And how did she die?"

"What matters—"

"How?"

"In childbed," he said. "But she had borne six children before her time."

"So, six children and her life is spent, and it was worth the spending because she left six behind her? Do you tell me that you have five brethren?"

"Nay, only two," he said. "Two sisters are still living."

"Hmmm," she said, nodding. "Would you give them up in childbed as willingly as you have given your mother?"

"I did not give her willingly! 'Twas God's will. I sin if I do fight against it! Would you encourage me in sin, prayer warrior?"

"Nay," she said, "I would not. Yet I would not so easily give my life for the brief pleasures of the marriage bed. Can you understand that, my lord? I do not want to die on my back, my body wet with my sweat and my blood and my urine." It was a truth. She did not want to die in such a way.

"It is how all men die, Elsbeth. There is no escape from it."

"But to fight, to have the chance to fight, that is something." And it was. He could act, taking a hand in his own fortune and future. What could she do but pray and hide? He would take even that sanctuary from her with a careless smile if she let him. She would not. Her life was worth more than a smile and a kiss from Hugh.

"You put too much weight on a mere possibility," he said, rising to his feet. She ducked her head to keep from staring at his manhood, which was predictably on the rise. His compassion was easily measurable by the hardness of his cock.

"Do I? I think it is very easy for you, my lord, who will face his death with his sword in his hand."

"I do not know the manner of my death. That knowledge is beyond us all."

"So it is," she conceded. "Yet many upon many women

die giving birth or in the fevers that come after; I would not be of their number." All she saw in that moment was the bleeding out of her mother's life. Ardeth had not wanted to die. Ardeth had not wanted to leave her children defenseless in a cold, dark world.

And Elsbeth would not bear a child that would be left alone when she died. Better to have no child at all. Had not Ardeth felt the same?

"It is not for you to decide," he said. "It will not be decided tonight."

"Why may it not?" she said. "Can we not lay this thing out between us now, giving peace to our tomorrows?"

"Only one thing will happen to you tonight, Elsbeth," he said, his voice as rough as sand. "Only one thing should occupy you."

"I know," she said, raising her head to look into his eyes. "I know the one thing that you would name. 'Tis the one thing that any man would name when faced with a woman, his prick rising hard and hot."

"By Saint Lawrence, you are grown coarse in your speech, Elsbeth," he said, lifting her to her feet, the stool tumbling noisily behind her. "Is this the speech of the cloister?"

"Am I in the cloister?" she retorted, pulling her arms from his hands. "What would you have of me, my lord? The maiden bound for the cloister, her heart in God's keeping? Or the wife, her legs spread to meet the lusty thrusts of her earthly lord? I cannot be both."

"Nay, you cannot be both. We both know what you are and what you will remain. You are my wife. That is who you are, and I will find my way into you—"

"Past my blood," she interrupted.

"Aye, past all barriers you set before me. I will not be stopped. I will have you, even if I do penance for a year."

"Even if I die," she said softly, looking into his eyes for a soul-shattering instant before lowering her gaze to the floor. He did not care what happened to her, not truly. Had she been tempted to believe that he might? She was a fool, and nothing she could say would keep him from seeing his will done upon her. But how that her blood, her gift from God, had not kept her safe? How that she had failed in her vow?

There were droplets of blood near the bucket, a smattering of tiny drops, fallen from her without her knowledge. Tiny bits of her, lost in the dark of well-worn wood and dust; tiny bits of her, cast free to become a part of Warkham, though none in Warkham would know whose blood had been shed in this chamber. None would know what had befallen or to whom. None would care even if they knew.

Only God would know. God knew even now in what place and circumstance she found herself. God had given her the miracle of blood to save her. But Hugh was determined that she not be saved, and what could God do when man decided to rebel against God's law and will?

Nothing. God did nothing. He only watched from the safety of heaven. It was left to man to dwell in the dust and the blood of earth.

She looked up and faced Hugh. He looked sad somehow. Perhaps it was true that he did not seek to harm her. Perhaps it was true that he only sought to obey divine injunction. Perhaps. What was certainly true was that his blood was up, his member hard, and his mind on carnal thoughts. There was certainly no escape from that, not for a woman. Never for a wife.

Yet perhaps there was an escape. He might think he knew her, but she knew something of him now, too.

Elsbeth smiled slightly and began unlacing her bliaut. "Very well, my lord. If it is my death you seek, take me and have it. I give myself to you, my life in your keeping. My blood on your hands."

Hugh lunged at her, grabbing her hands in his, and said, "Enough, Elsbeth! No more talk of death. It will not come by my hand."

"By your cock, then," she said, tossing back her hair with a flick of her head. "Choose your own names, my lord, but women die at men's hands and from a man's touch every day, every hour."

"You will not die!" he said huskily, lifting her face with his hands.

"Will I not? Did you not just instruct me that the hour and manner of my death is in God's hands? Do you know the mind and plan of God, my lord? Have you learned so much of God by living in Outremer?"

"Elsbeth, I would never hurt you," he said, running a hand over her tumbled hair, pulling her against his chest.

He was warm, as warm as fire and equally bright. He called to her with gentle wooing, with soft looks, with golden beauty. He called to her, asking her to run to her own destruction, a bright and shining Lucifer to tempt her to fall into damnation and death. She knew what he was, and still she listened. She was tempted by him. He had achieved much simply by tempting her.

Did her mother even now watch from heaven and weep at her child's walk into destruction? Nay, for there were no tears in heaven. Ardeth would be spared that, at least. Yet who would spare her?

"You are hurting me now," she said against the golden heat of his chest. His heart pounded beneath her cheek, and she fought the impulse to nuzzle against him. He would kill her if it pleased him. Let her remember only that. "Can you not see? This is not of my will."

"Give your will to me," he said, running his hand down her back to the slope of her derriere. "I will not betray."

"I am betrayed," she said, her breath heating his chest. "Can you not see? Betrayal is all around us, like a fire, licking at our skin, burning away all thought, all resolve."

"That is not betrayal," he whispered, unlacing her bliaut even further.

"What, then?" she asked, laying her face against his chest, soaking his heat into the cold fist of her heart.

"Only wanting," he said, lifting her face for a kiss. "Only passion and need and hunger. Do not fear, little one. I will not harm you. I only . . . want you."

Ghosts of old fears, old promises, blurred with the smoke from the fire, clouding her thoughts and her vision, sharpening her memory. Like a knife slicing across old wounds, the blood of sharp memory rose up to cover his words and his presence with other words, words she heard only in the blackest of nights when God was very far away.

She pulled away from him, freeing herself from his touch.

"I do not want you to want me!" she said, holding her hands out against him. "I do not want you to touch me! I would rather give myself to God than give myself to you!"

"You are given to me, Elsbeth," he said, his eyes as hot as flame. "You are not God's any more or any less than I am. He has given you to me, and I will take every gift He bestows upon me."

"He has not given me to you! He cannot have done," she said, her eyes welling with tears she could not even think to stop. Betrayal. All was betrayal. Had it not always been so?

Of course there were no tears in heaven. All tears had been spent on earth. She would have no tears left in her when earth was cast aside.

"He *has* done," Hugh said sharply. "No more of this. I am yours throughout this life. Take the gift of me, as I gladly take the gift of you."

"I will be no man's gift! I have more worth than that.

There is more to me than that," she said, holding out her hands to keep him off. But she could no more hold the turning of the tide.

Hugh stopped and studied her and then ground his teeth and grabbed her by the wrists, shackling her. "You are of great worth, Elsbeth. None dispute it. But you are mine, and if you do not want me yet, I will teach you to want me."

"Nay, this is a thing that cannot be taught."

"All things may be taught," he said, pulling her to his chest.

He kissed her through her tears, his mouth hard and hot and heavy upon hers. He was not brutal, but he was thorough, and that was a brutality in itself. She could not breathe. Her breath was stoppered in her throat, her tears the only thing that flowed freely. His hands went to her breasts, urging some response from her, and then he took her hands and put them on his shaft, hot and long and throbbing despite her tears and her terror, throbbing with passion though she cried to be free of him.

It was then that she began to gag.

Hugh released her with a jolt and stood away from her while she bent over and tried to find a breath to ease the nausea that hovered in the center of her throat.

"I sicken you?" he asked from somewhere above her.

Elsbeth straightened and flung her hair behind her. Looking at her husband, she said the one truth that would serve.

"All men sicken me."

Chapter Seventeen

"If you are seeking deliverance from me, you shall not have it," Hugh said, his anger and his hurt of a size to fill the chamber.

"Why? Because your pride is pricked?" Elsbeth asked.

"Rather say, mauled," Hugh said, running a hasty hand through his hair and swallowing hard.

"I do not seek your mauling, my lord, I only speak the truth. If it is a truth you cannot bear, then share the burden with me. I have no liking for it. Yet it is the truth. I can bear no other burden than this."

"Oh, aye, you can bear a burden, Elsbeth—the burden of my weight pressing you down, my prick puncturing your sheath, my body demanding your maiden's blood. All this you can and will bear, for I will have you. I will have you," he said, his voice strained and harsh as it tumbled against the rough stone. "And you will have me. I will make you want me. I have it in me to make you want me."

"So says every man."

"What do you know of 'every man'? You are a virgin, are you not? You are untouched by all but me. I know this to be true."

"You know this to be true?" she said on a harsh laugh. "How do you know? Wait, I know. My father told you. He told you all you wanted to hear, all you needed to know to make this match."

"Aye, he told me of his daughter, chaste and pious, devout and pure, and he told me true, did he not? You have not known a man. I would feel it if you had."

"*You* would feel it?" she said, her eyes hot in her anger

at his pride. "How wise you are, my lord, to know so much of me. Truly, the men of Outremer are prophets most holy. Do not come near me, my lord, else you be defiled by my blood and lose your gift of prophecy. For is this not all of you and none of me? All that you would have, you will take, but what Elsbeth wants—there is no room in you for that."

Hugh acted against her very words and came at her, his nakedness a weapon he wielded very well. "There is naught in you that can defile me, wife. I will have all of you, your blood and bones and very thoughts for my own. I will turn you to my will, making you mine, taking even your fear into myself, defeating it. I will take you, and you will have me."

Elsbeth curled down into herself, her very posture defensive and wary, like a cat being poked by a stick. Like a wolf about to strike. Like a woman pushed beyond all endurance and all forbearance.

"Nay," she said, every measure of defiance in the single heavy weight of the word. "I will not."

"Aye," he said, taking her in his arms, his scent coming at her like a salty fog, sharp and clean. "Aye, I shall have you and you shall have me. We will become one flesh. There is no more escape for you, Elsbeth. No more words; we have spoken enough on this. There are no words for what I shall do to you," he whispered in erotic threat.

She heard only the threat.

"There are always words to describe defilement," she said, turning her face from his, avoiding his eyes and his mouth. "It is only that men do not want to speak them."

"This is not defilement, wife, this is fulfillment. Trust me on that. I will not harm you. I will treat you with care, even now, when you have fought against every kind word."

"Kind words you have to spare as you plow your heaving way past my blood," she said, closing her eyes and wrapping her arms about herself, hiding from his touch, though he touched her everywhere.

"As I come into you, yea," he said, stroking her hair, kissing her brow and her closed eyes and the high rise of her cheek. "I will not harm you. I will do naught but what a man may do."

"What a man may do?" she repeated on a shivery laugh. "That will be enough, will it not?"

"Enough, enough," he whispered against her mouth. "Let me only love you. Let me teach you how little there is to fear. Let me find my way to you. The first of many findings. The first of many nights."

"Always at night," she said, clenching her eyes closed tight. "Why is it always at night that men speak of love?"

"Elsbeth?" he said, lifting her head with his hands. What did she say? Something rang harsh and loud within him at her words. This was more than fear of mating or even childbirth. This fear was old and grizzled, a knot of terror and dread that opened like a hungry maw within her heart.

She kept her eyes closed and her body hard and stiff against his caresses. Yet she did not fight. For all her resistance, she did not fight. Driven by fear such as hers, she should have fought him like a snarling wolf.

"You cannot touch me through my blood. God will not allow it. God has sent this to protect me," she said. "God will protect me. God will save me."

"Elsbeth," he said in command, "look at me."

She opened her eyes and stared at the wall; the stones made a pattern of shadow and light that was lost in daylight. The pattern of the stones could be best seen at night, if any cared to look. So much to be seen in the dark, if any cared to look. But none did. None ever did.

"What has befallen you?" he asked. "What harm do you fear?"

"Have you not told me, my lord? I fear death upon my childbed. I fear to die in bed," she said and laughed, the sound high and shrill with terror and tears.

Her bliaut and pelisse slipped from her to crumple on the floor. She stood in her shift, her hair a tumble of dark waves around her shoulders, sheltering her, as if she stood alone in the world with only the curtain of her hair to shield her, warm her, protect her. How that she seemed so alone, so vulnerable? How that a woman, this woman, seemed so in want of defenses and so desperately in need of them?

Her father had not told him of this. There had been nothing of this in Gautier's description of Elsbeth. Her form, her land, her piety had been discussed. Her reluctance to marry had been admitted. Her ultimate docility and submission had been assured.

This was not willing submission. This was blank and blind terror and the inability to fight against it.

Hugh took her in his arms and urged her to the bed. He said nothing. He did not know what to say in the face of such fear.

She followed him, her body stiff and cold, but she followed him, allowing him to lay her down, to wrap the blankets around her, to wrap his arms over her, to hold her close. He listened to her breathing and her heart, his mouth against her hair, his tongue stilled at last. He knew women, knew the paths into their very hearts, but Elsbeth was a maze. He was confounded by her, lost in trying to know her, his very purpose buried in the warm depths of her. Yet he could not lose his way, forget his purpose, forget Baldwin. He must find his way into Elsbeth and, finding, find his way back out.

"Have you relented, my lord? Will you release me?" she asked, her voice soft against his throat. "I have nothing to give you. There is nothing for you here."

Nothing for him? Nay, she said it wrong. There was

something for him in this place and in this bed; there was Elsbeth, and of a sudden that was all there needed to be. In just that moment, Elsbeth was enough and all that his heart could want.

He pushed that want, that weakness, from him and Baldwin rushed back in to his proper place. There was only room for one in Hugh's heart, and Baldwin held that place with a firm grip. Elsbeth was but a shadow cast by distant cloud. She could not hold sway. Baldwin was his sun, and Hugh was from a land awash in sunlight. The clouds of England could not encompass him. He would not lose himself in mist and shadow. His vow was stronger than the woman in his arms.

He could not let her go.

"Nay, little one, I have not relented. You are mine. I will keep you."

He felt her sigh at that and bury her face against his shoulder. She rested, stilled for the moment.

"I think you should reconsider. I am not fit to be a wife. Is it not proven even now? Let me go, my lord. You do not truly want me; you only want to win this battle in which we are engaged. I will give up the battle, giving you the victory, if you will only give me up. Let me go, Hugh."

"Why should I not want you, Elsbeth?" he asked. His question floated into the darkness like mist, hovering, uncertain.

She was silent long and then whispered, "Because I am God's."

"How are you God's?" he said, holding her against him, silently urging her toward revelation.

There was some darkness in her, some black terror that shaped her soul. He could not see it. Yet. But he would. He would find the heart of her, this little wife who carried so great a fear.

"I am God's because I gave myself to Him long ago.

'He alone is my rock and my salvation; He is my fortress, I will never be shaken.' "

"It is very safe, then, to give yourself into God's hand," he said softly. Did she not know she shook even now with fear? "He will protect you."

"He promises to protect," she said.

"And God keeps all His promises."

She did not answer. She turned in his arms, and he thought she meant to free herself, but she only turned her face to the ceiling, hidden above them in shadows and night.

"Does He not?" Hugh asked. "He keeps His promises well in Outremer," he said lightly.

"Then tell me more of Outremer," she said in answer, her own tone a struggling match for his.

Always she turned the talk away from herself, but he would not allow it. Not now.

"You know me well," he said, smiling. "I could speak of Outremer and Jerusalem for days and nights unending. Yet I would rather speak of you, Elsbeth. I find you more compelling than even holy Jerusalem."

"You need not lie," she said. "I would not dare to compete with Jerusalem for your attention."

"I do not have the habit of lying, no matter what you may think," he said with a soft chuckle. "Jerusalem is full of wonders, yet so are you. You need not hide from me. I am quite engaged by you, even now. Just think how enthralled I would be if you merely put some effort into enthralling me."

He could feel the easing of her, the opening into laughter, and was heartened by it. Her fear was running from her now, running back into the darkness from which it seemed to spring.

"Do I want you enthralled?" she asked.

"Of course," he said, turning her back into his arms, her head nestled beneath his chin. "If you are going to have a husband, it is best he be enthralled by you."

"Am I going to have a husband?" she asked softly.

"Aye, you are," he said. "For all your long life, Elsbeth. For all your very long life."

They were the words of a promise, a promise he meant to keep. She would have a husband and it would be he; even when she left for her life in the convent, when her life was given to God and she became the bride of Christ, she would still be married to him. Their tie to each other could be broken only by death; he was content with that. Let her hide away behind abbey walls. That was what she wanted, and he wanted it for her, though he would not be free to marry.

He had known from the start that this would be the way of it between them. They would marry, mate and part, each to his own purpose and future. No acrimony. No bitterness. No remorse.

But now he knew her, and she touched something within him that he had not known was there, some tenderness, some longing that did not serve Baldwin, and what did not serve Baldwin would not serve at all.

He did not know what course to take with her—to follow Gautier's counsel, to take her body and achieve what he must in the frigid North, then fly South to home and honor and legacy? Or to follow the hoarse whisperings of his heart, to wait, to hold Elsbeth in an embrace of tenderness and compassion for the dark shadow she held buried deep within her?

He was uncertain which path to choose, yet he knew that in all the plans of men, little Elsbeth of Sunnandune was less than the smallest part.

It was in his mind that she deserved better and more of this life. Yet he could do nothing; he could not change the world for her. He could not change destiny. He would not disappoint Baldwin.

"Tell me of your fears, Elsbeth. I can feel your fear, a

heaviness in your heart and soul, a burden that you should not bear in this life. Tell me all of it, for it goes beyond the childbed, that I may lift it from you."

"You cannot," she said, her voice as blunt and hard as a mallet of iron. "It is beyond lifting and beyond knowing."

"I can lift any burden, and nothing under God's sky is beyond knowing," he said. "Only tell me and I will strike it from you, splintering it past all power. It is the nature of a husband to perform such acts," he said, stroking her hair, pulling her against his chest. "I would be a worthy husband for you. I would not leave you to face this alone."

"A worthy husband," she repeated. "Is that what you are? And am I a worthy wife?"

"I am, or would be, and you are. You are a wife most worthy, beyond the worth of any woman I have known."

"Have you known many women, then?"

"Are the wives of England so different from those of Outremer that they would hear of other women in the heart of their marriage bed?" he said on a smile, stroking her hair, soothing her. "I will not compare you to any woman, Elsbeth. You are unique, beyond comparison."

"All things may be compared," she said. "I am a woman, flawed, imperfect. Unfit, if I could but convince you of it."

"You shall never convince me of that," he said. "We shall fit together very well, you and I."

Elsbeth sighed and turned within his arms, facing away from him. "You are very certain. Is there never any uncertainty in you, my lord? Can there be naught which gives you pause or causes you to stumble?"

"Nothing in this bed, surely," he said, urging her to lightness and the casual intimacy of two bodies bound by vows and sheets.

"Spoken like a man," she said, smiling.

"So you have noticed, then, that I am a man? I had wondered. You have seen scarce proof of it in—"

"In the heart of this marriage bed," they said in unison and then laughed softly.

Into the silence of that momentary peace they fell, resting in the falling, easy in each other's arms. After a time, Elsbeth said, "Will you take me against my blood? I bleed on, my lord."

Hugh considered. He felt the hitch in her breath and the rigid stillness of her as she awaited his answer. Did she fear him? He did not think so. Did she fear the act of their joining? Perhaps. That was a fear he felt, though muffled by darkness and shadow. Yet all maidens would have some fear of that bonding and its momentary pain. It may have been that Elsbeth feared only defilement at being taken during her blood time. The church was clear that to enter a woman's womb at such a time was to enter into sin. Would he cast them both into sin to please Gautier?

Nay, he would not. Elsbeth was worth more than Gautier's greedy pleasure. Elsbeth was his wife now; he would see to her. Let her father finally relinquish her into his hand, as was right and good by all church doctrine. Aye, that was the course he would take and follow to the end.

"I will not," he said, pulling her into his arms, his mouth against her hair, "though you try me sorely, little wife. I want you." He felt her shiver in his arms and pulled her in closer to his heat. "Yet I will wait until your time is past. Rest for now, Elsbeth, while I pray for patience and endurance. How long do you bleed, little one; how long must I wait?"

After a pause, she said, "A week, my lord."

"A week? I think a few days must serve, Elsbeth. And I think I will also pray against your most certain prayer that God extend your time."

She stilled, holding her very breath, and then chuckled. He joined her, laughing at her fears from the safety of the dark.

"Then we shall see whom God listens to best, my lord."

He heard the confidence in her voice and smiled. She was so certain, his little prayer warrior, of besting him at this game of prayers. Did she not know that God would heed the prayers of a knight of holy Jerusalem first and best?

Well, she would find out in time.

Chapter Eighteen

The night was shortened considerably by the arrival of two cold little feet and a cold nose pressed against him.

"Can I sleep with you?"

"Of course you can," Elsbeth said, turning to take Denise in her arms.

Of course Elsbeth would invite the child into their bed. Was she not ever and always seeking barriers to put between them?

"I think it is more proper for you to find your own bed, Denise," he said, running a hand through his hair. "This bed is . . . occupied."

"I was in my own bed, but I . . . woke up." Denise said. "Why can I not be in yours?"

"Yea, why can she not?" Elsbeth asked, pushing her hair off her face and facing him. Even in the dim light of a fire struggling for air, he could see Elsbeth's scowl.

Hugh got out of bed, as naked as when he had climbed into it, and bent to put more logs on the fire. The room was as cold as a frozen pond but without the beauty.

"Because this bed is occupied," he said.

"There is room," Elsbeth said.

"Aye, I am small. You said it yourself," Denise added.

This was getting him nowhere; two females were intent on fighting him for the right to stay in his bed. As to that, in other circumstances, with other women . . . Hugh shook himself out of that dream.

"What awoke you?" he said instead, climbing back into bed.

"I do not know," Denise said, burying her face against Elsbeth's side. "Something bad."

"Something frightened her," Elsbeth said.

"What?" Hugh asked. "You are in the safety of the tower. What can befall you here?"

Elsbeth spoke before Denise could answer. "What does it matter? The night holds its own terrors, and fear does not know to stay away from strong towers. She should stay with us."

"All night?" Hugh said.

"Of course, all night. Why should she not?"

"Aye, why should I not?" Denise said, turning from Elsbeth to look up at him, the hurt on her face readable.

Why should she not? Elsbeth lay in his bed, cloaked in blood, fear, and now the arms of a child. Even with Denise gone, he would not take her. He could not, not as she was; 'twould be a betrayal of the trust he wanted from her.

Let Denise stay. Nothing of import was going to happen in this bed tonight. It did not take a great blazing fire to see that truth.

"Stay, then," he said to them both, and when Denise flung her arms around his neck, he grumbled, "but keep your cold feet to yourself."

Raymond found them the next dawning tangled upon themselves, arms and legs entwined, Denise's head on

Elsbeth's breast, her feet tucked between Hugh's calves. Under all lay Elsbeth's hair, coiled and trapped beneath three bodies. Hugh was awake. He had been awake since the hour before dawn, thinking, considering, wondering.

His head was pounding.

Raymond came in quietly, as was his way, looked at the bodies on the bed, looked at Hugh and raised his brows in question. Hugh shook his head, rolling his eyes, and began the slow work of disentangling himself from the girls. They slept on as he eased from the bed and dressed himself.

When Hugh and Raymond were clear of the chamber, with the door closed softly behind them, Raymond spoke as they descended the stair to the hall below. All was quiet and empty at this hour, but that was but a momentary respite.

"Why was *she* with you?"

Hugh looked over at his squire and cocked an eyebrow.

"She? You mean Denise?"

"Aye," Raymond said tersely.

"She was afeared. Some mishap, some danger, in the night. It was not *you*, was it? You did not torment her, seeking some revenge against her whilst she slept?" Hugh asked half seriously.

"I? Nay, I would not waste a moment on that chit of a girl," Raymond said.

"Not even for torment?"

"My lord, I am no child—"

"I am pleased to hear my squire is no child, though he can be baited like one," Hugh said softly, making his point. "Now, what happened last night? Was anything amiss in the hall?"

"Nay, my lord," Raymond said, chastened. "I heard nothing amiss throughout the night."

"And when did you retire?"

"Past Nocturn. All was quiet. Only Lord Gautier was still about, and he in his cups most deeply."

"Not unusual for Lord Gautier," Hugh said. "And not unusual considering the loss he has sustained. A man often finds solace in wine when God deals him a blow."

"Aye, my lord, though . . ."

"Aye?"

"Though he did not speak of his wife. He spoke of you and of Elsbeth. He insulted you, my lord. He wonders if it is in you to consummate this marriage."

Hugh let out a breath and then smiled crookedly as he considered Raymond's face. "Did he? And did he also insult you, Raymond? Did he wonder if we share more than the bonds of duty?"

Raymond's blue eyes burned hot as he answered. "Aye, my lord. He did."

Hugh chuckled. "And what did you answer?"

"I answered only that you would do all you have vowed to do."

"Well done, Raymond. Well done."

And so Gautier ranted on, insulting him, his squire, his very manhood. And what of Elsbeth? She who bled in her woman's time had her own father prodding him to breach her through her blood and naming him a sinner most venal because she was not yet breached. What manner of man did that, and to his own kin?

"There is blood in the bed, Elsbeth."

Elsbeth woke with a start and the beginnings of a curse on her lips. She stifled the curse in time, but the blood from her sodden wrappings bled onto the linen sheet of her bed.

She was not a woman given to cursing. But being in her father's household seemed to have an ill effect on her. She was also not a woman given to sleeping so soundly. She could blame that on having a husband who was wont to talk and talk through the night, leaving her no chance to rest.

Aye, most of the problems she faced could neatly be placed at the feet of men.

She jumped up, her hands between her legs to catch the worst of the overflow, and waddled to the bucket. It was clean and empty of soiled linen. She had Hugh to thank for that, she supposed. Well, it was the least he could do since he tormented her at every opportunity. She hurriedly unwrapped herself, getting blood everywhere as she did so, and then dumped all in the bucket. She wiped herself with a clean, cold scrap of linen and then began the tedious process of binding herself anew.

She still bled, though more softly and hesitantly now. Still, the way to her was barred for the time. She had only hours now to wrest herself free of Hugh; her reprieve would not last much longer. Only hours, yet she could not find the urgency required within herself.

She was becoming comfortable as his wife. That was the stark truth of it. He was possessed of a firm and solid tenderness that burrowed into her heart with more force than passion ever could. Ardeth had taught her about passion, but of tenderness she had known no words. In Ardeth's life there had been no lessons in tenderness, and so her daughter stood weaponless in this unexpected battle with her husband.

She was half in love with him.

He could have taken her; knowing her father, she knew Hugh had been urged to take her many times in the past days. And he had not. He had not. He had honored her and not forced himself against her will and her blood.

But when her blood was stopped and her will was hanging by a thread?

Then he would take her. What would she do then, when all defense was stripped from her?

What could she do but pray?

"You are in flux?" Denise asked, buried within the blankets except for her eyes and nose.

"Aye. You have good eyes about you, Denise. I am in flux," she said with just the smallest bite of sarcasm.

She had not bled in her bed in an age. She had learned the lesson of light sleeping years ago. To fail was not pleasurable.

"Does it hurt?"

"Nay, it does not hurt. Be not afeared of that," she said, her wrapping done.

"I am not afeared," Denise said. "I only wonder." She was silent, watching Elsbeth look through her trunk for a bliaut. Then she said, "Does it hurt when Lord Hugh . . . pokes you?"

Elsbeth slowly straightened from her trunk, a deep rusty red bliaut in her hands, and turned to look at the girl.

"Pokes me? That is an . . . unpleasant word. Where did you hear it?"

"From Walter," Denise said.

"Walter Miller?" Elsbeth asked. "Why would Walter Miller speak to you of such? He speaks out of place. You stay away from the village, stay inside the gates, keeping to your prayers, Denise."

"With Father Godfrey? I do not like him very much," Denise said.

"He is our priest, Denise," Elsbeth said. "He deserves our respect, our reverence."

"I still do not like him. His breath is sour and he stands too close."

"Denise," Elsbeth said, "this is not proper."

Denise shrugged and buried her face in Hugh's pillow.

"I learned another word you will not think is proper," Denise said into the pillow.

"Oh?"

" 'Sticks you.' I think it must hurt when a man sticks you," Denise said, pulling the blankets up over her head, her body a small lump in the center of the bed.

Elsbeth slipped on a white linen chemise and then pulled on a wine red pelisse, lacing it up slowly as she considered what to say. Over all she slipped on the rust red bliaut and fastened a golden girdle about her hips with absentminded attention. This was not a conversation she wanted to have; such talk was very discomforting. She had no answer to give Denise, and she would not have wanted to give her the answer if she had one. Odd questions and unwelcome in one so young.

"What makes you ask?" she said, delaying.

"I am only . . . curious," Denise said from beneath the blankets.

Elsbeth sat on the bed, lifting her bare feet from the cold floor, and pulled back the covers.

"Why are you curious?"

"Because . . . because . . . it will happen to me one day."

"That is true, but not for many days."

"I suppose. But . . . it will hurt and . . . I will bleed."

This was most definitely a conversation she did not want to have.

Elsbeth sighed and lay down on the bed, laying Denise on her chest and wrapping her arms about her, holding her against all knowledge and fear of pain. As if she could.

"But not for long," Elsbeth said, hoping it was the truth. "And not very much."

Denise lay quietly, her breath a thin echo of Elsbeth's own. After a time, she whispered into the cold air, "What about . . . the blood?"

"It is not very much blood," Elsbeth said, repeating what Isabel had told her and praying it was the truth. "And it is only for the one time. The first time."

"But still, there is blood," Denise said. "I do not want to bleed."

Aye, and blood every month and blood upon childbirth and blood in dying. But there was no need to say such things to such a small girl. Those truths would come in their own time, a time far from now. Ardeth had held her just so, whispering the same comforts, the same hopes, in this very bed. And look where she had landed.

"Aye, there is blood," Elsbeth said, stroking Denise's flaxen hair, so soft under her hand, so smooth and cool. "And no one wants to bleed, and yet we must and do. Try not to think of it."

They were quiet after that. A cold wind from the east whistled past the wind hole and a stray gull was visible, white against the building clouds of gray. A silent and solitary traveler, far from the sea, yet riding the sky contentedly, unconcerned that another storm was building. Joyous in flight, untroubled by future storms; there was a lesson to be learned in that, most surely.

Yet was there not, in this bed, in this hour, trouble enough?

What was it in Denise's words that made Elsbeth tremble, her thoughts cast back to dark and shadowed memory? This talk of blood—that was what had set her back upon a path she had long forgotten, running hard from it as she had then. Even now, that path was shrouded and dark; she could not see what terrors lay at the end of it, and she did not want the gift of sight. That path was better left dark. Better left forgotten.

Except for the girl in her arms, who suddenly wanted to know about pain and blood and men who poked their fleshy sticks at her.

In the dark.

Always in the dark.

Elsbeth turned her face to the wind hole and filled her eyes with the light of day, gray though it was, damp and cold. Still, it was day and there were no shadows in the day. There were Matins and Prime and the Morrow Mass and then Terce and Sext and None and Vespers; prayers and chants in the solemn sanctity of the church to keep all shadows in their place. Compline was last, the last service before the dark, long hours of sleep. She stayed at Compline longest. She liked Compline least because then she had to leave and face the darkness on her own. Hours upon hours until Nocturn. Hours upon hours alone, fighting shadows.

Fighting fear.

"What made you fear last night?" she asked, holding the girl tight against her, molding her thin bones into a warm cocoon of safety. "Why did you run to us?"

Denise held her breath for a moment and then said softly, "I was afraid."

"Afraid of what?"

Denise said nothing for a long time. The gull had gone. The wind had died, the clouds held in their place by an unseen hand. All the world was still.

"Just afraid," she said.

Elsbeth stroked her hair and did not press. Some things were best left in the dark.

Gautier awoke with a throbbing head and a dry mouth. At least, he imagined he was awake. All was dark. It took him a moment to realize that all was dark because his eyes were closed. He cracked open his eyes with some difficulty and was instantly blinded by the dim, gray light of his hall on a dim, gray day.

Some things were best left in the dark. And he was one of them.

THE TEMPTATION

He closed his eyes again and took a shallow, sour breath. What he needed was ale. Ale would open his eyes and moisten his mouth. Ale would make all look and feel as it should; not this hard and bright awakening. Tonight he would sleep in his bed, leaving all memories of Emma in the grave, where they belonged.

That issue settled in his mind, he lifted his head from the table and looked about him. There was nothing much to see. It was uncommonly quiet. Another storm was building to soak all in rain and mud. With Hugh of the Bathwater in residence, rain provided rare amusement, watching him skip to avoid puddles.

He was not worthy of the rank of knight. Which suited Gautier very well. Hugh was the perfect man for Elsbeth. Between the two of them, they could open an abbey, their bodies barred from bonding by their very vows. That would suit Elsbeth well enough, he knew. She was a woman to despise the touch of a man. He knew that very well, though she would submit. She knew the value and the necessity of submission. It was in her submission that Hugh placed his trust, and in his pretty face. It was in her submission that Gautier placed his trust, though the untimely arrival of her flux confused his plans. Still, there were other plans that could be put into play to see his will accomplished.

Gautier smiled and lifted his head to rest against the back of his tall chair, the only chair in the room, as befitted his importance. If Hugh did not achieve his stated goal? Then all would still be well. Truly, he did not see how he could lose in this game of wills and power.

That knowledge alone was enough to clear his head and make him forget the sour foulness of his mouth.

Iovetta awoke with a hand across her breast. It was an unpleasant awakening because the hand was not her own.

"I must be up," she said, lifting herself from the straw. The hand pushed her back down.

"I am up," Edward said. "First things first."

He said that every time. She did not know why she bothered to let Edward lift her skirts, except that he was Gautier's chief man. That was why, if she were honest.

"Be quick, then, or John will be cross with me all day," she said, relaxing into the straw. It was moldy with such frequent raining.

"I am ever quick," Edward said.

That was true enough, and one of the reasons why she let him have her. He was quick and done and then a warm body at her side through the night.

He fit himself inside her, grunted into her hair while she listened to the birds calling from the rafters, and then slipped out of her. He was ever quick. Edward Quick they should call him, and some girls did, out of his hearing. He had a fearsome temper. It was a jest best left for women's ears. Edward would not have seen the humor of it.

"You will have to do without me one of these days," he said, kneeling between her opened legs and readjusting his braes.

"Oh?" she asked in mild interest, pushing down her skirts.

"Aye. I have Lord Gautier's ear, as you know, and his trust. I may do something for him which will earn me something special."

"Something special?" Jovetta asked. "You mean money?" Perhaps some would sift down to her. She was very accommodating with Edward, after all, and he was so very, very small and quick. She deserved something special, if she could judge.

"Aye, or favor," Edward said, standing. He did not help her with her clothing, which was just as well. Best if he kept his distance when he was not actually doing his quick duty. She did not like Edward very well, but when a man signaled his desire to a woman, what was she to do but lift her skirts and put on a smile of willing submission? 'Twas all that was required, and she knew it very well. "I watch Hugh even now, to give Gautier the word. He relies on me."

Watching Hugh? Hugh and his lovely squire? Nay, this was not good.

"Watch him do what?" Jovetta asked.

"Just watch him," Edward said with a smug smile.

"I think many in Warkham watch him," Jovetta said. "He is a man to watch by any maid's standards."

"Watch him all you may," Edward said. "The more you look, the less you will like what you see. He is not a man as they fashion them here."

"I had noticed that," Jovetta said wryly. Her humor was completely lost on Edward, which was just as well.

"He will not be here much longer, so look your fill now. Tomorrow . . ." He lifted his massive shoulders in a shrug.

"He cannot leave tomorrow. He cannot leave until Elsbeth's flux is past and—"

"Ugh. I will not hear talk about a woman's flux. 'Tis beyond the ken of men, or should be. Leave your woman curse among yourselves. A man need not abide it."

"A man who abides with a woman must abide it," she said, standing up and kicking the straw back into the corner.

Edward was already walking away from her, his need for satisfaction and bragging well met. He would talk with her again when he had need of her and not before. Which suited her well also.

But Elsbeth and Hugh to leave on the morrow? That she had not anticipated. That meant Raymond would leave as well. Lovely, blond Raymond. She would just seek him out and ask him straight. If she had interesting news for John, he would forgive her for being late. Perhaps. It was worth trying, as she was late already.

Jovetta left the stable, picking straw out of her hair as she went. The sun was struggling against a bank of low and heavy cloud that was yellow and pink in the morning light. Perhaps it would not rain today, though the smell of rain was in the air.

She found Raymond and his lord Hugh almost immediately. They were in the middle of the bailey, their heads lowered in quiet conversation, their manner thoughtful. Elsbeth was not to be seen, which was odd, as Hugh was ever hovering over his wife. If only Raymond and Hugh would part and each go to his own function; she had no desire to face Hugh, no matter what she had said to Marie. He was too far above her reach and he had never looked at her with anything close to lust. She was not a woman to reach beyond her grasp. But that was not true of Raymond. He was well within her grasp, and he had looked and looked again at her. Raymond she could approach.

At the thought, they parted, Hugh back to the tower and Raymond to the kitchen. She caught up with him before he entered and before John saw either of them. He slowed when he saw her coming. Aye, she could approach Raymond.

"Good morrow, Jovetta," he said. "You are in good time for Prime this day."

"As are you," she said. "But I did not seek you out to talk about the Morrow Mass, Raymond."

"You sought me out? I am flattered," he said, taking a step closer. "Let me now flatter you."

"Will you be in Warkham long enough to flatter?" she said, letting him gently pull a strand of straw from her hair.

"Oh, surely. Let me prove it to you," he said, running a fingertip down her arm.

"You can prove nothing to me now, Raymond, as the day builds all around us and I must be at my tasks or lose my place. Only tell me this for now—I have it from Edward, who is ever upon Gautier, that you are shortly to leave Warkham."

Raymond dropped his hand and his smile; he dropped all poses of flattery and adoration and stood straight and severe, looking down at Jovetta.

"What exactly did he say to you?" he asked, looking more the man and less the youth with every breath he drew. He became more attractive by the moment, though she would have not thought it possible.

"He does not expect you to be here on the morrow," Jovetta said.

"Why?"

Jovetta answered more than she was answered, yet she could not turn aside from such firm questioning. Raymond looked ready to kill, he was so wary and so suddenly sharp.

"He has some task set before him by Gautier; he thinks to be paid for it, and he thinks you will be gone from here, no matter the state of Elsbeth's flux."

"He said nothing more?" Raymond said, grasping her by the arm and pulling her close.

"Nay, nothing."

"You are certain? This is most important, Jovetta."

"I am certain," she said. "What befalls that you act so, Raymond? I did not think it in you to be so hard."

Raymond smiled slightly and set her from him. "Nothing befalls, Jovetta. It is only that my lord and I do not like tales told of us. We do not leave on the morrow. That is no part of my lord's plan."

"I am glad of it," she said, looking at him with hungry eyes. "You are a man I would know better. I am glad you stay in Warkham for a time."

Raymond smiled and ran his fingertip over the back of her hand. "I will stay. For a time."

Yet all he wanted now was to fly away to Hugh and tell him what he had discovered. This was not good. Gautier plotting with his chief man-at-arms; Edward boasting that he would have coin in his purse soon; and all tied to the departure of Hugh. Nay, it smelled of foul intrigue. It was a smell he had learned as a boy in the Levant, as had Hugh. They knew well how to act in such times.

"Jovetta! The bread will not leap out of the ovens!" John called from the midst of the kitchen.

Jovetta jumped and hurried through the door, Raymond forgotten. It suited Raymond well. He had to find Hugh. Hugh was always and ever with Elsbeth. Elsbeth was always and ever at her prayers or at her bucket. Raymond ran to the chapel; it was close upon Prime.

Chapter Nineteen

Hugh was in the chapel, praise God, and Raymond hurried to his side, the priest looking on with definite interest at such an eager entrance into the Morrow Mass.

"My lord, a word," Raymond said. There was no need to say more; Hugh understood his urgency at a look.

They withdrew to the shadowed quiet of the north aisle of the chapel.

"My lord, Gautier has whispered to Edward, who has murmured to Jovetta, that this is our last day in Warkham."

"Our last day? When he knows that I will not leave his holding without our bargain met in full? Aye, he plots mischief," Hugh pondered, running a hand through his hair. "Yet," he said, lifting his head, "yet I think I understand him. Does a man give up power unless forced? Nay."

"Yet he was going to give up—"

"But only to get something he held in higher value. If he doubts he will get it, then he will withdraw, hoping still to touch what he yearns to have. I always knew him capable of perfidy, as did Baldwin. Gautier's name for sharp bargaining has traveled far in Christendom."

"He would kill to keep from fulfilling a vow made between men of honor?" Raymond asked.

"He would kill to get what he wants," Hugh said. "What man would not?"

"You knew he would walk this path?"

"I suspected only," Hugh said, clasping Raymond on the shoulder. " 'Twas my pride and folly to defeat him at sword point within his own walls. I should have kept my name as the Knight of the Bathwater. 'Twould have served me better, yet I could bear no more of his insults. My sword is more than a match for his, and now he knows it."

"And so he speaks to Edward."

"To get his killing done," Hugh finished.

"My lord, I am ever at your side. I will not leave you, though we fight all of Warkham!" Raymond vowed, his blue eyes alight with manly passion.

"Nay," Hugh said. "That is not how this game will run. Does the wolf announce to the hart that he is on the scent? Nay, we will continue on as we have done. Do not betray our knowledge with action. Unless he set all of Warkham on our heels, we will win the day."

"He may do that, my lord. We are alone here, outnumbered."

"He will not do that. It is too open and his cause too dark. Between us, we can manage a score of men from this isle, can we not?"

"Aye, my lord," Raymond said staunchly.

"Then play your part, Raymond, as I play mine."

Elsbeth and Denise made it to the chapel in time for Prime, but just barely. They slipped into the back of the chapel, hiding behind the font, hoping to remain hidden so that none should note their tardiness. Hugh noticed. He stood at the front of the nave, just below the rood, and, upon their entry, turned and beckoned with a wave of his hand. Beckoned, though the throng of bailey, village and field stood between them.

"Look! Hugh wants us to stand with him!" Denise said, her voice joyous with childish pleasure at being so noticed.

Elsbeth felt no such joy. She did not enjoy being the object of so many eyes.

"We should stay at the back. We are late. Others are before us," she said.

"But he beckons!" Denise said, pulling on her hand, tugging her forward.

Elsbeth stepped on the foot of a cotter and mumbled an apology. Denise had dragged her forward before she could finish what was only to be a two-word apology in any regard.

"Denise!" she hissed, pulling at her bliaut, which had become twisted in their scramble. "There is no need—"

"We are come, Lord Hugh!" Denise trilled.

"Go, then, but I will stay here," Elsbeth said, trying to pull her hand free. They were in the center of the nave, the press of bodies heavy and thick.

"I will not leave you alone!" Denise said, grabbing again for her hand. "You did not leave me alone."

"What? I am hardly alone," Elsbeth said.

"I will not leave you," Denise repeated, catching hold of both her hands and pulling with a backward step, determined and strong. How could a child of such slight form be so strong?

"Go, I say. Leave me here. I am content," Elsbeth whispered, smiling awkwardly at Father Godfrey, who was staring at them in hesitation.

Denise paused. "Are you certain?"

"Come, Daughter. The very presence of God, it seems, awaits your coming," Gautier said with a hard smile. "Shall we delay our worship for you? Come. Stand where you are bid."

A flush of shame washed through her and she ceased her battle to stay in the anonymous center of the crowded nave, letting herself be pulled forward by Denise's suddenly hesitant hand. Before she had taken more than a step, Hugh was moving through the crowd toward her. The people of Warkham parted almost miraculously for him, as if he were Moses parting the Red Sea.

She stopped and stared at him, at the angelic, golden form of the man who was her husband. She stopped, and still he came on, smiling, his hand reaching out to her. His very heart was in his smile, or so it seemed. And so it seemed that her very heart answered him and her hand reached out to meet his, was taken in his gentle grip, resting there. Safe.

"Nay, stay where you are, little wife. You have the right of it," Hugh said, none too softly. "Let us humble ourselves before God, not raise ourselves up by crowding to the front. Did Jesus not say that he who is first shall be last, and he that is last, the first in the ranking of heaven? I follow your will in this, and gladly."

He did not mean a word of it. She knew him well enough to know that. These words of God and His kingdom flowed out of him without effort, and perhaps without thought. These words were his weapon in the battle to win her; she knew that, yet still they worked to win her. He could turn her heart with only a smile and the flowing gift of his approval.

Yet he did more even than that. He had done what she hungered for most and most often: rescued her from her father's will and censure.

He knew her better than she had supposed, and she could find no fault with the knowing. To be rescued every now and again was a sweet sort of pleasure. There could be no sin, no breaking of a vow, in that, could there?

"And do you think that God's own son meant that we should be last into worship?" Gautier said on a bark of laughter before turning to once again face Father Godfrey. "Come, Father, begin. We are past our time, and delay serves no one well."

"That is true," Hugh said, taking Elsbeth's arm and holding her to his side in the center of the nave, the space around them cleared of all save Denise, who kept tight hold of her hand. "Warkham's time seems to run to delay. Or rather, to creep to it."

Gautier gave Hugh a hard look. "You speak to me?"

"I do," Hugh said. Elsbeth trembled beneath his hand so that he looked down at her.

"Do not provoke him," she whispered. "It gains naught."

"Then speak out, Lord Hugh of Jerusalem," Gautier said. "I am certain all here would eagerly hear our discourse on matters of delay."

"Please," Elsbeth said, closing her eyes, squeezing his arm, "do not."

In that instant, Hugh made his choice, certain of the rightness of it. He had his own motives for pricking Gautier, but it was within Gautier's power and capacity to shame Elsbeth publicly. He would not open the door to that.

"Is this not the hour for prayer and have we not delayed enough? Pray on, Father Godfrey, we are yours to shepherd," Hugh said.

Gautier smiled, a hard, cold smile that Elsbeth knew well, and turned to face the priest. The hour of Prime was upon them, their hearts turned to God at the birthing of the day. Yet she could not find peace in worship. There was no solace here, not with her father and Hugh scrabbling for power and dominance. The world of men was a very exhausting place. Surely a life behind abbey walls would have more peace in it. She only prayed that she would one day know the truth of that for herself.

"I do not fear him," Hugh whispered to her.

Elsbeth bent her head and whispered to the stones at her feet, "You should."

She could feel his grumbling, as if his skin were writhing in irritation.

"You do not know me," he said as they knelt on the cold floor.

Elsbeth lifted her eyes to the rood before closing them to all sight of earthly things. "Yet I know him."

"What can he do? He can do nothing," Hugh said, his voice rising.

Elsbeth said nothing for the rest of the hour, her thoughts straining toward God and prayer and the perfection of sanctification. Hugh never did settle into prayer; she could feel his tension throughout the long hour of the service. He thought her father could do nothing? How that a man could be so blind to danger? Her father was capable of anything, at any time. All who knew him knew that of him.

Yet Hugh was her husband of an hour, a day, a week, but no longer. She would somehow break free of this false marriage, and then he would be gone, away from her father and all danger. An added benefit to setting Hugh on his way southward, away from Gautier. Away from her.

Then all was done and the people of Warkham were moving slowly toward the door, their eyes cast back at the two men who had been locked in a quiet battle of few words. She could see that Hugh wanted to urge her to feel a confidence in him that time and experience would not allow her. She knew her father well; more, he was lord of Warkham. There was nothing Hugh could do. He had little might beyond the strength of his arm in her father's domain. Gautier held all power here.

It was only one of many reasons for her wish to reach Sunnandune. Gautier could not touch her in Sunnandune; his arm did not reach that far. Who was Hugh to tempt her to think that he could gainsay Gautier in Gautier's own holding? That was a dangerous thought, and she would not walk on such treacherous and boggy ground. Not even for Hugh. He could not tempt her into forgetting what she knew of Gautier. That knowledge was old and dependable.

When they were clear of the chapel, her father striding back to his tower, Denise trailing behind to loiter with the pig boy, Elsbeth said in some irritation, "What can you do, my lord? My father is lord here. Whatever he will do, he will do. What power have you to stop him?"

Hugh took her by the shoulders and looked deep into her eyes. The green of them was as soft as marsh mist, inviting and mysterious. Deadly. If she was not careful, she would lose her footing and drown in such eyes. He called to her with even more power now than before.

His words of salvation and sanctity had been a balm, sweet words that suited her most well. But his words of power and safety and might were more potent still, for they promised what she could never believe: a world of rest and security in the arms of a man. He could not give her that. No man could give her that.

She was Ardeth's daughter with Ardeth's counsel ringing in her ears.

"I have the power of my arm and my will, Elsbeth, that is the power I have," he said.

He believed it; she could see it. Well, mayhap he had no cause to doubt. But she did.

"A mighty power, my lord," she said, taking his hands and lifting them from her shoulders. "You are most strong."

"Yet you cannot trust in me," he said, taking her by the hand and fingering the ring he had given her on their wedding day. It gleamed in the uncertain light like a promise.

She had worn it to please him. He seemed pleased by it. When had she ever worn anything to please a man? Never. Never until now.

"I do not distrust you," she said.

"Yet you do not trust. What ground do you tread?" he said, smiling softly.

Deadly ground. His smile could lure her to destruction, as could the softness of his words, the gentleness of his entreaty.

"Safe ground. Solid ground," she said. "Do not ask what I cannot give. You promised that it would be so between us."

"What can you give me, Elsbeth? Not your body, not your trust, not your love. What more would you have of me? I ask only this. Only tell me why you can not trust that I can manage the machinations of your father? I know what sort of man he is. I am more than man enough to manage him. Can you not give me even respect?"

"You know what sort of man he is?" she said. "Do you? You have known him slightly for a few weeks. I am his daughter. I have known him intimately for year upon year. My knowing of him is differently shaded, my lord."

She took a hard breath and faced him. "I give you what I can, my lord. I can do no more. If you want to repudiate me, you have cause."

"Aye, you have seen to it that I have cause, yet I will not, Elsbeth. I have sworn to keep you, and I will."

Denise and the pig boy were straying close to them, though they were ten paces from each other. The two pretended to themselves that they were not keeping distant company; the pretense carried no farther than themselves. Raymond, too, was in their sphere, even more distantly connected.

"Come, we are too closely watched here," Hugh said. "The sun breaks through. Shall we find patches of sunlight to bathe ourselves in? I would share the light with you, little one."

How could she not follow him when he invited so softly? Nay, she did not follow, but walked at his side, content. Safe. For now.

He would keep her. Why? Why would he not let her go? He said he had not her body or her trust or her love. Well, did she not suffer the same lack from him?

Nay, he would give his body quick enough, like any man, but nothing of trust or love was in him. He wanted something of her; some arrangement was in place with her father, yet Hugh would speak none of it. He spoke to her of trust? Nay, she would not trust, and never, never would she love. This half love, this half temptation would pass and she would rise above it. She had only to hold herself still and quiet and small and all would pass. She would survive even Hugh of Jerusalem.

She would ever and always survive.

They left the muddy bailey of Warkham and followed the villeins to their homes. And when the villeins disappeared inside their wattle-and-daub walls, Hugh and Elsbeth walked on. The road, High Bridge, led them away from tower and field to the distant bridge over the

Nene River, close upon Peterborough. Far distant from Warkham. All seemed distant from Warkham; her father's domain, yet his dominion remained as firm and unyielding as the unbroken mass of cloud above them.

The sun did try. White patches of warm light slipped through the high clouds, strands of silken light falling to earth in streams of promise. Promise that the clouds would break. Promise that the sun would blaze forth in triumph. Promise that there was more to the sky than cloud and rain and deadening fog.

But who was she to complain of fog? She was a child of England. She liked the rain. She had learned the beauty of clouds.

"I have prayed daily for sun," Hugh said, mirroring her thoughts. "It seems the Lord God has heard my prayer only in parts."

The sun shone, almost. The day cleared, in part. Hugh looked up at the sky and then at her as they walked along, their steps silent in the soft, damp earth.

"Yet I have little cause for complaint—"

"There is little proof of that," she said, laughing at him. It was a joyous thing to be out of Warkham; her very soul felt bathed and new.

"—with such a bride beside me," he finished. "See how you have ruined my compliment? A wife should keep still and let her husband speak his compliments in peace."

"If I did, I would have no chance to speak at all, since my husband compliments me with every motion of his tongue."

"Churlish woman," he said, running a hand through his hair. "The English are a strange race, yet perhaps they must learn churlish and grim tenacity to thrive in such a soggy clime. I find I can forgive you, thinking that."

"I am not churlish. England is not soggy and I do not—"

"A wise wife would not dissuade a man from forgiveness, especially when it is so freely offered," he said, tapping her on the bottom and then running a pace or two ahead.

"Running away?" she said.

"From you?" he asked, grinning back. "Never."

"Then running where?" she asked, watching him. Devouring him.

"Just . . . running," he said, turning from her, his hair lifting in the wind.

"Then run, my lord. I will be here when you do seek me out."

"Sweet words, little wife. You are learning the art of soft speech very well. I am a worthy instructor."

"Go!" she said, laughing in spite of all her best and most grim English intentions.

And he went, his long legs carrying him up the road. It was a long, straight road. He never was beyond her sight, though he went far from her side. Still, he was in her eyes and in her thoughts as he ran and ran from her.

It would be just so when he finally and truly left her.

And he would leave her. His life was in Jerusalem; he had not promised otherwise. His vow was to Baldwin, his heart set, his will unbroken.

She was not the woman to break a man's will or heart when they were set elsewhere. This was something she had always known. It was just that the knowing of it now was exquisite pain. She could not hold him, though she bled new blood with every pulsebeat of her heart.

He had won something from her, some small patch of ground within her heart that she had not known was there. She had guarded, she had prayed, she had fought with all the weapons she possessed, and still, still he had won something of her. A part of her was lost and would stay lost, no matter what befell between them.

Had she said she was half in love with him? A strange lie to tell herself. Was this love, then? This half pain, half joy, blanketed in aching sorrow and longing? How well the troubadours sang of it. She had thought it all of chivalry and none of truth, yet the truth was that love was a wound that bled, and the worst pain was in the healing of it. She would love him long, the pain of it her banner, and she could not find the will to turn from wounding. To lose this pain would hurt her worse than dying.

Had her mother taught her this? Had Ardeth even known of love? Of passion and of loss, she'd known, but what of love?

He had set out from the start to win her and he had done it. Why, she did not know. She was not worth such effort. For such a man, such victories must fill out every day, for what woman could resist Hugh?

Not she.

Forgive, Ardeth, if you watch from heaven. Forgive.

Yet was there still not a way? Her heart was lost, but not her life. If he would only return to Jerusalem, picking up the shards of his life there, leaving her to Sunnandune, all could still be well. If he would only go back to the life he had known before misty England had wrapped itself around him. If he would only run away from Gautier and the destruction that waited in every shadow when he was near. Hugh did not know her father and so he could be man-proud in his strength and sure of his victory, yet she knew better. She knew her father.

How long had she feared Gautier? She could not remember a time when she did not. He was not an angry man, nor given to brutish force or bellowing commands. In fact, he was a man much given to smiles. Yet it was a truth that when he smiled, she feared him most.

There was no logic to it, and she had prayed heartily and with goodwill to have her heart changed to a heart that was proper for the daughter of a respected baron or, barring that, to have her father changed into a baron she could love and freely obey. Neither of her prayers had been answered.

Her heart had not changed. Her father had not changed. Only one thing had changed: The hours spent in his company had shrunk, while the hours she spent in prayer had grown. In the end, those changes had been enough to satisfy. She did not see him. There was little to fear if she was not near him. There was little to fear in a life bound and devoted to prayer.

And so she had not feared.

Except from a distance.

The trouble was that she was not distant now.

When Hugh left her for Jerusalem and the life he had interrupted there, would he leave her with her father? He could not. Of all that he might do, he must not do that. She must have Sunnandune. He must give her that. He knew her better now, perhaps even cared for her a bit. He could lose nothing by giving her Sunnandune. He did not need it, not when Jerusalem held all his heart.

He came back to her then, running over the soggy earth, his cheeks red and smiling, his hair a tempest of gold. Just for now. He came back to her just for now. She must not forget that.

"You like to run," she said when he was near. "Do you run often through the crooked streets of Jerusalem?"

"I dare not," he said, huffing lightly, his hands on his knees, his head down. "I have a reputation to defend, and it is not for running through the streets."

Nay, it was through hearts he ran with never a look back to see the blood he left in his wake.

"What, then?" she said instead, forcing herself to smile. "What foundation is your reputation built upon, my lord?"

He lifted himself up and looked at her. "Say not you think it is for sodomy. We have covered that ground and laid all to rest there, have we not?"

"We have," she said. "Let us not talk of what is not, but of what is—that is all I ask."

"I do not know what you ask, Elsbeth. I do not understand what you want of me."

"Then let me speak plain, my lord," she said with a determined smile. He had his plan for his life and she had hers; it was time to put them both in play. This course they had run was nearing its end. She could play this game no longer; she had never enjoyed games, and this game of secrets and hidden purposes served her ill. He would leave her soon; she could feel it, like rain coming off the sea. Best sooner than later, while she still had some grip on her heart. "You will return to Jerusalem," she said, holding his gaze. "Your heart is there, my lord. Foggy England"—*and her grim women*—"will never claim you."

"Elsbeth, this talk is—"

"I release you to your king, my lord," she said, ignoring the ache that groaned from her throat to her womb, a pulse of loss that dripped blood and soul at once. "If you will release me to mine?"

He stood still, his green eyes a thousand times magnified by the forest behind him and the gray skies above him. He was a bolt of sunlight in the mist. He did not belong here. He would be consumed.

"What are you asking?" he said, his voice gone low and soft.

"I am speaking plain, as was your wish. Jerusalem is your home. England is mine. Baldwin is your king, and you love him with a love that will not be silenced or betrayed. Go to him, go back to the place that holds your heart and leave me to the place that holds mine. I only want Sunnandune. Nothing more. Release me to it, my lord, and you can run from this land of rain and fog and mud that ruins fine boots," she said, looking down at his feet and the remnants of his gleaming red boots. They did not gleam any longer. "Let this contest of wills between us end, Hugh. I am so very weary. Shall we not release each other, ending all battles?"

"You want this? This eternal separation across the very length of Christendom?" he asked hoarsely, his eyes holding hers, the red in his cheeks fading to stony white.

"We both want this," she said, making herself believe it.

"You said you would not seek annulment," he said, searching for a flaw in her. They were easily found, but not on this ground.

"And I will not. Go your way. I will not hinder you. Will you do me the same service? Go to far Outremer; I will never call you back." Except in her prayers. Except in her heart. "Is this not a fair bargaining?"

"Why?" he said, standing close to her.

"Why? Because it is what we both want."

He had all the time in the world to convince her otherwise. He had hours to reason away her plan. He had now and now, an endless now to tell her of his heart and his devotion and his love.

But he did not.

He did not.

His silence spoke all very clear. With a grunt and a scowl, he took her arm and walked with her back to the tower of Warkham in the far distance. It began to rain again, and with the first drops, Elsbeth began to laugh.

"I am not following you!" Denise said.

"You are here. I am here," Thomas, the pig boy, answered.

"That does not mean I am following you, you stupid boy," she said.

"I am not stupid."

"You look stupid. You act stupid."

"Then why are you following me?" he asked triumphantly.

"I am not!" Denise shouted, her blond hair flying wild in a sudden wind.

"I heard you had a black pig," Raymond said from far to the right of them.

They were out of the bailey of Warkham and into the fields before the village. How they had traveled so far from the walls of Warkham, Raymond could not say. Denise and Thomas had meandered purposefully away from the chapel, and he had followed them. Lord Hugh was gone with his lady, Raymond had naught to occupy himself, and so he had followed Denise, who had followed Thomas. It was the reason he gave himself because he could find no other.

He had a strong disliking for Denise. He was quite certain of that. Every time he spoke to her, he wanted to curse, blaspheming God's very angels. He had a very, very strong distaste for her company.

And still he followed. To protect her. Aye, that was a likely reason. She had no cause to be mingling with a pig herder.

"Aye, I do," Thomas said.

"He is not all black," Denise said, tossing back her hair. It looked like moonlight on the sea, white and shining. "He has a white bit on his chin."

"He *is* black," Thomas said, "and he is the smartest pig in Warkham. He knows his name."

"His name? You have named him?" Denise said, pouncing. "I thought you said you did not care what happened to your pigs."

"Of course I care! I care that they live long enough

and well enough to be butchered," Thomas said, tossing a stone into the millpond. "And I did not name him. He learned his name—he is that smart."

"What do you mean, you did not name him but he learned his name? That is impossible. I think you are a liar," Denise said.

"I am no—"

"What is his name?" Raymond asked, tossing a nice flat stone into the millpond where it skipped five perfect times.

Thomas rubbed a hand across his nose and said casually, "Blackie."

Denise looked around for her own stone, found a likely looking one and threw it into the millpond. It sank like a . . . stone.

"I could have thought of a better name than that," she said before digging around for another stone.

"I told you, I did not think of a name, it was only—"

"What name would you have chosen?" Raymond asked, skipping another stone. Six skips.

"Well," said Denise, finding a beautiful round rock with pink flecks. She held on to it and looked for another, less wondrous stone to throw into the pond. "I would have named him Spot, for the mark on his chin. The white mark," she said, looking pointedly at Thomas.

"Spot? That is a stupid name. Makes him sound like soiled linen," Thomas said, tossing a flat stone to land at her feet and turning away from her.

"It does not!" she said, picking up the stone and hurling it into the pond. Where it sank without a ripple.

"I think," Raymond said, "I think I would have named him Onyx, if he really is black. Onyx is special, precious. Black pigs are special."

"He has a white *spot*," Denise said.

"I did not *name* him," Thomas said.

"I would have," Raymond said, handing Denise a stone

and standing behind her to show her how to throw it, holding her hand in his, pulling her arm back, letting it loose. The stone skipped, only once, but it skipped.

Denise grinned and bent down to look for another flat stone.

"But he is going to be killed," Thomas said. "Stupid to name a pig marked for the blood month." He was very busy looking for stones and did not look up at them as he said it.

"People die," Raymond said, handing Denise another stone. She took it, but kept on looking for her own. "Horses die. Dogs die. We name them. Why not a pig?"

Denise looked up from her pile of skipping stones, four in all, and said to Thomas, "I think Raymond is right. This time."

They said nothing after that, just stood on the edge of the millpond, skipping stones. Denise got one to skip three times. She was just getting good at it when it began to rain. Walter Miller watched them from the corner of the mill, ignoring the rain, his eyes on Denise. Raymond stood closer to Denise and picked up a larger stone.

"Rain? Again?" Raymond said, scowling. "Is it never dry in England?"

"No. Never," Denise said. "You should go back to Outremer."

A retort was on his tongue, but he did not voice it. She was a very small girl, easy to ignore.

Thomas walked off to his cottage down the track from the millpond, but as he went, he turned and said, "Do they have black pigs in Outremer?"

"They have everything in Outremer," Raymond said.

"Except rain," Denise said, grinning wickedly at Raymond. He knew she was but a child and therefore could not grin wickedly. But she did.

"I would not mind a season in Outremer," Thomas said with a smile, turning to run toward home.

"And the women are quiet and beautiful in Outremer," Raymond said when they were alone and on the path back to Warkham tower.

Denise was quiet for a time, searching for an answer. When she found one, she delivered it grinning. "Do you name them? The women of Outremer?"

"Only the ones we do not mean to kill," Raymond said, grinning back at her.

He wanted to strangle her, but he shortened his stride so as not to leave her behind. It would not do if Lord Hugh's small charge was damaged in any way by his carelessness.

She began to gasp in shock and then choked when her gasp turned to a giggle. Raymond slapped her on the back a time or two and said, "Keep breathing, Blackie. Your blood month is not yet upon you. You have years in you yet."

"I do not!" she sputtered, and then, realizing what she'd said, they both burst into laughter.

Chapter Twenty

She did not want him, he realized.

No matter what he said or did, the answer was the same. She did not want him.

It should not matter that she did not. He had no need for wifely devotion.

He had wooed and he had not won. It should not matter. The wooing had been all for Baldwin, to win from Elsbeth what he needed to succeed in his quest. Her heart had been the path he had thought the surest and straightest to success. Perhaps it was not. There were other paths, other means.

Yet she did not want him.

He had not considered that such a thing would ever be so.

The rain came down in its relentless English fashion, soaking him through, his hair directing the water into his eyes most efficiently. His boots squished with each step and he had a hole in the right toe. They were long past saving. His sister had given him these boots. He had cherished these boots. He would leave what remained of them in England, along with his wife, whom he did not cherish and would never cherish. She was a wife, a means to an end, nothing more. She was never to have been anything more.

She did not want him.

She encouraged him with her dark, tearless eyes and serene demeanor to run back to Jerusalem on the next ship, leaving her behind in gray England, forgotten. Which was what he had planned to do from the start. But he would have left her tenderly, with great care, with solemn vows to cherish her always in his heart, and she, she was shoving him out of her life without even a frown. Nay, she laughed.

She did not want him? How that she did not want him?

Was he not a man worth wanting? Was he not a man worth keeping? Was he not a man worth a tear or two?

"You would let me go?" he asked, keeping his head down and the water out of his eyes as best he could.

"Did you not always plan to go?" she countered, keeping her own eyes on her footing. They were far from Warkham, and the way back was wet and dark.

He was not going to answer that. It put him in too harsh a light. And where a man spent his earthly days was not a wife's province. Where she would spend her days, that was his decision. She was the vessel to his needs, not the other way round. He did not have to answer to her what his plans had been or were or were to be.

"My plans were to earn your regard, to find a tender place for me to reside in your heart," he said, which was the truth, after all. "I wanted to win you, Elsbeth." He pushed back his dripping hair from his brow. "I have failed. I do not know any courteous words of high chivalry to mask the sharpness of my loss. I ask your pardon, lady."

"You have not lost," she said, looking quickly up at him and then down again, her eyes on mud and rocky track. "You have won what you sought—a wife in England—though I cannot see what you have gained."

"You speak very plain," he said. "I am unused to such. The women of Outremer speak a different tongue."

"I speak plain, that is true. It is the language of prayer, if nothing else. I ask your pardon if I offend."

"You do not," he said, taking her arm briefly and then letting go of her. And then taking her arm again. He liked to touch her, and she was his wife. He would touch her at his will and not feel guilt over it. Nay, not over that.

"Then do me the same service and speak plain to me, Hugh," she said, her head bent hard upon the ground, her eyes lost to him. "What did you seek in this marriage?"

The rain beat harder than before, cold and sharp against his skin, the trees moaning and thrashing in the wet wind of autumn. With every blast of water, more leaves were thrown upon the ground, their purchase in the treetops lost. It was a bare and bleak sky with naked limbs thrust upward in silent supplication. Their prayers unheard, their nakedness unrelieved as all soft and colorful covering was stripped from them by an unseen and relentless hand.

What had he sought in this marriage?

Not a wife of soft eyes and reluctant laughter. Not a woman who stole into his thoughts with every prayer she uttered. Not a lady of dignity and resolve.

Not this warrior of prayers and chants and holy sacraments.

"I came to find a wife," he said. That much she knew. That much was always true of men in need of land and power. "I came to find my future."

"And what future awaited you here?" she asked, her voice as soft as rain.

"Ask me instead of Jerusalem," he said, answering her well, though she knew it not. "Ask me what is the future of the very center of the world."

She was silent for a moment, even the wind slackening to consider his request.

"And should I also ask of Baldwin, my lord?"

"Baldwin and Jerusalem are one," he said, lifting his eyes to the horizon, unmindful of the rain. It was only rain. Rain would not beat him down. Rain would not defeat him, even if it be English rain.

"Then tell me of Jerusalem," she commanded, the softness which had cloaked her moments ago gone. Like the leaves. Like the promise of love he had tempted her with. Elsbeth was too wary to fall into that temptation. Other women, score upon score, were brought down by soft words and smiling promises, but not this gentle warrior of ardent prayer.

Hugh laughed softly and shook his head at his own folly. He had been blind, losing his way in the dark depths of Elsbeth. This was the path to win his way with her; this was the answer to his quest. Elsbeth was a holy child of God with holy aspirations, so she ever said, proving it upon each hour of sequestered prayer; she would grant him what he wanted. She would want the same as he. No path to love was needed with her. Why he had walked it, he did not know. It had been a waste of precious time.

Why had he felt the need to woo and win her? Why had he lingered in her company, pressing kisses upon her, learning the shape of her, the soft scent of her, the very rhythm of her heart? Why had he found such pleasure in the workings of her mind? Why had he wasted time at Elsbeth's side?

He had been a fool, and Baldwin had no need of fools. She wanted plain talk? He could give her that. If that was all she wanted of him, he could meet the desires of her heart. Was he not Hugh of Jerusalem? Was there ever a woman he could not satisfy?

"Jerusalem needs men, Elsbeth," he said. "She cannot stand and fight without men, and she is very light of men."

"You came to find men," she said, considering, not understanding.

"We are losing ground," he said, turning from her, scanning the indistinct horizon.

"My lord?" she asked, not understanding.

"We have lost Edessa complete, and Damascus, a needless loss. We are losing Antioch. What our fathers gained in their lifetimes, we are forced to watch slip away from us, their blood spilt for ground we cannot hold." He turned to face her. "We need men, men of blood, to hold the land."

"What of Ascalon? You are known for that battle, that victory," she said, not allowing his words to take root in her.

"Ascalon is ours, and from there we shall hold Egypt, but this is not a battle of prayers, Elsbeth. This is a blood battle, and men of blood are needed to fight it."

"And so you married a woman with one knight sworn to her?" she said sharply. "What merit could there be in such a plan? I have no knights to give you, my lord. I

320

hold a simple manor. I am not rich in power or men. I am only rich in prayer. Take my prayers; I give them to you freely."

"Elsbeth," he said, taking her by the arms and holding her fast. "There are things you do not know of Sunnandune. You have been long from there, by your own words."

"Aye, it has been long, but Sunnandune is mine. I know her. I know what I have in her."

"Nay," he said slowly, seeking forgiveness when he needed none. He had done no wrong. No look in her eyes would convince him otherwise. "You do not know. Your father has—"

"My father has what?" she snarled, pulling free of him, facing him in the rain and the mud, her hair rivers of black twisting over her breasts like beloved vipers.

"You were not here!" he shouted, as if she were to blame for her fostering and for her father's acts. As if he could make her answer for what had happened while she grew to womanhood. "The wars crippled the land. Maud and Stephen strove in war while the country bled. There was no one to stop him. No one to stay his hand."

"What has he done?" she shouted up at him. "Tell me! One truth from you, Hugh; can you manage even one truth?"

"Truth? You want the truth? The truth is he has increased Sunnandune, by any means he could. She now holds forty hides of land and ten knights," he said harshly. He was no liar. Never had he lied to her.

"Forty hides? That is three times more than Sunnandune," she said, staring into the middle distance.

"And ten knights," Hugh said, saying it all.

Elsbeth looked up at him, her eyes solemn and hard. "He promised you the ten."

"And twenty more of his own. Your uncle has promised fifteen and your——"

"Just tell me the total," she said harshly, looking across the rain-soaked land to the swaying trees.

"Between all your father's kin and the kin of your mother, I will return to Jerusalem with sixty-four knights to help us in our fight to save the holy land."

Elsbeth laughed softly and held her face up to the rain, letting the water wash her clean of all false hopes. "You will return to Jerusalem a mighty force with sixty-four knights at your back, my lord. Your king will honor you. Will the knights swear fealty to you, or is that honor to be saved for King Baldwin? Either way, you are increased in power and favor, are you not?"

"Elsbeth," he said, reaching for her.

She let him hold her body, but her heart and mind were far from him. She stood limp beneath his touch and let the rain take her.

"I was to fall into your hands, my heart in your keeping, and when you asked for the ten knights of my Sunnandune, I was to give them to you, was I not? I was to love you with so great a passion that all you asked of me I would give," she said. "Yet it will not be. I have been well tutored in the ways of men, and I will not give up Sunnandune to you or any man. Sunnandune is mine. You bargained with my father," she said stonily. "What else is required of you? I know there is more. I know him well."

Hugh looked at her for a moment and then said, "I am to have Sunnandune's knights and the knights of your kin. Your father wants only Sunnandune. I must deliver Sunnandune to him."

"You were to get Sunnandune for him." Elsbeth let out a sigh of pent-up breath and dropped her gaze to the mud at her feet. "Aye, he would want it; it was the sweetness of that place that made my mother so desirable to him. Now that he has multiplied its worth and might . . ." Elsbeth looked up at Hugh. "And what of me?

What plans were made for me?" Hugh took her hands in his. She pulled away from his touch and looked up at him, her face fierce and hard. "What of me?" she said again, more urgently.

"You were to be in your father's keeping until he found an abbey to your liking," Hugh said. "Did you not say you wanted an abbey life? I thought this would be little to ask of you. You love God as fiercely as I. You only wanted a life of prayer. How could you be harmed by this, Elsbeth?"

"How am I harmed?" she said softly. "I am wed to a man who wants only to rob me of my home and my wealth. I am bargained for between husband and father, my life of little worth beyond what I can surrender to the two men who are charged to care for me."

"No harm would befall you," Hugh said. "You would be safe in the abbey."

"Speak to me no more of abbeys," she said sharply. "I will not relinquish Sunnandune to you, and never to my father. He made that plain to you, did he not? That is why you were required. He bought you, my lord, a pretty toy to distract me while he eased Sunnandune from my grasp. Yet Sunnandune is mine and will remain so. I cannot be tempted to relinquish her."

"And I cannot be tempted to forget what I came to England to find," Hugh said, his voice sharp. "I cannot fail in this. These knights are mine. I have bargained for them, and they will come with me. Jerusalem's need is great, Elsbeth," he said. "The very heart of Christendom is in peril. You can grant me the ten knights of Sunnandune to defend the Levant and all the holy places of that land."

"Can I?" she said, staring up at him, her eyes as black as forest shadows and as dangerous. "Will I? I think not, my lord."

"Why will you not?" he said, shaking her lightly. "It is

a small thing and would do much to aid the cause of holy Jerusalem."

"Not to mention the cause of ambitious Hugh of holy Jerusalem," she said, wrenching herself free of him, throwing his hands from her with more force and will than he had ever seen in her. "Am I asked to bare Sunnandune, which I love with as fierce a love as you hold for your shining Jerusalem, of all her knights? Who then will protect her? How can I keep what I cannot hold?"

"Keep the one, then, but give me nine," he said, pressing against her will and her sodden skirts. She was obstinate of a sudden. When had Elsbeth ever planted herself so firm against his will?

"Keep the one? When I now hold forty virgates? And do you even now think that Henry will let Sunnandune stand at forty virgates without looking into the cause of her sudden increase? Pray that my father increased her size lawfully, or all could be lost in the fire of the king's anger."

She pushed away from him, her hands on his chest, but he was done with being pushed away from her. She would give him what he wanted. He did not want much, only the way to a higher place than the one he was born to.

"I can give you nothing, my lord. Your marriage to me was ill-advised," she said sharply, turning from him to walk away. "You bargained badly. Did you not learn better in wondrous Jerusalem?"

She would not walk from him, he vowed. Never in all the planning and plotting had it been possible that Elsbeth would walk away from him.

"You are for the convent," he said harshly, grabbing her arm and turning her to him. She crashed against his chest, and he held her fast against him. "You have wanted the convent from the start. Of what use is Sunnandune to you? Would you have kept it in the abbey?"

"I wanted only to be free of marriage, Hugh; that was my only prayer. I want Sunnandune. She is my home. I have waited for her all my life."

Had all been for naught? Hugh wondered. She would never relinquish Sunnandune, and it was the one thing she must do. He would have served Jerusalem better having stayed there. But he had not. He had come north and he had found Elsbeth. And now he had a wife who could give him nothing. Nothing.

"The road to Jerusalem is open to you. Take it and go home," she said, holding herself stiffly in his hard embrace. "Go home," she whispered as a single tear escaped to join the rain weeping down her face.

Go home? Go home without her? Leave her in England, this maid who was his wife? She had not been the wife he had expected. She had done nothing to win him to her side. She had not sighed or smiled or blushed in tempting modesty. Nay, she had fainted when he kissed her, prayed in competition with him, chided him for his vanity, and submitted unwillingly to every touch and kiss and stroke upon her skin. 'Twas not the way to win a man.

And he was not won. He could not have been won for so little cause and by such a solemn and stalwart maid. He had known women of greater beauty and sweetness, greater wealth and docility; it was not in him to fall for this chilly, formidable, vulnerable English damsel. And he had not fallen. He would not fall.

Yet he must touch her. Even now, when all looked lost, he had to touch her.

He had needed a wife because he had needed the right to claim knights of England for a holy cause, that was all. There was no more to him. He was Poulain, a knight of Outremer, and that was all. He had nothing to give a wife, and he needed nothing from a wife. Not even this wife. Not even Elsbeth.

"And when I go home, where will you go?" he said, lifting her high against him, feeling the soft weight of her breasts against his chest, hearing the hammered beating of her heart. Tormenting her. Taunting her. Tempting her. "How will you hold Sunnandune in the legal trials ahead? How will you hold her against the claim your father will surely press?"

"I will," she said softly, closing her eyes to the sight of him. But she could not keep him from her. She could not ignore the feel of him against her, the pure male power of the man she had freely wed in divine ceremony.

He kissed her throat, and she swallowed hard against his touch. Her hair hung down, wet and slick, and he pulled it with a single hand. Her throat arched back, exposed, and he kissed her hard, biting, letting the rain wash away the sting of him.

"And what of the abbey? What of a life devoted to prayer?" he murmured against her skin, shouting down the shame he felt at what he was urging her to do. He was Poulain. Nothing more. He needed the knights pledged to her. Nothing more. "If you give Sunnandune to me, I will see you settled in the abbey of Fontrevault. Think, Elsbeth; you could pray away your days, across the channel from Gautier. Is that not a life worth considering?"

She breathed a sigh and shook her head against his touch and his words, but he would not let her escape him.

"You know nothing of what I want," she said.

She smelled of rain and wood and wool, like wind and forest in the night, like the very earth itself. Natural. Warm. Dark. He buried his face in her and breathed hard, his mouth opening upon her like a babe's first breath, hurried and urgent and necessary.

That was wrong. She could not be necessary. Only

Baldwin was necessary. Only Jerusalem was urgent and urgently in need. His own needs did not signify. He could have no needs beyond the fulfillment of his vow.

But he needed her. In this moment, this now, he needed her.

It was her worst betrayal of all. She had made him need her. Made him want her. Tempted him to forget the beauty of golden Jerusalem in her dark embrace. Tempted him to stay.

"Aye, I do know. I know your wants very well," he said, holding her hard against him, pressing against her stubborn will.

"Sunnandune is mine," she said, trying to twist free of him. She was too small for that. He could hold her until the end of time. She would not work free of him. "I will not abandon Sunnandune."

"Not abandon her? You have not seen her for a decade," he said, setting her feet upon the ground and holding her hands in his, trapped. "Give her to me. I will see that all is well with Sunnandune while you are in the abbey."

She opened her eyes and looked hard into his. She shook the water from her eyes and shook back her hair. "You will keep Sunnandune, but you will relinquish me?" She laughed softly and her eyes flooded with sudden tears. "You must think me a fool, my lord. I will give you nothing. You will take nothing from me. Nothing," she said on a croak of emotion.

"Nothing?" he said, grinning without a trace of humor or goodwill.

She took the very heart of him, the part that made him a man, the vow he had made to Baldwin, and pressed it into the mud with every word she spoke. She would give him nothing? Oh, aye, that was true. She had given him nothing from the moment he had set his eyes upon her, but that was over. She would give him something. In that instant, it was the one and only thing he wanted from her, and he would have it.

Let Baldwin and his wishes wait; Hugh was done with waiting.

"Oh, you can and will give me something, little wife. You will give me what I have wanted of you from the start."

"I have nothing. There is nothing," she said, pulling hard against his hands. A fruitless resistance. He pulled her close to him, towering over her.

"I want you, Elsbeth," he said, his voice a whisper of raw intent. "I want your body under mine. I want your breath in me. I want your skin red with my caresses. I want your blood to cover me."

"Nay, I cannot give you that," she said, her eyes wide and black, like the very night itself.

"Then do not give," he said slowly. "I will take what I want from you."

Chapter Twenty-one

He was done with words. Done with vows. Done with careful, measured living. He had lost all. He would not lose this.

He dragged her by her hands, bound within his own, dragged her to the edge of the wood. Her feet slipped in the mud, her gown was soiled past knowing its color. Her hair was a tangled mass of black that hung around her face and torso like the fabled banshee of old.

He did not care. Let her curse him. Let her pray him into hell when this was done.

He would have her anyway.

She was his wife. He had the right to take her. God

help him, he had the will. Nothing she could say would stop him from this course.

Elsbeth said nothing to stop him; she only planted her feet and refused to walk to her own deflowering. He did not find that odd. He knew his wife as well as any man could know a woman. She would endure what was to come. She would not fight outright, yet she would not quite submit. Such was Elsbeth.

He did not care for any but his own needs, his own wants. He was miles past caring. Let her fear; she would learn that there was nothing to fear, learning what every woman since Eve had learned.

All had been denied him, including this. But no more. He would have her.

Holding her, trapping her, he ripped at the laces of her bliaut.

"I want to see your skin. I want to see it in the rain. I want to see your nipples rise in the cold, and I want to warm them with my mouth," he said. His voice was guttural. He hardly recognized himself. Well, he was far from Jerusalem, the place that had shaped him. He did not know himself in this strange land of water and cloud.

He did not care.

All he knew of himself was the wanting of her.

"Stop," she said, shivering in the cold. Or perhaps she trembled in fear. He did not care which. All caring had been washed out of him, leaving nothing but the fire of passion and need.

"Nay," he said.

"You will not stop?" she asked, her voice small and wet. He did not look to see if there were tears. He did not care if she cried.

"Nay, I will not stop," he said, peeling her bliaut from her shoulders and pushing the sodden fabric down. It was heavy going, but he was a knight of the Levant; he was more than a match for wet clothes on a frightened maid.

The linen of her shift was transparent in the rain and thin as a veil. Her nipples were dark and hard against the white of it, her skin slick with rain and cold to his touch. He looked quickly up at her face. Her eyes were closed, pressed tight against the world, her pulse racing in her throat. Her lips trembling.

"I am your husband," he said.

He did not need to say it. They both knew he had the right to her. They both knew his taking of her was long past due.

"I am your wife," she said, and he heard the pleading in her voice. She was his wife and he was stripping her bare along a well-trod track, taking her along the edge of a wood in the mud of incessant rain.

He did not care.

All he wanted was the feel of her around him, beneath him, part of him. He wanted her heat and her tightness and even her fear. Whatever he could have of her, that he would take, without regret. Without shame. Without guilt.

He had to have her. She had to adjust herself to it. There was no more to it than that.

"Then be my wife and give yourself to me," he said, pushing her down into the wet grass and mud that bordered the wood.

"You would take me here? Now?" she said, trying to lift herself up, trying to keep herself clean of the mud.

"I would take you anywhere, Elsbeth," he said, staring into her eyes. He wanted her too much to stop, too much to think or reason or hesitate. "Even now."

"Why?" she said, her legs pressed together against his seeking hand. "Is it because I will not give you Sunnandune?"

"It is because you will not give me yourself," he said,

knowing it was the truth the moment the words left his lips. "There is no thought in me for Sunnandune. Not now. Now, it is only you. Only us."

Her breasts were bared to him, white and soft in the rain, her veins blue in the cold. Her bliaut was tangled with her shift, twisted and wet; he could not free her of it. Well, he would take her as any eager man took a woman, by the simple lifting of her skirts, plunging into her warmth when all the world was cold and dark. So it would be with Elsbeth. She was his wife. He had the right to her dark heat. There was no sin in this, no matter the look in her eyes.

"In the mud you will take me," she said hoarsely. "Is that the way of it in Outremer?"

He pulled her hands from her skirts, holding her down, lifting the heavy weight of wet wool from her legs. He bared her legs and hips, until he could see all. Her linen wrapping blocked him. Ever it blocked him, but no more. Not now.

"Aye, in the mud and rain and even in blood will I take you. Set your mind to it, wife. I have it not in me to wait another hour for you. Make your peace with it."

He tore at her wrapping, ripping it from her, pulling it off her, this shield that had defeated him for so many days. She would have that shield no longer. He would prick her, marking her always as his. She could hide in the abbey for a hundred years and she still would be his.

The wrapping came free. White but for a tiny spot of dried blood. She no longer bled.

"You were ready for me," he said, accusing her.

"I bled just this day," she said, swallowing hard, facing his anger. She was bared to him now. There was no more escape for her. "I was bleeding this dawning."

"But you are not bleeding now. God is good," he said, and the very way he said it seemed to deny the certain truth of that statement.

"But not to me," she said, holding her face up to the rain, staring into the sodden sky.

"Will you fight me?" he asked, ignoring her blasphemy. Even that would not stop him. He wanted her beyond the reach of kings and angels.

The world was stripped of all but this need to have her. Yet he did not want her unwilling and unready; he only wanted her and, for once, wanted her to want him in return. Her heat matching his. Her need a match for his own. He wanted to prepare her, and he could do little to bring her to heat if she forced him to hold her down.

"I fight you even now, yet does it stop you?" she said in hoarse whisper. "I am a woman. You will force me to submit, is that not so?"

What was it about Elsbeth that tugged at him? She *was* his wife. This was her place, to give to him her body whene'er he had need of it. As it was his duty to give himself to her. That she did not seem to want him had no place in their vow.

"Yea, you are to submit, yet it is not my wish to force you. Give yourself to me, Elsbeth. Think not of Sunnandune or of Jerusalem. Let this be only of us," he said, slowly easing his hands from her.

The rain had slackened to a mist though the clouds stayed heavy and low upon the treetops. It was chill. His wife was lying naked in the mud and long grass of England. How that he could not feel shame at such an act?

Because he wanted her beyond any shame.

He was, indeed, far from Outremer.

"Will you fight me?" he asked again.

"My lord," she said, "I would bargain with you."

"A bargaining?" he said, his voice heavy. "You prove you are your father's daughter with the words. Are you so cold of heart, then, when all I feel is burning? I want you. I know little beyond that. There is nothing beyond that. Beyond this."

He was kneeling between her legs, the rain dripping from his surcoat and his hair, a penitent at the shrine of Elsbeth. Seeking succor. Mercy. Acceptance.

Her dark eyes huge, she said, "I bargain for my life, Hugh. Release me to Sunnandune and I will submit softly to your every touch," she pleaded.

"Do not ask it of me," he said. "Let there be only us in this mating, Elsbeth. No kings or kingdoms, no fealty and no vows, only us. Can you give me that? Can you give me just yourself, just this once? I have labored long and hunger much, I will confess," he said in soft entreaty. "Do I ask so very much?"

"I have little cause to trust you, my lord, and I fear the thing you ask with all my heart," she said, looking deep into his eyes. "I have run from what you ask all my life. I made a vow that I would not do this very thing."

"I understand the weight of a vow, little one," he said. "I do. Yet can we not leave even vows behind us? I want to take you to a place where there is only us."

"Is there such a place?" she whispered, laying her hand against his chest. "I have never heard of it."

"There is. With you, there is," he said, lifting his surcoat from him. "I will not hurt you, Elsbeth. Not in this. Never in this."

He was wet through. His mail he would keep, knowing the temper of the place and its lord, but he would remove what he could. A sign of respect or tenderness for her, he knew not. He cared not.

"All maiden's fear," he said, helping her to sit up, to sit on his thighs, her legs wrapped around him. "I will ease you through. If you allow it."

"If I allow?" she said, wrapping her arms around his neck and burying her face against his throat. Her nose was cold.

"Aye, for unless you want to be comforted, I can do nothing to please you. 'Tis in your power, little one."

The words, the thought, pleased her, he could see that. She had so little power in her life, except the power of prayer, and that was a power she pressed to the limit of time and endurance. She sought power, did Elsbeth, and found it in small measure. Well, what woman had power in this world? But if it pleased her, then he would give her what small power he could.

And suddenly that was all he wanted—to please her.

Had these English rains washed away all ambition from him, then? He did not know. Perhaps it was past knowing. For now, Elsbeth was entwined around him, reaching for her power with the mailed knight beneath her hands. He held himself still and let her find it.

"Will you hurt me?" she asked, her breath against his neck, warm and moist.

"I will do all to prevent it. Now and always."

"Then take what you will, my lord."

"There will be no taking in this, little wife, but only giving. Will you give yourself to me?"

"Aye, I will," she said, shattering her vow.

"A cherished gift," he said, laying his hands on her breasts. "I will not betray."

With a gentleness he did not know was in him, he caressed her, barely touching her, yet stroking her with so fine a touch that she could have been made of silk and he would not have snagged her.

She gasped, a small breath of sound that he felt against his ear.

"Have I hurt you?" he asked, knowing the answer.

"Nay," she breathed out.

She leaned into his hands but slightly, yet he could feel the step she took toward willingness and pleasure. He hid his smile and stroked her again, his hands fluttering like angel's wings over her, pleasuring her, showing her how little hurt there was to be found in him.

He kissed her softly, her rain-slick lips cool and smooth, her open mouth hot in the chill air, her body slack and loose beneath his hands. Such a kiss, such a willing, open kiss from hesitant Elsbeth. She had come far in her kissing since that first kiss in the chapel.

He laid his palms over her distended nipples, rubbing lightly against her as his tongue slid temptingly over hers. He was all soft seduction, all gentle wooing and tender touch. All for her, to ease her, to help her find her way into desire and need. For himself, he was as hard and hot as August in Damascus. This gentle easing of her fears was like to tear him up. Yet he would be willingly torn if it would help her. He would not hurt her, not even with fear, if he could ease her.

Gentle Elsbeth, who with a whisper drove every blood-thirsty instinct from a man; his every instinct was to please her, his every thought to . . . love her.

As Christ had commanded a man to love his wife. Nothing more than that. He was a Christian knight doing his Christian duty. He did not love her as he loved Baldwin. He loved her as a . . . as a weaker vessel, as Saint Paul had instructed. Aye, 'twas loving tenderness that he felt, and right that he should feel it. There was no sin in this, no turning from a vow in this.

He was not so far from Outremer that he could fall from Baldwin.

But Baldwin had no part in this; even he knew that. This was all of Elsbeth and her husband, Hugh. This was of blood and flesh and bone meeting as one. Becoming one. This was need, fed and met. Felt and fulfilled. This was Elsbeth. All was Elsbeth in this hour.

He could live in this hour forever and never want for more.

Was this how eternity would be? A forever now that

stretched out to touch all horizons, all needs, all hungers?

With Elsbeth in eternity, he would not want for more.

The kiss deepened. He wanted her. She was his, wanting him, wanting to want him more. He could give her that. He could give her all of himself and not note the loss.

She asked for so very little, and yet he would give her all; such was her power, such was the temptation of her.

She groaned and wrapped her hands in his hair, pulling his mouth down to hers with force and need, pressing her breasts into his hands, moaning, squirming.

He lifted his mouth from hers with some effort and said, "Have I hurt you?"

"Nay, nay," she whispered hoarsely, seeking his mouth blindly with hers, her breath hot with need.

With a groan, he kissed her. A devouring kiss, falling into her like rain into the sea, merging until they were one. Mouth to mouth, they were one.

His thumbs played against her nipples, as hot as her mouth, as urgent and demanding. She writhed against him, and he could feel the heat of her through his mail, through his tunic, through his braes. She was wet with need, as wet as rain, as hot as fire. With slow ease, he moved his hands down her body, over the bones of her ribs, the bulge of her girdle and skirts, to her open thighs. She quivered when he touched her thighs, laying his hands on her, stroking her, teasing her.

She groaned, a high, long groan that ended in a high-pitched moan of distress.

He ended the kiss and, kissing her neck just below the ear, whispered, "Hurt you?"

"Hugh," she moaned. "Hugh," she breathed.

"Have I?" he said, his hands still on her parted thighs, his mouth nibbling her throat.

"Nay," she said, blinking. Her eyes were the black of a winter's night.

"Good. I would not hurt you," he said, smiling as he kissed her.

Would not hurt her? He was killing her. Slowly, gently, tenderly killing her. She had never felt such hunger, such distress. There was no rest in such a place as he led her, no room to breathe, no soft falling. There was only hot need and twitching urges, bolts of searing want that left her breathless, restless.

But he did not hurt her. There was no hurt in this. There was only the slow torture of building desire.

She had not known there could be such agony without pain. But Hugh had known.

"What are you doing to me?" she sighed, turning her face to meet his mouth.

"Not hurting you," he said, keeping his mouth away from hers. Tormenting her.

Nay, he was not hurting her. His mouth on the edge of her jaw did not hurt. His hands on her breasts did not hurt. His thumbs on her nipples did not hurt, not in any way she had felt pain before. But she did not like it. She could not relax and be easy in his touch upon her, yet she turned into his hands, his mouth, with mindless, blind need.

He did not hurt her, yet she ached.

She did not want to ache for any man, yet she prayed the ache would never end. But if it did not end, she would surely lose all reason.

He was a demon to torment her so. An angelic, fallen demon. Angel of light. Lucifer's own.

With every throb of need, her thoughts tumbled, changing, as she was changing. Hugh was changing her into a woman of the flesh.

What of her prayers? What of the life she had planned, shunning all that a man could do?

With his hands and mouth on her, she could remember no plan beyond his next caress. All prayers were forgotten, snatched away, lost. She lived, holding her breath, for the next kiss, the next touch, the next embrace.

He was not human, to torment her so and smile as he did. Yet she had known that from the start.

"Please," she said, asking for mercy. Not knowing what deliverance would look like, feel like.

"You are not hurt?" he said, lifting her up to nibble her breasts. Her legs shook, and she cried out in soft distress at his mouth upon her.

"I am not hurt, yet I am in pain," she said when she could speak.

"I know," he said, licking her. "So it has been for me these last days. Wanting you, burning for you. Forbidden to have you."

"Please," she said again, her head lolling on her shoulder.

He was biting her softly, mouthing her, licking her. She was blind with desire. There was nothing else. No rain. No mud. No fear. Only Hugh and this endless sliding over pleasure that was not quite touched, not actually reached. Pleasure that tickled without penetrating. Without consuming. Without satisfying.

"I am here to please you," he said. "I will please you."

He dropped her down to his lap again, spreading her wide. The rain thickened and seemed to steam where it struck them, exploding missiles of mist, lost in the growing dark.

"When?" she said, pulling him to her, pressing her hips against him. She could feel the hard ridge of him, but he was not there, not where she needed him to be.

"Now?" he asked, pulling aside his braes.

She kissed him for answer, sliding her fingers through his dark gold hair. The very scent of him aroused her.

He stroked down her thighs, his hands gentle as his fingertips found the hot ache of her. She moaned at his touch, grinding herself against his hand, enjoying the pressure, needing the friction, hungry for the full weight of him on her and in her.

"Now," she said. "Now is good."

"With you, now is always good," he said, spreading her soft folds to find the narrow way into the heart of her.

She was wet. It was more than rain. It was passion.

She had spent her life running from passion and passion's result; now she ran into the very center of it. Because of Hugh. Her vow to Ardeth and to herself lay buried in the mud of Warkham, and she could not care past the yearning need for his touch. So her mother had feared it would be. And so it was.

Yet what could she do? She was a woman, and this was the way of it. Had not God promised that a woman would want a man? Had He not foretold all as He cast Eve and her man out of Eden? A woman would hunger for her man, and her pain would greatly increase upon the childbed. So it was. So it had to be. She could not stand against the very word of God.

This was a battle she never could have won. This was a vow that was destined to be broken. Had Ardeth known that as well?

"I will be broken upon this," she said, the knowledge washing over her, the last warning before the final fall.

He slipped a finger inside her, thrusting in and out. She moaned and moved against his hand, wanting it. Wanting more, all warnings fading into fog.

"Trust me," he breathed, kissing her face, her brow, her nose, her mouth. "I will not betray."

She could not answer him. She was lost to speech, to thought, to memory.

Using her body, she urged him. Using her mouth, she

silently spoke of her hunger and her need. She had to have him.

She had to have him, even for only this moment.

He had seduced her. She was lost.

Forgive, Ardeth, and pray for your lost daughter.

With a turning of his hand, he exposed himself. She knew the look of him, hard and high and hot. With a gentle nudge, he pressed himself at the entrance to her womb. He was huge. A siege engine would have been more likely to enter her. It was impossible.

With another nudge, a push, a groan, he was into her further. She could look down and see where they were joined. His manhood pulsed, thick with blood, gigantic. He was halfway lost in her, a miraculous joining of two bodies into one. She could see it now, how true God had been in describing this event. Two into one. Yea, it was that.

"Look at us," he said. "Watch me take you. Watch me lose myself in you."

She looked at him, his eyes green as the boughs above her, clear and bright with rain. He held himself still, letting her soften around him. With a slow smile, he kissed her. A tender kiss, a kiss of passion muffled, leashed and subdued. But living still, breathing, waiting.

"Am I hurting you?" he asked, caressing her breasts, her back, her face.

"Not enough," she said, squirming against him. She needed more. There was more of him and she wanted all.

"More?" he said just before he kissed her, his hands on her face holding her with tender ferocity.

When he released her mouth, she breathed into him, "More."

With a surge, he was in her. She felt a burning, a tight stretch, a rending that was sharp and hot. And then a fullness. A heat. A glowing heaviness that filled her up until she spilled out of herself onto him, losing Elsbeth into Hugh. Losing earth into heaven. Losing all.

"Hurt?" he asked softly, holding his hands on her derrière, pulling her onto him.

"Aye," she said, and he instantly let himself slip partway out of her. "Nay! I only know that I want you to stay. Do not leave me," she whispered against his throat, holding tight to him.

"I will not," he said, stroking her hair, pressing softly into her.

But he would. Yet his leaving was for later. For now, he was hers.

He held himself very still inside her, his breathing shallow, almost shaky.

"I am not hurt. Go to—I will not cry against it," she said.

"Cry against it? Nay, I would have you crying for it," he said, slowly pumping into her. "Fear not, little one. I take you to a place of wonders," he whispered. "Hold fast. I will not let you fall."

She needed this, needed him. This hot filling, this bonding, this oneness. She had not known how alone she was until Hugh filled her up.

Heat sank itself into her flesh, softening all her joints, stealing her breath, racing her heart. Her blood pounded against her flesh, searching for release, but there was no release for this ache. It only built and soared until all was shattered against it. Until she was blind in the white heat of it. Until she cried to be freed of the torture of her skin and breasts and mouth. Until the place of their joining, the open heart of her, was throbbing with want and need and finding none.

Finding none.

"Trust me," he breathed. "Follow me."

She tried. She tried to follow him, but it was too far,

too high, and she could not see where she would land from such a height if she did fall.

"Go. I cannot follow you," she said.

"Then do not follow. I will take you there."

He kissed her deeply, his hand snaking down her torso to find the source of all her torture. He touched her there, a gentle touch, light as sunlight, and she exploded into fire.

A burst of light and heat and force, and then she opened her eyes against it, squeezed her thighs against it, forced it away from her, so deeply afraid that she shouted out her fear. This was wrong. She could not do this.

"I have you," he said, pressing her hard against him, murmuring in her ear. "I have you, Elsbeth. It is nothing to fear."

"Please," she gasped, tears heavy in her throat. "I cannot do this."

" 'Tis done, Elsbeth. Fear not," he said, stroking her softly, kissing her cheeks and mouth and brow. "Fear not, little one. I did not let you fall. You are safe, are you not? All is well."

He slipped out of her, soft and small and wet, and then he pulled her close to him, sheltering her from the rain as best he could, his heat warming her.

"I did fall. I did," she said, wrapping her arms about his neck and holding him close.

"Perhaps you did," he said. "But it was only a little fall, and you were not alone in your falling. Did you not feel me holding you, sharing passion's fall together, keeping you safe? You are safe, Elsbeth. You are not hurt."

She was not hurt? Nay, that was wrong. This was wrong. All was wrong. She should not have done this, and she should not have found pleasure in it. This was wrong. All her life she had known it. This crying bond, this hot falling, was wrong.

Nothing Hugh could say would change that truth.

He lifted her to stand, and her skirts fell down to cover her. It was cold comfort as they were sodden and soaking. The sky was the dark of twilight and the rain was not abating. It was going to be a long, cold, sore walk to Warkham. She had to get back to Warkham and to her prayers. This had been a mistake. She needed to pray, asking for forgiveness for such a fall as she had taken.

She shook out her skirts, her back to him, her thoughts her own, and then she turned. There was something in his silence which struck her as false. He was upon his knees in the mud, looking at his cock. What there was to see, she could not have said.

He looked up at her. "There is no blood."

"Aye, my wrapping was clean. You marked it yourself, my lord. I bleed no more."

"And what of your maiden's blood? Where is that to mark me as the first to find my way into you? What of your blood, Elsbeth?"

Chapter Twenty-two

She had no answer to give him.

"I do not know, my lord. Washed away, perhaps?"

He seemed to consider it, looking up at her, speculating.

" 'Tis possible, I suppose," he said.

"What other explanation is open to us, my lord?" she said, her anger rising like smoke from a damp wood fire at his tone, his face, his very question. "I am no expert in these things, as you seem to be. What cause can there be for a virgin not to show her blood on her husband's cock?"

"*You* are angry?" he asked, rising to his feet, tucking his clean, white cock away from view. Small blessing.

"You are very astute," she said dryly, lacing her bliaut. The laces were leather and were slippery in the wet chill of the day.

"By the saints, Elsbeth, a husband has the right to know such a thing. There is no blood to mark my way into you. 'Tis something for a man to ponder, is it not?"

"Is it? I only know that you seem much taken with my blood, my lord. First, there is too much. Now, there is too little. You are very difficult to please in the matter of my bleeding."

Hugh took her by the arm, but she shook him off. Her patience and forbearance, certainly approaching legend, were thinned to breaking. He had pulled her off the roadway, stripped her naked in the rain and taken her virginity in the mud. And now *he* was angry, and all because there was not enough blood to soothe his vanity and pride? Had she not given him enough? Did he want still more of her, her very blood?

"A virgin bleeds, Elsbeth. There is no mystery in that. But if she does not bleed . . ."

"Then she is no virgin?" she snapped. "I am, or was, a virgin, my lord Hugh. No man had made his way into me. I was pure and would have joyously stayed pure, yet you would not give me that, would you? You would not let me have my heart's desire. All my life, all I have ever wanted was to keep my distance from men, yet you had to take and hold and touch and make me your own, by blood. By my blood. What have you lost here today? Nothing. And yet you will gain nothing. I will not give you Sunnandune to toss into my father's keeping. If you thought that you would take my will when you took my body, you were wrong. This seduction has gained you nothing you sought."

"Do you mock me, little one?" he asked sharply, taking

her arm again and helping her over the bracken to the roadway. "I would not mock what we have shared just now, and let me say again what I sought from you in this joining. Not Sunnandune. Not knights. Not power. I sought only you, Elsbeth. I wanted only you. Will you say now that you regret your choice? Will you mock this bonding we have forged in our heat?"

"You would not mock? Yet you question my very purity. I was a virgin. No man had touched me, until you. No man had fouled my purity, until you. No man! None! Only you," she said, her voice hard and harsh with the first true anger he had seen in her. "What more would you have of me than that? You have taken me, entered me, branded me with your touch and scent. I never wanted such. I only sought to be free, and now I am . . ." she said, her voice sliding into soft despair.

"Mine," he finished for her. "Mine, Elsbeth. Always you will be mine."

She looked up at him, her eyes furious and black. "Always? By your very words your wish is to leave me to my father, broken of my will and of my wealth while you seek fame in Jerusalem. How do you find 'always' in that? Did you give no thought to me at all when you plotted with my father and spoke your marriage vows?" she finished softly.

"Aye, I thought of you," he answered her. Too much he thought of her. Too little was there of Baldwin in his thoughts of late, and much too much of Elsbeth.

"And now you think I have deceived you. You think I was no virgin, yet when have I ever lied to you, my lord, and why would I lie over this? Is this not the perfect escape for me? If I had told you that my maidenhead was a memory, would you not have sought nullification of this marriage, and is that not all I have ever wanted of you? If I had not been a virgin, my way would have been clear. I would have told you. I would have been served most well by telling you."

A telling point, yet why should he believe her? There had been no blood, and a man counted much on such a sign.

He looked down at the ground at his feet, at the mud that rose to engulf his ankles, and sighed. He knew Elsbeth. She sought prayer, not men, and she did not lie. He had never known a woman who held so hard to truth. Besides, she was a woman who did not run to temptation and the fall that surely followed. His wooing of her was the boldest proof of that. If ever there was a woman who would not tumble heedlessly into passion, it was Elsbeth.

He would believe her. She had been a virgin, a bloodless virgin. In any other woman, he would have doubted. But not Elsbeth.

"I believe you," he said, looking down at her. "You were a virgin. A man looks for blood, yet Elsbeth is more than blood, and her word is all the proof I will ever require."

"You take me at my word, my lord?" she asked, looking at him, understanding the weight of what she asked of him. It was a rare man who would take a woman at her word, especially in the matter of her purity. Indeed, he could not think of a one who would do it.

"Your word is all I require. I do not doubt you. You were a virgin until I found my way into you. You never knew a man's kiss or a man's touch or the flare of desire."

"Until you," she said, looking into his eyes.

"And so it shall remain," he said softly.

"And so it shall remain," she said, sealing the vow.

If he lived out his life alone in Jerusalem, she would be his English wife. If she lived out her life in the abbey, she would be the wife of Hugh still. Whatever befell, they were one. He would take no other wife, and he would never release her to take another man. Even if he could only have her distantly, still she would be his.

They stood in the rain, letting themselves be washed of all anger and doubt. It did not take long; the rain was falling heavily, and there was more trust shared between them than he had known.

How that she had come by his trust?

He did not know how he had come to this place with her; it had been no part of his plan. He was vulnerable in such a place, this trusting of a woman, yet he could not climb back to where he had been.

"So, then," he said lightly, forcing the weight of his vulnerability behind him, "let us make our muddy way back to Warkham. I will need a bath and dry clothes and a hot fire, in that order. And a new pair of boots. Does Warkham have a proper bootmaker?"

"My lord, I do not know," she said, a grin slowly finding its way to her face.

"Well, I shall find out, and soon. I cannot be about in these poor boots for another day. They are fit for the ashes and nothing else. I shall mourn them, Elsbeth. 'Twould not be amiss for you to say a prayer that my sister will forgive the destruction of her gift. I would not face her wrath on earth or heaven," he said, grinning and taking her by the hand. "You will pray for me, my boots, and my sister?"

"Aye, my lord, I will pray," she said as they walked hand in hand together in the rain. "Yet what of Sunnandune and your bargain with—"

"Let us leave all that for now. Let us stay in this place of only Hugh and Elsbeth for a while more. Let us think of nothing beyond the rain, my pitiful boots and our next step upon this muddy track."

But it was not to be.

"You have lost," came a voice from out of the wood.

Hugh turned and pulled his sword free in one motion, pushing Elsbeth behind him as he faced the man who owned the voice.

Edward came out of the wood noisily, his sword out, his hair hanging on his brow. Edward, as was his way, had been too quick. Silence would have served him better.

"The day is done and you do not have Sunnandune," Edward said. "My charge is clear. I bear you no offense, Lord Hugh, yet still, I have my duty to my lord."

Hugh wasted no words in reply but charged the man who stood with drawn sword, while his wife shivered at his back. He knew what this was about. He knew the man who had set all in motion, and he knew that there was no more need for courtesy. When next he saw Gautier, they would face each other over steel.

Hugh lunged before Edward could leave the wood, his feet mired in brush and mud, his sword arm shadowed by low overhanging branches. For just a moment, Edward could not strike. It was in that moment that Hugh cut him down. A single thrust and Edward fell, his blood springing up from a wound to his neck where it joined with the shoulder, his mail buried into the flesh in bloody rings. With a grimace, he stumbled into the bracken, wet and slippery. His purchase lost, he tumbled to the ground, his sword still up and seeking, yet his legs collapsed beneath him.

He was done.

"You are quick," Edward said as he stared up at the sky. He dropped his sword and clutched his wound, but there was no stopping the flow of blood. Nay, it sprang from him with a will and charged down his body to slide into the mud, dark and wet. "I had not thought it of you, a Poulain."

"Nay?" Hugh said, holding his sword to be washed by the rain. "You are proven wrong. A hard lesson."

Edward smiled on a sigh and then he died. The rain came down. Elsbeth shivered at Hugh's back and said nothing.

Hugh turned to her, his sword still out and shining in the uncertain light, and clasped an arm about her shoulder.

"My father did this," she said through chattering teeth.

"Aye," he answered, smoothing back her hair with a single hand. "He wants Sunnandune, his wanting taking him beyond all caution and all reason."

"We must go to Sunnandune! We cannot stay in Warkham," Elsbeth said. "Even now he could be out there, looking for us, searching . . ."

Her skin was white with fear, and Hugh took her in his arms and closed her against the sight of Edward and his blood and the chill rain washing over them all. If he could have swept her up and away into the clouds, he would have done so, yet he was but a man, his place upon the earth.

"We shall go," he assured her. "Yet can I leave without Raymond and the trappings of my knighthood?"

"Nay, I suppose you cannot," she mumbled distractedly. "Yet we must fly from here. Warkham is not safe."

"And so we shall fly, but first we must return and make a proper departure."

"But—"

"I will not lose you, Elsbeth. I will defend you with my life," Hugh said, stroking her arms and back. "I will not leave you to him. Trust me for that. All will be well. I have some skill at arms, if I may boast."

Elsbeth laughed and shook her head at him. "You jest, and I know it is done to ease me, yet you do not know him as I do. We are not safe. We must away."

"And so our leaving begins with our preparations," he said, turning them to face the return walk to Warkham. "I will let no harm befall you."

He believed every word he spoke, yet he did not know Gautier as she did, and so his sincerity, his certainty that all would be well, did not give her any peace at all. These were the fears which dragged at each step on the long, wet walk back to Warkham Tower.

"Here they are!" Denise said, running across the bailey, leaving Raymond behind her. Raymond followed more sedately, if no less eagerly.

"Here we are," Hugh said, reaching down to rub a hand across Denise's hair. He looked at Raymond, and they shared a glance of meaning and flickering alarm. "Where is Gautier?" Hugh asked quietly.

"It is almost dark! Where were you?" Denise said, pulling at Hugh's hand.

"My lord, he rode out past the gate at None and has not returned," Raymond answered.

"Did he ride alone?" Hugh asked, handing Denise over to Elsbeth.

"Aye, my lord," he answered.

"Keep watch then upon the gate while I stay close upon Elsbeth. We leave at once, for Gautier has broken all bargains."

"You leave at once?" Denise said plaintively. "Where are you going?"

"My lord, I have much prepared even now. It will take me but a moment to saddle the horses," Raymond answered and then ran off into the darkness.

"Where are you going?" Denise demanded of Hugh, her voice becoming shrill. "Do not go! Do not leave me."

"We must, Denise," Elsbeth said, caressing the girl's head. "You will be safe here."

"I am not!" Denise said sharply. "I do not want to stay without you."

"Yet you must," Elsbeth said. "This is the place of your fostering. You must remain. You will be well."

"Elsbeth, do you not go to collect your things?" Hugh asked as he watched the gate for the arrival of Gautier, watched the men-at-arms for signs of aggression, watched the skies for the emerging stars and the end to endless rain.

All for Elsbeth. Every thought for her. When had she captured him so completely? There was no room for Baldwin in his mind when Elsbeth had so firmly entrenched herself within his heart. He had no plan for Sunnandune or for his promised knights or even for Jerusalem; he only sought her safety, certain he could make good on his promise.

"Please," Denise said, her voice rising into tears, "do not leave me. I hate Warkham."

Elsbeth looked down into Denise's shining eyes, something pulling hard at her heart with the girl's words. She felt the same. She hated Warkham. Even now, she longed to run past the gates, empty of all but speed, her hands free of every possession, every bliaut, every girdle, every comb, all to rush free of Warkham and her father. Could she blame Denise for feeling the same?

"Can we not take her?" she said to Hugh.

"She is not ours to take," Hugh said softly.

"I will take her," a voice said from out of the darkness. It was Father Godfrey, and he was holding a torch whose flame was swept wildly in the swirling wind. The rain disappeared in an instant, leaving behind only wind. "She should not be left alone to Warkham's courtesy. I will watch over her."

"Nay, I want to go with you," Denise said, burying her face against Elsbeth's ribs.

"Thank you, Father," Hugh said briskly, content that the matter was settled so well.

Yet Elsbeth was not content. What could the priest do? Was not his life circumscribed by prayer?

Should not prayer be enough?

351

"Do not leave me with him! Please take me with you," Denise cried, hanging onto Elsbeth's skirts.

"We cannot, Denise," Hugh said, taking her arms from Elsbeth and kneeling in the mud to face her. "We dare not. There is much amiss between the lord of Warkham and the lady of Sunnandune. Would you make it worse? For so it would be if we stole you from your proper place."

"I do not care," she sobbed, burying her face against his shoulder. "I only want to go with you."

"Denise," Father Godfrey said, laying a hand upon her head, "God will suffice for this. You must trust in His goodness and His bountiful provision for you. All will be well for you in Warkham. God will see it so."

God would see it so? Nay, these words struck dull and deep in Elsbeth's heart. Nothing was ever well in Warkham. Not even prayer could surmount Warkham's walls and escape the grip of Warkham's lord.

'Twas blasphemy to think it, and she shook the ache from her heart. God was mightier than Gautier. God was a strong tower and a fortress for the righteous. It was so. It had always been so.

Yet it was not so, not in Warkham when Warkham's lord was in residence.

"I do not believe you," Denise said, her crying becoming wildly desperate. "I do not believe anything you say."

Hugh looked at Elsbeth in expectation. Would she not soothe the child, admonish her not to speak so to their priest and guide in the affairs of heaven? He looked in vain. Elsbeth had no words to speak against that charge.

"In belief there is rest, Denise," Father Godfrey said, unoffended. " 'May the Lord of peace Himself give you peace at all times and in every way.' So he gives us His promise, for all times and in all ways."

Aye, God gave His promise, yet what was a promise but a vow, and did not vows shatter? Would God's word shatter when thrown against Gautier? 'Twas blasphemy to think it, yet she could not find the strength to control her thoughts. Her shattered vow to Ardeth seemed to break all vows, all controls within her heart and mind.

"All is ready, my lord," Raymond said, coming from the darkness into the torchlight. He had prepared three horses, one for his lord, one for himself and one pack animal. There was no horse for Elsbeth.

Elsbeth turned to look at Hugh, and within her arose the same plaintive cry that had come from Denise's mouth. *Do not leave me. Take me with you.* Yet she said nothing, she only stared.

The bargain with her father was broken, had been broken upon Hugh's sword. There was no hope of his getting Sunnandune, and so there was no hope of claiming the knights of Gautier's promise. Hugh had no more need of Elsbeth. He had even taken her body, proving his manhood upon her. Nay, of what more use was Elsbeth?

"Elsbeth? You are staying?" Denise asked, sniffling. "I do not mind staying if you are with me."

Still, she said nothing. She could only stare at Hugh in the darkness.

Hugh stared back at her, frowning. "You thought I would leave you," he said softly. And then, "You thought I would leave you?" he growled. "You are my wife. I swore to you time and again that I would not betray, and I will not. I will not, Elsbeth," he whispered. "You are mine. Did I not swear that I would keep you? Did I not tell you that we had traveled far beyond Sunnandune? Did you believe none of it?"

"There is no horse for me," she said. What more needed to be said? No matter what he had vowed, there was no horse for her. She could not fly to Sunnandune, though she had often wished it.

"Do you have a horse that is not Warkham's?" he

353

asked. "I will not steal from him, giving him cause in this battle we must face."

Nay, she did not have a horse of her own. She had come to Warkham in a cart sent by Richard and Isabel; cart and driver and accompanying knight had returned to Dornei long ago.

Hugh read the answer in her eyes.

"You ride with me, Elsbeth. You stay with me," he said. It was a promise.

The warmth of feeling that pulsed through her at his words shamed her. She should not need him. How had she come to need him?

"What of Denise?" she asked.

"Denise must stay," he said.

"Nay!" Denise said, clutching his hand.

"Aye, it must be so," he said to the child. "I have no just cause to take you from here. You must stay; Father Godfrey will attend you as best he may, and I will write your father and urge him to make another fostering for you. I can do naught else, Denise."

"You could if you wanted to!" she said, pushing away from him, rushing into the penetrating dark of Warkham. "You can do what you want. I know you can!" she shouted.

Guilt pulled hard at Elsbeth, and she turned her face from it. There was naught she could do. They could not take Denise with them. They had to leave Warkham, and if a rebellious and contrary girl could not understand that then she was to be pitied, but still they must go. Her own relief at being rescued from Warkham she did not look too closely upon.

"My lord, we must away," Raymond said, laying a hand on Hugh's shoulder.

"Aye, go. I will attend her and calm her," Father Godfrey said.

It seemed unlikely. Denise had never been overfond of Father Godfrey.

"My lord?" Raymond urged.

Hugh mounted with a sigh of frustration, and Raymond helped Elsbeth to mount behind his lord. It was a precarious perch as she was behind the high rise of his saddle, yet there was nothing to be done about it. Elsbeth hung on mightily as Hugh urged his mount forward, piercing the darkness of Warkham's bailey. Gautier had not returned, had not called his men down upon Hugh's head, but that could change in a moment. They had to leave or risk losing their very lives.

Raymond hesitated and called out softly to Hugh's back, "I will come anon. Do not slow for me. I come." And then he was gone, blending into the shadows of the bailey.

He knew where to find her. In the solar.

He entered, though it was not quite proper for him to do so, but these were not proper times. She sat upon a simple stool and looked into the fire. It flickered halfheartedly and only increased the shadows in the corners of the chamber. Denise, with her fair skin and light hair, lit the chamber like moonglow.

"I thought you were leaving," she said, looking down at her fingers, entwined upon themselves.

"I am leaving," he said, crossing to her and kneeling at her feet. She would not look at him.

"Go, then."

Raymond stood but did not leave.

"I will come back for you," he whispered.

Denise looked up at him, her eyes bright, and then they dulled and she shook her head. "You cannot make that promise. You go where he goes, and he goes away from Warkham."

"I will not serve Hugh forever," he said. "I know you

hate it here. I will come and take you wherever you want to go."

"I want to go home," she said, her voice very small and tight.

"I am certain that you will go home. Hugh will write the letter to your father. You would aid yourself if you sent a letter of your own. Ask Father Godfrey if he will aid you."

"Why should he aid me?"

Raymond smiled and said, "Do you think he wants you about Warkham? You cannot be a favorite of his, your soul being so very rebellious."

Denise smiled slowly. "You are no more a favorite of his than I. I think you were chased out of Jerusalem for fear that you would foul the very air."

"The air of Jerusalem cannot be fouled; it is the air of God Himself. You would know that if you knew anything at all."

"I know that you are a very"—she was searching for the perfect insult, and then blurted out—"a very able squire. I think you shall be a wondrous knight."

Raymond said nothing. He and Denise looked into each other's eyes for a time, the fire dying a slow and quiet death, and then he grinned.

"You flatter me so that I will walk with you to the chapel, in search of Father Godfrey."

"And so that you will ask him to write the letter," she said with a grin.

"You are a very cunning damsel," he said as she stood up from her stool.

"Will you do it?" she asked as they walked toward the door.

"I will," he said.

"Then I do not think being called cunning is an insult."

Raymond laughed softly as they crossed the hall and said, "You are right. It is not."

Chapter Twenty-three

They rode through the night, the rain gone but for the rich moisture in the air. The stars glimmered out from behind the clouds, white and silver and blue in the black of night. They rode to Sunnandune, south and east of Warkham, leaving the sea and the River Nene behind them.

"Where are we bound?" she asked.

"To Ely," Hugh answered, "on the Ouse River. Yet we cannot fly that far in a single night. We will stop at Crowland Abbey for the night. Tomorrow will we reach Ely."

"Do you think he will follow?" she asked, turning to look behind her. Only Raymond rode behind, a stalwart heart who would not fall without hue and cry to mark it, nay, nor blood. He would fight hard for his lord.

"Aye, I think it in him. His will is thwarted. He cannot be pleased," Hugh said.

As Hugh's own will and quest had been thwarted. He had bargained for Sunnandune and had lost. How pleased could Hugh be at this turning?

"Where is he now, do you think?" she asked softly, more to herself than to Hugh. She could almost feel her father running behind them, like a wolf in the wood, running after them, hunting them.

Fear and the irresistible urge to run and hide swelled like the rising tide within her. This was what Denise had felt at being left in Warkham. Elsbeth knew that fear. She remembered it. It was no small thing, this fear of Warkham. It was no small fear to be a child, without voice, without power, without succor in Warkham Tower.

She remembered that, though she remembered little else of that time.

She had left Denise to that. She had left on a running horse with a strong knight to defend her. Denise had been robbed of aid so that Elsbeth might escape.

She was coming to understand an unpleasant truth about herself. She was a coward. What of Elsbeth, Prayer Warrior? All mist and cloud, a name built on whispers, a legend built on boggy marshland: a lie. An unpleasant truth, yet one she could not ignore as she had ignored Denise.

"Turn back," she said in her husband's ear. "Turn back to Warkham."

"Did I hear you aright?" he said, slowing his horse to a stop.

"Turn back," she said, laying a hand upon his arm. His arm was mighty. What had she to fear? "We cannot leave Denise. You know that we cannot, no matter what befalls us."

"You risk all, little one," he said.

"And you do not?"

"I am a warrior," he said. "It is my function and my desire to fight, risking all."

"And I am Elsbeth. Have you not heard of her? She is a prayer warrior of some merit. It is time she earned the name. Take me back," she said.

"I cannot put you in harm's way, little one," he said softly, laying his hand over her own. "If I die in this, what would Gautier do to you to get Sunnandune for his own? I cannot take you back to that."

Aye, there was much her father could do to her, but she would not think of that now.

"You will not die. You are a fearsome knight; does not the world know that for a truth? I have no fears which are greater than your might. It is for Denise that I fear now."

"What of Denise? She is safe there. No harm can befall her in that strong tower."

"It can," Elsbeth said. "We must go to her. Her fear is great."

"Her fear is not so great as it was," Raymond said. "I left her in the care of Father Godfrey. He is writing a letter to her father, begging her release from Warkham with all haste."

"Father Godfrey? Nay, we must return," Elsbeth said, all pretense of serenity flown. "Hugh, trust me as you have urged me time and again to trust you. We have little cause for trust between us, yet I have trusted you when all counsel has urged me down a different path. Give me now the same. Trust me. We must return to Warkham."

Trust her? All was lost because of her. His quest a failure, his good name in Jerusalem spent, his future torn from his grasp to lie in her half-closed hands. She had given him nothing that he wanted and had taken from him all that he had hoped to find, and now she asked for his trust.

His trust. To walk into a battle he could not win. Gautier would not fight him, that had been proved. Nay, Gautier would use the men of his holding to fight for him. Odds of a hundred to one, if Raymond were discounted. There was no winning here. This was not a matter of trust; it was of logic and of might and of men, yet she made it a matter of trust between them.

"Of course we must return," he said against all logic and all reason and all wisdom. Because Elsbeth asked it of him. Because she trusted him to make all right. Because she believed him able to meet all odds. Because she asked him, and in her eyes he saw all the victory he would ever need. "Come, Raymond. We ride for Warkham Tower."

* * *

He had come looking for her, of course. She was not very difficult to find, not if a man knew where to look. The solar was oft used, as were the kitchens, but the chapel was the favored place for young girls to find a place of seclusion. He did not mind the chapel; 'twas quiet and full of heavy dark. Nay, he liked the chapel well enough.

He watched her as she slept, her blond hair shining like a streak of moonlight in the candle's glow. Such pretty hair.

He reached out a hand to stroke her hair, a gentle touch, hardly touching her at all. Yet he did touch. He had the right.

She stirred and mumbled in her shallow sleep.

He crouched down and swept his cloak over them both, a cocoon of dark warmth in the vaulting darkness of the chapel. She awoke with a sharp start, moving away from him instantly.

"Sleep on, Denise," he said. "I will warm you."

But she did not sleep on. She tensed, stiffening against him where he held her hip close to his own.

"Why are you here?" she whispered.

Gautier smiled in the dark. It was good that she whispered. She knew that what he wanted from her had to remain secret. In secret and in whispers he came to her. In secret and in whispers would she remember this night. "I am here to find a girl who needs comfort and warmth."

"I do not need anything," she said, squirming from his side. Unsuccessfully.

"Nay, you are chilled. I will warm you," he said, stroking her hair. Beautiful hair, soft and white, and her skin smelled like . . . flowers, like summer.

"I am not chilled," she said.

"You are, Denise, and you must not lie. 'Tis a sin to lie."

"I do not lie!"

"Yet you are cold. I can feel it," he said, running his hand over her body, over the slim and perfect line of her form, over the softness of her skin.

"I do not . . ." she said, stammering, her teeth chattering, her body beginning to tremble. "I do not want you here."

"Nay?" He grinned, holding her firmly. "Have I asked what you want? It is what I want which should concern you."

"I do not care what you want!" she said loudly, pushing at his hands.

"Then you are in sin, Denise, for a woman to show her lord anything but docility is sin. Obedience. Submission. This is the mark of a godly woman. Is it not your mission on this earth to be as holy as Christ Himself?"

"I know not," she said.

"The path to that righteous holiness," he said, continuing on as if she had not spoken, "is submission. You must obey your lord in all he says. You must submit to his will, Denise. That is what is required of you."

"I do not care!" she said, trying to find an opening in the cloak, her hands frantic within the long folds of the fabric.

"Yet you must," he said, running his hand down her smooth, straight form. "I must show you the right path in this. I will instruct." She was as slender as winter grass, supple and unmarked by disease or childbearing. Unblemished. Pure. Untouched.

Until now.

"Stop! Raymond!" she cried, her voice muffled by the cloak and the darkness, by the celestial reaches of the stone itself. There was no one to hear her. And if they did? He was lord here. His will was law. "Hugh! Hugh!" she cried.

Aye, she would cry for the Poulains. They had kept him from her, always at her side. Yet now they were gone. Even Emma was gone, she who had kept this girl shunted away in the solar, dirty and forgotten. But he had not forgotten her. He had only waited for his time. His time was now.

"Hugh? Hugh has fled. You are alone, except for God. He has not left you. He sees you even now. Cry instead to God, little one," he said, reaching between her legs to feel the hairless place of her womanhood. "Pray and see if your prayers are answered. If you are righteous, He will deliver you. Pray hard and pray long, that is my counsel. But I will tell you now what God will say. Submit. Submit and you will be blessed."

"God would not say that!" she screamed.

She struck out at him, a tiny flurry of hands and feet and screams. This was new. Never before had he been fought with such fierce terror. He did not find it worrisome. She was small and smooth; he could take her at his will with none to stop him. So it had always been. So it would be now.

The cloak whirled in a sudden cold gust, and then there was the stamp of sodden boots drawing nigh. The cloak was pulled from him, the shelter of dark stripped off. The light of the single chapel candle was blinding for an instant, and he blinked hard, shutting out the light and finding temporary solace in the dark. A tall shadow rose up against the stone shadows. Blond hair shimmered softly in the flickering light. It was the Poulain. Gautier would not have thought it. Should Hugh not even now be running from Gautier's anger and the long reach of his sword?

"Hugh!" Denise cried out, scrambling against him.

"Be gone," Gautier growled out at the intruders, holding her fast.

Denise bit his hand, crying out, "Let me go!"

Gautier stood, taking Denise with him by the back of her thin neck. Hugh stood with his squire at his side, his look dark and cold as surely he had never looked before. Elsbeth appeared from out of the shadows. She was holding a lighted taper before her, pushing the darkness from her and from them all. It made a circle of light that she carried like an angel into the blackest portion of hell.

Yet Gautier knew that for a lie. Elsbeth was the key to it all, the weak, soft spot upon which rested his victory. Gautier smiled at seeing Elsbeth.

"Help me!" cried Denise, twisting in Gautier's grasp. Never had a child shown such fight. He did not know what to make of her.

"Release her," Hugh commanded, coming up to him and grasping hold of Denise to take her in his arms.

Gautier hesitated and then let Denise go; the fight now was for Elsbeth, and if Hugh did not see that, so much the better. The child threw herself at Hugh, who pushed her from him and away from his blade. It was in Elsbeth's waiting arms that she found the warmth and comfort Gautier had promised.

Gautier stood to face Hugh and his anger, watching him tighten his grip upon his sword. And then Gautier smiled. This would not be a fight of arms. This battle was all of hearts, and hearts were turned with words, not steel. Hugh was outmatched.

"Returned? You have met the bargain, then?" Gautier said softly. "You have won Sunnandune from her, as you said you would."

"This is not of Sunnandune. This is all of Denise. What were you about with her?" Hugh asked.

"This is not of Sunnandune? All is of Sunnandune. Sunnandune is the key upon which all riches open. Do you care nothing for your knights, Hugh? They are ready. I have only to drop them into your hand," Gautier said softly, his smile relentless.

It was a temptation, Hugh could not deny it. So many knights, so much glory, so well received by Baldwin, the best man of the age, and all to be had for the price of forty virgates. It seemed a paltry price for so rich a prize.

"What of Denise?" Elsbeth said from behind Hugh, her voice rising to the smoky heights of the chapel. "You will not turn from that charge. Not with me. I cannot be tempted with a prize of many knights."

Hugh was jerked back from temptation at Elsbeth's words, and in his heart he thanked her. He would not be bought for so paltry a price as forty virgates.

Gautier turned to her and said easily, "I am about the training of this girl in the ways of a woman, though I do not answer to you, Elsbeth. Best you remember that."

"What training is it that takes place beneath the dark mantle of a cloak under the very rood of Christ?" Hugh said, shaking temptation from him, even as it clung to him like rain. With every shiver, he was doused yet again by visions of knights and glory and power. He did not know how to shake free of what permeated his very skin.

"I do not answer to you, Poulain," Gautier said, still grinning.

"Answer to this, then," Hugh said, twisting his sword to press it against Gautier's throat. His sword gleamed silver in the dim and holy light, throwing light and divine menace like the very sword of God.

"Will you kill me?" Gautier asked. "And lose all you came to find? I think you are wiser than that, Hugh. I know you well."

"You do not know me," Hugh said.

"Aye, I do. I chose you from among many, and I chose very carefully—the perfect man for my daughter. And the perfect man for me."

Hugh looked back at Elsbeth standing frozen in the

center of the nave, the soft glow of the taper embracing her in light. She looked at him, her dark eyes wide and solemn, her arm tight about Denise.

"You will not turn from this, Lord Gautier. Not this time. Answer me! What have you done to her?" Elsbeth said to her father, her eyes devouring him as surely as the hawk devoured the hare.

"Nothing but what any man may do when his eye is captured by a comely lass. Even your pretty husband may find warmth with other bodies in other places," Gautier said. "Do you not remember, Elsbeth? Do you remember none of it? I remember," he said with a tender smile.

"Nay, you lie," she said, her voice loud and strong, pushing memory from her, chaining it in the dark. He said that Hugh was like him? A bold lie, boldly told. Hugh was nothing like her father.

Nothing . . . except that they had bargained together to rob her of her legacy.

"A lie? When have I ever lied to you, Elsbeth? Never. It is this man from Outremer who is the Prince of Lies," Gautier countered.

"Nay," she said. "Hugh—"

"He has lied with every breath, Daughter—you know the truth of that. His words were nets of entrapment, woven of gold and silver strands of flattery, fit to catch the most wary of women. You, Elsbeth, he sought to catch your heart and you know why. He had to have Sunnandune of you. He never meant to stay. He never cared for you. And still does not. See how his eyes shine when he thinks of the glory of Jerusalem?"

"He lies, Elsbeth!" Hugh said. "He seeks to save himself."

"Aye, but only with the truth," Gautier said softly, looking hard at Elsbeth. "I have no other weapon, nor need one. Come, Elsbeth, you know 'tis true. I have never lied to you."

Nay, he had never lied. He had instructed her in duty and taught her the weight of it. He did not lie now. She knew the truth of what he said regarding Hugh. She had ever known these truths, yet she had thought, deceiving herself most willingly, that things had changed. That Hugh had changed.

Yet what had changed? Did not Jerusalem still need men of blood? Did not Hugh still love Baldwin? Did not Elsbeth still cling to Sunnandune?

Nay, nothing had changed. There was no lie in that.

"There are other crimes and sins beyond the sin of deceit," Hugh said, turning from Elsbeth to face the charges of her father. "Worse crimes. Dark sins. Speak to that, if you would speak, Lord of Warkham."

"He is very much like me, Elsbeth," Gautier said to her. "How does that sit with you? Well, I would think. Did I not arrange all well for you, Daughter?"

"He is nothing like you!" Elsbeth said sharply, her flame flickering. She disliked Gautier for some dark reason, and she was drawn to Hugh as to a bright flame on a cold night. Hugh could not be like her father. She had always and only wanted to escape her father. He was nothing like her father.

But had she not always and only wanted to escape Hugh?

"Leave, Elsbeth," Hugh said. "Raymond, see it done. Get them gone from here. I will not have her drink in his lies."

Raymond turned to Elsbeth, Denise wrapped within her arms. But Elsbeth would not move. Her eyes were trained on her father, and she would not be moved.

"Nothing like?" Gautier said and laughed. "Your mother could argue better for my cause. I won her heart as he has won yours, and in just such a fashion, by passion and by artful courtesy. Can you not see it, Elsbeth?

Aye, we are alike. Why else did you fall but that this falling was so familiar?"

A light came into Hugh's eyes, a light of holy horror, and then all was shadowed and shuttered, shut against the awfulness of truth.

"Raymond!" Hugh shouted. "Take Elsbeth out! No more will she hear this man's lies."

"Lies?" Gautier said, backing up a step from the drawn sword. "I do not lie. Look to yourself, Poulain, to see the Prince of Lies, Deceit, and Flattery."

"*You* are all lies," Hugh said, "all deceit, all trickery."

"Did I lie about Elsbeth?" Gautier said, dropping his hand down to his dagger. "Did I not speak true of her? Did you not find her submissive, compliant, a dutiful wife in all ways? Do not say you did not note her devotion. I take much pride in her ardent devotion. She is most prayerful, my daughter. I taught her well the power of prayer and the delights of divine seclusion."

"My devotion and my prayers?" Elsbeth asked, her brow lowered in confusion. "My devotion is my own; my prayers are my solace. There is naught of you in it."

"Nay?" Gautier asked. "I would have said that it was all of me."

"Elsbeth," Hugh said, turning toward her, his hand out in entreaty, "leave. Do not listen to him. Raymond! Do as I say. Take Elsbeth and Denise away."

"Enough," she said sharply, casting off Raymond's hand. "I will not leave. This is of me, and I will be part of it. You decide my fate, do you not, when you speak of Sunnandune? I will not leave you to it."

"You see," Gautier said to Hugh, one man to another as Raymond lifted Denise in his arms and carried her from the chapel, "she begins to cast off your net of seduction even now. You tempted her for a time, but she has thrown free of you. Did you not say that this would never happen? Are all your vows so easily tossed?"

"Prick me not, old man, or I shall prick you in return," Hugh snarled, clenching his swordhilt.

"I would stand amazed if you could prick at all, Poulain," Gautier said. "You could not prove it on my daughter."

Elsbeth looked at Hugh and at her father. They were alike. They were. It was so plain to see when the scales of desire were fallen from her eyes. She felt newly sighted, so clearly did she now see.

Handsome men, smooth of speech, easy in their arrogance and pride, and with a knack for seduction. Had her mother not told her of this, of how she had fallen into Gautier's hands, soft and willing, captured by his flattery and his beauty until all the world grew dim in his arms? Until all dreams were shattered when arms betrayed and let a lover fall. Until Sunnandune was signed away. Until passion called elsewhere, to other arms and other beds. Until all illusion died.

They were alike, Gautier and Hugh, but Elsbeth would not be like her mother. Had she not sworn a thousand times to walk a different path, to hold herself secure against all invasion, against all threat, against all men? Aye, so she had, and she had stumbled badly in her vow yet all was not lost, not completely.

It only felt that way.

The men battling over her looked into each other' eyes, reading each other, and Hugh could not ignore what he saw in Gautier's eyes. It was as if Elsbeth were laid open for him, all her fears and secrets lifted from shadow into light.

So this was the cause of her fear. This answered all yet he would give Jerusalem itself to have stayed in ignorance. But what of Elsbeth, who had lived, and live only to forget? How had she survived?

In devotion and in caution, as she did now; lesson learned in childhood and never to be forgotten.

"You fouled her, did you not?" he whispered hoarsely. "When she was a child, you took her and ruined her," he said over the sharp taste of his own bile. "As you attempted with Denise. How many girls have you ruined? How many girls have fought against your touch?"

"Ruined? Ruined Elsbeth?" Gautier answered high and proud. "I made her perfect, as I made them all. Elsbeth is all that a woman should be. A perfect wife, is she not? Compliant? Devout? Ever ready to do your will?"

"Nay—"

"Aye! Let us not lie, not to ourselves, brother knight," Gautier snarled, his dark eyes glittering in the light. "You have the wife you sought and found her perfect for your needs. This I did for you, long years past. You had only to ask and she gave you all you desired. Her wealth. Her body. Her will. All given unto you. Is that not so? Yet you mangled it somehow. She would have thrown all into your hands if only you had pushed past her blood and made her sing in sweet torment for you."

"Speak not to me! You foul the very air with the pestilence of your putrid soul."

"What fault did you find in her?" Gautier pressed, looking at Elsbeth over the rim of Hugh's shoulder. "None. None, because I had taught her better. I taught her what it was to be a woman."

"Nay," Hugh said, raising his sword again. "You taught her how to fear and how to live in the shadow of sin. That is no gift."

"You complain now? When you have won a wife men dream of?" Gautier said, softly laughing. "Aye, you would complain, having lost Sunnandune and the knights of your quest to clumsy handling. You are a man as I imagined them to be in the Levant. Soft. Womanish."

"Womanish?" Hugh said. "You have misjudged. I will kill you, Gautier, and by your blood, all sin will wash from Elsbeth and she will be healed."

"Will you?" Gautier asked. "You will lose your life in Warkham if you kill Warkham's lord, and you will lose the knights you came so far to find. Is Elsbeth worth all that? Is she worth your very life?"

It was true—he would lose all if he murdered Gautier. Was not Jerusalem worth more than a single girl?

"Lift your sword," Hugh commanded. "Let this be a battle of honor."

Gautier laughed. "Nay, I will not. I am no fool to give you a way out of this without a price to pay. Kill me and you pay with your blood. That is your choice. I know you have the skill to best me. You showed it to me so proudly, did you not? That was foolish, Hugh. I had thought better of you. I ask again, is Elsbeth worth your very life and the lives of all the souls who dwell in Jerusalem? Can a woman be worth all that?"

The answer should have come easily. Jerusalem was all he lived for. Until Elsbeth. Solemn dignity and quiet strength, that was Elsbeth. Stalwart beauty and devoted warrior. A tongue that scraped against his pride, honing him to brightness. A woman who resisted falling into the polished and practiced lure of him until he would fall with her.

"Elsbeth is worth all that and more to me," Hugh said slowly, the truth coming slow upon him, like an English dawn, heavy and soft.

"Ah, how ardent you are, yet did you not hesitate? There is more to this than Elsbeth. There is all of Jerusalem. Will you risk losing Jerusalem for the wavering shadow that is Elsbeth?"

"Elsbeth is no shadow," Hugh said softly.

Yet had he not thought much the same? Who was dark and shuttered Elsbeth when held against the golden light of the holy city of God? How long had he thought so little of her worth? From the very start, from the very

370

first look and the very first word of shining flattery he had poured into her heart.

When had that ended? He did not know. He had not been looking for it, and it had stolen upon him like mist in shadow, soft and quiet. Like Elsbeth.

"When held against shining Jerusalem?" Gautier asked. "I think she must fade away completely when compared to such a citadel of holiness and light."

Hugh looked down the shining length of his sword into Gautier's face. He did not like what he saw.

Gautier spoke Hugh's very thoughts and with his very words as they had been. As he had been. They *were* much alike. When had he ever given thought to any but himself? When had he ever put Elsbeth and her needs above his own desires? In twenty years, would he be like Gautier was now, this man who used all for gain and who thought of no one but himself? Would he use his smiles and his power to achieve all he thought he deserved in this life, abandoning his soul to polish his pride?

What of Elsbeth?

Yet what of Jerusalem and of Baldwin? 'Twas no light matter to toss aside the kingdom of God's earthly Son.

"You are like enough to be my son, Hugh. Why else do you think I chose you for her?" Gautier said. "We do what we must in this life, to get what we must."

Nay, there was more to this life than that. There was Elsbeth.

Elsbeth and his ill-timed love for her was the temptation he faced and must surmount.

How long had he loved her?

It could not matter. He could not lose all for loving Elsbeth. He could not renounce his king, his vow, his quest for a mere woman. For a wife. For Elsbeth. Even Elsbeth would not ask it of him.

Of course she would not. She asked him for nothing.

She set him free to find Jerusalem, yet what was Jerusalem against the beauty of Elsbeth's heart?

She would not ask, yet he would ask it of himself and give no less than the heart of his dream for her. She deserved so much more than a city and a kingdom. She deserved the very world.

Would he be like Gautier twenty years hence? He had lied too easily and too often. The truth of it was, he was Gautier now, unless he shattered that mold, breaking free.

He had fallen very far, very far, since coming to England, but he was Hugh of Jerusalem still and he would fall no farther.

With a wry grin, he faced Elsbeth's father. With a soft smile, he answered him.

"Elsbeth is worth more to me than a thousand Jerusalems," he said softly, his voice a ringing that chimed against the stone.

And with those words, Gautier threw his dagger.

He aimed it true and he was quick. It hit the mail covering Hugh's shoulder, piercing the links before falling, spent, to the stone floor. Before the dagger had even fallen, Hugh sliced his way into Gautier, leaving a bright wet arc of blood across his belly. He bled all over the stone of the chapel, sinking down into the wet stink of his own urine, fouling the place. As he had always done.

"What have you done?" Elsbeth asked softly.

Hugh turned to face her, this fractured woman who bore so many silent scars. He loved her. There was no other truth than that.

"I have killed your father," he said. "Will you forgive the act?"

"Forgive?" she asked slowly. "Do not mock. I am so black with sin that I cannot forgive any man."

"Elsbeth, you are as white as snow, washed clean by a

thousand prayers," he said, Gautier's blood dripping from the tip of his sword. "No sin clings to you. All sin rested hard in Gautier's hands."

Elsbeth said nothing, only looked at her father's body, at the blood flowing out of him to find small paths between the stone. He was going white, his cheeks sunken, his jaw punching against the sky. He had died very quickly and very easily by Hugh's hand. Perhaps Hugh had been right; he was a man to match her father. Perhaps there was nothing more to fear. Yet without her fear, what was left of Elsbeth? Had she not been ruled by fear and the hunger for safety all her life? Where was God, the strong tower for the righteous? Nowhere she could find Him.

Prayer upon prayer she had cast upward in her longing for deliverance and there had been no deliverance from Gautier of Warkham. There had been only the long falling that had marked her life. The sparrow fell and God did mark the fall, yet He did not stop the falling and the sparrow died. He did not stop it. The sparrow fell and fell. Denise had the right of it. There was no safety to be found on earth.

"The sparrow falls," she said softly, her eyes filled with tears. "Is that not so? I am that sparrow," she said, her anger rising. "I fell and fell and God let me fall. God did not save me. Where was God when I needed saving?" she demanded, her tears hot on her cheeks, falling to the stone, shattering against the cold.

Hugh stood very still, a weight of soul and muscle bound into a man. Her accusation hung in the holy air of the chapel, weighing heavily upon the very stone.

"Elsbeth, into this temptation I will not let you fall," Hugh said, his voice deep and strong. "Gautier caught you up in his long falling. God did mark it and God did send a rescuer from His right hand; He sent Hugh from His own city of Jerusalem. God did not fail you."

"Denise was saved," she said. "I was not. God's rescue is slow, too slow for me."

"Elsbeth," Hugh said, his voice stern and heavy, "look up. What do you see?"

She looked and saw what she had seen a thousand upon a thousand times, in every prayer and at every mass. The rood of Christ rose above them both, arms outstretched, face turned to heaven, body broken upon the cross.

"I see Christ upon His cross," she said.

"Aye," Hugh said. "Christ upon His cross. So often we see and so seldom do we remember what it is we are seeing. He was beaten savagely, was he not? His own mother did not know His face. He was lifted up for us, taking the blows meant for us. Yet will His servants have an easier burden than their Master? Nay, Elsbeth, it cannot be so," Hugh said, his own eyes filling with tears. "The earth is a hard place, a hard and brutal place awash in sin. How can we escape this life into the promise of eternity without a few blows to mark our passage? I would take this from you if I could," he said. "I cannot. But does not Christ heal as He Himself was healed? All wounds are washed clean, Elsbeth. All things made perfect in His sight, as you are perfect."

"I only wanted to be safe," she said, crying softly, wiping her eyes with the back of her hand. "God could have saved me from this."

"I know," he said, "yet even Christ was not protected from the sins of the world. There is no refuge from sin, Elsbeth, not on this earth. His blood is the only safety we have and you have been given the gift of His blood in full. And another gift, besides, I think," Hugh said. "He took all memory of this from you, is that not so?"

"I remember nothing," she whispered, staring at the blood of her father. "Yet he touched me, did he not? He marked me, staining me, and felt no shame," she said in horror. "That is why there was no blood. I could not bleed for you. He had bled me long ago."

Her hands began to shake, and Hugh stepped near to take the torch from her, placing it in a bracket on the stone wall of the chapel.

The memories shifted in the dark, rising up, formed and bleak, until she pushed them back into shadow, commanding them into disremembered mist. This was her daily battle, this battle of mind and soul. Like worms crawling into her heart, like maggots in her flesh, like the very decay of death, she was hounded and hunted by memory, praying for memory to die and stay dead.

Praying for release from the world of men, as her mother had taught her. Praying to be strong against the temptation of desire. Praying to resist the lure of a man's beauty and the charm of his smile. Praying to survive, as Ardeth had taught her the means and methods of survival in a world ruled by men and their lusts.

She had survived.

She had survived and been taken by Hugh of Jerusalem, and she had not found the way out of the temptation of loving him. And so she fell into the very pit her mother had warned her of. Worse, she gloried in the fall.

Ardeth would have been so disappointed in her.

Yet the world Ardeth had prepared her for had been all of Gautier and none of Hugh. Her mother had known naught else. Her mother's lessons had been true in a world ruled by Gautier, yet for a heart ruled by Hugh, they would not serve at all. Perhaps that was the final truth.

And perhaps this falling was not so hard a fall when two fell together, their very souls entwined about their hearts.

"If there be any man who has seen enough of Elsbeth's blood, that man is I," Hugh said softly, trying to cheer her. When that failed, he said, "He touched only the part of you he could reach, little one. Your soul he could not reach. The part of you that is eternal was never in his grasp. That is why you cannot remember. God has given that as His gift to you, a proof that Elsbeth is innocent and clean. Accept the gift and do not search in shadows, Elsbeth. Let lie. Let lie, little one," he whispered, holding her in his arms under the outstretched arms of Christ.

"What of my prayers? He said he touched my very prayers," she said, beginning to shake from her spine until her teeth chattered together at the force.

"He lied," Hugh said. "Only God can touch our prayers. And the prayers of Elsbeth, Prayer Warrior, are very dear to Him. Is that not so? Do you not defeat me at every prayer in our competition?"

"Do not mock me," she said, hanging her head. "He always mocked me. I would not see him in you."

Hugh dropped his sword to the stone and took her hard into his arms. "I would be whate'er you ask. Tell me never to jest again and I will walk in frowns. Tell me to lift my face unto the sky and I will gladly drown in English rain. Tell me to love you all my days," he said, urging her face up to his, "but, nay, do not ask me that, for that quest is done. I love you, Elsbeth, and will for all my days."

"Men say such things," she said, shaking her head in teary dismissal, "and such things are never meant, especially not to me. I know what I am."

"Mine, Elsbeth," he said. "You are mine. For now and for always. What more do I need to know?"

"Why would you want me, knowing what you know? Did I not keep saying I was unfit? Did I not speak true?"

"Did I say I wanted you?" he said, his smile weak and lopsided. "I need you, Elsbeth. I need you beyond all things this world can give. Beyond air, beyond sun, beyond rain, beyond the very blood of my heart, I need you. All polished words of chivalry have flown from me, there is only this hunger and this need to have you in my life and in my arms."

Elsbeth had no answer beyond the tears she could not stop. He pressed her to him, crushing her body against his own, his hair tangling with hers, golden strands, wet with rain, twining with curling black; shadow and light. Memory and truth.

They stood so and loved. Loved against kings and kingdoms, loved against wisdom and loving counsel. Loved against all and still loved on.

"That is lust, I think, and you will not die of it," she said, sniffing back her tears and smiling crookedly, leaving her past in the past. Letting lie, as he had urged.

"Churlish woman," he grumbled with a grin. "Then live your life at my side and prove me for a liar if you can. This is a game I will win, little wife. I cannot lose. Unless I lose you," he whispered against her brow. "That I will not do, no matter what else is lost."

"Jerusalem," she said. "What of Baldwin?"

Hugh rested his chin on the top of her head, his arms lightly about her, and said nothing for a while. It took some time for him to say farewell to Jerusalem and Baldwin and all he loved in far-off Outremer. It took some time for him to banish all the golden glories of his dreams to be buried in the dark quiet of Elsbeth and England. It took some time. Perhaps a moment.

"Baldwin will forgive," he said softly, his eyes lost in the shadows of the stone. "And Jerusalem . . . Jerusalem will fall. Yet I choose Elsbeth."

"I would not ask it of you," she said, bowing her head into the shadow of his arms.

"You would ask nothing of me, and there is so much in me to give. Let me give this to you, Elsbeth, a gift to us both," he said. "You are my Jerusalem, little one. You are all I seek in this life. You are every honor and every prize. It is your name I want linked to mine. Let me be no more Hugh of Jerusalem, but only Hugh, the heart and blood of Elsbeth. Having you, I am content to have nothing more. But I will not live on having less."

"Such pretty words," she said, shaking her head gently as the tears ran down her cheeks. "And so many of them. Can you not say it plain? I require no such speeches from you. Have I not said so from the start?"

Hugh released her to kneel before her. He was a golden glow of strength and force in the dark weight of Warkham. So he had always been to her. So he would always be.

"Then hear me, Elsbeth of plain speech," he said. "I will love you for all my life. I want no life that takes me far from you. Let Jerusalem fall. Let Baldwin curse me. Let us never make a child between us. So I will live with you, little one, satisfied to only be where Elsbeth is. First wife. Only wife."

Elsbeth smiled down at him and then laughed softly over her silent tears.

"This is plain speech? You promise to love me over words of Jerusalem and curses? You promise to love me yet not do the deed that makes a child? These are vows of love for courtly rituals of love. I am your wife, my lord. You need not flatter."

Hugh surged up from his knees and lifted her in his arms. Without a word, he carried her from the chapel and across the dark and muddy bailey.

"You are more churlish by the hour," he said, shaking his head in the dark of another soft night. She could feel his hair moving on the backs of her hands; it felt warm and golden even in the dark. "I do not know why I love you. What makes other women swoon, you find tedious. There is no finding my way with you. I am lost in dark Elsbeth and have no will to break free."

Elsbeth grinned as he kicked in the door to the hall and crossed the floor to the stair tower. The men of Warkham watched, the priest in their midst. Hugh slowed and faced them, Elsbeth held tight against his chest.

"I have killed your lord," he said to the men. "It was a matter of honor, and he was armed. My blood marks the wound he dealt before he died."

All eyes watched, and all hands were stilled at the pronouncement.

"My lord," Father Godfrey said, "all here know what befell in Warkham chapel. Raymond and Denise were not hesitant in declaring it," he said, holding his head high. "My shame is great that I could do naught during all the years of my time here. I came out of the abbey at Warkham's behest. I took the orders of the priesthood and was made to bear the burden of hearing his confession for these nineteen years. My burden was great, my lord, and there are few here who do not know of it, though I kept the honor of my vows."

"You knew what he did and you did not stop it?" Elsbeth said, and then fought the urge to hide her head when all eyes looked at her. They knew she had been fouled. Everyone knew. She felt stripped and shorn of all dignity.

"There were many who tried," Father Godfrey said, "but the manor courts in the time of King Stephen did little. Gautier was not the only man of those times to push past the boundaries of law and honor."

"So you did nothing?" Hugh said, his anger rising to heat them both. "In all of Warkham there was not a man among you who would kill this viper?"

"He was lord," Walter the miller said from the corners of the room. "What was there for us to do? Am I a knight? Do I have the skill of arms? Does this priest?

Speak not to us of what we did not do," Walter said heavily. "We did all we could."

"Which was very little," Hugh said sharply.

"Do you think your wife was his only victim? He took my Allota, ruining her past all hope. She died from his attentions. She was but six. If I could have done something, I would have done it then, but he left Warkham and was gone for more than a year, bringing new men of blood with him when he returned to guard him well, they who knew not whom they served. I watched him when he dwelt with us, as did we all, and watched out for the girls of Warkham, trying to keep them out of his way. Some escaped him. Elsbeth, his own daughter, God forgive, did not."

"Say no more," Elsbeth said. "Please."

"One thing more," Walter said. "I found you in the chapel once, your skirts torn and your thighs bruised and marked with blood. I held you in my arms and prayed with you for healing and for forgetfulness. I thank God with every Mass that the prayers of that hour were so well answered. Live on, Elsbeth. Give no thought to the man who bound you to his sin."

"Good counsel," Father Godfrey said. "Heed it well, Elsbeth, and forgive us if you can. We strove to find a path of escape, of justice, and could only pray that God would see it done. And so He has. He sent Hugh of Jerusalem to us and to you."

"What of the men who served this lord?" Hugh said. "The knights of Warkham—will they seek vengence on me?"

"Nay, they knew not what he was. The knights of Warkham change upon the seasons as they come to know their lord. These knights will do nothing, now knowing what they know. All fighting upon Warkham soil is done," Father Godfrey said.

And so it would remain. She closed her heart against

all memory of Gautier, accepting God's gift of forgetfulness. Let the dead stay dead and let the living cherish the gift of life.

"That is well," Elsbeth said to all within the hall. "All is well," she said more softly, for her husband's benefit.

When she felt the rage within him tremble against his skin, she whispered, "Let lie, Hugh. All is past. Let lie."

Hugh shook his head at her and breathed out a sigh before kissing her softly on the brow.

"And if Elsbeth speak it, then so it shall be," he said. "If I would give you all the world, then I can surely give you this."

"Give me this and I will not ask you for the world," she said, running her hand against his cheek, loving him with a touch.

"Done," he said, staring into her eyes.

"One thing more I ask of you," she said as he started to walk to the tower stair.

"Aye, and did I not know that with a woman there is ever to be 'one thing more'?"

Elsbeth grinned and buried her face against his neck.

"Take me to bed," she mouthed against his neck.

He ran up the last few stairs.

The fire was lit, awaiting them. He set her on the bed and lifted off his tunic. She put out a hand to stop him and said, "Yet one thing more."

"So begins my torment," he said on a growl.

Hugh ran his hands through his hair and grumbled, eyeing her on the bed. She smiled up at him, unrepentantly amused.

"Would you try again? Would you try to tell me how you love me in ways that are pleasing to my ears?" she asked sweetly.

"Nay," he said, his grin sudden and wide. "I will not. I will show you. My words do not reach Elsbeth's heart. Perhaps my hands will serve her better."

"Your hands will serve me better? I think that is a man's reasoning," she said.

"Lady, I think you are right," he said, leaning down to her, clasping her small face in his hands. "Now let us see if I can make you faint again."

Epilogue

"Things were easier when you kept fainting," Hugh said.

"I did not faint!" she huffed.

" 'Tis not a good time to argue, wife. I am very busy now."

"*You* are busy?" she snapped. "I can do this birthing with only Winifred to attend me. I am quite adept at birthings."

"Ah, but, wife, this is different, is it not?" he said, grinning.

Aye, it was. He had crossed the seas to bring to her the very best of midwives, cajoling the woman into settling herself in the damp soil of England when her roots were in Antioch; yet when Hugh was set on wooing, the woman was won. None knew that better than Elsbeth, and so Winifred attended her now and would stay for every birth beyond this first. The first was more than enough to occupy her.

She would have hit him most soundly if she could only move to reach him. The bulk of her stomach surged up and blocked even the sun. Even the moon. Even the very stones of Sunnandune. Yet it could not block Hugh. Nay, his face was looming above her girth, and he was grinning.

Well, he had good cause to grin. He was not the one

with pains ripping through his very bones. Nay, she had that hard honor.

Though she could not help smiling when the pain eased. He was so very determined to have her laughing through her labors. And he was so very successful. At least for now. She knew better than he what was to come. No woman laughed when the pain was sharp and low and long. Nay, 'twas all of screaming then.

"You are not going to scream, are you?" he asked, frowning.

"I may, if it suits," she huffed as he wiped her brow with a damp cloth. "Give me the cloth," she said, panting. "It eases the nausea to have it over my mouth. 'Tis the damp cool, I think."

"The damp cool? By the saints, you are going to give me an English child! Confess it, Elsbeth! You are conspiring to bring forth a child of fog and rain."

"I confess," she said as another pain began to slide its way over her belly. "I confess to having an English child, but he is not formed of fog and rain. Which is a pity."

"Perhaps now would be the time for another woman to attend; even little Denise," Hugh said, speaking to Winifred. He knew Elsbeth would not grant him leave. "I am ill-trained in such business as this."

"Leave Denise to Raymond, my lord. I want only you here with me now. Were you not with me at the start? And besides, what need have I for another woman when a knight from the Levant is near?"

"Have I just been insulted or flattered? I cannot discern," he said with a jaded grin.

"Oh, flattered, surely," she said as a pain built and washed over her like slow fire.

"Come, tell me," he said when the pain had passed, leaving her limp and drowsy. "We made this child that day in the wood, did we not?"

"What day in the wood? You have an appetite for

woodland rompings, my lord. I lose count."

"You must remember. I know you must," he whispered as Winifred felt her belly and pressed to feel the babe's head. It was low and turned. All was well, to judge by her look. "It was May Day last, the only day that month without a cloud to mar the sun. You cannot have forgot."

"I remember it was cold," she gritted out, holding fast to his hand.

"I remember only the sun."

"You would. 'Twas I who was bared from nipple to knee."

"Ah, so you *do* remember!" he said on a chuckle. "I think that was the day this child began. You screamed loud and long upon your release. I remember a flock of birds flew up in terror at the sound."

"I remember that one of them left the white signs of its terror upon my head," she said, throwing the cloth at him.

It hit him in the face squarely. Still grinning, Hugh bent to freshen it and then placed it, damp and dripping, over his wife's mouth. She breathed in deeply, her nausea quieted.

"There is a chance, then, if this child be conceived in light and sun, that he be more of Outremer than England."

"I wish only that he be of smaller head," she said before the pain overtook her.

"Would you take some ale?" Winifred said, holding the cup to her mouth. " 'Twill soothe."

"I would he were out of me. That would soothe better," she said, grasping the cup and drinking down a swallow before the next pain assaulted her.

"Not much longer, little one," he said, rubbing his hand down her thigh in a long caress. "He comes."

"He comes too slow and too hard," she said. "If I had the strength, I would . . ."

"Would what?" he asked.

Elsbeth smiled weakly and lay back on the mattress. "Sleep. Do you think I will sleep ever again?"

"Not for another year, at least."

"Oh, husband, you are cruel. A lie would have been sweeter."

Hugh shrugged and grinned and watched as Winifred spread Elsbeth's knees to feel of the babe between her legs. There was so much fear in this room; he bantered with her to keep the dark at bay. There was so much to fear. If he lost Elsbeth, the sun would die.

"I only repeat what my sister told me," he said. "She may have lied. But I do not think so; there was too much prideful anguish in the telling."

"Can you see the head?" Elsbeth asked.

"Yea, dark and wet and only just coming," Winifred said.

"What do you need of me?" Hugh asked the midwife.

"I need you to take my place on this bed," Elsbeth gritted out as another pain struck her fast and hard.

"That is a prayer I will pray God does not heed," he said, kissing her knee as he stroked her legs. They were trembling. She was trembling. And cold.

"What color is my skin?" she asked, suddenly deeply afraid. Why was she cold? Emma had been cold.

Hugh looked up from the progress of the babe and stared into her eyes, comforting her by his very calm. "The same color as when I first described it to you, little wife. The color of rising dough, warm and golden white, though now there is the flush of berries on your cheeks and chest. A repast for any man."

"I look of stout health?"

"You look robust," he said. "If you were not otherwise occupied, I would take you now."

"Not for another year, at least," she said, sinking back into the bed. "I quote."

"Oh, wife, you are cruel. A lie would have been sweeter. And truer," he said, grinning. "I quote."

"You misquote," she said.

"He comes," Hugh said, bending down to watch, his head lost to her sight and only his shoulders visible.

"Hurry him, if you would," she said, and then she screamed. The pain was unlike any she had expected. Sharp. Deep. Long. And then done.

"The head is out," Winifred said. "I have him by the neck. Slippery, like an eel, he is."

"By the saints, he is all of England, this one. All wet and soggy," Hugh said.

She could feel something coming, coming, and then it was out and the child sliding with it.

"God above!" Hugh roared "A great spill of water has just come washing out of you, Elsbeth!"

" 'Tis the water of the womb. 'Twas trapped behind him," Winifred said.

The pain was a swiftly receding memory, praise God above. "Is he out?" Elsbeth asked.

"Aye, she is," Winifred said, handing the babe to be clutched to Hugh's chest, the cord a twist of blue and red.

"A tiny English lass born in a crashing wave of bloody water," Hugh said, his eyes swimming in tears.

Elsbeth felt the pain of her afterbirth trying to break free. A dim pain when compared to the birthing of a child. She leaned up on her elbows, suddenly renewed in strength.

"A girl?" she said, smiling, her eyes tearing so that she could not see a thing.

"Aye," he said, laying the babe on her belly, the cord holding them together for just a few moments more. "A daughter."

She stared at her daughter for the length of time it took to deliver the afterbirth, whole and intact, for Wir ifred to cut the cord that bound them, for her to slide her child up her belly to find her breast. For an eternity. For an instant. She could not take her eyes off her miracle.

She was tiny and red and wrinkled and black of hair, which was curled and wet at the top of her head, bare and bald around the ears. She was perfect. Beautiful. She even smiled.

"She is certainly your daughter," Hugh said, coming to wrap an arm around her shoulders.

"She is that," Elsbeth said, grinning so hard that her cheeks hurt.

"See how she smiles? See that? That is pure English wickedness, my wife."

"Oh, she is not wicked. She is . . . perfect."

"Aye, perfectly wicked," he said, winking down at her. "That great rush of water? Ruined my boots. My new boots from my sister. All the way from Jerusalem. Ruined in a moment."

"My lord, must we discuss your boots? Can we not discuss the perfect daughter I have given you?"

"Well, of giving, I would say that *I* have given you a perfect daughter."

"Aye, I will not argue it," she said, nestling into his arms, her daughter finding the nipple and pulling hard to find her milk. "Her name?"

Hugh kissed the top of his wife's head and ran a fingertip down his daughter's cheek. "I think Ardeth would suit her well."

"Ardeth, aye, it suits," Elsbeth said, taking her husband's hand in hers and kissing the base of his thumb.

They watched Ardeth while she nursed, the nipple falling from her pink mouth as she fell suddenly into sleep. Winifred had cleared the room of all the blood and water of the birthing, leaving them alone. Leaving them together, a family.

Hugh took Ardeth from his wife's arms as she slid down into her bed, sleep pulling at her eyes. He bent to kiss her and pull the woolen blanket up over her shoulders. Through the wind hole, the wind rose and pushed before it the smell of rain.

"New boots, most definitely," he said as he left the chamber with their daughter.

In her sleep, Elsbeth smiled.

If you like Claudia Dain, you'll love . . .

CARNAL GIFT

by

PAMELA CLARE

Her body and her virginity are to be offered up to a stranger in exchange for her brother's life. Possessing nothing but her innocence and her fierce Irish pride, Bríghid has no choice but to comply.

But the handsome man she faces in the darkened bedchamber is not at all the monster she expected. His tender touch calms her fears while he swears he will protect her by merely pretending to claim her. And as the long hours of the night pass by, as her senses ignite at the heat of their naked flesh, Bríghid makes a startling discovery: Sometimes the line between hate and love can be dangerously thin.

Coming in March 2004